When we reach the next town the Stukas have already visited it, and prepared it for the taking. The dust of pulverized bricks and mortar hangs like a red-grey cloud in the air. Artillery and Cossack horses lie in the shattered streets, stiff-legged and with swollen bodies. Guns lying on their side, wrecked lorries and mountains of tangled equipment, are scattered among the heaps of bodies. Dead and wounded Russian soldiers lie against walls, or hang from gaping window openings.

Dispassionately we stare at the bloody scene. It has become an everyday sight. In the beginning we puked and felt sick to our stomachs. It is a long time since any of us puked.

By Sven Hassel

THE COMMISSAR

SVEN HASSEL

Translated from the Danish by Tim Bowie

CASSELL

Cassell Military Paperbacks

an imprint of Orion Books Ltd,
Orion House,
5 Upper St Martin's Lane,
London WC2H 9EA
An Hachette Livre UK company

First published in Great Britain in 1985
by Corgi
This Cassell Military Paperbacks edition 2008

British Library Cataloguing-in-Publication Data.
A catalogue record for this book is available
from the British Library.

ISBN 978-0-7538-2255-5

Printed and bound in Great Britain by
Clays Ltd, St Ives plc

The Orion Publishing Group's policy is to use papers that
are natural, renewable and recyclable products and
made from wood grown in sustainable forests. The logging
and manufacturing processes are expected to conform to
the environmental regulations of the country of origin.

www.orionbooks.co.uk

This book is dedicated to my old friend
the Scandinavian film producer Just Betzer
who has thrown himelf enthusiastically
into the filming of my books.

Sven Hassel

Many have suffered in war – from hunger,
  from wounds and from frost
But they suffered most who bore no arms, who
  died unseen – lost.
Those who suffered at human hands. Their
  torturers saw each heart,
And around them the land they sprang from –
  then – tore them slowly apart.

Nordahl Grieg
(freely translated)

CONTENTS

* The Soviet Secret Police, now the KGB

> *A soldier's conscience is as wide as Hell's gate.*
>
> *William Shakespeare*

The Gauleiter was in a hurry. He drove recklessly, taking no heed of the refugees choking the roads. His triple-axled vehicle was heavily loaded. He was the first to have left the city. The vehicle had been loaded for several days. Then, the sound of tank-guns in the distance persuaded the Gauleiter that the time to start on his travels was now. The only member of his large staff whom he took with him was his young secretary. She believed in the Führer, the Party and the Final Victory.

She pulled her mink coat closer about her. It had once belonged to a rich woman who had died in Auschwitz.

They were stopped four times by the Field Police, but the Gauleiter's golden-brown uniform was as good as a password. At the last stop the guards warned them against proceeding further. The next sentries they would meet would be Americans. Their road-block was where the road turned off from Hof to Munich.

A coarse-faced sergeant of snowballs* stuck a gun-barrel through the vehicle window. The Gauleiter had changed into civilian clothes.

'You *ain't* gone hungry, have you, sausage-eater?'

'He is a Gauleiter,' smiled the secretary, who no longer believed in the Führer, the Party and the Final Victory.

The snowball sergeant emitted a long, low whistle.

'Hear that boys?' He turned to his three-man MP guard. 'This civilian sausage-eater's a Gauleiter!'

They all laughed.

'Come on,' said the MP sergeant, prodding the Gauleiter with his gun-muzzle. 'Let's take a stroll into the woods, and see how the spring crocuses are coming along.' His breath stank of cheap cognac.

* *Refers to the white MP helmet*

9

The secretary heard three bursts of automatic fire. White helmets appeared again from the woods. She was halfway across the fields towards the farm, and never heard the next burst of fire which came from behind her. She was dead before her face hit the ground!

'What the hell you shoot her for?' shouted the sergeant, in an irritated voice.

'Escapin' wasn't she?' said the corporal, cheerfully. He cracked a fresh ammunition clip home with the heel of his hand.

Soon afterwards the next loaded vehicle arrived.

PANZER ATTACK

'Section, halt!' The Old Man's voice comes hoarsely over the radio. He throws up the flap of the turret with a metallic crash, and pulls his battered old silver-lidded pipe from his pocket in one and the same movement. Hard-boiled as our Section Leader is, he is still a carpenter at heart. An aura of sawdust and wood-shavings hangs about him.

'Blast these bloody things!' he swears, turning round with difficulty in the narrow turret aperture. The new, heavy winter underwear makes a man twice his normal size round the waist. 'Where's Barcelona and his lot got to?'

I open the side hatch and peer tiredly down the long column of tanks rattling along the cobbled road. They are our heavy tanks, mounted with flamethrowers. There must be something very well-defended up in front of us, or the heavies wouldn't be in the lead.

'Noisy lot o' bleeders ain't they?' growls Tiny, showing his sooty face cautiously at the loader's hatch. 'Jesus'n Mary!' he shouts, ducking quickly inside again as the muzzle flames of a pair of *degtrareva** spit from the windows of some business premises further down the street. Our machineguns begin to chatter back immediately. The clatter of running feet is heard on all sides, mixed with shouted orders and screams. It sounds as if the gates of hell had suddenly been thrown open.

A figure in an earth-coloured uniform, carrying a T-mine, comes scrambling up over our front apron. Tiny sweeps him away, with a burst from his machine-pistol, before he can place the T-mine under our turret ring.

---

* *degtrareva*: Russian machine-gun

11

Suddenly the street is swarming with Russians. They come flooding out from every door and window.

I catch sight of a Russian helmet on our open side. Reflexively I empty my pistol into a twisted face. It shatters like an egg.

'Grenades,' shouts the Old Man, ripping a stick-grenade from its clip.

I pull personnel grenades from my pockets, and throw them through the hatch. The little eggs explode, cracking sharply in our ears. Human screams split the darkness.

A 20 mm coughs angrily from an attic window. The small, dangerous shells ricochet between the house walls. It is as if devils were playing ping-pong with exploding balls of fire.

Without awaiting the Old Man's order I swing the turret, and aim our gun at the building from which the 20 mm and the *degtrareva* are spitting their pearly rows of deadly light.

Our long gun roars, violently.

With a certain feeling of pleasure I see two uniformed figures whirl down from the third-floor windows. They catch for a moment on the overhead wires of the tramlines, then fall to the cobblestones, landing with a soggy thump.

I send three more rounds of HE into the building. Flames commence to roar up from the roof. Tiles fall in the street like enormous hailstones. They splinter on the cobblestones.

The fire runs quickly along the houses. In the twinkling of an eye the whole row becomes a sea of roaring flame. Terrified men spring from the windows, preferring death on the cobblestones to burning alive.

'Who ordered you to open fire?' rages the Old Man, hitting out at me with a stick-grenade. 'Fire when you're ordered to, an' not before, you powder-mad sod, you!'

'They'd have done us up for sure, if I hadn't fired,' I defend myself, hurt. 'The gun's to shoot with, isn't it?'

'That building you've just disposed of so thoroughly was 1 Battalion's billet. Get *that* through your thick skull! *You* just shot it all to hell!' shouts the Old Man, despairingly.

'Sabotage, that's what it is,' says Heide, triumphantly, 'or I don't know what sabotage is! Kick him in front of a court-martial so we won't have to look at *him* any more!'

'Must 'ave rotten eggs where 'is brains ought to be,' barks Tiny, jeeringly. 'Shit on 'is own doorstep when 'e could've done it in the snow'n only shit icicles. Let's blow 'is 'ead off!'

'Shut up!' snarls the Old Man. He puffs fiercely on his pipe.

'See that sky-pilot over there,' grins Porta. 'Runnin' like mad with a bible under his arm, and a crucifix banging on his navel. The speed he's going you'd think the devil had his pitchfork up his arse!'

'I cannot ever understand why chaplains is just as scared of gettin' knocked off as all us ordinary shits,' Tiny wonders. 'Them lot 'as got *connections* to the 'igher regions!'

'The holy and righteous are just as scared of blowin' their last fart as we heathens are, my son,' philosophizes Porta. 'In reality only very good people indeed can permit them-selves to become religious.'

'*Panzer, Marsch*,' orders the Old Man, pulling his head-phones down over his ears, and settling his throat micro-phone in place. '2 Section follow me!' From old habit he lifts his clenched fist over his head. The signal to move forward. Maybach engines howl up into whining upper registers. Broad tracks churn forward over the dead and wounded lying in the street.

A Panther tank stops over a foxhole, where two Russian soldiers have taken cover with an LMG. The tank waggles on its axis, like a hen settling on to her eggs. There are screams, sharply cut off. The Russians have been crushed to a bloody pulp.

The noise of the tanks is deafening. The guns and auto-matic weapons drown out every other noise.

'*Anna* here! Here *Anna*,' the Old Man says to the radio. '*Bertha* and *Caesar* make safe on flanks. Fire only at clear targets! I repeat: fire only at clear targets. And I'll want an exact ammo' count from all of you. Now, fingers out, an' get

13

moving, you sad sacks!'

Flames lick at the houses. Bullets rattle and clang on the sides of the tanks. Machine-gunners fire at them, in the wasteful hope that they can do the steel giants some damage. Poisonous yellow smoke penetrates the tanks, making the crewmen's tired eyes burn and sting.

A burning roof crashes down on top of a P-III. Flames shoot up, and in a few seconds it becomes an exploding ball of fire. Reserve petrol drums lashed to its rear shield turn the tank into a travelling bomb.

The cold, damp night air stinks of explosion fumes, blood and dead bodies.

'Here Hinka, here Hinka,' comes from the scratchy loudspeaker. The steely voice of the regimental commander cuts through the racket in the tank. '5 Company will do clean-up. Prisoners will be sent back to grenadier battalion. I warn you! No looting of any kind! Breach of this order will be punished most severely!'

'Always *us*,' grumbles Porta sourly, speeding up his motor. 'It's bloody wonderful! They chase us poor bloody coolies, till even our soddin' socks are sick of it. Why am I so rotten *healthy*, and why do all them lovely Commie bullets go *round* me? I'm never, *ever* goin' to get away from this shitty war, and into a lovely, clean hospital with lovely clean, anti-septic nurse's cunt all round me just longin' to get across a wounded, bloody Ayrab like me!'

''Ot shit!' growls Tiny, bitterly. 'Risk your bleedin' life, every day in every way, for a fucked-up mark a day.'

'It's the rotten German army,' snarls Porta, angrily. 'Why, oh why, was I ever born in a war-crazy country like Germany!'

I feel dog-tired, but a rage of energy still courses through my weary body. They've filled us up with benzedrine. For the last six days we have been unable to snatch more than a few minutes of sleep at a time, and we walk around in a queer sort of haze. The worst of all is that every time we have almost fallen asleep we wake up with a start, and the bitter taste of fear is in our mouths.

Tiny hangs over the guard rails. His eyes are wide open, but see nothing. From one loosely hanging hand dangles a P-38. He's like the rest of us. He dare not fall asleep. Now we are close to the danger point. The point where we can no longer be bothered to keep a watch for approaching death. It's waiting out there for us somewhere; perhaps in the form of an explosion; perhaps in a hysterical hail of machine-gun bullets.

Shells come whistling over the town in great arcs, despatched from invisible batteries to strike at distant targets far behind us.

Tiny jerks awake and cracks his head against the roof of the tank. He swears bitterly and long. Dark blood runs down beside his left ear. He dabs at it, irritably, with an oily cloth.

''Oly Mother of Kazan, what a bleedin' dream,' he mumbles. 'I was walkin' around in a wood tryin' to find the Red bleedin' Army. Up comes a commissar an' shoots the shit out o' me.' He looks around at us, quite out of touch. 'Stone the crows,' he says, feebly, 'now I *know* I don't like gettin' shot up.'

The tank stops. Mud and remnants of bodies drip from the tracks. Its white camouflage paintwork is a dirty grey from powdermarks and filth.

We stretch ourselves in our steel seats, and throw open the shutters to let in some fresh air. But all we get is poison-yellow smoke and the stink of death.

Tank grenadiers sneak along the house walls. They have the dirtiest job of all. Not a bit of glory. Their reward is more often than not a bellyfull of machine-gun bullets. They start in cleaning out the cellars for fanatics, crazy fools who fight to the last man and the last bullet. Their reward is a throat slashed open. Brainwashed idiots filled with Ilya Ehrenburg propaganda. The same kind of people as ours. The ones who die whispering 'Heil Hitler' from between crushed lips.

From where we are lying in ambush, we can see a long

15

way out over the steppe. It is like a whitish-grey sea, fading away into the distant horizon. Far, far behind us, towns and villages, set on fire by shell-fire during our savage attack, burn fiercely.

Wherever we look, fiery red and yellow flashes split the darkness of the night, marking clearly the deadly path of the armoured attack.

Halfway down some cellar steps hangs a US Willy's jeep with five headless bodies in it. They sit to attention as if on parade. It seems as if a huge knife has slashed the heads from the four Russian officers and their driver in one enormous sweep. There is something strange about the headless bodies. They are not wearing battle khaki but dark green dress uniforms, with broad shoulder distinctions which glitter in the flames from a burning distillery nearby.

'See now. Sights like that,' says Porta, spitting accurately out of an observation slit, 'make a man glad to be alive, even when life is monotonous and weary.'

'Where you think that lot was off to, togged up in them uniforms an' all the cunt magnets they c'd get their 'ands on?' asks Tiny, interestedly. He leans out of the turret opening. 'They must've lost their way to end up 'ere where there's a war goin' on.'

'My guess is they were on their way to a party with some field mattresses,' says Porta. He licks his lips at the thought.

'Let's give 'em a goin' over,' suggests Tiny, jumping down from the tank. 'They're goin' to a 'ores' party, they'll 'ave some pretties on 'em. Count on it!'

Porta inches up through the turret opening, eagerly, and bends over a headless first lieutenant with a row of ribbons on his chest.

'A hero,' he laughs, putting the ribbons in his pocket. Buyers for them are easy to find behind the lines. His quick fingers go through the officer's pockets, regardless of congealed blood and crushed bones.

'Not a lot o' gold teeth in *this* lot,' remarks Tiny dis-

16

appointedly, nosing around in the blood-spattered vehicle.

'Perfumed officers' cigarettes with paper mouthpieces,' says Porta, putting some blue packets into his specially-made poacher's pockets.

'Any *seegars*?' asks Tiny, turning over a body, with an unpleasant squelching sound.

'Are you out of your mind, man?' answers Porta. 'Stalin's officers don't smoke cigars. That's capitalistic!'

'Lucky for us then we're bleedin' capitalists,' Tiny laughs noisily, picking up a bottle of vodka, one of the finest kind with the old Russian czarist eagle on a royal blue label. A vodka which only the top party leaders get supplied with.

Two grimy panzer grenadiers come along, dragging a screaming, half-naked woman with them. She tries desperately to tear herself loose, but they only tighten their grip on her.

'You're goin' with us, you little cat, whether you want to or not,' grins one of them, lasciviously. 'You're gonna get the chance to enjoy the war in our company. We're gonna 'ave an orgy, with sighs'n everythin' else as belongs with it.'

But the terrified girl obviously does not want to take part in an orgy. She kicks one of the grenadiers on the knee. He lets out a chain of shocking oaths, and grips her roughly by the throat with one filthy, wet fist.

'Listen to me, you little wildcat,' he snarls, wickedly. 'Get civilized or I'll smash your pretty little face in. *Panjemajo**, you Bolshevik bitch? It's a long time since me'n my mate've had any fresh goods. *Panjemajo*, Bolshy? You're goin' to an orgy, an' you're gonna be the main attraction. *Panjemajo*?'

'*Da*,' she whispers, in terror, and seems to give up all attempt at resistance.

'The party's over,' snarls the Old Man, swinging his mpi muzzle round to cover the three. 'Let 'er go! Now! Or would you rather we had a fast little court-martial?'

---

* *Panjemajo*: Russian for understood?

17

'Now I've heard it all,' shouts the biggest of the two panzer grenadiers, pushing his helmet to the back of his head. 'Been chewin' on wood, 'ave you? Belt up, you puffed-up excuse for a dragoon, you!'

They have let go of the girl and fumble for the machine-pistols hanging across their chests. They have not seen Tiny and Porta standing behind them.

'Get 'em up! Let's see you try to tickle the angels' foot-soles, my sons,' trumpets Porta, grinning happily.

Both panzer grenadiers swing round with mpis at the ready. Bullets snarl angrily past Porta's face.

Reflexively, Tiny cuts the grenadiers almost in two with a scythe-like burst from his *Kalashnikov*.

One goes down, internal organs flopping from his open gut. The other is thrown onto his back, and tries to crawl under the tracks of the tank.

'Bye-bye, then,' grins Tiny. 'See what 'appens to little boys as gets caught tryin' to pinch a piece o' cunt!'

'*Was* that necessary?' asks the Old Man, fretfully, pushing his helmet up from his face.

'What you bleedin' want us to do, then? Them two blue-bollocked bastards was gonna shoot us to death,' protests Tiny, outraged.

'The way of the world,' sighs Porta. He pushes at the nearest body with the toe of his boot. 'Him as shoots first lives longest!'

The Old Man takes a deep breath. As he crawls back down through the turret opening he breaks into a mad burst of laughter. He knows very well that this war is eating us all up. To protest against the cruelty of death is completely useless.

'Where'd the bint get to,' asks Porta, looking searchingly around him.

'There she goes, runnin' like mad,' laughs Tiny, pointing. ''Ad enough of us Germans, seems like.'

Bullets from an MG whip along the fronts of the houses, throwing earth and mortar over the jeep. The big, soft lump

18

of fear is back in our throats.

'Come on,' says the Old Man. 'Let's move!'

'Can I borrow that big feller's uniform?' asks Tiny.

'What the devil do you want with that?' asks the Old Man, wonderingly. 'Haven't you got uniform enough in the one Adolf's lent you?'

'You ain't forward-lookin' enough,' grins Tiny, cunningly. 'When *"Grofaz"** 'as lost 'is war, and we get enrolled in the other FPO's lot, it'll be a good thing to 'ave a uniform of your own to start off with.'

'You're lookin' for a miracle, son,' laughs Porta.

'Are we to understand then,' asks Julius Heide, his eyes narrowing to slits, 'that you're turning your back on the Führer and the Reich, and no longer believe wholeheartedly in the Final Victory? I wonder what the NSFO'll† have to say to *that* when I hand in my report.'

'What a shit that Julius *is*,' Tiny bellows with laughter. 'The turd o' the world, an' never goin' to get no cleverer.'

'He's what he is,' Porta takes it up. 'A real man o' the new times. A well-trained German soldier who shits an' eats by numbers, an' turns his toes in an' feels happy as a sodding lark long as he's in company with patriotic nuts'n close-cropped generals with a window in one eye. Heil Hitler!'

'I've got all that written down, mark my words, Obergefreiter Porta,' snarls Heide, affrontedly. 'You'll have to repeat every word of it at your court-martial. The day you dangle'll be the happiest day of my life!'

'Better get crackin' then, my boy, 'fore the *untermensch* turn up. Or it'll be me, Obergefreiter by the grace of God Joseph Porta, who'll be puttin' his weight on the *other* end of the rope,' answers Porta, blowing down the barrel of his mpi.

'Up, you lazy men!' the Old Man scolds them. 'Here comes Löwe. Get your thieving fingers off them Russian

---

* *Grofaz*: Greatest Leader of All Time (nickname for Hitler)
†NSFO: Nazi political officer

19

bodies! It's a court for you, else! You know what *that* means?'

'Bye, bye napper,' says Tiny, patting his own cheek lovingly.

Porta has just time to lift the Russians' identification papers.

'Also saleable,' he grins as he sidles down through the tank turret opening.

'When this German world war's all over, there'll be coppers in personal documents. Everybody'n his brother'll be standing in line to get a new start in life.' He chuckles away to himself at the idea.

'Jesus, but I'm *tired*,' groans Barcelona, when the section makes a halt, a couple of hours later, in an open square. They are all hoping the halt means a rest period for them.

Suddenly the square is swarming with Russian soldiers. Some are armed to the teeth, others only half-dressed under their long khaki cloaks, which stream out in the wind. They have one thing in common. Their hands are stretched up above their heads and they are shouting: '*Tovaritsch**', the universal appeal for permission to remain alive. Strangely enough life seems only to begin to be really valuable to us when we have given up all hope and all ambition.

The Old Man swings down wearily from his turret onto the slush-covered cobblestones.

Hordes of Russian infantrymen, with grey, hopeless faces, push and shove their way past him. Only with difficulty can he keep himself from being carried along with them.

'Think they were rushin' to get in an' see the latest porno movie wouldn't you?' crows Porta. 'Mind *you* don't get taken prisoner along with them, Old Un. We don't want to lose you like that!'

Tiny's huge body blocks the side hatch of the tank. Mouth agape, he stares at the khaki-clad flood of humanity streaming around the vehicle. It fills the whole street from side to

---

* *Tovaritsch*: Russian for comrade

side. There is the burnt-out wreck of a tramcar in its path. The stream goes over, not round, it.

''Oly Russian mum o' Kazan,' cries Tiny, in amazement. 'It's the 'ole bleedin' Red Army, it is. Never 'ave I ever laid eyes on that many Russians at one time in all me German bleedin' life!'

'Hold on to your maidenheads, my sons,' says Porta, dropping back down into the tank. 'If that lot o' tired heroes gets to thinkin' how many *they* are an' how few *we* are, then our heroic participation in this fucked-up war'll be over 'fore we know it.'

'Stone the crows,' howls Tiny fearfully. He slides rapidly back into the tank and clangs the shutters to. 'Let's get *out* of 'ere!'

Barcelona's eight-wheeled Puma armoured clean-up waggon slides to a crashing halt. Its long, 75 mm gun juts threateningly from the low turret. It sideswipes the burnt-out tramcar with a screech of metal. Some Russians are caught under the heavy wheels. They scream heart-renderingly. Other soldiers pull them free and help them away. We hardly notice. This is everyday fare for us. There are too many prisoners anyway. Who cares about a few more or less?

Barcelona leans from the turret, pushes his huge dust-goggles up onto his helmet, and shouts something indistinguishable.

Albert's black African face bobs up out of the driver's aperture.

'Bow-wow!' he barks, with a flash of shiny, white teeth at the Russian prisoners. They jump back in alarm at the sight of a German negro.

'They think he's goin' to eat them,' grins Porta in Berlin gamin style. 'It'll all be in *Pravda* in a few days' time. Capitalist foes using cannibal troops!'

'Stop that cursed motor,' the Old Man boils up, irritably. 'You can't hear yourself think!'

'You *are* in a bad mood,' says Barcelona, with a broad

21

smile. 'Liven up! This war's only the start of something much, much worse. I've got a little message of greetings with me from Staff HQ. Get your arses in gear, boys, an' fast. Up front you go, and knock off some of the godless heathen, so those who're left alive can sneak off back where they came from. This is what we're getting paid for, you know. I'm to follow on as number three.'

'Who's two?' shouts Porta from his driving-slit.

'The "Desert Wanderer" in his P-IV,' giggles Barcelona, happily. 'He's used to lookin' out for camels, from his apprenticeship in the Sahara.'

'*Camels?*' asks the Old Man, blankly. 'There's no blasted camels in this war? *Are* there?'

'You'll see,' answers Barcelona. 'Before you know it you'll have a camel's nose up your jacksey, my friend. Ivan's sent over a whole camel division from the Kalmuk steppe.'

'Holy Mary, mother of Jesus,' shouts Porta, delightedly, 'then I can do us camel steaks. I've got a wonderful recipe for them that was given to me by a Bedouin, in grateful appreciation of my not running him over when we invaded France. Listen . . .'

'Not a blasted word will I hear out of you about food,' states the Old Man.

'What shiny-arsed bastard's found out it 'as to be *us* again?' asks Tiny, peeping cautiously over the edge of the hatch. The pure number of Russian prisoners going past us is still making his blood run cold.

'The Divisional Commander,' answers Barcelona, with a look on his face so haughty you'd think that he himself was the Chief of Staff. 'Herr General Arse-an'-Pockets wants some new silver to hang round his neck, an' we're the boys who're goin' to put it there. By the way, I hear Gregor got four threes in the black hole for smashin' up Arse-an'-Pockets Kübel. The general ended up in a tree, boots, cap an' all, an' frightened the black ravens half to death. Gregor's got the boot, and'll soon be back with us.'

The Legionnaire's P-IV can be heard starting up behind

the tram terminus. The Maybach motors stall again and again. Ignitions whine time after time. Then thunderous explosions crash down the narrow side street. The horse-power of the mighty engines begins to take hold. The roar of exhausts splits the air and fills the whole street.

Our motor catches immediately. A stench of petrol and hot oil spreads on the slush-damp air. The steel giants rattle up the steep alley, the earth shaking under their treads. Barcelona waves happily from the turret of his clean-up waggon, then disappears down inside and clangs the hatch shut behind him.

With a swing, graceful as a skater's figure-of-eight, the heavy eight-wheeled armoured vehicle disappears down the alley, slush spurting up from under its wheels.

We roll recklessly on, behind us the Legionnaire in his P-IV. Cobblestones and earth fly up from our tracks. They tear grey wounds in the poorly-paved road surfacing.

'Jesus, Jesus!' cries Tiny, banging his fist down on a shell. 'What a bleedin' bill we'll get if we ever 'as to pay for all the damage we're doin' in this country. Reckon it'll be clever to keep out o' sight for a bit, when we've lost the final bleedin' victory!'

'What a lot of *shit* you talk,' hisses Heide. He hammers viciously on the communicator, which has gone on strike again.

'Listen to it,' Porta laughs, jeeringly. 'The Führer's soldier's goin' sane. He's calling *Grofaz*'s radio programmes a lot of shit.'

'It's no fault of the Führer's,' Heide corrects him. He shakes the radio. 'It's sabotage to install a pre-war radio in a brand-new Panther tank!'

'Complain to Speer, then,' Tiny suggests, grinning broadly. 'It's 'im as is doin' the sabotage! Bleedin' barmy to give a soddin' 'od-carrier the job o' runnin' the 'ole war-industry, any road!'

'Idiot,' snarls Heide, beginning to dismantle the radio with quick, sure fingers. It begins to splutter, suddenly, and a babble of excited voices fills the tank. The whole network is overloaded with the voices of hysterical tank-commanders. They have all sighted the enemy positions at the same time, and guns begin to go off unordered. A 75 mm siege gun is hit by a German shell and goes up. Red-hot metal rains down.

All at once we are wide awake. Tiredness disappears from our bodies. In a tank battle the fastest crew wins.

I pump the foot-pedal and ready the gun. Then I see Barcelona's Puma come roaring back toward us. Heide's MG rattles nastily, sending a rain of tracer bullets across the river, which is covered with a heavy gruel of thick broken ice.

'Get your finger out,' shouts the Old Man, impatiently, banging his fist on my shoulder.

'You've got your target! Fire at the muzzle-flash. Get *on* with it, man, *if* you don't mind! Or do you *want* to get roasted alive?'

Nervously, I rotate the turret a few degrees, but can still see nothing. Nothing but darkness and whirling snowflakes. Snow lies on the edges of the viewing-slits like wet cotton-wool.

'Fire then, you blasted idiot,' shouts the Old Man, angrily. 'D'you want to get the lot of us killed?'

The brutal hammering of the two MGs fills the tank. Tracer tracks fumble about, with long silvery fingers, searching for enemy flesh.

Barcelona's Puma zig-zags back down the wide avenue, now cleared completely of Russian prisoners.

Its three MGs spit out a heavy, rapid rain of tracer towards the grey-white river banks. The Russian infantry over there send back a storm of fire at us.

'Give 'em three HEs,' orders the Old Man, brusquely. 'That'll give the gun-crazy bastards something to think about!'

A huge spout of mud, blood and snow goes up, as the HEs land between a couple of machine-gun nests. Tracer comes back at us, ricocheting in a mad dance between the trees lining the avenue.

Two P-IIIs and a P-IV go up in a roaring sheet of petrol-explosion flame. The crews hang from their turrets, bodies crackling and bubbling like torches dipped in fat.

A new sound mingles with the cacophony of this devil's concert. The hollow, whining howl of Stalin organs.

Forty-eight rocket shells come sailing through the air towards us. Long comet-tails of flame stretch behind them. Then, like clowns in a circus, their tails tip forward, and they drop vertically to the earth. They give us no feeling of being dangerous, but seem more like some strange kind of firework device. When they strike the earth our impression changes. The holes they make are tremendous, and the blast from them presses the air from our lungs.

Cutting through the roar of the Stalin organs comes the shrill scream of an armour-piercing shell on its way towards us. With a deafening crack it strikes, boring through the front shield of Feldwebel Weber's P-IV. It goes through it at an angle, and up into, and through, the turret, taking Weber with it. He lands, with a soggy splash, out in the road. The lower part of his body is completely crushed. Blood pours from his shattered face.

Two blood-spattered crewmen scramble from the P-IV, which has burst into flames. The driver has his hands over his face. He runs in circles, screaming like a madman, then collapses into the slushy snow.

A P-III comes rumbling along at top speed. It passes over the driver, leaving nothing but shreds of flesh and bloody rags of uniform.

'Come death, come sweet death,' croons the voice of the Legionnaire from the radio speaker.

The other crewman goes down across a heap of twisted metal rods, pierced through and through by a burst of tracer which seems to last for an eternity. -

Roars and howls fill the air like mad organ notes. The long tram terminus collapses in on itself like a house of cards. Nothing remains of it but twisted girders and an enormous cloud of brickdust and pulverized mortar. In the middle of the desolation a tramcar stands comically on end. I stare fiercely through the optical sight, but can still not find the target. I feel like tearing open the turret hatch and running, running as fast and as far as my legs can carry me.

'Let's take 'em,' rages the Old Man, impatiently. 'Can't you see they're rangin' in on us? If you're tired of life, then for Christ's sake *die* an' get it over with!'

'I only wish the devil had that rotten swine who invented smokeless powder,' I curse, furiously, and rotate the turret a further couple of degrees. 'You used to be able to *see* when they fired their shit at you.'

'Stop your complaining, son,' says Porta. 'World wars are as world wars have to be, and not the way *you* want 'em to be. Now we have smokeless powder, and that is what we have to live with.'

'You can't explain any bleedin' thing to *'im*,' rumbles Tiny. ''E thinks with the tip of 'is old John Thomas, *'e* does!'

I stare until my inflamed eyes hurt with staring. I turn the sights slowly and catch sight of the muzzle-flash of an 85 mm. Without removing my gaze from it for a second I adjust the sights. Lines and figures dance before my eyes. The long barrel of the gun sinks, as if it were nodding a greeting to its target.

The Old Man steadies his night-glasses on the rim of the turret.

'Heaven have mercy on us,' he mumbles. 'It's a whole PAK* battalion!'

'Shovel shit at 'em, then!' shouts Porta from the driving seat. 'Else *we'll* get shat on, an' from a great height. Gettin' shot up ain't nice, let me tell you.'

All my attention and energy is concentrated on the busy gunners on the far bank. Four muzzle-flashes illuminate the small bushy-topped trees with a ghostly blue and blood-red glare. For a second I see the PAK gun-crews clearly. Shells whine across the flat terrain and explode in the avenue, tearing up blue-grey cobblestones and sending them flying

---

* *PAK*: German abbreviation for anti-tank gun

to all sides like new, runaway projectiles.

Explosions roar, thunder and crash. The few remaining windows tinkle to bits.

A human shape whirls up into the air. It looks like a woman, but the incident is merely an intermezzo in the hell of explosions.

'What a trip *she* got,' sighs Porta. 'Qualified her for the air-to-land forces, that did.'

I am only half-listening to Porta, so taken up am I with my target.

The long gun-muzzle, with its new smoke-shield, turns slowly and silently. I make a fine adjustment of the sights, and zoom in on the bustling men over there. Now I can see the Russian battery commander quite clearly. He looks like an actor on stage, illuminated by blue light-beams, rather like spotlights.

'Weird,' I mumble, unconsciously, almost enjoying the sight of the tall, slim officer in his ankle-length grey-brown cloak. His fur cap is cocked cheekily over one eye. He corrects the fire of his battery, completely unaware of our new optical sighting device which can see through fog and darkness as if it were clear daylight. 'Weird,' I repeat, and feel wildly exultant over the fact that I am the one who is going to decide just how long the tall Russian officer will remain alive.

'What d'you say?' asks the Old Man, leaning down inquisitively from the turret hatch.

'Dreamin' about 'is field-marshal's baton 'e is,' jeers Tiny, with a hoarse laugh.

'Gone to sleep, have you?' asks the Old Man angrily, hitting me hard on the shoulder with his night-glasses. 'What're you waitin' for, then? Why don't you fire? Fire, I said! Fire, damn your eyes! Shoot their arses off!'

I grip the firing release with unnecessary force . . .

With an earsplitting crash the gun goes off. A yard-long flame licks from the muzzle. The enormously heavy vehicle is pressed back on its tracks, as if it were bobbing a curtsey to the projectile which leaves its gun-muzzle.

'Loaded, safety off,' rumbles Tiny, as the breech clangs shut. The hot shell casing clatters over the steel deck plates.

With an oath Tiny kicks out at it, sending it flying toward Julius Heide. It hits him in the back of the neck. Heide jumps to his feet, violently angry, and rushes at Tiny with a stick-grenade swinging in his hand.

'I'll smash your skull for you some day, you stinking Hamburg sewer-rat,' he hisses, white with rage, and strikes at Tiny with the grenade.

'Stop that and shut up,' orders the Old Man. 'When this lot's over you can *kill* one another for all I care. Until it *is* – stay soldiers. Why, *why* did I ever let them wish 2 Section on me? God curse the day!'

'You love us really,' grins Tiny, pleased. 'If we was to take you serious an' leave you, you'd be dead as a smoked 'errin' 'angin' in the chimney-place 'fore we was out o' sight. Drowned in tears you'd be, an' never see 'ome no more.'

I press my eyes to the sight, and follow the course of the shot. A gout of snow and flame goes up close to the bushy-topped trees.

Khaki-clad forms fly up into the air. A gun-carriage is thrown away to one side, taking a whole row of bushes with it.

The Old Man is firing orders into the radio, to the other vehicles of the section. Panthers and P-IVs stream into the broad avenue, and down the side streets, with popping exhausts. Broad tracks scream and clatter over the blue-grey cobblestones. Sections Three and Five halt on each side of the street. They are so close to the walls of the great houses lining it that they scrape plaster from them, with a tearing, nerve-wrecking sound.

A window on the second floor opens. An old woman with a comical old-fashioned nightcap on her head screams with hysterical rage, and shakes a clenched fist at us threateningly.

'*Ssvinja*,' she shouts, and throws some object down at the

nearest tank. It explodes with a roar. A blinding sheet of flame goes up.

'The mad bitch is throwin' grenades,' shouts Porta. He shakes his head at the fact that anyone could be so foolish.

'Soon put a stop to that,' snarls Heide, murderously. He throws open the radio hatch and presses his mpi butt into his shoulder. Coldly he sends three short bursts at the furious woman in the green nightdress.

With a rattling scream she falls from the window and splashes onto the snow-wet cobblestones. As she falls her old-fashioned nightcap comes off. It flutters down a little behind her body and lands, like a wounded bird, on our gun-barrel.

'Jesus,' yelps Tiny, stretching his neck up, 'that's a lucky omen. I remember when me and the Yid furrier's son David from *'Ein'Oyer Strasse* was beltin' along one time on delivery bikes with a load o' fur capes. As we passed Zirkus Weg, some sod slung a used pro' out a third-floor winder. 'Er drawers come off on the way, float down light an' pretty an' land, neat as you please, right smack on me ol' nut. There was a couple dizzy coppers on bikes breathin' down our necks. They'd seen us "borrowin'" the capes from "Alster 'Ouse". Any rate as soon as the cops saw this fuckin'-machine comin' down from the third floor they drop us an' we get away clean. So that bleedin' nightcap's gonna bring us luck!'

Barcelona's Puma opens fire. In the next few minutes 2 Section sends a storm of high-explosives into the Russian anti-tank position.

A cloud of dust and all kinds of debris lifts on the far side of the river. The earth has been literally shaved clean of everything standing up.

The countless Maxims fall silent. As the cloud of dust dissipates, we see a huge pile of scrap where the PAK battery used to be.

'That's that,' says the Old Man, lighting his silver-lidded pipe. He pushes his helmet back tiredly, and rumples his shock of greying hair.

'Hell, I'm *itchy*,' he swears, scratching his head violently with both hands. 'It's these blasted leather helmets.'

Tiny rubs a grimy hand across his soot-streaked face, and fishes a fat cigar from his gas-mask pouch. With the flamboyant gesture of a movie gangster he lights it and blows the smoke down Heide's neck.

Porta passes the vodka bottle over his shoulder. Tiny takes the first long pull at it. I have hardly set the bottle to my lips when there is a deafening explosion. A 120 mm at least.

''Oly Mother o' Kazan, Jesus'n Mary!' coughs Tiny, dropping his cigar in alarm. 'That musta took 'arf the bleedin' world with it!'

'KW-2,' says Heide, superciliously.

The Old Man whirls round in the turret, searching for the source of the threat.

The night is ripped open again by a crashing shot from the KW-2's 120 mm gun.

One of 3 Section's P-IVs is hit. It is thrown like an empty cardboard box along the street. There is a gaping hole in its flank. Two of the five-man crew tumble from the wreckage; they are living torches. The P-IV goes up into a huge fireball. Chunks of tracks and armour rain down on us.

'Where the hell *is* that Commie bastard?' comes Barcelona's hysterical scream over the communicator.

The Puma come whirling up over the hill and into cover behind the rubble of a former cannery. The rest of the section scatters in all directions. The KW-2 is slow-moving but its shells make scrap-iron of anything they hit.

Porta is the first to grasp the situation clearly. There is reason behind the selection of the quickest-minded men in a tank company for the job of driver.

'Back o' that house,' he shouts, speeding up his vehicle. 'The shit's down there. Jesus what a gun. A Cossack with a jack on could lie on his back in comfort in the muzzle of it!'

'Yes, devil take me,' cries the Old Man, in alarm. 'There the beggar is. Standing there lookin' at us. Gun round 70 degrees. Pointblank at 80 yards. Turret five o'clock. Got it? *Move* man, damn you!'

'Got him,' I whisper, feeling a cold shiver run down my spine as I make out the giant, grey-white silhouette, with its bulldog-like gun sticking out of the huge turret.

'Holy Mary, Mother of God!' Barcelona's voice comes over the radio. 'Lookit that bastard there? If he gets us, with just one, our feet won't touch till we hit the *Potsdammer Platz* in Berlin 'n get scraped off it by the Eytie street sweepers.'

I hold my breath anxiously as I sight in on the armoured monster. Its clumsy turret is beginning to turn slowly. There is no doubt it is us he is after.

'Fire!' I give myself the order.

Before the muzzle-flash has died away our shell strikes the KW-2. It explodes on its armour in a shower of glowing splinters. Harmlessly! We have forgotten we were loaded with HE.

'I give *up*,' shouts the Old Man furiously, banging his fists on the turret ring. 'That greenhorn trick'll get you a court! I've no *time* for you lot any more!'

'Oh, great!' Porta bellows with laughter. 'Hit 'im bang up the jacksey, an' you're loaded with HE, an' don't even tickle his piles up for 'im. Try hittin' him with a marker this time, an' splash some paint up his arse. He'd like that I reckon!'

'Jesus'n Mary, what's up then?' asks Tiny, chewing violently at the butt of his dead cigar.

'I've had it! I've bloody well *had* it!' screams the Old Man, blue in the face with rage. 'What's *up*? You loaded with HE, you habitual criminal oaf, you! You mad-brained, illiterate, anti-social ape! HE he throws at the world's biggest bloody tank! I *won't* stand it any more!'

''Old up now Old Un'. You'll 'ave a stroke an' drop dead if you go on like that,' says Tiny in a fatherly tone. 'Anybody can make a mistake. Even in a world war small mistakes can 'appen. 'Ere's an armour-piercin' S-shell, *see*? We can get it off at 'im 'fore 'e's woke up. The neighbours ain't all that quick off the mark where 'eadwork's concerned. We seen that plenty o' times. It's us Germans as 'as got it up top in this man's war!'

'I'll get you a court-martial,' the Old Man promises him, white with rage, '*and* I'll take you to Germersheim personally, when they give you life!'

'Arse'oles to that,' grins Tiny, carelessly. 'They'll let me out anyway when Adolf's lost the final victory. *An'* they'll probably make me *Bürgermeister* in some funny town somewhere or other.'

'If that should come about I'd like to live in the town you get to be *Bürgermeister* in,' grins Porta. 'It'd be fantastic! An' it'd certainly go down in history as the best practical joke ever played in Germany. Send him to Germersheim, Old Un', so we can get to see a *Bürgermeister* nobody's ever seen the like of before.'

Barcelona and I fire together. Our S-shells strike the huge vehicle simultaneously, tearing the turret half-off. The commander appears in the hatchway just as the gun of the Legionnaire's P-IV spits out a long muzzle-flash. The Russian is cut over as if by a circular saw.

'*Panzer, Marsch*!' orders the Old Man, and stamps impatiently on the steel plating of the floor.

Our tank swings out and rumbles thunderously after the Panther. We leave behind us a hell of flame.

We crunch over furniture thrown from the houses by blast. A body lying spread-eagled across the tramlines, with a Schmeisser gripped in one hand, is minced under our tracks. Two turkeys dash from a pen, and run in front of us, heads bobbing.

'Jesus Christ and all the prophets,' shouts Porta, in a strangled voice. 'There goes, God help me, our Christmas dinner! Suspend the world war a minute. Those two *tovaritsch* turkeys are more important!' Before anyone can stop him he has pulled the tank to a halt and has the driver's hatch open. 'Come on Tiny, leave them shells be! Roast turkey's in the offin'!

'What's in what bleedin' oven?' asks Tiny, opening the side hatch without considering the bullets which are flying around outside. 'Jesus'n *Mary*!' he shouts happily springing out of the tank.

Before the Old Man has time to react, Tiny's huge, filthy ackboots are splashing up mud as he chases after the terrified birds.

'This beats everything,' shouts the Old Man, in a rage. 'Leaving their post in the waggon during battle! This is the worst thing they've done yet!'

'I'll swear to it for you,' offers Heide, his face lighting up. 'Desertion in the face of the enemy. That's the charge!'

'You shut your trap, you!' orders the Old Man, grinding his teeth together. He puts his head up cautiously over the rim of the turret to try to get a sight of the turkey hunters.

'It is your duty to charge them, so that those two can go before a court-martial,' shouts Heide, his bloodthirsty non-com mentality coming to the fore.

'I told you to shut up,' hisses the Old Man. He draws his P-38 from its holster. '*Do* it, or I'll shoot your head off for refusing to comply with an order.'

'You gone nuts over there?' comes Barcelona's voice scratchily over the communicator. '*Cojones**, they've got 'em! Let's get this caper over with quick so we can get our chops round some roast turkey!'

'Beg to report two prisoners taken,' cries Porta, jubilantly, as he crawls back through the driver's hatch with the maddened Russian turkeys dangling from his hand.

In a moment the whole interior of the tank seems to be filled with panic-stricken turkeys. Wings flap across our faces like whip-lashes. Blood is running down Tiny's cheek from a turkey's pecking beak.

''Elp!' he howls. 'The sod's tryin' to *eat* me. *Shoot* 'im!'

The terrified turkey flies up onto Heide's back and begins to hammer away at the back of his head as if it were trying to peck its way through to the other side. He screams in shock

* *Cojones* – Spanish for balls (testicles)

and pain, and thrashes at it with his fists.

'Fanatics, that's what these two are,' cries Porta, desperately. He aims a blow at one of the turkeys, which seems to be running completely amuck.

'I can't stand any more of it,' sobs the Old Man, bending over the turret rim despairingly. 'Dear God above, help me to go far, far away, far away from 2 Section! What have I done to deserve so hard a punishment?'

The communicator scratches and howls.

'What in the name of heaven have you stopped for, Beier?' comes the company commander, Oberleutnant Löwe's, angry voice. 'Get on, damn it, man, or you'll be for it. It's always your cursed section that's out of step. Clear that road-block away at the bridge, and clean out the nests. Take care, now. The area's mined. But *get on* with it, gentlemen!'

He pauses for a moment to get his breath. 'You're the lead, Beier. You and that shitty section of yours, that I'd like to see slowly roasting in hell. Your job is to go – and to *keep on going*. You stop and everything else stops. The Divisional Commander wants this job over fast, repeat fast!'

'Rotten rat-race,' mumbles the Old Man angrily. He peeps cautiously over the turret rim. 'The bridge,' he hisses. 'But fast!'

'Two more dead un's for the list,' grins Tiny, proudly, holding up the two dead turkeys.

'2 Section follow me,' the Old Man says into the communicator. He is so angry we can hear the sound of his teeth grinding.

'What you mad at?' asks Tiny, looking up at him with his head on one side. 'You're gonna get 'ot roast turkey with all the trimmin's, just like it was *really* Christmas. Enjoy the war, the peace'll be terrible! There won't be no parties 'eld in the synagogues for us thousand-year soldiers.'

Porta pulls to a halt just before the bridge and falls back resignedly in his seat.

'The tour makes a temporary stop here,' he says, with a

short laugh. 'The neighbours've dropped half a forest across the road. Call the Pioneers. That's what *they're* for.'

'They don't give a damn for us,' snarls the Old Man. 'Two of you get out and sling a wire round those tree-trunks so's we can pull 'em out of the way.'

'Not me,' cackles Porta. 'The driver is not to be used for any work other than driving, and is to be rested on every possible occasion. I'm bein' rested!'

'Julius and Sven! Outside! Quick's the word, *please*!'

Super-soldier Heide is out of the tank in a flash. I hesitate before opening the hatch and leaving the protection of the tank's steel walls. There one is safe from the bullets and hand-grenades of the infantry at least. The air outside hums with the sound of them, like a nest of angry wasps.

'What if the neighbours attack us?' I ask nervously when I am outside.

'That's an easy one,' grins Porta, racing his motor. 'We go into reverse. The 1000-year Reich didn't entrust us with this valuable tank to let any silly sod of a neighbour go smashin' it up. Far as you two are concerned you can be proud an' happy. You'll fall like heroes, an' *Grofaz*'ll send your families a postcard. *Heil*! *Sieg*!'

We look up fearfully at the rough sides of the tank as Porta crashes the hatch cover shut.

'Cowardly swine,' hisses Heide bitterly, as the Old Man follows Porta's example and closes the turret hatch.

'The vaunted heroic death comes to us in a dirty snow-drift,' I whisper to myself.

'What the hell are you mumbling about?' snarls Julius, staring at me. We take cover behind the huge tree-trunks, and work feverishly to get the wires into place.

I cannot be bothered to answer him. He would never understand, anyway, with his *herrenvolk* mentality.

Tracer from the turret MG whines over our heads, drawing firefly chains into the Russian tank defence positions. In a hail of whistling shrapnel fragments we finally manage to make the tow-wire fast around the first of the tree-trunks. We haul the wire after us to the tank and loop it over the tow-hooks. Our hands are cut to pieces, and blood drips from our fingertips. I drop the wire for a second to blow on my mutilated hands. Heide explodes into a howl of rage.

'You lazy pig. Letting me do all the work.' He rips his pistol from its holster, and points it at me with outstretched arms, like a film actor. 'Get up, you cardboard soldier, or I'll shoot your head off!'

At that moment I hate him so much it hurts, the puffed-up shit. How annoyingly pompous he looks, standing there tall and slim, with lips so thin they are almost invisible, and icy-cold, blue eyes. Not even the newest war-mad recruit could be so regimentally correctly dressed as Julius. When it came to it what did he know more than a recruit does? Nothing!

Raging I climb back onto my feet, murderous thoughts whirling through my brain. I know Heide is crazy enough to really shoot me if I don't get up quickly. And worst of all he would get away with it.

The Maybachs howl in top output, and the wire is drawn tight as a violin-string. After several attempts the logs begin to roll. We jump like madmen to avoid being crushed by them.

A Russian MG sweeps the road with a short burst. Bullets ricochet, howling, from the steel sides of the tank. It sounds as if a group of drummers have suddenly run amuck on their instruments.

We have almost finished clearing the road-block, and look forward to getting back to the safety of the tank when Heide gives a yell, and goes down into the ditch in one long spring. He slides like a bulldozer through the gruel of ice and water in its bottom.

'Mines!' he screams.

I stand gaping, out on the road between two enormous logs, without understanding a word. I see a large grey-red box with cyrillic lettering on it. A lever sticks up vertically

36

into the air. The mine is armed and ready to explode. For a moment I am completely paralysed.

Our tank is rolling backwards at full speed. Porta has obviously also seen the wicked piece of machinery which is waiting to spread death and destruction on all sides.

Suddenly I am on my own in the middle of a tangle of great tree-trunks and wrecked trucks. I stare, as if hypnotized, at the flat grey-red instrument of death. Then I come alive again.

'Mines!' I yell, 'mines!' As if they didn't know it. When the lead vehicle runs into mines, the news travels back fast.

I throw myself face-down into a large, half-frozen puddle, and hardly notice the water running down into my felt boots. Soon it will turn to ice and my feet will begin to burn like fire.

'God help me,' I pray. 'Help me! Don't leave me to die here!'

There is complete silence. Even the heavy Maxims have ceased firing. It seems as if the whole world has stopped dead. As if the war is holding its breath and waiting for the mine to go off.

An eternity goes by, and still nothing happens. It should have exploded long ago. A count of five is usually enough. I have already counted to thirty-five.

The turret hatch opens slowly, and the Old Man's head appears.

'Get off your arses, you weary warriors. Get rid of that mine.'

'You must be off your rocker,' Heide shouts back furiously. 'You can see the bastard's got delayed-action fuses.'

'Shut up, and obey my order,' shouts the Old Man, impatiently. 'Get that thing out of our way, and I mean *now*. I don't care if it's got *ten* delayed-action fuses. I want it out of the way! D'you think they'll stop the war just because you lot trip over a mine?'

Porta peers cautiously through the driver's observation slit.

37

'What're you playin' at? Don't you *want* to get your heroic names on the big porous stone in front of the barracks at Paderborn? Very big honour that is, let me tell you. A great, national reward!'

I lift my head and take a look at the strange menacing thing. The lever points up in the air like a warning finger. I take a grip on the insulated pliers in my pocket, and ready myself to crawl over to the mine and dismantle it. It is at times like this that a man feels he never should have taken that bomb-disposal course.

The next moment everything disappears in a roaring jet of flame. Pieces of logs whirl through the air and rain down everywhere. I am totally deaf for several minutes, and feel as if my insides have been squeezed by a giant hand. Two minutes later and there would not have been a shred of me left. But the road-block has gone.

We jump up onto the tank as it comes rattling past.

'Nice job you did, there,' the Old Man praises us, with an approving smile. 'Speed up, Porta, give it more gas. We've a long way to go yet!'

'Yes, if it's China we're headed for that *is* a bit of a way off,' grins Porta, exuberantly.

'China?' mumbles Tiny, racking shells in the ammunition locker. 'Ain't that the place where they eat with sticks an' fatten up on rice? Let's get movin'. I can't think of anythin' better'n boiled rice with tiny 'errings.'

'I can give you the address of a good eating-house in Pekin,' grins Porta, putting on speed.

The armoured division rolls relentlessly on, pushing deeply into the Ukraine. Many fall, more are mutilated. The landscape is grim. The grey coldness of a Russian winter is approaching. Tanks rattle and roar through sooty-black villages, plough past huge piles of coal. We do not see a single tree. Vegetation, grass, all green things are gone. Not the least trace, even, of the much vaunted sunflower fields is left. The wild madness of war has eaten up everything in its path. Omnivorously.

The company halts for an hour before a middle-sized provincial town. We have never heard the name of it before. A Russian armoured division has taken it over and turned the town into a hedgehog defensive position. Then our Stukas come roaring out of the grey, snow-filled clouds with sirens howling relentlessly. Heavy bombs whirl down through the air. One swarm of dive-bombers follows the other. The town disappears from the face of the earth – *ausradiert* as they say in the propaganda programmes.

Then the tanks pass over what is left of it, killing everything left alive and crushing the dead to pulp under their tracks.

When we reach the next town the Stukas have already visited it, and prepared it for the taking. The dust of pulverized bricks and mortar hangs like a red-grey cloud in the air. Artillery and Cossack horses lie in the shattered streets, stiff-legged and with swollen bodies. Guns lying on their side, wrecked lorries and mountains of tangled equipment, are scattered amongst heaps of bodies. Dead and wounded Russian soldiers lie against walls, or hang from gaping window openings.

Dispassionately we stare at the bloody scene. It has become an everyday sight. In the beginning we puked and felt sick to our stomachs. It is a long time since any of us puked.

'That's the way to take a town,' shouts Julius Heide, enthusiastically. He leans triumphantly out of the forward hatch. With a jeering smile he stares at a Russian soldier sitting up against a wall and looking blankly at his crushed legs.

'You're wearin' the wrong uniform,' says Porta. 'You talk like those puffed-up arseholes in the shit-brown uniforms, an' the yellow leather equipment to hold their fat guts in. You're a shit of shits, you are, Julius! You're blinded by your crazy belief in the Führer. I really think you'd be glad if one of the shit-brown sods knocked on your mother's door one day an' screamed: "Heil Hitler, Frau Heide! Your son,

Unteroffizier Julius Heide, has fallen for the Führer and Greater Germany! We feel for you in your proud sorrow, Frau Heide! The Führer thanks you!"'

'Old Man, you are my witness,' explodes Heide, in a rage. 'This is an insult. I will not stand for it!'

'Sit down then,' says the Old Man, indifferently. 'There's a lot of things *I* won't stand for. Come on, *Panzer Marsch*! And keep your traps shut, too! I can't stand the sound of your voices. And you, Porta, stop insulting Adolf!'

The night is dark. Snow and rain fall at the same time. It is cold on the way to Nikolajev.

We stop in the middle of a huge factory. It is Porta, of course, who discovers it to be a vodka distillery. Half an hour later we are stoned out of our minds. We reel around, falling over one another, pour vodka over our own heads and lick it into our mouths like cats lapping up cream. We dip our bread in vodka, and become more drunk than ever.

A Feldwebel dies of alcohol shock. A Gefreiter sets fire to himself, to convince a friend that vodka can be ignited just as easily as petrol. We try to put it out by throwing more vodka on him, and laugh foolishly at his screams of pain.

Some of 3 Section come along, dragging four women with them. They throw them across a packing table.

An infantry Feldwebel threatens them with a court-martial. Even in the madness of war there has to be some order and discipline. The punishment for rape is hanging. This is the case in every reasonably civilized army. Nobody listens to him. He is pushed to one side, and drunken soldiers threaten to cut his throat.

'Pricks at the ready!' orders an Obergefreiter with a bloodstained bandage round his head. He throws himself lustfully on top of a half-naked screaming woman, old enough to be his great-grandmother. '*Cunt!*' he roars, and collapses, helplessly drunk, between her thrashing legs. Others pull him away from her and fight to take his place.

We wake up next morning depressed, and with the most horrible hangovers. Soon the military police arrive with their shiny helmets, and the crescent emblem dangling on their chests.

The court-martial is over in four and a half minutes. Eight soldiers dangle, each at the end of his rope. The whole battalion is paraded to see the show. The dead men hang there, with strangely elongated necks, wearing only their uniform trousers. Greatcoats and boots have been taken from them. There is a shortage of such things. They hang there still, turning and swinging on the end of their ropes, as we rattle past, mud churning up from our clattering tracks, on the way to Nikolajev.

'*C'est la guerre*! Come death, come sweet death,' hums the Legionnaire, sardonically, from the turret of his vehicle.

'A dear fuck that was,' sighs Porta. 'Better to pay for it in coin of the realm, if they won't do it for love.'

'There's more'n you'd think get it for takin' cunt what ain't theirs,' growls Tiny, looking thoughtfully at the hanged men.

Raindrops spatter on the armoured sides of the tanks. It is a cold and miserable day. The air reeks with death, and stinks of wet clothing and leather. The clouds are dirty grey. They seem to be rushing towards the west, away from the melancholy Russian day. It is no longer really day. More a kind of twilight.

The little Colonel general is standing on a thrown-up mound of earth, observing his 4th Tank Army. As usual he is wearing his battered silk field-cap, with its short peak pulled well down on his forehead. Beneath it his eagle nose juts out like a beak from the middle of his narrow skull of a face. His boots seem unbelievably long on his short legs. He stands, stiff as a statue, with his map-case under his arm. A hugh pair of binoculars dangle from his neck, partly covering the red tabs on his cloak. To look at this tiny man, with the oversized binoculars and the almost comically high-topped riding boots, you would never dream that he is the greatest tank general who has ever lived.

The Old Man gives the Army Commander a regimental eyes right.

41

'If only the neighbours'd send a 150 mm down on his napper,' Porta wishes, with an abrupt laugh, 'an' send him up to give the angels a big smackin' kiss on the arse.'

'We'd only get another of the same sort,' says the Old Man, tiredly, '*and* most likely one worse'n little short-arse there!'

'He's standing right on top of a busted shithouse,' laughs Gregor Martin, who is now back with us. He is turret-gunner on Barcelona's Puma.

'Wish 'e'd drop down through the top an' fall into it,' growls Tiny, 'so 'im an' 'is fancy silk cap'd get drowned together in Russian shit.'

Barcelona both salutes and gives the eyes right at the same time. The sight of the Army Commander has made him nervous.

Colonel-general Hoth lifts his hand an inch or two.

'Who's that fool?' he asks his Adjutant, who is standing to attention at his elbow as usual.

'I will find out, sir,' barks the Adjutant, smartly.

'Don't you know your men?' asks the General, irritably. 'My Adjutant ought to know every man in my army.'

'Mad bastard,' thinks the Adjutant. 'There's 80,000 men in 4th *Panzer*. I don't know every silly sod on the staff, even.' He is, however, an old hand. He barks out the first name to come into his head.

'Oberfeldwebel Stollmann, sir!'

'Charge him,' snarls the General. 'He can be punished for unregimental saluting. I've never seen anything like it! Saluting! As if the fool was on parade. I want you to look after that man. Properly, understand!'

'Very good, sir!' replies the Adjutant, scribbling in his notebook.

As Barcelona's Puma swings round at the entrance to the long connecting road, the General catches sight of Albert's black face in the open driving hatch.

'Why's that man's face black?' he asks the Adjutant.

'*Black*, sir?' mumbles the Adjutant, in surprise. He puts

his glasses to his eyes, to get a closer look at Albert. 'Looks like a negro, sir!' he says, doubtfully.

The entire staff put up their binoculars. For a moment 4th *Panzer* is forgotten, and all interest is concentrated on Albert in the clean-up waggon's driving-seat.

'A *negro*?' snarls the General, irritably. 'What nonsense! Germany's had no colonies for the last twenty years.'

'Twenty-five, sir,' the Chief-of-Staff corrects him, 'and the last of the colonial troops were retired years ago.'

'Charge that man for having blackened his face without orders,' snaps the General, brusquely. 'I don't want my army turned into a lot of circus clowns!'

The Adjutant writes feverishly: Driver in Puma 524 to be punished for blackening face. He adds, on his own initiative: and for laughing.

In the course of the day we push on through stretched-out villages lining the sides of the roads. White sheets hang from every window as a sign of capitulation.

The inhabitants stand pressed up against the walls of their houses, unsmilingly, faces marked by the fear of the future.

Late in the afternoon we make a halt. We refuel, ammunition is issued, and benzedrine tablets are handed out to each man. There is still no time to waste on sleeping.

Porta and Tiny are long since inside the houses, ransacking boxes and cupboards. They do not really know what they are looking for, but are just sniffing around like inquisitive dogs.

'Funny things they drink out of in this country,' says Tiny, gazing in astonishment at a large pink irrigator and holding it up. 'Couldn't empty that bleeder very often 'fore your bleedin' brains blew out through your ear'oles. What's the tube in it for though?'

'Anybody can see *that*,' answers Porta. 'Ivan's a practical feller. He lies on his back when he drinks, so he doesn't hurt himself when he falls down. We Germans can learn a lot here in Russia.'

43

'I gotta try that,' says Tiny, enthusiastically, hanging the irrigator from his belt like a second gasmask pouch. 'Think o' lyin' flat on your bleedin' back an' gettin' the biggest drunk on the world's ever 'eard of! Maybe a bloke ought to turn Russki an' forget all about old Germany?'

'Holy Virgin Mary's Mother,' cries Porta, in surprise. 'Here's a dead woman, and she's wearing a hunting cap with a feather in it. Going travellin' perhaps when she died. Did go too, only a bit longer trip than she'd reckoned on.'

'Smells like murder,' he murmurs, after taking a closer look at the body. 'Took one in the guts, she did. Can't have been an execution, or she'd have got the pill in her neck. That's how they do it in this country.'

''Ow dreadful!' says Tiny, turning up his eyes. 'Such wicked bleeders ought to be put in jail!'

'Here's her handbag,' Porta goes on. He picks up a lady's bag made of reindeer skin. He shoves his nose right into it, and rummages round.

'Out of here immediately! That's an order!' yells Heide in his best NCO's voice. He positions himself in the doorway with his hands on his hips and bobs up and down on his toes.

'Up you, Moses,' says Tiny, unimpressed.

The blood flashes up into Heide's arrogant Teutonic face.

'I'm warning you, Obergefreiter Creutzfeldt, call me Moses one more time and I'll shoot you! It's dishonouring!'

'Dis'onourin'? Gettin' shot?' laughs Tiny, swinging his *Nagan*.

'*Moses*! You look like the feller as falls on 'is arse at the village fair.'

Heide fumbles furiously for his pistol, but luckily for Tiny it sticks in its holster and he has to use both hands to get it out.

'*Moses*! You'll never get to be a big cowboy star in the pictures,' Tiny screams with laughter. 'The bleedin' rustlers'd've shot you fulla 'oles 'fore you knew what was goin' on!'

A salvo of howling rockets from a Stalin organ drops in the next street, and sends a wall crashing down across the roadway.

'Jesus'n Mary,' cries Tiny, throwing himself down into cover close by the wall. 'Ain't them barmy bleedin' neighbours *ever* goin' to get tired of shootin' at us?'

A German SMG begins to bark in wild, hysterical bursts.

'Hell man, stop that!' the Old Man's voice rings through the noise. 'The tracer'll tell 'em our position!'

'Julius 'as 'ad it,' shouts Tiny, pointing with the muzzle of his mpi at Heide's body stretched out on the floor.

'The Führer lost a faithful soldier there,' says Porta, sadly.

'Hold his forehead while I take his three gold teeth. I've had my eye on 'em for a long time now!'

'You gonna do that? 'E *is* a kind of a mate when all's said an' done!' says Tiny, suddenly turning moralist.

'How's he to know what's happening? Dead isn't he?' answers Porta, bending over Heide. He is just about to take a grip on one of the teeth with his forceps when Heide comes to with a shout. 'Damnation!' cries Porta, in astonishment, 'I thought you were dead!'

'Corpse robber,' screams Heide, gazing with open disgust at Porta's rusty dental forceps.

'Corpse robber?' says Porta, blankly. 'Couldn't *be*! Not dead yet, are you?'

'I'm going to charge you,' snarls Heide, furiously. He dabs at his neck, where a shell-splinter has dug a deep furrow.

'Outside!' shouts the Old Man. 'Get this area cleaned up and quick about it. It's full of aspiring heroes looking forward to dyin' for the great Stalin!'

'I'm on my way,' shouts Porta. He runs off along the houses with the LMG in his hand, supporting grip out.

A clumsy Russian hand-grenade comes flying through the air and falls, smoking, at Tiny's feet. With a resolute kick, worthy of a soccer international, he sends it flying back. Not for nothing is he the regiment's top goal-scorer.

Porta sends a couple of short bursts up at some gaping window-openings, and jumps to cover behind a burnt-out transport vehicle.

'Either them shits're down in the cellars,' yells Tiny, falling full-length in a shower of mud and half-melted snow, 'or else they're upstairs.'

'Where?' howls Porta, crossing in long jumps to the opposite side of the street. He goes down, like lightning, flat in the gutter as he hears the feared mooing of a 'cow' on the way. A row of cobblestones flies into the air.

'Get down, damn you,' shouts the Old Man to the section, signalling with his arms.

Albert is behind a pushcart lying on its side, firing away with an MG-34 as if he were aiming at breaking the world war record for disposal of most ammunition in the shortest time.

Barcelona drops down beside him, panting. 'What the hell are you shootin' at, you black ape? We got to *account* for that ammunition!'

'Shit on that, man!' wheezes Albert, grey-faced with terror. 'No fucking Commie bastard's gonna pull the carpet out from under *my* fallen, fuckin' arches!'

'Stop it, you mad sod,' shouts Barcelona, giving the LMG a kick which sends it flying out of Albert's hands. Shaking his head from side to side, Albert leans up against the wet wall of a house and stares with a lost look at his LMG, which lies hissing in a drift of filthy snow.

'What're you sitting here moping for?' asks Porta, emerging from a house behind two prisoners with hands raised above their heads. 'You look like Frankenstein playin' the part of the Mummy.'

'Now I'm not supposed to shoot any more,' grumbles Albert. 'This is the shittiest war that ever was, you know that, man!'

''Course you can shoot,' answers Porta. 'Bang away at 'em, son. That's what the army's paying you for.' With a broad grin on his freckled face he disappears round the

46

corner with his two prisoners. He will sell them to a prisoner collection squad, out looking for medals.

'Mount!' orders the Old Man. '*Panzer Marsch!*'

'The Führer has won the war,' declares Heide, proudly, as we roll past long rows of Russian soldiers standing with raised hands. They have a lost look about them.

'There'll only be room for two kinds o' people, now,' grunts Tiny, bitterly. 'Them peacocks as does the orderin' about, an' all the other bleedin' idiots as stands to attention, in the sacks as 'olds their bones in place, an' screams 'Eil 'Itler!'

After a short, bloody battle we push forward straight through Poltawski. At the edge of the roads lie corpses clad in grey prison uniforms. All of them have small bullet entry holes at the back of their necks. Cheekbones jut sharply through the thin parchment skin of their faces, and their teeth are bared in ghastly skull-fashion.

'Liquidated,' confirms the Old Man. He sends a long, brown stream of tobacco-juice over the rim of the hatch. 'They're as bad as our rotten lot.'

'Not long since,' says Barcelona, leaning out of the clean-up waggon's turret to get a closer look. 'Blood's still fresh and drippin'.'

'But why've they shot 'em?' asks Gregor. 'And right out here on the road, where we're coming bashin' along.'

'Couldn't keep up,' says Porta, knowledgeably, 'caused trouble and slowed down the rest.'

'They bloody well can't do *that*,' says Gregor, bending over the body of a woman. 'They bloody, fuckin' *can't*!'

'You'll see worse than that,' answers Porta, laconically. 'Wait till the pendulum swings back, an' it's us who're on the run with the neighbours snapping at our arses. Then you'll see what *we* can do!'

The Old Man lights his silver-lidded pipe in silence, and wishes inside that he could get his fingers on the man who had carried out this massacre.

The rows of dead seem never-ending, but no more than

47

an hour later the maelstrom of war has driven the episode out of our heads, like many other things.

Physical death lies in wait for us round every corner. We cannot choose death, but must live, and carry on as well as we can. War is a disease, and it is best not to think of it too much, but to forget the impressions its symptoms leave on us. If we didn't we would all very soon go raving mad.

The section takes up position alongside a small river, which runs, yellow and cold, down to the distant sea.

Porta has placed the SMG behind a heap of potato-sacks. Potatoes are as good as sandbags for stopping bullets, he says. Barcelona wants the vehicles ready to go, so that we can move off at short notice if necessary, but meets with wild protests when he demands that the drivers remain in their seats.

'There's not gonna be much time,' he tries to explain to the angry drivers, who are afraid of remaining alone in their vehicles. 'I want those bloody waggons ready to move while there's still *time*!' he orders, raging.

'Up you and your time,' shouts Porta, disrespectfully. 'Sit in your sardine-can yourself if you want to. I'm staying here with the popgun. When the neighbours come knockin' on the door'll be time enough to take off. I'm gonna be one of the survivors of this world war. I'm not goin' to get fried in me own fat, if some Commie sod or other gets the idea of tacking a magnetic onto my backside.'

In the light of a huge fire, which is raging down at some grain storehouses, Tiny comes crawling out of a window opening dragging a large chest behind him.

A Maxim sends a line of tracer bullets at him.

'Stop that bleedin' waste o' bullets,' he yells, waving a threatening fist at the invisible Russian positions. 'Got earth where your brains oughta be? Or shit, is it, maybe?'

'I'll smash you to bits, if you don't leave that chest lie,' shouts the Old Man, furiously. 'Get back to your rotten squad. I see you looting one more time an' you're for a court!'

A flare goes up. A slowly sinking comet with a colourful

tail of smoke behind it. Everyone stands completely still in the blinding white light. There are sounds all around us. Heavy boots tip-toeing, nervous hands cocking weapons, battle-knives ringing, bullets being pushed into breeches. The mumbling noises of death. We see nothing, hear only the noises coming from the darkness. We are never quite sure whether they are real or whether our nervous imaginations are deceiving us.

Porta raises his head and sniffs like a tensed-up hunting dog.

Slowly, unbelievably slowly, the cursed flare sinks down towards the earth.

Without making the slightest noise I turn the LMG.

'Holy Saint Agnes of Bielefeld,' whispers Porta, in open excitement. 'If what I'm smellin' is right, I will burn a candle in the synagogue of my heart for the God of Germany for the rest of my life.'

There is a sharp cracking explosion above our heads, and we press ourselves down into the mud. One of the very largest flares flowers against the night-dark heavens.

'Life ain't nothin' but one wide-open, stinkin' black arse-hole,' curses Albert, his teeth chattering, from a deep cellar opening. 'Tonight my girl'll be dancin' at the *Zigeunerkeller*, an' they'll all be starin' straight up her clean-shaven black cunt every time she swings her legs. After that she fucks with the whole rotten garrison. *That's* what a man has to put up with!'

'She black, too?' asks Gregor interestedly, his eyes watchful above the MG barrel. He is certain there are several companies of Russians sneaking around out there in the darkness, getting ready to storm our positions and cut all our throats.

'I'm a paleface compared to her,' mumbles Albert, running his hand over his face. 'She's black as only God's own people *can* be!'

'She a whore?' asks Porta bluntly, showing his face over the top of a sack of potatoes.

'You say that once more, man,' snarls Albert furiously,

49

'an' I'll pull that maggoty white skin of yours down over your stinkin' German face! She's an *artiste*, man! She dances French in the *Zigeunerkeller*. And she's got her name on the posters outside! An' I love that girl, man, even though she *is* a French nigger woman.'

'Holy Mary, Mother of Jesus,' shouts Porta. 'Can I believe my ears. Get that flare out quick. Sucking pigs, God dammit, *sucking* pigs!'

As soon as the flare dies, Porta and Tiny race off like hungry hounds on the scent with tongues hanging out. They take no notice of the Old Man's angry shouts ordering them to come back to the unit.

'It's desertion,' shouts the Old Man into the dark. 'I've had it now. My patience is at an end!'

'They smell food, *mes amis*,' the Legionnaire chuckles merrily. He lights a long cigarette from the butt of the previous one. 'The whole of the Red Army, even, would not be able to stop them now!'

Tiny falls only once during his mad rush forward, but tumbles twenty yards on down an incline, and brings up against a tilted tractor. Soon after he runs across a Russian answering a call of nature behind a bush.

The Russian's pistol has only half cleared its holster when Tiny's close combat knife thuds into his chest. 'The good die young,' growls the big man, as his knife goes home.

> 'I was so lonely,
> You were so charming,'

sings Porta, happily, in a hoarse Louis Armstrong voice, as he bends over a litter of six grunting sucking-pigs. One of them rubs itself lovingly against Tiny's jackboots. He lies down in the mouldy straw, and begins to play with the piglets.

'Cut that out, now,' warns Porta, 'or it'll be the same game as with that big sow we got fond of. The one that died of old age!'

'Why d'you sing that foreign stuff?' asks Tiny, wrinkling his brow.

'*I* dunno,' answers Porta. 'I think it sounds nice. I love Louis Armstrong. Nobody can sing like them darkies!'

'Adolf's black-listed 'im too,' says Tiny, sadly. 'I 'ad a good record of 'is. They knocked the shit out o' me once up in *Stadthausbrücke 8* for 'earin it. Gawd, 'ow they did belt me. Then they made me eat the bleedin' record afterwards, just so I'd understand that that kind o' *untermensch* shit wasn't what us Germans listened to.'

'Adolf's mad as a hatter,' says Porta, 'but we'll get him some day. Be patient, my son. The sun always comes out again after the storm.'

'I can't stop thinkin' about it,' says Tiny, scratching one of the pigs thoughtfully behind the ear. 'I reckon we ought to shoot 'is Austrian bonce off. But break 'is left leg first. Then 'is right. Then both arms from 'is finger joints upwards, so 'e'll know we mean it serious. In between times we 'it 'im in the balls, if 'e's got any. Then we wind up by pourin' petrol all over 'im an' puttin' a match to 'im like a bonfire. That's exactly what *I* think we'd 'ave to do to 'im to make everythin' even steven!'

'Take it easy, we'll fix him when the time comes,' promises Porta. 'He'll be sorry he ever took on the job of Führer. Vote for Adolf and die young,' he laughs out into the night.

A shell explodes, with a crash, somewhere inside the town. A couple of machine-guns rattle viciously, but soon go silent. The plopping of a mortar sounds as a finale.

The Old Man bursts in on them in full battle-kit. He is covered with mud from helmet brim to boot-tops.

'You gone stone bonkers? What the hell are you up to?'

'Take a look,' grins Porta, pleasantly. 'We're engaging some Commie pigs.'

'Heavenly Father,' groans the Old Man, despairingly. He throws his mpi, clattering, across the mud floor. 'What have I done to be made leader of such a lot of crazy sods as 2 Section? The neighbours are attackin' along the whole front, and close to rollin' us up, an' what are *you* doin'? Sitting here playing with some bloody pigs. You go on

51

report for this, blast your eyes, you do!'

'Why're you always so mad at us?' asks Tiny. 'You think too much about the army an' the bleedin' war, you do. Enjoy life. It's short enough as it bleedin' is!'

'Shut your trap, you,' hisses the Old Man, viciously, pointing at Tiny with a stick-grenade.

There is the heavy thudding of distant shell-fire. In between the sharper crack of tank guns can be heard.

'Maybe it's about time a feller got 'is valuable arse movin',' says Tiny, listening critically to the guns.

A couple of Maxims start up a crossfire, but it is nervous shooting and does us no damage.

Porta tucks a kicking piglet under his arm. Tiny slings his mpi and takes one under each arm.

'You take one too,' he says to the Old Man. 'We ought to 'ave enough to be able to give everybody a bit, so they won't get snotty!'

'You can't run about carrying pigs in the middle of an attack,' rages the Old Man, copper-coloured in the face. He strikes at one of the piglets.

Porta peers out of the door, but quickly closes it again.

'What's up?' asks the Old Man, his face twitching nervously.

'Nothin' special. Only a Russian colonel, with a machine-popper under his arm, and his eyes full o' German corpses!'

A rain of bullets strikes the walls of the house, almost tearing the door off its hinges.

'Nice way to knock on a door,' growls Tiny, getting behind a heavy supporting tree-trunk, still with his squealing piglets under his arms.

The plopping of mortars sounds continually. The whole area is bombarded with earth, stones and shrapnel from the explosions.

'Let's get out of here,' says the Old Man. 'The neighbours'll be here before we know it!'

'Jesus'n Mary,' shouts Tiny. 'Them crazy neighbours is shootin' with 'eavy stuff! You'd think they was tryin' to kill us poor bleeders or somethin'!'

One of the piglets intensifies its squeals. Its side has been cut open by a piece of shrapnel. Tiny is covered with blood.

'Kill that blasted pig,' shouts the Old Man. 'They'll hear it all over Russia.'

Tiny slits its throat quickly. The squealing dies away in a few small final grunts.

'To die so young,' he says, compassionately.

It is a heavy, icy-cold morning, and fog lies like a blanket over the landscape.

Porta stops behind the cover of some bushes. He withdraws the flare-pistol from its canvas holster.

'None o' that shit,' the Old Man warns him, nervously. 'We can't see anything by it anyway.'

'*I* know *that*,' answers Porta, stretching his arm upwards at an angle with the flare-pistol clutched in his hand. 'It'll just make Ivan know we're awake an' ready. Then, while the silly sods are sittin' there afraid they're gonna get their arses shot off any minute, we sneak quietly away from the party.'

The flare hangs, for a few short minutes, over the terrain. Then it is dark again, and we can see nothing at all.

'At the double, that way, along the old position,' the Old Man orders me.

Panting with effort, I rush along the narrow trench, in mud up to my ankles. I stop for a moment at a corner. I need a cigarette. I see Russian faces under funny-looking helmets. They are looking straight down at me from the parapet of the trench. Everything happens faster than my eyes and brain can register it. The dark morning fog is filled with flame, smoke and wild cries. Behind me and in front of me there are Russians who have jumped down into the trench. The muzzle-flash of a *Kalashnikov*, going off just in front of my face, blinds me for a second. Maddened with the fear of death I fall over backwards, come up again and engage a Russian who is just as frightened as I am. I strike at him blindly with my combat knife, and feel it get home in his guts. In a close embrace we fall to the muddy floor of the trench. I wrench my knife out of his body, and stab at him

53

again and again. Hot blood spurts into my face. Then I am up again, and run in panic, without knowing which way my feet are carrying me.

The Russians behind me throw hand-grenades. The night lights up with their explosions.

Porta and Tiny come rushing towards me. I throw myself down to avoid their rattling machine-pistols.

The Old Man is behind them. Close behind him come others.

A wild, bloody hand-to-hand fight begins. I rip a *Kalashnikov* from the hands of a dead Russian lieutenant, and begin to fire blindly at whatever is in front of me.

We thirst for blood and revenge. We *want* to kill. We are happy to have hit the hated enemy in the back.

A bare-headed Russian corporal stands in front of me, with both hands above his head. I empty half of my magazine into his chest, and smash the butt of my weapon into his face.

Suddenly everything is still. The fighting is over as suddenly as it began. Some minor skirmishing, the report will say.

Porta has a bottle of vodka in his hand. He pulls the cork with his teeth, takes a long, gurgling swig at it, and gives out a long, rolling belch. The blood comes back into his thin cheeks, and his eyes begin to look more lively. He wipes his mouth with the back of his hand. Then he bends down and picks up a rifle-grenade. He screws off the cap, and puts the grenade into his pocket. Ready for use, if we run into any more surprises.

With mpis at the ready, and fingers on their triggers, Porta and I jump through a street-door, ready to mow down anything moving. We know that those left behind in such towns are crazy fanatics, totally insane, completely regardless of their lives as long as they take some enemy soldiers with them.

Silently we sneak along the walls of the houses, straining our eyes to pierce the dust hanging in the air. I strangle a cough, afraid to give away our position to some madman waiting with his finger on the trigger.

The first room is empty. The next one, too.

Quietly, I catfoot up a narrow spiral staircase. My heart seems to stop beating for several minutes when a heavy hand falls on my shoulder. Luckily I am so frightened that I forget the weapon in my hands.

'Mustn't shit in Adolf's trousers, now,' whispers Tiny, calmingly. 'It's only me! If it'd been Ivan you'd 'ave been kissin' the angels in the arse by now!'

'Lord preserve us! You nearly frightened the life out of me,' I stammer, knocking his hand away, roughly.

'Look what I found,' he says, happily, holding up an oblong box filled with cigars for me to see. 'A bleedin' colonel belongin' to the neighbours was sittin' there dead with 'is 'and on top of it when I come by.' With a flourish he places one of the fat cigars in his mouth and lights it with a lighter made out of a bullet casing.

'You must be mad,' I whisper fearfully. 'With everybody out there lying in wait, ready to shoot our heads off, you . . .'

'Worth dyin' for a good cigar,' says Tiny, calmly. He holds his primitive lighter above his head like a torch, and looks inquiringly around him.

The staircase creaks treacherously, as we tiptoe on up it.

'Rotten old shit,' he rages, kicking noisily at a loose plank.

Porta is waiting for us on a landing with a half-empty vodka bottle in his hand. He takes a long swig at it, before handing it on to Tiny, who leaves only a drop for me.

'Anybody here?' I cough, nervously, from the fiery spirit.

'How should I know?' asks Porta. 'Think I'm a bloody clairvoyant or somethin', p'raps?'

'We'll soon find out,' says Tiny, taking a couple of heavy drags on his cigar, and sticking his head out of the door-opening, like a Red Indian trying to look round corners. 'Hey, Ivan there!' he roars in a voice which echoes through the house. 'Come on out you *tovaritsches*. We got somethin' nice for you.' He thumbs off the safety on his LMG and waves the muzzle about. 'Not as much as a limp prick,' he chuckles and enters the room with long, confident strides. It is a mess of shattered furniture. Shards of porcelain and glass crunch under our hob-nailed boots.

A doll, of the kind which can open and close its eyes, lies in the middle of the floor. Porta picks it up and places it carefully on what is left of an old-fashioned sideboard.

The sweet, sickly stench of death hangs over the whole house.

An LMG rattles wildly out in the street. Two others start up. Mortars plop. The sounds die away again into a waiting silence in which death watches from every hiding-place.

'Hell, my arm hurts,' I complain, trying to roll my sleeve up.

'Where?' asks Porta. 'Let's have a look at it.'

'Gawd, you're bleedin',' says Tiny, opening his eyes wide. 'Who's cut you, then?'

'Must have been down in that rotten trench, when those murderous swine jumped down on me,' I answer.

Porta puts on a dressing, first washing the wound with some beer from an opened bottle standing on the sideboard.

'That's quite a slash they give you there,' says Tiny, pityingly. ''Ave a officer's cigar will you? It 'elps.'

I shake my head, and bite my lips with pain as Porta scrapes the long knife-cut clean.

We continue slowly on through the house with machine-pistols at the ready. In the attic we find a double bed with a body lying on it. It is swollen up and lies with staring, glazed eyes.

Tiny pushes at it inquisitively with his bayonet.

'You nuts, or somethin'? Head full o' earth, is it?' Porta scolds him. 'Put a hole in him, an' we get corpse-gas straight up in our faces. We won't be able to stand ourselves. Take a look if he's got any gold teeth, but careful! *Don't* bloody puncture him.'

Tiny opens the dead man's mouth, with the mien of a professional dentist.

'Not a sod,' he says, shaking his head, sadly. 'Proletarian shit with steel teeth. Them bleedin' Commies knows 'ow to do the people in the eye, all right. The bosses gets gold in their kissers, an' the coolies 'as to make do with bleedin' iron. An' that's what they call equal rights? I ain't never goin' to turn Commie. You can put that in the soddin' 'eadlines!'

Most of the roof has been burnt, and we can see the dark sky through it. A flare explodes into a spreading white flower of light. Immediately, the heavy guns begin to thunder. A row of red fireballs blinks into existence.

'Jesus'n Mary,' shouts Tiny clattering rapidly down the narrow spiral staircase. 'The neighbours are comin'!'

Plops and crashes intensify, as a rain of shells falls on the town.

I almost fly through the door and throw myself flat down into what I hope is cover, but turns out to be the remains of two Germans. My stomach rolls over and I puke heartily. I beat at my clothing in a hysterical attempt to rid it of the human rubbish.

'Take it easy, *mon ami, c'est la guerre,*' drawls the little Legionnaire. In one long jump he is beside me. 'It is only more human offal on the muckheap of the war.'

After a short while the artillery fire dies away. Only the mortars continue to plop away, dropping their shells around us.

A couple of Maxims bark angrily, sending lines of tracer along the street.

'Where the hell they shooting from?' asks Gregor in wonder. 'Can't see their muzzle-flash anywhere.'

'The wicked sods are shooting through tent canvas,' Porta explains, knowledgeably.

Three tank grenadiers come running noisily, weighed down by field equipment, and throw themselves down, panting, alongside us.

'Feldwebel Groos,' one of them introduces himself, putting his new-looking steel helmet straight.

'Obergefreiter, by the grace of God, Joseph Porta,' grins Porta, raising his yellow topper slightly.

'Fuck off, you silly sod,' snarls the Feldwebel, inching away as if Porta had the plague.

The sucking noise of a mortar bomb sounds again. It falls a little way in front of us. A spout of water goes up and a red fire hydrant goes spinning across the street to smash against the wall just behind Tiny.

I hunch down behind the LMG, my stomach cramping with fear. I drop my head and rest the rim of my helmet on the stock of the weapon, afraid to look up.

Another flare wobbles into the sky. The sound of the shot rings in my ears. It is the Feldwebel of grenadiers who has sent it up.

'What in the name of all the devils in hell are you up to, you dopey idiot?' rages the Old Man. 'D'you want the whole of Ivan's blasted army on our necks?'

''Ead-full o' rotten, bleedin', cat-shit's what 'e's got,' growls Tiny, looking wickedly at the grenadier Feldwebel. 'Want my advice, Old Un', you'll cut 'is balls off!'

'Who do you think you're talking to, Obergefreiter?' explodes the Feldwebel, in a fury. 'Can't you see *these*? You're talking to a Feldwebel. I'm putting you on report for speaking improperly to a superior!'

'Shut your arse, mate. Tie a knot in your prick,' Tiny suggests from the darkness, cackling with laughter.

'I won't stand for this,' bellows Feldwebel Grooss. 'I demand that this man be punished.'

'Get out of here 'fore I shoot you,' hisses the Old Man, irritably. 'Nobody invited you. This is 2 Section, and you've nothing to do with us here!'

'This *is* the same war,' Feldwebel Groos says, defensively, staring furiously at the Old Man.

'Got cloth ears have you? Didn't you hear the man? He said to beat it,' shouts Porta, happily. 'Are all Saxons as hard to dance with as you? To hell, Fido! Get back in your basket an' go to sleep!'

'Don't you let 'em talk to you like that, sir,' says a tall grenadier with a voice as thin as his body, and a uniform still stinking of depot moth-balls.

'Ivan'll be here any minute an' shoot your backsides off,' says Gregor with a long, happy whinny of laughter.

'Up on your feet! We're moving,' decides Groos, sharply. He gets to his feet with the air of a leader of men, and does not hear the treacherous whine in the air. We hear it and press ourselves down as close to the ground as we can get. 'Cowardly pigs,' he just manages to get out, before an 80 mm shell explodes right in front of him.

His body is silhouetted briefly against the glare of the explosion. The shell blast cuts him in two, and sends the upper half of his body, with binoculars and steel helmet, far off to one side and through an open door.

'Christ a'mighty!' shouts Tiny. ''E was lucky that bleedin' door was standin' on the jar. 'E *woulda* got one on the nut if it'd been shut!'

'What do we do now?' ask the other grenadiers, looking uncertainly at the Old Man.

'Find yourselves some good Russian cunt,' suggests Porta, pleasantly, 'and fuck yourselves out of this world war. That's the best way, short of gettin' out of it alive!'

'Get back where you came from,' orders the Old Man, brusquely. 'I don't want you here with my section!'

Grousing, they get to their feet and disappear into the darkness.

Quite slowly the firing dies away, and a waiting, threatening silence falls over the ruined town.

Swearing and grumbling we pick up our automatic weapons and our heavy equipment, and trudge on.

I swing the LMG up onto my shoulder, and wipe melting snow and mud from my face.

'God love us, but it's cold'n wet,' says Gregor, as he folds up the tripod legs, and blows on his fingers, which are blue with cold.

With his machine-pistol in the crook of his arm, like a man carrying a shovel, and his wet helmet pushed back on his neck, the Old Man rolls along bow-leggedly in front of 2 Section.

'Come on, my sons! Let's see if we can't find the Red Army an' get the war over quickly,' Porta emits a death's-head laugh. 'That's what we left home for!'

'What a bleedin' life,' sighs Tiny, tonguing his cigar over to the other corner of his mouth, and shaking the snow from his light-grey bowler with a great sweep of his arm. 'No sensible bloke ought to be forced into livin' through everythin' as goes on in a fuckin' world war like this'n,' he moans, pessimistically.

'Know what I'd like?' asks Gregor, impulsively, as he trudges along close to the walls of the houses. 'I'd like to visit General bloody Arse-an'-Pockets, and stick a grenade into his fucking bed. God rot him, I would! Then I'd stand outside an' watch the fun when the little sod hit the ceiling along with the *Kraft durch Freude** whore he was sleepin' with.'

'Get on, get on,' the Old Man pushes along impatiently. 'What the devil d'you think you're getting paid a mark a day by the Army for?'

Some Russians get up and come to meet us with arms stretched above their heads. But others, who were with them, disappear into the darkness, throwing grenades behind them as they run.

Tiny kills eight men in one long burst which seems to go on forever. He crushes the skull of an officer, who is screaming, '*Stalimo!*'

The section halts near a burnt-out corn silo. It is still smoking a little, and it is nice to warm oneself at it.

Soon we begin to feel alive again.

I throw myself down behind the LMG in a heap of blackened corn. Gregor lies alongside me, flat on his back. His eyelids flutter. He blows a tiny pin-feather away from his face.

The Old Man stares gloomily into space. He knows there are thousands of kill-crazy men all around us, out there in the darkness.

I watch him through half-closed eyes. As long as we have the Old Man as our Section Leader we still have a tiny chance of getting out of this madness reasonably unharmed.

* *Kraft durch Freude:* Strength Through Joy (Nazi holiday organization)

He doesn't want to see any of us killed uselessly in some idiotic caper devised by a madman a long way behind us, who is only looking for medals and a new row of salad dressing on his chest.

A 37 mm strikes and ricochets off with a howl, but does no damage.

Porta leans tiredly against the still-warm ruins of the silo and spits foolishly into the wind.

'Holy Saint Agnes, is there anything as beautiful as a fucked-up world war which loses its breath for a minute, and has to take a break? What d'you say to coffee with somethin' a bit stronger in it?'

'Got beans?' asks the Old Man, lighting his silver-lidded pipe.

'What do you take me for?' Porta laughs, hoarsely. 'The day I *haven't* got beans enough for a cup of coffee, that'll be the day they pull the world from under my feet.'

'We haven't really got time,' says the Old Man, puffing away at his pipe. 'But to hell with it, make it anyway. We're not the blasted Moscow Express, we're only 2 Section!'

With nimble fingers Porta rigs up his American petrol-burner.

'The people who sailed across the Polar Sea with this nice little thing couldn't ever've dreamed that Obergefreiter by the grace of God Joseph Porta'd be makin' coffee on it some day,' he grins with satisfaction.

'That blasted silence,' mumbles the Old Man, blowing into the metal cup attached to his water-bottle.

'Nothing like a "little black"* on a cold morning,' says Porta, adding a dash of vodka to each cup.

Albert takes a big gulp of his coffee, to leave more room for the vodka.

'If I do thirty years in this war, I'll never get used to them rotten flares,' he says, thinly, cupping his hands and blowing warm breath up along his cheeks. 'They make me think of corpse candles. Life ain't nothin' but one great big shitter,

* A cup of black coffee with a dash of schnapps (or vodka).

man, an' it gets blown out from under you 'fore you even know it, an' they still say "God is good!" Enough to make you grin your tripes into knots! In all my black life I never learnt as much about bein' scared as since I got into this rotten excuse for a war, and always soakin' wet I am, too! If only a man could get pneumonia, at least he'd have a temperature an' all that, but the good God has decided otherwise and here a feller's got to go creepin' around on the stinkin' face o' the earth and waiting till the neighbours shoot his black arse off!' He takes a slug at the vodka coffee, and looks around him mournfully. 'Sometimes I wish they'd just come and kill me an' get it over with. When it comes to it, man, life ain't worth livin' with, anyway!'

'*C'est la guerre, mon ami*,' sighs the Legionnaire, the eternal *Caporal* bobbing between his lips. 'You are no more than the garbage which goes to make up the military muckheap. That is as Allah has willed it!'

Porta laughs quietly and pours more coffee and vodka into our cups.

'Heide's Führer certainly took us for a ride when he promised us eternal peace and *Kraft durch Freude* with all the trimmin's!'

'Shall we place the machine-guns?' asks Barcelona, stretching out in the warm corn.

'No, sod everything,' says the Old Man, uncaringly. 'Let the neighbours come and beg us to shoot at them for once. I couldn't care less!'

It is still dark when we turn out again, and wriggle into our wet capes. They smell of mud and ancient sweat.

The Old Man is standing outside in the clammy morning mist, waiting for us. The flaps of his field-cap are turned down over his ears, and the silver-lidded pipe hangs slackly at the corner of his mouth. It is one of those miserable mornings, which Russia has such a wealth of. A morning fit to draw both the soul and marrow out of a man.

Grumbling and moaning at one another we pull our equipment together. We seem, by now, to have assembled a fantastic collection of gear. Light and heavy machine-guns, clumsy gun mountings, machine-pistols, combat knives, collapsible spades; cartridge belts criss-crossing our bodies, grenades filling our pockets and stuffed into the tops of our jackboots. Add to this, wire-cutters, magnetic charges, batteries and signal telephones, field-lamps, map-holders and compasses.

'God what a load of shit,' pants Porta, struggling with his gasmask pouch. 'Stay here, while I bring up the limousine!'

'That's in order,' answers the Old Man. 'Drivers pick up their waggons, but quick's the word, mind! Let's get this lousy war over with, so we can go home again!'

'Let's hope the neighbours' nasty boys haven't pinched the chariots out from under us in the course o' the night,' chuckles Porta, as he goes off whistling with the other drivers of the section at his heels.

'If anybody wants my opinion,' says Tiny, importantly, 'I reckon we ought to set a guard on them waggons when we're in the sack. If we don't the insurance won't cover us. Well that's up to you fellers. I'm goin' to go down an' get the bleedin' pigs.'

'You'll stay here,' the Old Man flames up, furiously, but Tiny doesn't hear him. He is already out of sight, with a grenade in one hand and an mpi in the other.

After a while the days and nights flow together into one grey blur. We cannot remember the difference between one town we have stormed through and another, and it is a long time since we stopped counting the dead. There are too many of them for us to keep up any interest.

Out in the fields lie the carcasses of piebald cows blown up like balloons and with legs jutting upwards stiffly.

Porta almost cries at this insane waste of good food, and embarks on a lecture on the correct preparation of *Osso Buco* with rice and a piquant sauce.

27 Panzer Regiment is withdrawn from the attack. Most of its companies have shrunk to reduced section size. Our company has three vehicles left. The rest are junk.

> *When we left the soil of our father-*
> *land, they told us that we were*
> *going out to defend the holy rights.*
>
> *Marcus Flavius*

It was early in the morning. He ran wildly down through the valley. He was the last man of his section. Most of his comrades had already fallen, crossing the stream, when a Russian SMG which was covering its banks opened up. The water rippled a deep red behind him. He reached the top of the hill, and felt a burning pain in his side. It had been ripped wide open. Everything went black.

Well into the afternoon he came to himself again. The air was shimmering with heat, the sun burning down on him. He attempted to turn his head away from it. His greatcoat was torn open. Buttons gone. His right side was one bloody mash; minced flesh, crushed bones and tatters of uniform.

'Water,' he groaned. 'Water,' he repeated, but nobody heard him. The battlefield was silent.

A short distance from him lay two Russians. One of them had died several hours ago. His face was a mask of blood. The other soldier still moved slightly now and then, and a rattling sound came from his ruined mouth. His stomach had been slashed open.

A swarm of flies crawled busily about on the protruding entrails.

'Water!' he mumbled again. 'Thirsty!'

The whole of the long valley was a jumble of empty cartridge cases. Down by the bank of the stream stood a burnt-out T-34. A little further off lay the shot-away turret of a German P-IV. The lush, green grass had been flattened by the tread of countless heavy boots; tank tracks had slashed open the soft earth.

A swarm of flies buzzed up, suddenly. Some of them lighted on his face, crawling between his parted lips, and up into his nose. He tried to raise his hand, and then to shake his head, but the orders from the brain resulted in no more than a slight tremor of his body.

'Water!' he thought. He kept on thinking about water until the moment he died.

Two weeks later his mother, a war widow of World War I, received the obligatory postcard:

In the name of the Führer, Adolf Hitler, we regret to inform you that your son:

> *Lieutenant Georg Friedrich,*
> *Platoon Commander of Infantry,*

has fallen fighting bravely and in line of duty for Führer, Volk and Fatherland.

The Führer thanks you. Heil Hitler!

THE FAT LEUTNANT

The town which has been chosen for us to recuperate in looks neat and clean. The war has moved through it quickly, leaving only a few wrecked houses to mark its passage. The gasworks had been blown up, of course. Gasworks are always blown up during a retreat. But we don't care. Who wants gas, anyway? Not us!

The Hotel *Ssvaeoda** hums with activity. The owner, Tanya, stands behind the bar, dressed in an ancient mauve party dress, and flanked by three attractive, short-skirted waitresses, ready to welcome the German liberators. She has an interesting, and very ripe, vocabulary which she has picked up from the Mongol troops who were stationed here before we arrived.

Porta and Tiny start immediately to teach her the equivalent expressions in German. Two days later she is welcoming everyone who enters the bar with a pleasant:

'Lick my arse?'

Tiny has his hand up under the mauve party dress. He is trying to persuade her to tell him where the commissars hid their vodka and caviare when they left.

'Fuck?' he tempts her, lasciviously, in a whisper which makes the rafters ring, and the stuffed bear by the fireplace blink its blood-red eyes.

With the proud gait of a Czarina, Vera Konstantinovna comes through the door. She keeps her expensive fox fur on indoors, despite the heat of the room. She is said to be a woman of rank, married to a high-up commissar, who has

---

* *Ssvaeoda:* Russian for freedom.

gone off with the Red Army. The others address her, jeeringly, as 'Your Grace', but cannot hide the fact that they are really not a little afraid of her.

'Shag, then?' suggests Porta, making the international sign for copulation with his thumb. 'A trip on the old pork dagger? *Panjemajo?*'

On their way upstairs Porta already has both hands searching about under Vera's skirt.

'I will just wash *ma petite soeur*,' she murmurs, pouting her lips for a kiss. 'My husband installed a bidet here, before he had to leave. You know what bidet is?'

'A trough to wash out ol' Porky Pig's kennel in,' laughs Porta. 'They're all over the place in France, but they fuck more there too.'

While she is in the bathroom Porta takes off his clothes. He throws his heavy Russian pistol clattering on to the dressing-table, but, as usual with him, retains his yellow topper and his boots.

From down in the bar Barcelona's heavy bass voice can be heard:

Wir, im fernen Vaterland geboren,
nahmen nichts als Hass im Herzen mit,
Doch wir haben die Heimat nicht verloren,
unsere Heimat ist heute vor Madrid . . .*

She has nothing on but her shoes and stockings when she returns to the room. Her reddish-golden hair swings loosely around her shoulders.

'What a peach,' shouts Porta, admiringly, smacking his tongue. 'Come with me to Berlin. You could make a fortune

---

* Very freely:
   We're from many a distant homeland.
   But we feel no loss in our hearts.
   For we have not lost our homeland
   It is here before Madrid . . .

in the *Zigeunerkeller*. They pay 200 for a single, and 500 for a round trip there!'

She comes slowly toward him, her lips parted in a sensual smile.

'Oh Jesus, Jesus,' he mumbles in a hoarse voice, his small eyes rolling round in his head. 'You're enough to make a dead man get it up again!'

'You are a sweet man,' she whispers, seductively. 'But why you wear the boots?'

'Helps in a quick getaway,' he grins. 'Think now if your husband, who has gone on his travels, was to put his commissar's head in here with a *Kalashnikov* in his hands. I'd be quicker over the cobblestones with me boots on!'

She kisses him. Small, feather-light kisses, which tickle his face. She falls back on to the bed taking him down with her.

'Like my old stick o'rock, do you?' he asks, after a while. 'It's all the way from Berlin, an' can do most anything!'

'You are nice, man,' she whispers, enticingly, and runs her fingers over the bristly hairs at the back of his neck.

When Porta comes back down to the bar, several hours later, he is met with cries of admiration.

'What'd it cost you?' asks a Wachtmeister of artillery, interestedly. He is wondering if the 25 marks he has saved up is enough.

'She did it for love!' Porta brags. 'But *you*, you can count on slipping a grand at least for the pleasure.'

'Fuck her then. She ain't my type,' snarls the Wachtmeister disappointedly. He goes over to chat up one of the short-skirted waitresses.

'Take cover!' shouts Tiny, swaying drunkenly to his feet. 'I'll shoot the bleeding cocks off the lot of you, else!'

The machine-pistol seems to go on chattering forever. A huge mirror carrying the old Czarist eagle shatters to pieces. Bottles fall from behind the bar. Ricochets leave splintered tracks in the floor. When the magazine is finally empty he stands for a moment swaying uncertainly on widespread legs.

'Are you dead?' he asks the empty bar-room, changing magazines. 'Maybe you know now 'oo it is as 'as invaded this bleedin' country?' With another long burst he blows all the windows out, shoots a cow in a landscape painting hanging on the wall, and makes a colander of the plank wall screening the bar from the kitchen. Then he falls to the floor, clutching the machine-pistol lovingly in his arms.

A quartermaster with only one boot on exits rapidly through the door. He thinks the Russians have come back.

Tanya helps Tiny to his feet, embraces him and tells him with false friendliness that she has always loved Germans.

'A world war's not all wickedness,' says Porta to Vera, straightening her garter. 'Does that commissar feller of yours know you dish out his private crumpet to the German liberators while he's away? He might send you to *Kolyma* for unRussian behaviour if he found out. But p'raps you'd like the work, down in the state mines?'

'We've got visitors,' yells Gregor, happily, as a Kübel comes skidding sideways through the slush of the square with tyres whining.

Five military policemen spring eagerly from the Kübel. Carefully as ballet dancers they pick their way through the melting snow, to avoid marring their mirror-bright jackboots. Their helmets sparkle, throwing flashes of light to all sides. As they cross the square they draw Walther pistols from their new, yellow holsters. They tramp heavily and with assurance across the planks of the floor, chests well out to display their brightly-polished headhunter insignia for all to see. They are big, well-nourished men, who enjoy the fear they are accustomed to engendering.

The guard commander, a brutal-looking, beery Saxon

70

with the Blood Order* over his right breast pocket, marches round in a circle and sends field court-martial looks at us.

'You don't know *me*, you sons of pigs,' he roars, with a self-satisfied air, spitting on the floor. 'But God help you when you do!' He draws a long police truncheon from its special pocket in his trouser-leg, flexes it like a rapier with both hands, and swishes it menacingly through the air. 'Let's see the bastard who was shootin' in here without orders!'

'I'm the bloke you're lookin' for, Herr Wachtmeister, sir,' grins Tiny, round a fat cigar. As he answers he presses the muzzle of a heavy *Tokarew* pistol hard up under the MP's fat jowl. 'Look, you stinkin' excuse for a 'uman bein', you sod off, an' take your bleedin' shower of coppers with you! 'Cos in just one minute I'm goin' to start shootin' again.'

'You're bloody *mad*!' stammers the Wachtmeister, nervously, falling slowly back toward the door.

'No I ain't,' grins Tiny, sending a bullet into the floor between the man's feet. 'I'm Frankenstein's bastard, bleedin' son, I am, an' I drink blood every mornin' for breakfast!'

'Arrest that man!' gabbles the Wachtmeister, chalk-white in the face. There is no reaction to his order. His four MPs have fled out of the door. He gives out a shrill scream, as Tiny closes in on him with a deep snarl, and hammers his helmet down over his nose with a closed fist. He gets out of the door so quickly that he falls over his own feet and slides a long way on his face in the slush.

'There'll be trouble *now*,' predicts Barcelona, darkly. 'They'll *kill* us, when they come back with reinforcements.'

'Pick up your gear, and let's get out of here,' orders the Old Man, squaring his cap on his head.

'We are closing now,' says Tanya, decisively. 'Get off

* The Blood Order: An early *SA* decoration

71

with you. We see you again tomorrow. This is a *nice* place, I must tell you arse-licking Germans!'

She rattles the iron venetian blinds shut, and turns off the stuffed bear's wicked red eyes.

On the way out Tiny smashes his fist through one of the remaining window-panes. He shakes his hand, which is covered with blood, and licks at it like a cat lapping up cream.

'What the hell did you do *that* for?' the Old Man scolds him, angrily.

'It was a Commie bleedin' window, that's why,' yells Tiny. He kicks out at an empty bucket, which rolls noisily over into the opposite gutter. 'You're always grumblin', Old Un'. You don't want us poor, lonely soldiers to 'ave any fun. I *love* smashin' windows. 'Ave done since I was a nipper. If I 'ad to pay for all the windows I've busted, I'd need a big, bleedin' loan in the National bleedin' Bank to do it. You ought to 'ave been there the night me an' the Jew furrier's son David from *'Eyn 'Oyerstrasse* busted all the windows in the David Station, an' showered the bleedin' coppers all over with busted glass. It was their own fault, really. They was 'avin' a gaspipe repaired, an' the silly bleeders 'ad piled up all the cobblestones just ready to 'and for us when we come out o' the "'Appy Pig"!

'"'Ere we go, then!" shouted the Yid's kid, an' 'e threw the first stone. It landed smack bang on Superintendent Willy Nass's bleedin' desk, knockin' over 'is personal coffee-pot an' smashin' 'is inkwell, so a 'ole lot of documents important to the soddin' state gets covered with coffee an' ink. Nass went bleedin' barmy, an' went off 'Amburg-style so all the Schupo coppers started puttin' on their armour an' artillery. On their way out o' the door leadin' to the *Reeperbahn* they got stuck, there was that many of 'em. David an' me borrowed a couple o' bikes, as was leanin' waitin' for us, up against the wall of the variety theatre, an' spurted off down the road with a posse o' blue-lights chasin' our arses. Jesus, but they was narked when they copped us. Me that is, 'cos I was the only one they copped. The Yid's David 'e'd gone off to Buxtehude. Said 'e 'ad to 'elp 'is auntie with 'er tomatoes. Nass, 'e threatened me with 'eavy punishments for pinchin' bikes an' wanton destruction of property while escapin'. There was somethin' too about old women an' a paperstand. I tried to explain to 'im, best I could, as it couldn't 'ave been me 'cos I couldn't ride a bike.

'"It's a *lie*," 'e screamed, an' smashed the top of 'is desk in two with 'is truncheon. But we'll soon find out what's what, 'e promised me, an' pushed me out the door an' down the bleedin' stairs. Out in the street they give me a national police force bike, which Nass 'ad to give a receipt for. We started off from *Davidstrasse*, as goes down on the slope into the Elbe.

'"Get on!" said an Oberwachtmeister with a moustache the spittin' image of Adolf's.

'I pretended to fall off a couple o' times, an' they beat me up a bit to make me understand as 'ow this bike trip was important to 'em. They set me up on the saddle then an' give this national bleedin' bike an 'ell of a push.

'"Ride, you stinkin' cycle thief," Nass ordered me, out from under 'is 'at-brim.

'"Very good, sir," I yelled and 'eld me feet out to the sides. The bleedin' bike did the rest. It went like a bat out o' bleedin' 'ell down *Davidstrasse*, an', 'angin' over on one side, round the corner o' *Bernhard Nocht Strasse*, as is pretty steep. I nearly kissed a number 2 tram on the way, as it come pissin' up the 'ill there where all them 5 mark 'ores from *Fischermarkt* does their business.

'Down by *Landingsbrücke*, I 'ad to leave the police bike, which carried on on its own down into the bleedin' Elbe. You should've 'eard 'im, Nass, go on when 'e found out 'is bike was drowned. I 'eard later as 'e 'ad to pay for it. It was 'im as 'ad 'is name on the receipt.'

'Stop all that shit about *Davidswacht* and Nass,' sniffles Porta, who has caught a cold. 'We'll be shot before we know where we are. That commissar bint I had social

73

relations with, told me there was a mob of NKVD who'd gone underground here when the Red Army lighted out.'

'Latrine rumours,' says Gregor Martin, off-handedly. 'Our friends have lost their courage. We have won the war. All we've got to do is make our way straight across Russia, and meet up with the rice-eaters on the other side o' the earth.'

'I want to see the MO first,' sneezes Porta. 'My feet are killing me *now*, an' what a walk *that'll* be! Have you any idea just how big Mother Russia *is*?'

'Know what I think,' trumpets Tiny, banging himself on the chest. 'We ought to burn the arses out from under them NKVD bastards, so's we could get a bit of bleedin' peace for once in a while!'

'*Up* you,' groans Porta hoarsely, clearing his nose between his fingers, noisily. 'I'm about tired of fucking about on the crust of this sodding earth at everybody's beck an' call. Think of all the things that're going on in Berlin while I'm wastin' my time out here playing soldiers!'

He blows his nose again, and takes a big swig of vodka. 'Our German God ain't all that smart. If He'd been clever He'd of took out a Bohemian Gefreiter named Adolf Hitler in the First World War!'

'Watch your mouth, Obergefreiter Porta,' Heide warns him, sharply. 'It is my duty to report you to the NSFO. I have no doubt of what the result of that will be.'

'See into the future, can you?' asks Porta, ironically, wiping his nose with the back of his hand.

A revealing click sounds in the quiet night, and we go to cover alongside the wall.

'An mpi, a bleedin' mpi,' whispers Tiny, as he goes down.

Like a wise old tomcat Porta moves straight across the street and forces his way down some wrecked cellar stairs, where half a door hangs swinging.

As he moves, explosions erupt from another cellar opening.

74

'A *Balalaika*! God rot me, a *Balalaika*!' howls Gregor excitedly, and fires reflexively at the flash.

Just as reflexively I tear the ring from an egg-grenade, and sling it towards the cellar. There is a hollow thump, and a yellow-red flame blooms in the darkness. Its reflection comes back at us from wet steel helmets.

Tiny rushes straight through a glass door, with a deafening crash. Glass splinters fly around his ears. His *Schmeisser* explodes, chatteringly. It takes only a few minutes. He comes back out through the door-frame, kicking glass out of his way. He sneezes twice, violently.

''Ere's the bleedin *Balalaika*,' he shouts, holding a *Kalashnikov* up above his head. ''Im as played it's dead!'

'The bloody neighbours are that fucked up by this war, they ain't able to do much more'n get in the way,' coughs Barcelona. He has a cold, like the rest of us. He coughs up phlegm, and spits on a dead horse, which is lying in a pool of frozen blood.

'Don't you be too sure of that,' sniffles Porta, taking another swig from his vodka bottle. He regards vodka as an alternative to vitamin C, and thinks it will help his cold. 'Never trust the neighbours. Before we know where we are those rotten lice'll have started up all over again, and we'll be back where we kicked off!'

'Know what I think?' shouts Tiny, from inside the remains of a delicatessen. 'This war is a new Thirty Years War, like the time Jesus landed 'Is army in the Red bleedin' Sea to give the Turks a beatin' up.' His biblical knowledge is, as usual, slightly off-centre.

Heavy infantry fire sounds from the far end of the town.

'They've got shit between the ears,' sneezes Gregor. 'War-mad bastards. Why they got to always be shootin'? I wish I was back with my general. With him, war was *fun*!'

'Not allowed to shoot MPs, is it?' says Porta, mysteriously, and scrapes frozen snow from his boots.

'Too true it ain't,' laughs Barcelona, swallowing a whole

handful of throat pastilles. He has 'found' them on a body.

'There's a lot o' things as ain't allowed,' shouts Tiny. Angrily, he picks up an unexploded hand-grenade and throws it through a window. 'Fuck 'em all!'

Jesus, Jesus, why is everybody always sneezin' and freezin' in this God-awful country,' sniffles Porta. 'Anybody know a cure for it? I feel as if hair's growin' out of the sides of my head, an' the germs've built a barbed-wire entanglement in my throat!'

'A Russian grenade up your backside, or perhaps a *Kalashnikov* burst straight into your napper'd clear that cold away in a second,' says Gregor, with a less than humorous laugh.

'They're a certain cure, at least,' the Old Man admits, scraping at his silver-lidded pipe with his combat-knife. 'Colds are hell, and worst of all they're not enough to put you in sick-bay.'

'You're right there,' puffs Tiny. 'I saw the MO yesterday. Threw me out 'e did, an' threatened to 'ave me jailed for bleedin' sabotage o' the war effort.

'"I got a fever sir," I said. "52 degrees at least."

'"Up your arse, man," 'e yelled.

'"Where else, sir," I answered, and then 'e went funny an' started shoutin', Off I went then, 'fore anythin' irregular could start 'appenin'. I did manage to sneeze straight in 'is face, though. Give 'im somethin' to think about when '*is* thermometer registers 52°C.'

'Whose people are you?' barks a monstrously fat Leutnant, with a monocle flashing in his fleshy, white face.

'Who the fuck's askin'?' comes, anonymously, from Porta, off in the shadow of the houses.

The Leutnant goes into a rage, and demands to know their unit.

'Push a gun-barrel up his arsehole,' cackles Gregor, hidden in the darkness. 'He'd love it! He looks like one o' them as likes to get their shitters reamed out now an' then!'

'You're insulting a superior officer,' rages the Leutnant, his face tightening. 'Who are you, you filthy man?'

''E's a colonel in the Chinese bleedin' Army,' roars Tiny, happily. '*Panjemajo, grabit**'

'Shut it!' warns the Old Man, well aware that their joking can have serious consequences.

'Yes, but he *is* a Chinese colonel,' roars Porta, whinnying with laughter. 'In command of two regiments of Pekin paratroops, but all very secret, Herr Leutnant, sir. Even the Chinese ain't been told, sir!'

''Ey there, Leutnant!' Tiny bellows with laughter, and bangs his hands on his knees. 'You gone the wrong way, you 'ave. Any minute now ol' Ivan Stinkanovitch is gonna shoot that bleedin' winder-pane out o' your fat bleedin' kisser, an' send you flyin' up to 'ave a fuck at the angels!'

The Leutnant tears his pistol from his holster, cocks it theatrically and aims it at Tiny, who is lighting a big cigar with the air of a captain of industry.

The Legionnaire swings his mpi down from his shoulder and sends a burst into the ground at the Leutnant's feet. Bullets ricochet in all directions.

The Leutnant drops his monocle. It smashes to pieces on the cobbled road surface.

'*We'll* get you a glazier, sir!' offers Porta, as the Leutnant's squad disappears down the street in disorderly flight.

'You're under arrest!' screams the officer hysterically, grasping the Old Man's arm.

'Take your hands off me!' snarls the Old Man, pulling away angrily. 'You're not in garrison here, Herr Leutnant, and we're not your recruits! This is a front-line unit, and I'm its commander. You have nothing to do with us. We don't *know* you!'

'I'll have you stripped,' whines the Leutnant hysterically. 'This is mutiny. I'll get you a field court-martial!'

* *Panjemajo, grabit.* Russian: Understand, arsehole?

'Do as you wish, sir,' answers the Old Man, his eyes slitted with rage.

'Knock 'is bleedin' teeth out,' suggests Tiny with a wicked laugh, 'an' kick 'is arse'ole up round 'is ears afterwards!'

An amphibian comes rushing down the street and skids to a halt in the slush, its nose pointing back in the direction from which it came.

Oberleutnant Löwe springs lightly from the vehicle and walks, with long strides, towards the Old Man, who is standing with dirty, soaking wet boots and looking very sour.

'So here you are,' smiles Löwe. He touches his helmet brim with a large, mittened hand. He stares inquisitively at the fat Leutnant. 'What are you doing here?' he asks harshly, fishing a bent cigarette from his breast pocket.

The Old Man gives him a light, and nods his head in the direction of the fat Leutnant.

'This officer came rushing down here, and started to tell me what to do with the section, sir,' he said. 'I've just been explaining to him that I would prefer him not to do that.'

Oberleutnant Löwe blows out a cloud of cigarette smoke, takes a quick look around, and understands the situation immediately.

'Come with me,' he orders the Leutnant, who is just about to open his mouth and give vent to his repressed rage. Löwe is already back in the vehicle alongside the chief driver, Obergefreiter Brinck. The Leutnant is hardly in his seat before Brinck stamps the accelerator down and is off in a shower of mud and snow.

'Single file. Follow me!' growls the Old Man sourly, moving off at the head of the section.

'There 'e goes again. *Rotten*!' says Tiny, with a hopeless gesture. 'It ain't *my* fault this time, any road. It was that bleedin' officer as started it an' then couldn't take a bit o' fun!'

'It's always the officers,' says Porta, blowing his nose on

his fingers. 'They can't keep their mouths shut when we're talkin'. That's *their* trouble.'

Gregor finds a furniture store, and we take up temporary quarters inside it.

'Inspect for booby-traps?' asks Heide, zealously, looking under a sofa.

'Don't change the positions of the furniture, an' don't, repeat don't, touch the pictures,' advises Porta. 'If there's a picture of Stalin, let it be. Our treacherous enemies like to plant small surprises under furniture and behind pictures. Turn Stalin's face to the wall, my sons, an' you'll get the surprise of your young lives!'

'Gawd, yes!' cries Tiny. ''Member the time we moved that dead bleedin' pig, an' the entire village went up in the air, an' took a motorbike platoon with it. The neighbours 'ad tied the pig with a lead to the ammo' depot. It was like the soddin' world went off its axles, an' I went up an' kissed the soles of Jesus's bleedin' feet. There wasn't nothin' left o' the pig, either. Not even a bit o' pork to add some life to a fried egg!'

'Anybody got any rifle oil?' asks Heide, who is dismantling his machine-pistol.

'Rifle oil?' grimaces Gregor, contemptuously. 'Pull your fucking pud, brother, an' use what comes out of it. That's what the rice-eaters use. Their army don't let anythin' go to waste!'

'Shut up, you rotten swine,' snarls Heide, in a rage, sending him a wicked look.

'That's enough,' orders the Old Man. 'I don't want any more trouble. Shit between your ears, that's what you lot've got! Every one of you!' He throws himself down on to an embroidered sofa, and stares emptily at the ceiling.

A distant rumble brings our heads up.

'Tanks,' says Porta, reaching for his topper.

'Train goin' through a long tunnel,' says Tiny, stretching himself out comfortably.

'Train? You must be wrong in the head,' shouts Gregor,

throwing himself down on the floor in terror. 'It's a shell. A *big* un!'

There is a deafening explosion.

'Jesus'n Mary,' yells Tiny, rolling himself into a ball and laughing madly. 'Little bit closer this way, an' we'd never've ever seen 'ome again. An' poor ol' Julius's gun'd never 'ave been cleaned, neither!'

'Fucking *shit!*' screams Gregor, pushing his turkey-cock face through the broken window. Suddenly, he goes completely amuck, and empties a whole magazine into the darkness. 'Shoot me!' he yells, throwing a hand-grenade. 'It takes twelve men to shoot one rotten, lousy soldier who don't want to fight no more in this man's army!' He waves his machine-pistol in the air. 'Get *to* it! I've *had* it! Fuck your rotten fuckin' war! Stuff it! Stuff it up your arseholes, an' shit it out again in a load of South American revolutions. Then stuff it down Adolf's fuckin' throat an' make him thank you for the gift parcel.'

The Old Man and Barcelona wriggle across the floor to get hold of him. He is standing on the spring mattress of a double bed, hopping up and down. He has a fresh magazine in his hand, but cannot get it into his machine-pistol. 'Oh God!' he screams. 'There's none of us ever goin' to get home again! The neighbours'll shoot our fuckin' German arses off!'

The Old Man slaps him hard, twice, across the face.

'Nazi bastard,' shouts Gregor, his eyes rolling madly. He swings the muzzle of his mpi round in circles. 'You don't know who I am. Me an' my general's took out a patent on this war. You lot's only here to get shot at!'

'Battle strain,' says the Old Man, slapping him again across the face. Barcelona twists his arms up behind his back, and forces him to drop the machine-pistol.

'Get your traitorous hands off me!' howls Gregor. He kicks a steel helmet from one end of the furniture store to the other.

He fights furiously with the Old Man and Barcelona. He

thinks they are a firing squad come to carry him off to execution.

'Death makes a man want to meet death!' he screams out into the room. His eyes are bulging wildly. 'But it's easier if you take some of 'em with you, an' can get down there where God an' the Devil's barterin' souls!'

'Always the bleedin' same,' sighs Tiny, from his resting place in a broad four-poster bed. His grey bowler is pushed down over his eyes, and a fat cigar hangs from his lips. 'Goin' under together is also a kind o' pleasure, as Moses said to the soddin' Gyppos, when they all drowned in the Red Sea!'

'Up my fuckin' black arse,' yells Albert suddenly, jumping to his feet with a long howl. He rushes across the floor of the furniture store and bangs into Porta who falls across Heide, scattering the parts of the machine-pistol across the floor.

Heide lets out a roar, and tackles Albert just as he is about to go through the door.

'You stinking black rat,' he rages. 'Nobody gets away with that with me!'

A new, giant shell comes roaring over, and we all go down on the floor. The night becomes one long, shuddering, thunderous explosion.

'What the hell's happening?' shouts Barcelona hysterically, as the great concrete building begins to shake like a sapling in a storm. Shrapnel splinters come from all directions. They hammer against the walls, showering us with mortar dust.

The grey office windows at the far end of the long storehouse tinkle to pieces in a rain of glass shards.

'Halt! Who goes there?' roars the Legionnaire, releasing the safety catch on his machine-pistol.

'The Beast of the Apocalypse,' answers Obergefreiter Brinck, happily, coming crawling in through a shattered window. 'You hide yourselves real good. Took me two hours to find you.'

81

'You must be mad,' the Old Man scolds him. 'You could've got yourself shot!'

'War is a risky business,' grins Brinck carelessly, starting to rig up a field telephone on the floor.

'What's this, then?' asks Porta, wonderingly.

'Army field telephone model 1932,' declares Brinck happily. 'The Signals coolies've put down a cable. I've suggested code name "*Sauerkraut*" for you. Command's got code name "*Eisbein*". If Ivan gets on to it he'll think we've opened up a chop-house. Try to ring an' order a table he will, I shouldn't wonder. Don't get too worried, though. The neighbours're shooting off like mad, and the cables are gettin' shot up quicker'n Signals can repair 'em!'

A little later Gregor goes amuck again. He is halfway through the shattered window before the Old Man and Barcelona get hold of him. They give him a going-over with their fists. It is the only effective treatment for front-line madness.

They have hardly finished with him before Albert starts up again, howling like a wolf. He runs his head into the wall. Then he draws his combat-knife, and begins to stab and slash madly at a sofa. Screaming wildly, he cuts it to pieces. Springs fly up and hit him in the face, driving him even crazier. In the end he becomes so entangled in wires and furniture webbing that we have the greatest difficulty in freeing him.

'That black monkey's gone out of his mind,' rages the Old Man. 'Take away his weapons, before he kills some of us!'

The scream of a shell makes itself heard from out in the darkness. The flash of the explosion lights up the night. It is followed by another explosion, and then another. Shells continue to hammer down, seemingly endlessly. Beams and tiles crash around us. A large door comes flying across the room and cuts off the head of an infantryman who is on his way up the stairs.

'And they tell us this shit of a town's been cleared,' yells

Porta, wriggling further down in the four-poster bed along-side Tiny.

'I think they're gonna attack,' says Barcelona, listening carefully. 'Listen, that's 75 mm!'

'Jesus'n Mary,' mumbles Tiny, burying his head under a pillow. 'Those bleedin' shells drive a feller barmy!'

From the street comes the clatter of rushing boots.

The Legionnaire peers cautiously out of the broken window.

'*Par Allah*!' he cries, fearfully, 'it is Ivan! He is all over the street, out there!'

'Ivan?' asks the Old Man. 'Impossible! That means the whole division's been turned back!'

Porta's constantly surprised, birdlike face peers carefully from the window niche in the end wall. The hair seems to stand up on his head. He closes his eyes and emits a grunt of fear.

'The devil, it's the whole neighbour's army,' he shouts, gripping his LMG, and dashing straight across the store-room towards the street door.

We take the plank fence almost together. Hand-grenades explode, hollowly, behind us. From the darkness comes the muzzle-flash of an mpi.

I throw a hand-grenade at the flash, and take a row of empty dustbins in my stride. They go clattering away into the night.

A figure whirls up into the air, and seems to hang for a moment on the top of the flame from an explosion.

We throw ourselves flat, as their artillery lays a carpet of fire over the large park.

With fear gripping at my entrails I press myself down into a small stream, without knowing how I have got there. I don't even feel the coldness of the water, or hear the ice cracking under me. Huge shells fall behind me. A burning house crashes in on itself.

I realize I must get away from the stream. The artillery will centre in on the burning row of houses behind which I am lying.

Immediately after the next rain of shells I jump to my feet and rush straight across the road through the park. I throw myself down, senselessly, into a shell-hole which still stinks of iron and powder smoke. The shelling rises to a furious crescendo. It is as if the entire world is being turned inside out.

They are using everything they've got. Field-guns, howitzers, mortars, tank and infantry weapons. The mortars are the worst. They come almost silently and explode with a wicked sound. I am so frightened I feel like screaming, and running away as fast as my legs can carry me. But I have been long enough in this filthy war to know it would be certain death if I did. I force myself further down into the narrow shell-hole, making myself as small as possible. I rest my chin on the butt of my machine-pistol.

A shell falls not far away from me. My steel helmet is pushed back by the blast. I am unconscious for a second. The helmet strap has almost strangled me. My brain feels empty. My hands are cold as ice. It seems an eternity before life flows slowly back into me.

Now the tanks come. They are not far from my shell-hole. I hear the rattle of their tracks. T-34s and the enormous KW-2s speed through the park. The screams of men dying under their treads cut through the noise.

I hear German machine-guns firing madly, sending glowing lines of tracer through the darkness.

Five or six flares explode in the heavens, and turn the night to a ghostly, pale sort of day.

I look up cautiously and catch sight of the T-34s on their way through the park, alongside the path. Infantrymen can be clearly seen sitting up behind on the tanks.

Now the anti-tank guns start up. When the 88 mms go off, the sound is that of a huge steel door clanging shut.

A T-34 explodes in a ball of fire; another one goes up.

I hear tracks rattling close to my shell-hole, and the ticking ring of an Otto engine.

A T-34 stops close by, and I feel the warmth of its exhaust

blow down over me. It is so close I could put out my hand and touch its tracks.

My heart almost stops beating from fear. Shivering with terror I bore my fingers into the earth and try to get even closer to it. The T-34's gun goes off, and it feels as if my head is about to burst open. The force of the explosion is impossible to describe. A tank-gun is the devil's own personal invention.

An Unteroffizier from 3 Section arrives at a run. A machinegun burst from the T-34 rips across his chest. He is smashed over backwards. The LMG flies from his hands, his steel helmet following it.

A Fahnenjunker runs, limping like a winged bird. He stops, and stares in panic at the huge, armoured colossus. The tank-gun flames again. The Junker falls forward like a log.

I think for a moment that he is dead, but there is still life in him. His fingers claw at the earth and he begins to crawl slowly towards my hole.

'No,' I whisper. 'Not here. If the tank sees him, we're *both* finished!'

Engines howl, and the T-34 begins to move forward slowly, the earth shaking under its steel tracks.

The tracks come slowly towards me, cowering there in my shell-hole. Feverishly I tie two grenades together to make a heavier charge.

The T-34 swivels halfway round. Its tracks throw earth and stones high in the air. They rain down on me.

The tank slides sideways down into a ditch. I am about to throw the grenades, when it turns half round again on its own axis, and rattles toward the Fahnenjunker. He presses himself down, desperately, behind a large round stone, then gets halfway to his feet. The tank knocks him back down and crushes him under its tracks. A bloody pool is all that is left of him.

The T-34 makes off with a thunder of engines. It smashes over a wooden bridge, which collapses under its weight in a rain of splintered planks and beams. Two infantry men, who were hiding under the bridge, are crushed into an unrecognizable mass.

How long I run before I come to a halt I never know. I have lost all idea of the passage of time. My knees tremble under me; my thigh muscles are hard and knotted. My mouth feels as if it were full of sand. In a panic I spring across the ditch, and push my way through the bushes lining it.

Porta catches me by the ankle, and I fall forward.

'Calm down,' he says, easily. 'It's not *that* bad. The neighbours are just pointin' out to us that they're still around. They don't want us to go thinking we've won the war just yet!'

'Where's the Old Man?' I ask, breathlessly.

'Lying over there, enjoying the cool of the evening together with the rest of the boys. We didn't get off too badly, but there's not a button left of 3 Section, and they say the division's got its balls shot off. Arse-an'-Pockets has made a real mess of this one!'

The Old Man comes sliding down between the rose beds, with Gregor at his heels.

'We've got to get through now,' says the Old Man, breathlessly. 'Ivan's over on this side with all his pots an' pans. Half the division's got the shit shot out of it. Let's move. Go down behind that furniture factory. There's a bit more room there.'

'There's tanks behind us,' I put in. 'Both T-34s and KW-2s, and they're banging away like mad.'

'Sod *them*,' snarls the Old Man. 'Don't look at 'em. We've *got* to get through.'

'Tiny,' he calls, softly.

''Ere I am!' answers Tiny, avalanching down past the rosebeds.

'Got the stovepipe* still?' asks the Old Man.

'Too right,' grins Tiny, '*an*' a packet o' acid drops for it. Its Dad's Day in Russia y'know!'

* Stovepipe: Bazooka

Barcelona looks over the top of the roses. 'Adjutant's just been here. Wants us to work our bloody way up to the sunk road.'

'That clever sod could make a pancake without breakin' eggs,' snarls Porta, furiously. '*This* feller's not goin' anywhere near any sunken, rotten road. All the bloody Red Army'll be goin' that way an'll shoot us full of holes. Those people from the officer factory'll kill the lot of us before they've done!'

'We're going back,' says the Old Man, getting to his feet with his mpi at the ready.

'Follow me!' he orders, jumping over the roses.

Suddenly I begin to feel the cold, and the water which has seeped into my boots.

'Heavens above, but I'm *cold*,' I mumble, pulling my collar up around my ears.

'You'll soon get warmed up,' grins Porta.

'Spread out, blast your eyes,' commands the Old Man. 'How often do I have to *tell* you. Don't crowd together!'

Behind us we can hear the rumble of the field-guns, and, in between the sharp crack of tank-guns.

Two tanks are on fire. Tall flames shoot up from them. One of them explodes in a rain of red-hot steel splinters.

A Russian in a flapping brown cloak rushes past us with his long queerly-shaped bayonet fixed.

I raise my machine-pistol and send a short burst into his back. He gives out a long, ululating scream, and his rifle and bayonet fly from his hands.

I follow the others down a partly overgrown path, jump over a wrecked anti-tank gun and go head over heels down a steep flight of steps.

'Keep your distance,' shouts the Old Man. 'You want to all get killed at the same time? Spread out, you rotten sacks, spread *out*!'

'Mines,' shouts Barcelona, warningly, stopping short as if he had run into a wall. 'Mines,' he says again, standing as if rooted to the ground. He is in deadly fear of mines, having been blown up by them several times. Even though these experiences occurred a long time ago, he has never forgotten them.

The whole section has stopped. It is best not to think too much about mines. It can stop you moving forward altogether.

'Get on, get on,' the Old Man shouts, giving me a push.

A flare bursts above our heads. The 25 men of our section turn into 25 statues. We stand, for several minutes, defenceless, bathed in its deathly white glow. Protecting darkness falls around us. The night seems to be filled with running, leaping figures; everywhere is confusion. We run around in the dark, Russians and Germans together. Hand-grenades are thrown into houses. Wounded and dying soldiers scream shrilly.

In the middle of the street a T-34 spins wildly round. It explodes in a blinding flash of light.

From the centre of the town come explosions and the noise of battle.

'Hope they don't smash up Tanya's place with all their shooting,' says Porta, worriedly.

'P'raps it's the commissar, on his way to pick up his woman,' says Gregor, with a short, sad laugh.

'It's all a fart in a colander,' sighs Porta. 'The longer I live the more I realize that the only thing of value anybody's got, is his own poor, rotten life.'

We throw ourselves down, tiredly, behind a small hillock.

'Ducks!' cries Porta, assuming his pointer attitude. He is right. The quiet quacking of a flock of ducks can just be distinguished.

'If we can get hold of a couple of 'em, I'll do you duck an' Portuguese rice,' he promises, licking his lips hungrily at the thought. 'It's a feast for the Gods! First you take some rice – that *is* when you've got your ducks – then some onions they're easy enough to find – and so is a bunch o' carrots. Finally some tomatoes, oil, salt an' pepper. The rice has to be boiled in duck-fat, adding water slowly as it comes to the boil, says the recipe, but I prefer wine to water. Smooth out

88

the rice nice an' even, an' lay your portions of duck carefully on top of it. Then, chop your tomatoes fine together with the onions and spread 'em out over the whole thing. I tell you, my sons, the aroma is that beautiful you'd think it was a Christmas Eve before the war.'

'Shut your trap, man,' snarls Albert viciously, from the darkness. 'You make everybody more hungry than he is, just listenin' to you talk.'

'Shut it the *lot* of you,' snarls the Old Man, in turn. 'Ivan's smack in front of us!' He takes his cold pipe from his mouth, and beckons me over to him. 'Listen good, now' he whispers. 'You go first over the stream, but quietly as possible, understand? The rest of us'll wheel round in an arc behind the ruins over there.'

'Why me?' I protest, nervously.

'Because I say so,' answers the Old Man, nastily. 'Get off with you! But keep your ears open and send up a green flare if you run into the neighbours.'

The ducks scatter, quacking, in front of me, as I wade cautiously into the cold water. The icy teeth of it bite into me. After a few minutes I can no longer feel my fingers. I stop for a moment by a deserted MG position, and pour water out of my boots. They're the most stupid boots in the world, these German leather dice-cups. I wish the devil had the genius who invented them. The Russian puttee over a shorter boot is a thousand times better. Our boots are only good for goose-stepping in.

Behind a large farmhouse I meet the section again.

'Spread out,' orders the Old Man, waving his mpi at us as if we were a flock of hens he was shooing out of his way.

Cursing we crawl between bramble hedges. The thorns tear our skin, and it hurts more than ever because we are so cold.

'You two stay here,' the Old Man turns to Gregor and me. 'But don't, for God's sake, start shooting all over the place. Fire only at muzzle-flashes. Albert! Crawl over to that turnip heap, and cover the house, but God help you if

89

you make a noise! They're here, an' we can count on 'em being frightened all to hell. Frightened people've got sharp ears an' sharp eyes, and they let off at any sound they hear.'

'I'm frightened all to hell, too, man,' whines Albert, piteously. 'Jesus but I'm frightened! Think of gettin' knocked off here. And the little I've got out of my short life.'

A hoarse, stifled cough, out in the darkness, makes us start and listen shakily.

Like a couple of snakes the Old Man and Barcelona glide away over the wide field.

Porta presses his face down into his cupped hands to stop himself sneezing, while Albert puts both hands to his ears in terror.

Porta draws his breath in deeply a few times and smiles happily, at having succeeded in stifling his sneeze. It would have been a catastrophe. It doesn't need much to set the guns going off at you, when you are lying right under the noses of the other army.

A loud sneeze comes from the pig-sty. It is followed up by three or four more, sounding loud as gunshots in the night.

'Ivan's as snotty-nosed as we are,' whispers Porta pityingly. 'Shame for him, it is.'

'It's this rotten war that's to blame,' mumbles Gregor sourly. 'If you don't get your turnip shot off, you catch all sorts of aches an' pains. I hurt all over, and I can't get a pill even for any of it. And they talk about human rights. A feller's hardly started living before they get hold of him and knock every single, individual trace of a thought out of his head. I'll never forget Paust, the Feldwebel I was a rookie under. He'd got a face as red as a lobster, and his breath stunk like a shithouse. He had gaps between his teeth, an' the teeth were yellow as ripe cheese. I was dumb enough to jump to one side instead of catchin' a fuckin' dummy gun he threw at me.

' "I'll remember you," he screamed, breathin' cheap beer and stinking fish straight into my face.

'Later in the afternoon I complained that the helmet

they'd issued me with was too little, the greatcoat was too big, and the boots pinched my toes. That started something, all right. For the next three weeks we had our gasmasks on from morning to night. We only 'ad 'em off when we were eating. In the latrine we still had 'em on. When the rest of the company got fifteen minutes rest, Paust nobbled me.

'"Attention!" he screamed, "gasmasks on! Forward march! Double march! One-two, one-two, one-two!"

'I'm doubling straight for the barracks wall. Then comes the next order.

'"Down! Forward crawl! Get that arse down. Prick an' balls into the ground, you wicked little shower o' monkey's afterbirth, you!"

'Straight through a pool o' mud he drove me, an' down through a water-filled tank trench like I was some kind of a submarine.

'"Back an' start again," he shouted, disappointed that I'm still able to breathe.

'When we'd got to the middle of the day and the sun was so high there wasn't a single patch o' shade anywhere on the parade-ground, I wasn't runnin' any more, I was staggerin'. The rubber facepiece of the gasmask was going in and out like a bellows. My rifle felt heavy as lead and was slippery all over with sweat. The heavy uniform you could've wrung out like a dishcloth, an' God help you if you so much as loosened a button of it. In the afternoon they took us for a walk in the country. I got promoted, straightaway, to number one on the MG. Paust chased me on an' on over them ploughed fields with that fucking machine-gun on my back. When he shouted "*Down!*" I went down like a log, never caring where I landed. Then we practised advancin' in short rushes. I tell you, sometimes I'd run straight into a tree and the machine-gun'd give me a real welt across the back o' the neck.

'Then one day I gave up.' Gregor throws his arms wide, and stares, cautiously, towards the long wing of the farmhouse where we know the Russians are taking cover. 'That afternoon, when I went down I stayed down. I'd got it into my head that I wasn't going to take any more of it.'

'Feldwebel Paust came rushing over to me, blowin' on his whistle for dear life. I didn't see him, but I could hear him. I'll never forget that voice. I've often prayed to heaven to let me meet him out here somewhere.

'"So you won't get up then, machine-gunner Martin?" he howled at me. "By God, I'll smash you, man, I'll finish you right off! I won't leave you be, till you're nothing but a lump o' quiverin' jelly, beggin' to be let die!"

'I lay there in the middle o' the ploughed field, and got my strength back with the help of hate. I didn't know then, that that was just what he wanted. To be a good soldier you've got to be a good hater! If you don't hate with all your might you can't kill. Hate's the strongest source of human energy. But there I was now, lying in the middle of a fuckin' Westphalian field, outside the old Papal town o' Paderborn. My whole face felt like a glowing, bubbling pancake, and I was near drowning in me own sweat inside the gasmask. The glasses of the eyepieces was so wet you couldn't see through them. The heel'd fallen off my one boot. My uniform was torn to ribbons. My knees hurt, and blood was pouring from them. I think I'd sprained an ankle, but I forgot that when Paust an' three others got me up and chased me on.

'I threw myself down beside a tree, and could hardly hear Paust's voice screaming at me. I knew he wouldn't stop 'til tank-soldier Gregor Martin was crushed like a fly on the wall. I'd really wanted to be an officer, that's why I'd volunteered, but that day by the tree on the bank of the river decided me that I'd never be an officer.

'"Into the river," he ordered me. "Forward, *march*! One-two, one-two, you sad sack!"

'I got halfway to my feet, but fell again. My legs were simply unable to carry me.

'The whistle shrilled.

'Then I crawled. He wanted to see me before a court-martial for refusing to obey an order, and you know how frightened we all are at the thought of a court-martial. Better the traditional Hell of the priests than Germersheim. I got to the water and crawled out into it like some fucked-up kind of crocodile. On the way I lost my steel helmet, but Paust kicked it in after me.

'"Helmet, *on*!" he bawled. "*I'll* tell you when to take it *off*!"'

'I crawled on the river bed, followed it down, I hadn't strength enough left to swim. Two Unteroffiziers had to pull me out. An ambulance picked me up a little later. At first I thought it was taking me to the mortuary! The MO asked me who'd done it to me. But I knew the answer to that one. I said I'd fallen out of a window.

'Eight days I was in hospital, and ten minutes after I got back with the rookie company they started again where they'd left off. I was out there goose-steppin', with instep stretched, in the Westphalian bloody fields.

'"Chest out! Tighten your arse!" screamed Feldwebel Paust, his voice echoing back from the woods. The instep had to be up at the level of your waist-belt.

'Yes, we learnt it, and so effectively that we could have marched straight to our deaths with our insteps *still* pointing at the sky.'

'*C'est la guerre*, we are the human offal of the war,' whispers the Legionnaire, quietly. 'It is our fate, so has Allah willed it, and this we must accept!'

We lie silent for a while, thinking over his hopeless soldier's philosophy.

'What's this, what's this, now,' the Old Man scolds, softly. 'Still lying here?'

'We're gone,' says Albert, and disappears quickly into the bushes.

Gregor is at my heels. It is so dark we can only see a couple of yards in front of us.

I stumble over something which proves to be a tipped-over wheelbarrow. I curse quietly. A battered helmet with a comb on top comes up on the far side. Faster than thought Gregor throws his bolas. It wraps itself round the Russian's throat. He manages no more than a hoarse rattle before he goes down.

'What the hell are you up to?' asks Albert, nervously, pressing himself to the ground in fear.

'Oh, Jesus, Jesus!' he cries as he catches sight of the dead Russian. 'I'm soon gonna get a nervous breakdown! The devil take that ol' pappy of mine as just *had* to beat the drums for the Prussian Hussars! He shoulda stayed home in his grass hut, he should, and not gone gettin' the best son he had mixed up in this terrible German war of revenge.'

'Hell's bells!' shouts Gregor, in terror, as a colossal red flame splits the darkness. Like a fiery spire it shoots up towards the heavens. It folds out into a huge mushrooming cloud, like some horrible mirage, suddenly appearing from nowhere.

Half-blinded and deafened we stare into the devilish redness. It grows and grows, and becomes a brilliant carmine umbrella of enormous proportions. It spits out yellow and white spurts of fire, like flaming sprays of roses. Slowly the giant, raging fire-flower becomes millions of licking tongues of flame. The whole of the heavens and the battleground around us are coloured red.

Porta and two Russians come running out from the glowing redness; it is one thunderous, indescribable inferno.

'Run dammit!' cries the Old Man, desperately, tugging at my shoulder.

With a feeling of unreality I follow him. My feet move automatically.

A Russian, with a *Kalashnikov* slung across his chest, runs past us. A blast of heated air throws us to the ground.

In shock, we run and creep our way out into the ice-cold water of the stream. It is beginning to warm up, slowly. I dip my field-cap in the water and hold it over my face for protection.

'*Tovarisch!*' screams a terror-stricken Russian, as we run

into one another out in the middle of the stream. 'Idiots!' he yells, pointing to the roaring sea of flames. Then he dashes on, the water splashing up around his running feet.

After a while the rest of the section begins to collect around the remains of a shattered fountain. The granite Cossack on it has now not only lost his head, but also the rest of his torso. Only his stone trousers and boots are left standing in the basin.

'What the devil was all that?' I ask, dabbing burn ointment on the blisters which seem to be eating into my flesh.

'It was that madman Porta who pulled the chain on us,' snarls the Old Man, sending Porta an angry look.

'But who the hell could've guessed it was a bloody great petrol dump,' pants Gregor, pouring water over his red, blistered face.

'I thought it was the handle of a safe I was turning,' Porta excused himself. 'It *looked* like one. You *know*, a bit of a turn to the left an' a bit of a turn to the right and you're a rich man. In this case, however, the result was a little different. I got a bit of a shock there, when I found myself in the middle of the world's biggest bonfire, together with a coupla Ivans!'

'What a lot of lying, rotten sods they all are,' whines Gregor despondently, creeping down into his coat-collar against the icy cold. 'They said we were coming here for a rest, and we fall into nothing more or less'n the worst kind of a shit-heap. They keep on tellin' us the enemy's crushed, and then what happens? Half the rotten Red Army's pissin' around back of the German lines. Oh god, what a rotten war! They've all got nothin' but crap where their brains ought to be!'

Albert comes sauntering along, with his machine-pistol dangling from its sling round his neck. He is wearing a lady's fur coat, a crazy-looking, gingery object, with fox-tails hanging down from its lapels. He has lipsticked his heavy mouth, and drawn big red circles around his eyes. He looks like a painting from the brush of a mad, surrealist artist.

'What *do* you look like?' asks the Old Man, open-mouthed.

'I look like what I look like, man,' he answers. He snatches a piece of bread from the fingers of a corpse and takes a bite of it, but spits it out again immediately.

'Why can't those mad geniuses back there send some Stukas over, an' put those blasted guns out of action?' asks Barcelona. He begins to kick a punctured football about.

The battle noises of tank-guns and field artillery can still be heard from the outskirts of the town.

It is easy to tell the sharp crack of tank-guns from the heavy boom of the field artillery. In between comes the characteristic sound of a bazooka, and when the heavy guns pause for a moment, the hysterical hammering of machine-gun fire.

'Two men! Over to the park!' the Old Man orders, pointing with his silver-lidded pipe.

Albert and I plod away. We have not gone far when we catch sight of a coal-black cat, crossing the road slowly and self-importantly with its tail erect.

'We stay here,' says Albert, decisively. 'That's bad luck, that is, a black cat crossin' your path. Death and destruction'll hit us, an' *hard*, if we go on!'

'You're right. We'll wait here a bit,' I say, shivering in my wet clothes. 'Then we'll go back and tell the Old Man we've been all through the town and haven't observed anything.'

'He'll just about kill us, man, if he ever finds out we've took the piss out of him because of seein' a black cat,' chatters Albert, trying to think of a way out.

A house crashes down, tall fingers of flame shooting up from it. Not far away we hear the confused noise of hand-grenades exploding.

As we turn a corner we see Porta, tiptoeing down a narrow alley, bent over strangely and grunting all the time: 'Oink! Oink!'

We halt in amazement and stare inquisitively after him, as he clambers up over a huge pile of rubble, and bends down to look through a hole in a wall.

'Oink! Oink!' he grunts, just like a real pig.

'Gone mad!' whispers Albert, his eyes round and shining whitely in the darkness. 'I knew it'd happen. He's been queer in his ways lately. Believe you me, man, it's that cat that's done it. The devil's in every black cat.'

'Must be a lot of devils then,' I answer him. 'Because there's certainly a lot of black cats!'

'Don't you know that ol' devil can turn himself into thousands of little devils if he wants to? Gotta be able to. Else how could there be a German devil an' an American devil, an' one in this place too?'

I shrug my shoulders, and watch Porta disappear, still grunting, behind the rubble-heap.

'He thinks he's a pig that's been issued with an mpi,' mumbles Albert, shaking his head despondently. 'I see darkness, when I think what this war is on the way to turning us all into.'

When we get back the Old Man has no time to listen to our report. He is too busy giving one of the new men a talking-to.

'I'm goin' to look after you,' he shouts, angrily. 'Why'd you shoot those three prisoners?'

'Isn't that what we're here for?' asks one of the new boys, a Fahnenjunker-Gefreiter.

'Get them heels together,' rages the Old Man. 'Stand up straight when you talk to me, you lazy man. And remember it's Herr Feldwebel!'

The Fahnenjunker-Gefreiter clicks his heels together, and places his hands rigidly down along the seams of his trousers.

'Very good, Herr Feldwebel,' he replies, with a look of hate.

'Why'd you shoot those prisoners?' repeats the Old Man, in a penetrating voice. 'They'd got their hands up, and they were unarmed, and you shot 'em like lousy rats. That's *murder*!'

'I never saw their hands were up, Herr Feldwebel, and I

97

believed they were armed.'

'Liar!' hisses the Old Man. 'I was further off from them than you were, and I saw them clearly coming out of the house with their hands up!'

'I saw 'em an' all,' shouts Tiny, from a corner.

'You shut up!' the Old Man snaps. 'I can do without your help. Hand over that machine-gun,' he turns to the Fahnen-junker-Gefreiter. 'You're no longer number one machine-gunner, you're a runner for Command Group. I'll make your backside so red-hot it'll *burn* that killer streak out of you. If I did what was right I'd turn you straight over to a firin' squad, you filthy murderin' little swine. Now get out of my sight! The very sight of you makes me want to spew!'

Albert sits by the window, wrapped in his crazy ginger fur coat. He looks tired.

'Lay down and get some sleep,' I say, giving him a push.

'Sleep?' he cries, staring cautiously out through the window. 'You must be crazy, man! That black cat was a warning to us. The neighbours are comin' over tonight. Count on it. I don't want to get *my* throat cut the way that Section 4 lot did.'

'Cool down. Get that black blood of yours off the boil,' I comfort him. 'Nothing's going to happen. The neighbours are just as tired as we are.'

'I don't know,' he answers, 'but I got a funny, creepy feelin'. Those wicked sods've got somethin' brewin' for us. Take a look down that rotten long street over there. Before we can blow a fart they can be coming at us from hundreds of holes an' corners.'

'You're soft in the head,' I answer him. 'Come on, now! Let's get some shuteye!'

We roll up close together, like two dogs, for warmth. It takes only a few minutes for us to fall into a deep, troubled sleep, plagued with nightmares.

A long, scratchy, nerve-racking howl brings us to our feet, clutching at machine-pistols and hand-grenades. The whole of one wall disappears in a thick cloud of dust, and a

98

blast wave throws us across the room. An upright piano comes flying through the air and breaks up with a confused jangle of notes out on the landing.

I am rushing for the door, when Julius Heide grabs me and pulls me flat on my back to the floor.

A giant orange-yellow tongue of flame shoots up. The double door to the street flies off its hinges, and goes twisting away over the housetops like a piece of paper in the wind.

'The fuckin' neighbours are lettin' us know they're still alive,' gasps Barcelona, spitting out mortar.

Albert goes down on his belly by the window, and sends wild bursts down the street.

'Who the devil's that black idiot belting away at now?' rages the Old Man. In two long strides he is over to Albert and pulls him away from the window. The LMG clatters to the floor.

'It was a Russian,' Albert defends himself, wiping the back of his hand across his mouth. 'A mad sod in a topper just like Porta's!'

'Rubbish!' says the Old Man, angrily. 'You shoot that thing off one more time just because you're shit-scared, and I'll blow the black head off you, you shakin' sack o' bones! Understand me?'

Slowly we begin to relax again. Cigarette ends glow in the dark. We try to get back to sleep, but none of us can.

'Where *is* Porta, anyway?' asks the Old Man, looking searchingly around.

'He thinks he's turned into a pig,' answers Albert, pulling the ginger furs closer about him. 'He's goin' round grunting!'

'Grunting?' asks the Old Man, unbelievingly. 'Has he gone off his rocker? What's he grunting for?'

A salvo of 155 mms falls close to us, and the noise drowns Albert's reply.

'God help us, aren't they ever gonna stop that racket?' asks Gregor, pulling his cloak up over his head. 'Any of you ever thought what a shell like that *costs*? It's bloody expensive I can tell you, and most of the ones they shoot don't do any good. Christ in Heaven, they *must* all be mad!'

'You believe in God?' asks Albert suddenly, from over by the SMG, popping up his head from the depths of the ginger furs.

'You gone mad too, 'ave you?' asks Tiny in a hollow voice. He is down inside a large chest which he has taken over for a bed. He has pulled the lid down after him and left only a narrow crack through which we can just see his eyes.

'Believe in God yourself?' asks Gregor, looking at Albert with a crooked smile.

'If he does it's gotta be a darky God,' says Barcelona, with a short laugh. 'I once saw a picture of a black God in an American magazine. He was an old feller with a big white beard, and went round with a stick and a top-hat.'

'God's always old, whether He's black, white or yellow,' says Gregor, gesturing with his machine-pistol. 'He's simply *gotta* be old. Think of all the things He's been through to get all that experience.'

'If God's the way they say He is, then He must be very tiresome an' not very tolerant,' philosophizes Albert thoughtfully, polishing away at the machine-gun as he talks. 'He must be an officer or he wouldn't expect us all to bow down before Him, and always be prayin' to Him for somethin' or other!'

'What God does is not a subject for discussion,' says the Legionnaire who is sitting reading his Koran, as usual. 'What Allah does is right and must be accepted!'

' "*Gott mit uns*", it says on our belt-buckles,' Albert goes on stubbornly, after a short silence. He seems quite fascinated by his thoughts on the subject of religion. 'Why ever should God be with *us*? The English an' the Yanks go to church a lot more'n we do, an' what about all the atheists? God's helping them, seems like, just for the minute! It's enough to make a man laugh his head off!'

'Why in the name of all hell're you bothering us with all ¬hat God rubbish? Change the subject or shut up!' explodes the Old Man, puffing furiously at his silver-lidded pipe, and sending up billows of smoke.

'Religion is a kind of opium,' Gregor trumpets, importantly. 'Me an' my general were always agreed on that. It makes people soft. Parsons should be refused admission to Heaven, my general always said. They ruin all the hardheaded people with their preaching, and all that's left are the soft-headed ones.'

'Oh I don't know,' says Albert, thoughtfully. He pulls his head back down inside the ginger-coloured furs, like a snail going back into its shell.

'What the devil do you mean by that?' asks Heide, looking up from the LMG which, as usual, he has dismantled and is cleaning.

'I mean I don't know whether there's a God, or there isn't,' answers Albert. 'An' I mean too that I don't understand a word of any of it, man!'

'Now I'm *ordering* you to decide on what you really believe in, you black monkey,' the Old Man foams, removing his pipe from his mouth. 'Either you *believe* in God, or else you *don't* believe in God. Make up your mind *now*, an' then shut up!'

'I have done,' says Albert, stubbornly, pulling his head in again. 'I made up my mind a long time ago that I was gonna believe I didn't know whether there was a God or there wasn't a God, an' that's what I believe in. And now you get mad at me because of me admitting "I don't know" is what I believe in.'

'You will have some explaining to do at any rate, *mon ami*, when you one day stand face to face with Allah,' laughs the Legionnaire, heartily.

'I don't think I will, you know,' says Albert assuredly. 'I'm a nice, decent sort o' feller, who's only killed people he's been ordered to kill, and not pinched anything if he didn't really have a need for it!'

'Shut it, shut it, shut it!' shouts the Old Man. 'A bit more of this and they'll shoot you without needing an order to do it!'

'Oink! Oink!' comes from out in the street.

'It's Porta,' laughs Gregor, looking out of the gaping window opening.

'Seen a pig go by?' asks Porta, from the opposite side of the street. 'One with black patches on it, and light blue eyes just like mine?'

'Now I've heard that, too,' the Old Man breaks out, fiercely. 'God help us, he's running about the place looking for a pig with black patches on it, while the neighbours're knocking the whole damn place down round our ears! Come back. Come bloody *back*!' he roars through the broken window. 'That's an *order*!'

But Porta is lost in the darkness, still hunting for his black and pink pig with the pale blue eyes.

More and more soldiers from other units arrive, and sit down round the fire Tiny has started in the middle of the floor.

Tiny shakes a tin of signal powder into the blaze, and the flames turn bright red.

We chuckle with pleasure at the brilliant sight.

Porta comes barging noisily through the door.

'That rotten pig must've been at the commando school,' he yells. 'I've been on his tail all night, and every time I called to him he answered me. Then, just when I thought I'd got him, down by the suspension bridge, he goes over to the attack an' dashes off across the river to the neighbours. They're sitting there chewin' on him now, I shouldn't wonder!'

'That fat Leutnant with the monocle. He's the cause of all this,' says Barcelona, staring into the red flames.

'I thought he was in jail,' says Gregor. 'That was the cook-waggon gossip.'

'Latrine rumours,' Barcelona shakes his head. 'That shit's got his feet under the table with the red-tabs. Two hours after they'd turned the key on him they had to bow him out again with an apology.'

'Better shoot his blubbery chops off him, then,' says Porta, drawing the heavy *Nagan* demonstratively from his holster, and aiming it at Heide, who ducks instinctively. 'Well, I'm off,' he goes on, returning the *Nagan* to its holster with a flourish.

'Where the hell d'you think *you're* goin'?' growls the Old Man, pushing tobacco down into the bowl of his silver-lidded pipe. 'I won't have it. I won't *have* you running around over the whole of Russia. I want you here where I can keep an eye on you.'

'Be back in two shakes,' promises Porta, elevating three fingers vertically. 'Just off to have a look-see if the war hasn't come to a stop all of a sudden. It's that still.'

Gregor flips the cards round with practised fingers. We play quietly for a while.

Suddenly Tiny crashes a petrol-can down on Albert's head. Albert is sitting opposite him in his ginger fur coat, looking as if he had stepped straight out of a coloured cartoon strip.

'That black ape's more of a twister'n a 'ole Jew colony,' rages Tiny, swinging the heavy can round his head. ''E keeps stickin' them klepto-bleedin'-maniac fingers of 'is out over the coppers, but 'e don't drop no soddin' money into the pool.' The can lands on Albert's head, for the second time, with a reverberating clang. He falls out of his chair and knocks over the card-table.

'Stay where you are, so's I can kill you dead, you stinkin' Congo German you,' screams Tiny furiously, lifting the petrol-can for the third time.

'You *have* killed me,' bleats Albert, holding both hands protectively over his head. 'Can't you see I'm dead already, and I'm *bleedin'* man!'

'Get up, you black soddin' corpse,' shouts Tiny, kicking out at him.

Oberleutnant Löwe bangs through the door, followed by the monocled Leutnant.

'Where is Obergefreiter Porta?' asks Löwe, with a steely glint in his eye. 'Where *is* that wicked man?'

'Pluckin' geese, sir,' says Tiny, with a sloppy attempt at a salute.

'*What* is he doing?' asks Löwe, gaping at Tiny.

'Pluckin' geese, sir,' explains Tiny, making feather-plucking movements with his hands.

'I've got some geese to pluck with *him*,' snarls Löwe, straightening his dirty field-cap. 'He's to report to company immediately, and tell him to keep away from Oberst Hinka. The CO doesn't want to *know* him any more. He's for a court-martial and Germersheim!'

''Ow about division then, sir?' asks Tiny owlishly. 'The General an' Porta's good friends, sir!'

'I'll look after you too, Creutzfeldt,' splutters Löwe. He turns on his heel and disappears, with the monocled Leutnant close upon his heels.

'What the hell's Porta doing now?' asks the Old Man, bitterly. 'That crazy sod's enough to drive a man up the wall. He goes on as if he owned the whole blasted army. Now I'm gonna tell you *all* somethin'. You're nothing but a shower of shit, the lot of you! I won't be finished with you till you've all seen the inside of Germersheim with lifers on you *an'* a death sentence laid on top of 'em!'

He is interrupted. The door crashes open and in comes Porta, dragging a squealing pig after him.

'He came back, after all,' he grins, happily.

'A few hours of that Commie lot was enough for him. Pretty, ain't he? That squealing's just an expression of how happy he is at having managed to defect!'

'You're to report to the OC,' says the Old Man, tiredly. 'That means now!'

'Who says you've laid eyes on me?' asks Porta, casually. 'Löwe's only a sodding officer. That lot can wait till I've got time for 'em, and time's what I haven't got enough of just now!'

'You're to report to company,' sighs the Old Man, 'whether you've got time or not! Call company,' he orders Gregor, who has communications duty.

'Connection broken,' Porta shakes with laughter, as he wrenches the telephone cable loose. 'Come on Tiny, we got to get food on!'

We eat and eat – for four hours together. Grease runs down from our mouths on to our chests. In between we take a trip outside to make room for more. We are so ravenously hungry that we are unable to stop eating.

Gregor almost chokes himself. Porta recommends that we hang him up by his heels. He coughs up a large chunk of pork.

We do not stop eating until only the gnawed bones remain. Gasping and belching, we sprawl on the floor, totally gorged with food.

War is a disease.

Sven Hassel

The train was struck by a bomb only a few yards away from the shelter of the tunnel. The railwaymen and the torn-off boiler of the locomotive were thrown 400 yards away into the ripe corn.

The leading carriage stood up vertically in the air. The next in line had been squeezed into the semblance of a closed concertina.

The Jabos came back. The leading machine dropped phosphorus bombs. Incendiary sticks skipped across the Red Cross cars. In seconds they had become a roaring sea of flame. Most of the patients burned to death in their beds.

The Jabos turned and swept the cornfield with their machine-guns. Before leaving they dropped the last of their incendiaries. The corn blazed up.

The black smoke of the conflagration was visible all day, even from many miles away. Not a single man or woman on the hospital train escaped alive.

VERA KONSTANTINOVNA

'I don't *like* this joint,' grumbles Porta, pulling the cork from a bottle of vodka with his teeth. He takes a long swig of the fiery spirit and wipes his mouth on his sleeve. 'Is this a billet to give *us*? Not even a rotten stove! It's cold as an Eskimo's arsehole! An' they call us the *herrenvolk*! Don't make me die laughing!'

'Section leaders to OC,' sings out the clerk, Gefreiter Voss, sticking his pointy nose in to us through a broken window.

'The devil,' growls the Old Man, sourly, buttoning up his long winter cloak, and slinging his machine-pistol over his shoulder, muzzle down. 'Look after the shop while I'm gone,' he turns to Barcelona, 'and I want that SMG in position. Those wicked sods could be on us again before we knew it!'

His breath clouds out around him, as he wheels away on his clumsy bow-legs through the deep sludge. His hands, contrary to all regulations, are pushed down deeply into his pockets. Anyone seeing him rolling along with his cap pulled down on his head, round-shouldered, bow-legged and wearing clumsy infantry boots, would think him no more than a stupid yokel. But they would be terribly wrong. In reality he is a deadly dangerous, battle-trained soldier, with a quite superhuman faculty of calmness, despite his frayed nerves. His face resembles a squashed orange, but still, somehow, engenders confidence. He is an old trench-rat, who doesn't trust many people; and that is one of the most important reasons for his having got us out of the dirtiest corners imaginable. And with amazingly few losses.

A little grey cat follows him, meowing, part of the way.

He kicks the door of the company office open disrespectfully. Here Hauptfeldwebel Hoffmann reigns, fat and vain as a South American dictator. He is wearing a tankman's black uniform, despite the fact that it is reserved for line troops and is not for echelon.

'You're supposed to knock three times before you come in here,' says Hoffmann angrily, swinging half-round and then back again in his American swivel chair. 'This isn't a brothel, man, it's Company HQ. This is where the brains live!'

'Brains?' grins the Old Man, in an insulting tone. 'You're sitting on 'em! Don't get too blown up, will you! Just remember we're short of men up the line. I might just ask for you down there with me, so you'd get busted to an ordinary Feldwebel an' lose your two silver stripes!'

'*You* get *me* out in your lousy section?' jeers Hoffmann. 'No Beier, I'm this company's Hauptfeldwebel, and I'm gonna stay being that as long as there *is* a 5 Company. They need an empty-headed key-swinger to look after the prisoners at Germersheim. Fancy the job?'

'Shit!' growls the Old Man, tramping on in to Oberleutnant Löwe without knocking.

'*Grüss Gott*,' Löwe greets him, leaning back in his rickety, creaking chair. 'Like a "little black" to warm you up?'

'Yes, *please*,' answers the Old Man, filling a mug half-full with coffee and topping it off with vodka. He throws his helmet down on the trampled earth of the floor, sits down on a hand-grenade box, and stretches out his legs and his filthy boots in front of him. He leans his machine-pistol up against a table leg.

'You look tired, Beier,' says Löwe. 'Been rough the last couple of months, hasn't it?'

'We've had our hands full,' says the Old Man, blowing on his coffee. 'That bloody 2 Section'll soon have me climbin' up the wall. No sooner we've got away from the blasted war than I'm standin' there with me mpi at the ready keepin' the rotten lot away from the temptations of the soddin' flesh.

108

Sometimes I can't hardly understand what's going on. About a week ago Unteroffizier Julius Heide goes raving, an' mows down a couple of hundred civvies with his machine-gun. Even if I was to charge him for it nothing'd happen, except me gettin' a bawling-out from the NSFO. That spit an' polish follower o' the book, Unteroffizier Julius Heide's a valued member of the party, so why shouldn't he get his funnies murdering a few women and children! They're only *untermensch*, anyway. Soon as we're finished with the murdering an' killing, Porta and Tiny enjoys themselves with a couple of willing Russian girls. What happens? They get punished for fraternizing! The laws in this war are really *strange*!'

'I didn't hear what you just said, Beier,' smiles Oberleutnant Löwe. 'Neither of us wants a court-martial, do we?'

The four other section commanders enter, and bark out short reports.

'More than half the company's gone up in smoke,' Löwe says, looking at the casualty lists in front of him. 'So! Until further notice we remain inactive. There's fresh supplies and replacements on the way to us. But don't take that inactive business too seriously. There's strict orders from regiment to keep the men constantly on the move. Otherwise they'll get up to all sorts of monkey-tricks. Herr Oberst Hinka wants no complaints, either civil or military.' Löwe throws a glance at the Old Man, who is still sitting on the grenade box, warming his hands on his coffee. 'And I'm thinking of 2 Section in particular, Feldwebel Beier, and also in particular of those two madmen Obergefreiter Josef Porta and Obergefreiter Wolfgang Creutzfeldt. And, while we are on the subject of 2 Section, we've received a long message from Army HQ.' Löwe throws three closely-written folio sheets over to the Old Man.

'That's to do with Gefreiter Albert. They want us to wash him white!'

The four other section leaders double up with laughter.

Only the Old Man and Löwe remain serious and straight-faced.

'There's nothing to laugh at,' Löwe tells them, buttoning his greatcoat. 'This is a very annoying business. Answer it Beier, in a manner which can bring them to understand that a negro cannot be washed white. Before I forget it, there's another annoying matter between the NSFO and Joseph Porta. I thought I'd be able to stop it, but, unfortunately, it's already gone to regiment. Division's heard about it too. If the worst happens it could cost Porta his head. A bitch of a case. You *must* keep your people in order, Beier. I'm punishing your section by giving them burial duty. Don't forget, now, Germans and Russians are not to be buried in the same grave, and civilians are to be buried on their own. *Don't* make the same mess of it as you did last time, when they mixed officers and other ranks together. Officers get their own individual graves, and such graves are specially decorated. The men go into a common grave, and may be buried in three layers, as long as there is a 30 cm layer of earth between them.'

'Lord help us!' mumbles the Old Man, grinding his teeth. He fills up his mug again with hot coffee.

Almost an hour later, his pipe billowing smoke, he tramps back down the muddy, tracked-up road.

The cat meets him again, and stand up on its back legs, pawing at his trousers.

'All right for *you*,' he says, scratching his neck. 'You haven't got 2 Section! You've only got yourself. Shit, that's what it is, pussy!' He becomes more and more angry with the section, the closer he gets to the billet. 'I'll *bury* 'em!' he promises himself. 'God damn it, if I don't. I'll make 'em crawl round the world three times, an' it'll be over the North Pole an' the South Pole. *That* ought to cool 'em down a bit!'

Fuming inside, he kicks open the door, throws his machine-pistol down in a corner, and looks angrily around. He sees immediately the almost unbelievable disorder in the great hall.

Untermensch Albert is having a furious verbal battle with *Herrenvolk* Heide. 'You're always after me, Julius, but now I want to know the reason why,' snorts Albert. 'Even if I *am* black I'm just as much a German as you are, and I've got all the rights of a German. So if you're after me for bein' a Reich-nigger then I'm gonna report you for it!'

'If *you're* a German, then *I'm* a Chinaman,' rages Julius, contemptuously. 'I'll tell you what you are, you black ape! You're a charcoal cartoon of a human being, a trained, performing man-eater, who chews bones for dinner like a hound-dog!'

''E's more'n that!' trumpets Tiny. ''Is gran'dad was a French Yid from Senegal, with a bleedin' great 'ook of a snitch, an' the skin of 'is cock cut off. 'E used to clean up in the synagogue every Thursday!'

'It's a lie,' howls Albert, insultedly. 'It was my *great*-grandpappy was a French Jew, and he *married* a girl from Senegal!'

'Now I've heard everything,' gasps Heide. He is on his feet and over by Albert in three long strides. He stands over him with legs straddled and fists planted on his hips, stinking of Unteroffizier.

'*Are* you a Yid? Answer, you black mongrel, or I'll crack your skull wide open, as I have the right to do!'

Albert creeps further down into his ginger furs, in terror.

'My great-grandpappy was a French Jew. I'm a German,' he whines, fumbling for his machine-pistol. Before he can get hold of it Heide kicks it clattering out of his reach.

'*French* Jew!' sneers Heide. 'There are no *French* Jews. Either you're a Jew or you're not a Jew. You've sneaked your way into the German *Wehrmacht* under false premises. God knows what the Racial Commission'll say when I report this.'

'They'll kick you out,' grins Albert, assuredly, 'an' they'll tell you, man, to go wipe your Nazi arse on your report! I've *been* in front of 'em, an' they've looked down my throat an' up my arsehole, an' measured my face, an' held me by the bollocks an' pulled my prick for me. And they declared me

111

80% German when they'd finished. I was close to gettin' put in the SS, where I might've ended up an officer!'

'What *is* all this piss you're talkin',' shouts the Old Man, irritably, pushing Heide angrily to one side. 'I don't want any trouble with you lot, whether you're Jews or whether you're Germans. You keep yourself to yourself and go polish your machine-pistol, Julius! You're nothing but trouble to me. And you, Albert, go out and wash your face and make sure you rinse it several times! That's an order from Corps HQ, and you come back in here to me after and prove your black colour's *real*! You, Barcelona, you're guard commander for the next three days!'

'Why?' asks Barcelona, his mouth dropping open. 'What've *I* done?'

'Saluted the General when you shouldn't have, you sloppy fool! Do it again and they'll put you inside! Porta! Where the hell's that madman got to?'

'Cookin' food.' answers Tiny. 'Pork chops à l'Alba!'

'I don't *care* where his blasted pork chops're from,' rages the Old Man, flinging his steel helmet down on the floor. 'He's halfway inside Germersheim, an' they'll hang him there! Nobody goes anywhere, you hear! Everybody stays here! In an hour from now you parade for grave duty, and in the meantime you clean this place up. Nails in the walls for uniforms an' equipment an' regimentally hung up. Beds made up out from the wall at equal distances. Helmets on gasmask pouches accordin' to regulations. No missing nails in your boots!'

'We ain't got any nails.' protests Gregor, weakly.

'Shit some, then.' orders the Old Man.

Tiny jumps up, clicks his heels together, and lifts his pale grey bowler courteously.

'We 'ear an' obey, 'Err Feldwebel, *sir*!' he trumpets.

'Cut that play-acting *out*!' snarls the Old Man, viciously. 'There'll be early parade tomorrow mornin'! All illegal weapons to be handed in! Anybody running round with enemy guns'll be for it!'

'For it!' echoes Tiny.

For a second it looks as if the Old Man is going to throw himself at him. Then he gives up. The energy of his anger seeps out of him. He drops down on to a creaking bed, runs his hands through his hair, and begins to fill his pipe.

'What a shower of shit you lot are,' he mumbles, looking round at us.

We dig the common grave in the park. There is no more room in the churchyard.

The Old Man sits on the remains of a pedestal, on which a statue once stood, and blows out great clouds of tobacco-smoke.

Porta and Tiny are sorting bodies, and talking quietly to one another.

'You as much as look at a gold tooth, and I'll shoot you!' The Old Man aims at them threateningly with the stem of his pipe.

'Perish the thought,' lies Porta, with one finger inside the mouth of a corpse. Tiny stands ready with the forceps.

'Two in this one,' whispers Porta. 'Wait till he's down in the grave before you take his savings. Then the Old Man can't see it. How many we got?'

'A lot,' answers Tiny. More than five is a lot where he is concerned.

The partly decayed body of a woman slips from my hands as I pass it on to Heide and Gregor. They are down in the grave lining up the bodies regimentally.

Heide goes amuck when the heavy corpse knocks him over into the middle of the grave. Snorting with rage he throws a torn-off arm at me.

'You did that deliberately! God help you when I get hold of you!'

I hide behind a toolshed, and stay there until he goes off the boil. He is mad enough to carry out his threat.

We have to dig two more common graves. There are many more dead than we had thought.

During the sorting process Tiny comes to an SS-Haupt-

113

sturmführer who has had the lower part of his body shot away. Since orders are that parts of bodies are to be buried together with the person to whom they belong, Tiny begins to search for a pair of legs which could fit the Hauptsturm-führer's body. Not finding them, he takes two torn-off legs which, by the boots, must have belonged to a Russian officer.

Porta scratches his stiff red hair doubtfully, and looks critically at the legs, with their Russian riding breeches and high brown boots.

'Don't really fit, do they?' he says, spitting over the edge of the officer's grave. 'If they ever open this one up, they *will* be confused. They'll think it's a wrong 'un they've run across. An SS officer who was going to desert and had started changing into Ivan's uniform. No it won't do, my son. We'll have to get him a couple of German legs!'

'I'll 'ave another look, then,' grunts Tiny patiently, crawling, with difficulty, up out of the grave. He stops in a kneeling position on its edge, and turns an ear toward the low-hanging clouds. '*Jabos!*' he shouts. 'Bleedin' arse'oles, *Jabos!*'

Porta stretches his neck. His cunning, foxy face sniffs towards the east.

'*There!*' yells Tiny. He is back in the grave like lightning, and burrows down between the bodies.

They seem to jump up from behind the trees, and, with a nerve-shattering roar, they pass over our heads. Their stubby wings sparkle as they rise vertically into the sky and come back round for a return run. They open fire with all their automatic weapons: machine-guns and light cannon. Hundreds of spurts of dust fountain up from the ground, as the projectiles whip across the park. Two of the machines bank, and fly along the row of open graves. They are so low that the faces of their pilots can be clearly seen.

I drop down flat on my face behind the toolshed. A machine-cannon salvo splinters into it, throwing all kinds of dirt and muck over me. I turn my face up for a moment to see where the battle-planes have gone to.

Both machines seem to rear up on their tails in the air. They describe a great arc and come roaring back at us. This time they drop bombs. The shattering noise of the explosions almost burst our eardrums. The earth shakes. Clods of earth and stones rain down on me.

Someone gives out a long, rattling scream. It drowns in the roar of the Jabos, as they attack again. The projectiles spitting from their wings seem to roll up the asphalt path like a carpet.

The machines flash over us again. More bombs fall; deafening us.

They come in twice more. Then they fly off towards the east, back to their base.

We wish everything far, far away, as we start in again collecting bodies.

Tiny finds a pair of German legs which will do for the Hauptsturmführer.

It is far into the night before we have finished filling in the graves. We sit down, tiredly, on the soft earth of one of the common graves. The vodka bottle goes from hand to hand. We are soaked in sweat despite the biting cold of the evening.

The Old Man is sitting with Barcelona, sorting dog-tags. German here, Russian there. They put them separately into large bags, and tie the service books of the dead men in bundles. There are also letters. A lot of letters. Barcelona unfolds one and reads it aloud:

My beloved boy,

It is a long time since I heard from you. Did you get my parcel? There is a woolly sweater in it to keep you warm. Don't forget to change your socks if you get your feet wet. You know how you are with colds. Claus the foreman's son who you went to school with is back from the Army. He lost one arm but they are not sending him home. When his leave's finished they are putting him on barrack

115

duty. Even the ones who lose a leg aren't getting sent home now. We had an air-raid alarm again yesterday. They dropped some bombs on the railway station and they say it's flattened. I'm going down there this afternoon with Mrs Schröder to see how bad it is. Now look after yourself won't you. Now your dad's gone I've only got you. I'm glad you're on a part of the front where there's not a lot happening. Mrs Schultzes two boys are in a place where a lot of terrible things are going on but we mustn't talk about that. Our new Gauleiter is very strict and hard on people who talk too much. They came and took our neighbour Mrs Schmidt in the middle of the night because she talked about something called *Nacht und Nebellager*. So you have to be careful what you say. My dear, darling boy, it's twelve months since you went away but thank God you'll be getting leave in two months time. I am counting the hours. Write soon. I get so disappointed when the postman goes by and there's no letter for me. I know you're not allowed more than one letter every eight days, but promise me you'll write then at the least.

See you in 58 days time.

Your loving
Mother

'Shit!' says Tiny, as Barcelona refolds the letter and places it inside the soldier's service record book.

'Up you get,' commands the Old Man, coming to his feet. 'Sling arms! Broken step! Follow me! Quick march!'

Chatting as we go, we walk in a disorderly column down a narrow path. We keep to its sides, under the shelter of the trees, in cover from the air.

'Shall I cook the grub when we get home,' offers Porta, from the darkness under the trees. By 'home' he means the factory hall we have taken over for our quarters. 'I'm going to do us "Pork Chops à l'Alba",' he goes on, enthusiastically. 'It's a dish that Kings an' Emperors prize highly,

116

Orthodox Jews do it with beef cutlets, but that spoils the effect. It needs character to do "Pork Chops à l'Alba", I can tell you. First of all it's out in the fields and find your shallot onions. These you have to chop very fine, and the right song for doing that to is the "Georgian Harvest song". When they're nicely chopped up, you sprinkle 'em, with an elegant flip of the wrist, with parsley, sage, salt an' pepper. But, for heaven's sake, *black* peppers! The man who uses *white* pepper should have the devil let down through his throat with a roll of barbed wire on his back! Then you make small cuts on each side of your pork chops with a good sharp knife. I usually use my combat knife. It's always got a good, sharp edge to it. I prefer to hum "The Song of the Volga Boatmen" during the next operation, which is rubbing the onion mix into the pork. Now we come to the next step, which can be difficult. Borrow some butter from your next-door neighbour, which, of course, you never intend to pay back. A lot of people live high on borrowing from their next-door neighbours. It's cheaper an' also saves storage space. The butter you've borrowed you then melt. Take your pork chop between two fingers, I recommend the thumb and forefinger of the right hand, and dip half of it in the melted butter. Turn it, then, on a fire-proof dish for about ten minutes. After this, you pour your wine over it, but light an' easy. *Don't* drown it! The chops only need to be slightly, but happily, intoxicated. Whip in the remainder of the borrowed butter and pour the sauce over the meat.'

'What *kind* of wine?' comes Gregor's voice from the back of the section.

'White, of course, you excuse for a driver!' snaps Porta.

'Any special sort?' Gregor enquires.

'How that fool goes on! You can see he's been around generals too long! Use what you've *got*. The main thing is it's white, and what's left of it you drink yourself.'

A despatch-rider comes round the bend ahead of us at top speed and stops in front of the Old Man, who is out in the middle of the narrow path with his arm raised.

'Russian tanks, Herr Feldwebel!' shouts the despatch-rider, straddling his motorcycle. 'Coming this way to get back to their own lines. Orders from Regimental HQ. Stop and destroy!' With a roar the motorcycle is off again.

'God damn and set fire to it,' rages the Old Man. '*Tanks*, and we've got the job of wiping 'em out! Of course! Who else?'

Tiny takes a sausage from his pocket, snaps it in two and gives Porta half.

'There's some blood on it,' he apologizes, 'but they say as blood gives a feller strength!'

'Where'd you get it? asks Porta, suspiciously.

'From a dead un',' answers Tiny, chewing on his half of the sausage.

'What kind of a dead un?' asks Porta, sniffing at his half.

'Russian bleedin' lieutenant,' mumbles Tiny, looking towards the trees.

'The sausage ought to be all right then. Officers only eat top-class stuff,' says Porta, taking a large bite.

'Come on,' orders the Old Man. 'Things'll soon be humming. Get your magnetics ready! Stovepipes in the lead! We attack from the right of the road, and don't let me see any itchy trigger fingers. Wait for the order!'

'We getting anti-tank support?' asks Heide, pompously.

'Yes, up your arse,' Porta laughs noisily. 'If they'd got anti-tank guns to spare, they wouldn't send us, now would they?'

Part way into the wood we meet a couple of sections from 7 Company. They are wildly excited, and go on about hordes of Russian tanks.

'And they've infantry with 'em,' shouts a Feldwebel to the Old Man. '2 Company's been steam-rollered to bits. Not a dry eye left in the lot!'

'Sounds pleasant,' answers the Old Man, with a short laugh. 'But that's what we're here for. To kill or be killed.'

'Down!' shouts Barcelona hoarsely, as half a dozen flares suddenly open up in the sky, making everything as light as day. The whole section is flat on the ground before he has finished saying the word.

An SP comes rushing along at top speed, bumps over the top of the hill and lands with a jangling crash on the far side.

'Up with you,' bawls the Old Man. 'Move! Open line abreast! March! March!'

The section spreads out and lumbers, panting, across the uneven ground. I have the MG under my arm, supporting it on my hip. My finger is along the trigger-guard. My heart is beating so fast it is almost painful. I go rushing straight through some bushes, which tear at my face and hands. Blood runs down.

A little way in front of me Porta is running, his idiotic yellow topper on the back of his neck. Down in the valley the SP wheels round as if the driver had gone mad. The night fills with heavy thuds and brilliant muzzle-flashes. They give light enough for us to be able to glimpse half a score of T-34s. The SP stops with a jolt, and replies to the fire immediately.

From a row of ruined houses, long bursts of Russian Maxim bullets rush at us.

Some of the rookies throw themselves to the ground, and try to creep away from the hell of fire.

'Get *up*! Get *on*!' roars the Old Man, striking at them with the barrel of his mpi. 'Who the devil told you to fall down?'

Breathing heavily we break into a run. We are now not much above a hundred yards from the closer of the T-34s.

Blue-green lightnings flame from the muzzles of Russian machine-pistols: Maxims spit wicked yellow flashes as they pepper us with their deadly, pearly chains of tracer.

I go down so heavily my face smashes into the lock of the LMG. I wipe my hand over it. I am bleeding freely, but have no time to think about that. I sight in on the muzzle-flame from the Russian SMG, press the butt of my gun into my shoulder and grip so tightly with my left hand that I almost get cramp in it. I send three short bursts at the Russian SMG. Then I'm up like lightning, run to the left and fall into new cover. I am hardly into it before a grenade goes off where I was only a moment ago.

A shell from a tank-gun passes close above my head and cuts Fahnenjunker Kolb in two with the efficiency of a circular saw. The blast from the exploding shell throws me far off to one side and tears the LMG out of my hands. I sob with terror and press my face into the ground. When the rushing in my ears stops, I put my hands out to feel for the LMG. Instead, my fingers find themselves touching a naked leg. I feel at it and cannot believe my eyes when I open them to look. A naked leg, torn off at the groin and blown out of both boots and trousers. I start to scream, and beat my fists on the ground, hysterically.

'Get *on*! Get *on*!' the Old Man chases me, bringing his mpi-butt down on the small of my back.

'No!' I protest, 'I *can't* go on!'

Heide grabs me brutally by the collar.

'Get up, you yellow swine,' he snarls, viciously. 'Where's your LMG? Don't tell me you've lost your weapon?' He throws me from him, as if I were a sack of rotten potatoes.

I fall, sobbing, on one knee, completely finished.

He points the muzzle of his machine-pistol at me, and cracks me hard across the face with the back of his hand. My helmet goes back on to my neck. Then, suddenly, it is all over. I am a normal, well-disciplined soldier again. The MG is back in my hands with the strap regimentally across my shoulder. My legs are going like runaway pistons.

I literally fly past Porta, who is in cover behind a wood-pile, readying the stovepipe.

'Hey there!' he shouts cheerily after me. 'Hang on. Don't want you getting to Moscow before us an' grabbin' all the good cunt!'

A T-34 is hit just in front of me. A blinding sheet of flame goes up, and the tank breaks up with a metallic sound, like a giant fist crashing down on a tin roof. The explosion illuminates a whole row of wrecked houses. From off to the left come the hard cracking explosions of German stick-grenades. It must be Heide's squad who've got within throwing distance.

Porta's bazooka howls, and the passage of air from the speeding rocket almost tears my helmet from my head.

A T-34 goes up in a volcano of flame. Porta's rocket must have scored a direct hit on its ammunition locker.

I am deaf for several minutes from the violence of the explosion.

'Come *on*! Forward!' roars the Old Man, his bowed legs cranking away.

I rush forward, shooting as I run at the dark figures over by the wrecked houses. Between bursts I hear the short, stammering bark of the Old Man's mpi. A couple of yards in front of me I see a shadow which resembles a mole-hill, but is really a Russian helmet with its funny steel cockscomb. I shoot so low that the tracer scorches along just above the ground, cutting the Russian's head in two.

'Forward!' the Old Man chases us on. 'Forward!' He pumps his arm up and down in the air, signalling to us.

I take cover behind a concrete balustrade, and lob a couple of hand-grenades over the rosebeds, in which leafless bushes stand closely ranked. I push forward between the flower beds.

'Back!' I scream, desperately, rolling head-over-heels down the slope.

I have run into three Russian SMG gunners, and they are sending a hail of bullets along the length of the hill.

'No, damn that,' roars the Old Man. 'Forward! We've no choice! Up with you! Grenades!' I look around me, timid and frightened, and I feel like running, dumping that cursed machine-gun anywhere, and running; running till I reach home again.

'Come *on*!' shouts Porta, waving to me. 'Let's kick Ivan's arsehole up round his ears, so he won't get to thinkin' he's winning the war!'

I jump to my feet and press on up the steep slope. A couple of hand-grenades, and the Russian machine-gun nest goes up in a fount of flame. My feet seem suddenly light, as if they had grown wings.

Tracer bullets snarl and hiss past me. It seems incredible they can all miss. Running madly I reach the opposite stone balustrade, am over it, and rolling down the slope on the far side. Round about me I hear the sharp crack of tank-guns, and the hollow droning of the stovepipes.

Another T-34 explodes in a sea of red, glowing flame.

The rest of the section comes rolling down the slope after me.

Russian MGs hammer wildly. Three or four shadows flit past.

I thread a new belt into the LMG, and smack it shut far too noisily.

'Give me some covering fire,' the Old Man demands, hoarsely. 'I'm going over that balustrade there, and as soon as I'm gone you come after me! And get the lead out!'

'Very good,' I mumble, pressing the butt of the LMG into my shoulder and sending off five or six short bursts. The Old Man struggles up on top of the stonework, rolls over it and disappears. I jump up, and rush, bent over at the waist, across the open stretch, sweeping the LMG from side to side.

A green flare goes up, hangs in the heavens, and slowly dies away.

'Done it again,' pants Porta, pulling up alongside me.

A number of Russians come slowly toward us with arms above their heads. They stare at us fearfully as we search their pockets with nimble fingers. They have nothing on them worth bothering with. A few evil-smelling *Machorkas*, one or two greasy, much-thumbed letters.

'They're poor as us,' sighs Porta, patting a shaggy *Kalmuk* on the shoulder. He is an elderly man with a large moustache, drooping sadly down over his mouth.

The last of the T-34s goes clattering off through the park. In the distance sounds of fighting can still be heard, but they ebb slowly away, and the silent blanket of night falls again over the scarred town.

The next day passes with one parade after the other. We are continually sent back to do it all over again. Which we don't of course do. Instead we sit and play cards. In the end the people who lay on parades get tired of all the work it costs them. The hidden foreign weapons come back out again. A *Kalashnikov is* really better than a *Schmeisser*. For one thing it has a magazine holding a hundred rounds, and the *Schmeisser* holds no more than thirty-eight.

After a while everything is back to normal. Porta and Tiny tramp around again in their private headgear – tall hat and bowler. Albert is packed into his ginger-coloured fur. Heide is almost normal, and is no longer indignant over Albert's racial cocktail. He does not speak to him more than absolutely necessary, however.

'He looks like a shit-fly that's burned its arse on a storm lantern,' says Porta, as Albert sits down alongside Heide and starts showing him some photographs. Heide conceals his disgust, but cannot help studying them closely.

Leave is handed out generously, but only to married men with children, so that the Old Man and Barcelona are the first to go. We follow them all the way down to the leave train, and stand, waving, long after the train is out of sight, and even the sound of it has died away.

We go back to our billets feeling like small children who have been left at home on their own. Without the Old Man we feel lost.

Then something else happens, which almost knocks our pins out from under us.

Gregor is leaving us, and for ever. We think it is a lie. Even when he is packing his gear, and sharing out the things he no longer has any use for, we can't believe it. He shows us it in black and white. Army Staff has asked for him. He is again to be driver and bodyguard for his famous general. We go with him to the train, too. He is wearing a completely new uniform. They dare not send him off to report to a general in his worn-out front line kit.

'You *do* look nice,' cries Porta, admiringly. 'They could

123

put you straight on to a recruiting poster to bullshit idiots into the Army at a mark a day!'

We take leave of him on a platform filled with holes. Gregor leans far out of the window shaking our outstretched hands. As a general's driver and bodyguard he has been allocated a seat in a real passenger compartment. He treats the MPs who examine his papers accordingly. Condescendingly, he looks the spit-and-polished MP up and down, and tells him to say Unteroffizier when he speaks to him, and stand to attention.

'Anybody can bloody well see you're General Staff now,' Porta nods, approvingly. 'Give 'em some stick, the shits, but don't forget you're still one of us! If you happen to run across anything good, don't forget Joseph Porta, Obergefreiter by the grace of God, is in the market for everything!'

The train departs and we slouch back to our regular routine. Soon, however, we are beginning to feel the need of excitement again.

We do not see much of Porta. Hauptfeldwebel Hoffmann is continually sending out office runners – hounds we call them – looking for him, but it is not often they find him. When they do find him it is because he wants them to.

He is spending most of his time with Vera, the deserted wife of the commissar. She is beginning to feel herself very truly liberated by the German Army, in the shape of Porta.

It is Sunday afternoon, and everything is peaceful and quiet. Snow falls softly and silently. There are no noises from the front line, which is by now far away and almost forgotten. Out on the parade ground Tiny is playing with a large, ugly dog, which resembles him not a little.

Hauptfeldwebel Hoffmann has his trackers out after Porta, as usual. He wants to put him on 24-hour guard duty. But Porta is lying, stark naked, on his back in a large, red four-poster bed, with angels blowing celestial horns on each bedpost. He resembles more than anything a long, thin, forked radish as he lies there on the pink bed-clothes, warming his long, bony toes between Vera's thighs. They are both dozing and seem to purr with satisfaction like a couple of well-fed cats.

Porta is dreaming that he is lying on the shore of an azure lagoon, wearing a white tuxedo, and surrounded by a group of willing ladies wearing no clothes at all.

'*Zolloto*,' mumbles Vera, rolling over in her sleep.

Porta chuckles with laughter, and moves the tips of his fingers as if he were counting money.

'*Zolloto*,' smiles Vera, happily.

Porta sits up in bed, wide awake, and suspicious as an old, experienced alley-cat.

'What do you do?' she whispers, sleepily, ruffling his red hair.

'You said *Zolloto*!' says Porta, bending over her. '*Zolloto*!'

'I say *Zolloto*?' she asks, seemingly carelessly. She swings her long legs over the edge of the bed, and pushes her feet into a pair of high-heeled white fluffy mules. With a lazy movement she takes a Russian cigarette, with a long tubular mouthpiece, from the drawer of her bedside table. 'I can *trust* you? You villain!' she says after a long silence, blowing smoke into his face as she speaks. 'I mean – *really* trust you? Can you keep silent, if the world falls down on your head, and they stroke you and they promise you the moon and all the planets, if you play canary for them?'

'What the hell d'you think I am?' grins Porta, holding up three fingers. 'In my short but exciting life, I have brought literally scores of plain-clothes coppers to the brink of the screaming meemies. I've been chucked out of the glass-house for disturbin' disciplinary routine. One General, two Obersts, six Leutnants and a whole *army* of Feldwebels and that kind of *shit* have been driven out of their minds by me. A couple of 'em put a hole through their heads after they'd chatted with me for a bit, an' an *untermensch* like you wants to know if *you* can trust *me*? Ask instead if *I* can trust *you*? Even though you've got race, you're still an *untermensch* talkin' to one of the *herrenvolk*!'

She takes two long, thoughtful pulls at her cigarette, and

pinches the long cardboard mouthpiece between her fingers. 'Watch out, *herrenvolk* man. You could choke on that stupid grin,' she says, sourly.

Porta is across the floor in two jumps, and fills two tumblers with cognac.

They raise their glasses and toast one another silently. She lights a fresh cigarette, and exhales smoke slowly.

'It does not make you nervous to get into something both Russians and Germans will not like?' she asks him. 'What I talk about is so unlawful, a crook lawyerman from the Mafia even, would shake with fright just to think about what could happen to him if he got caught!'

'*Me*? *Nervous*?' Porta laughs, heartily. 'Losin' my good German life's all that worries *me*. Where breaking the law's concerned I don't give a shit for that. I work for me, *and* I know how to fix people who blabber too much. I remember one feller. Talked as much as a flock o' canaries in mating-time. We took him for a sail one day when we had a hot engine to drown. We put a rope round his neck, but that was only so's he wouldn't fall overboard and get lost at sea. But when we got out there where we were goin' to lose this engine, we somehow forgot our mate's safety line was tied on to it, and the canary went down to the bottom along with the motor. The last we saw of him was a pair of shoes, round-heeled they were, waving goodbye to us.'

They lie naked on the bed for a while, drinking rum laced with cognac, while they convince one another how grey and melancholy the world is when you haven't enough money.

'I was born to be rich,' breathes Vera, a deep, thoughtful wrinkle appearing between her eyebrows, 'so that you must understand the Soviet Union is not altogether suiting me.'

'Only fools choose a life without money,' Porta agrees, filling up their glasses again. This time he chooses *Slivovitz* to get rid of the cheap cognac taste.

'My father was Imperial officer, a general,' she sighs proudly, looking sideways at Porta. 'If Lenin stay in your damned Germany I would be at the Imperial court now.

Why you do not shoot him for the devil's sake?'

'May I just touch Your Grace?' asks Porta, rolling over on top of her.

'My mama was from the best circles,' she goes on, swinging her legs up around his skinny thighs. 'Her family was much at the palace. We all believed in God.'

'God didn't help you much though, when Lenin's boys got there an' shot your blue-blooded arses off,' says Porta, biting her nose gently.

'Everyone know my father. His division was the best. He won the St George Cross. You Germans fled from him as fast as your legs could go . . .'

'Hold it,' Porta puts in, holding up his hand. 'I wasn't in that fight!'

'My father was a wealthy man! He gave his life for the state. He sign death penalties, send criminals to Siberia, was lover of fine horses and women, the Tsar and God.'

'I've met one or two generals like that,' says Porta, laughing shortly. 'They think they were born to the job. They never get round to understanding that that's something we made 'em into!'

'You talk like a filthy *Bolshevik*,' she spits, angrily.

'You're wrong there, girl,' he laughs, emptying his tumbler. 'Don't forget you're the wife of a commissar with gilt-edged red stars all over you. The Tsar's generals are all gone upstairs an' are kissin' Ivan the Terrible's arse part now. Stalin's commissars are the boys that're steppin' light an' easy around on the stage these days.'

'What would you say to making 30 millions? Maybe more!' she asks him, sipping thoughtfully from her glass.

Porta picks up the cognac bottle, and takes a long swallow. Then he takes up the rum and washes the cognac down with a still longer swallow. He looks at her for a long time. Then he asks, in a quiet voice:

'Did you say millions? You're not kidding me?'

'Yes. 30 *millions*!' She smiles mysteriously. 'But I think more. Much more. We have worked all out, so there is nothing to get worried about. It is what you call a sure thing. We are already rich!'

'You've no idea,' he says, in a knowing voice, 'just how many clever chaps I've met who've told me just exactly what you're telling me. And what they were talking about was small potatoes compared to your millions. But they're all tucked away behind bars now, and wondering what it was went wrong with their sure thing!'

'You are frighten, then?' she jeers at him. 'I am wrong about you? Take your rags and get out of here. I don't know you any more!'

'No my dear, it ain't that easy,' he grins fiendishly, shaking the empty rum bottle. 'When Joseph Porta, Obergefreiter by the grace o' God, gets on the trail of a job with 30 million iron men, he wants to hear 'em chinking! I've dreamt about something like this all my stinkin' German life. You realize how long it'd take just to *count* 30 millions? A hell of a long time I can tell you. It'd make even the Yids in the state bank sweat just to think of it.'

'You go with us in sledge, and are ready to run a little risk to be rich and independent of politicians and other foolish people?' she asks, taking a deep pull on her cigarette.

'You can bloody well believe it I'm ready.' He roars with laughter. 'An' if your sure thing *is* a sure thing, then I swear by the Holy God above I'll burn seven candles for you forever in the synagogue of my heart!'

'Light them now, then,' she smiles, offering him her cigarette-lighter. 'You can get helpers? Good men? Not stumbling bums?'

'Too true I can,' he nods with assurance, lighting one of her cigarettes. 'I have a kind of friend in Berlin who can open any kind of safe or strong-box, from the most advanced model to the primitive ones the municipalities buy in bundles of twelve. We called him "Plastic Man", because he usually worked with plastic explosives. I once saw him open a safe that belonged to some people who didn't trust the banks after Adolf moved in to Berlin. He stuck a coupla little balls of plastic explosive on the door of it by the hinges. We stepped into the next room, where he set it off with a natty little radio an' "BOOM!" it said. When we went back inside there's this impenetrable armoured door lyin' on the floor inside out. All we had to do was empty the box. That door couldn't have been opened quicker with the proper key.'

'This has nothing to do with safes,' she corrected him. 'It is much bigger than such things!'

'Do we have to send somebody off in a natural manner, then?' he asks, with a pleased expression. 'I can fix that, too. My adjutant, Tiny, is a very handy fellow with a garrottin' wire. People drop dead from it. An' if there are any really *big* problems attached to removing somebody from this world in a hell of hurry, then I've got a mate we call "Sudden Death". When I was last in Berlin, I took him with me to "talk" to a feller who thought he could put one over on me. We arrived, just when they'd got to the dessert, with a couple of Stens. It went off that quick, we hadn't even said hello before the chap had fell over from the weight of the lead in his body. The landlord of "The Half Donkey", who was standin' there waiting with pancakes on a plate, got his tie shot off by a bullet. He was that shocked he was still standing there in the same spot, with his bloody pancakes and the shot-off bit o' tie in his hand, when Inspector August an' his posse arrived to discover who it was'd got shot.

'"Shot?" he whined, dropping his pancakes. "Nobody's been *shot*!" He didn't know a thing about the body under the table. He swore to it. Said it must have got left there, somehow!

'They closed the case as bein' disorderly conduct, when they found out where the bullets in the body came from. They were from *Prinz Albrecht Strasse 3*.'

They sit back together on the bed, propped up on pillows, and drinking steaming-hot coffee.

A large map is spread out in front of them.

'Here,' she says, 'are our millions. They lie there waiting for us.'

'Prikumsk,' he mumbles, bending closely over the chart, as if he were nearsighted. 'Prikumsk! Sounds like some kind of a drink. You sure all that glitterin' Commie gold is really hidden away there? I don't like that river. There's another town over there on the other bank. Reminds me of a beartrap ready to snap shut and hold you fast while you shit yourself waiting there to get shot!'

'You can be easy,' she says. 'My husband lead the convoy, and nobody put wool on his eyes!'

'And now your reliable husband has decided to go fetch the 30 million again?' grins Porta, sceptically. 'And *you* can trust him, of course. But can *I*? Good an' faithful servants of the state who steal with both their fingers an' their toes I do not feel happy about!'

'He is a good friend to his friends, true as steel,' she declares grandly. 'He *never* cheat!'

'No! I don't suppose so,' Porta laughs, heartily. 'What kinda feller's this commissar husband of yours, anyway? Is he from Moscow?'

'Are you mad? You believe I trust a man from Moscow?' she screams, insultedly. 'He is Georgian. His mother was Jewish from Crimea. The grandfather on mother's side from Salonica. The family was Italian.'

'If you tell me now there's Irish on his dad's side,' he says jokingly, 'then I'm sorry to say your commissar ol' man's goin' to have to go through the process of natural death. A knife in his back, or somethin' like that. A cocktail like him can be a dangerous mixture.'

'What in hell you mean by that?' she asks, her eyes narrowing to slits. 'You are some kind of racist pig?'

'No, I can't afford to be,' answers Porta. 'But let me tell you I know just what goes to making a good Mafia boss. 90% spaghetti blood, preferably Sicilian. That's the beginning of the dodgiest of the dodgiest. 2% Irish, to make him a good fighter. 5% Jew juice, so he understands figures an' knows

130

how to alter 'em to his own advantage. Spot o' Greek on top of that lot an' he'll be one o' the worst villains on earth, with the big advantage of trustin' his fellow human beings as far as politicians trust one another. D'you understand now why I have doubts about your husband's reliability?'

'You think the gold bars are perhaps not there?' she asks suspiciously.

'I believe it's there all right, and I'm in no doubt that your good husband, with all the advantages of blood the Lord has granted him, will be able to pinch it off of his mates in the Kremlin. But I'm also in no doubt of his also having found out how he can also take a silly sod of a German. It'd be nice not to have to share with *anybody*, wouldn't it now?'

'He never do that,' she shouts, insultedly. 'You must not forget that he is a Russian officer!'

'Yes, I realize that,' he laughs, heartily. 'But just you watch out you don't find yourself sitting on your bare butt in a very cold snowdrift, watchin' honest hubby making off as fast as his legs can carry him with the shekels. Why in the world would he want to share 'em with *anybody*, when he could hang on to the lot with no bother?'

'He would not dare to do that with me,' she shouts, furiously. 'I would kill him completely! Step on him like a piece of shit!'

'D'you really believe all that?' he asks, staring at her. 'You couldn't do a thing to him. You weren't thinkin' now of going to the OGPU, were you? And I'd recommend you to keep far, far away from the Gestapo. *They're* not a very tender-hearted lot. If he does you out of it, you'll have to swallow the pill no matter how bitter it is. He's got the laugh on you all ways. He's *rich*! You don't get back on rich people. Not often. The best weapon in the world's money!'

'You think he would do that,' she asks, with growing suspicion.

'No trouble,' he answers, laughing shortly. 'Can't see why he shouldn't. Money can change the best of us.'

'I am his wife, whom he loves,' she protests, shaken,

looking at Porta in shocked fashion.

'When you've got a big bag of money, it's easy to get yourself a new wife. He says he loves you, does he? A man says a lot of things on his way down the thorny road of life.'

'You have evil in your mind,' she snarls, bitterly. 'I should never have told you about this thing!'

'Maybe it would've been cleverer not to,' admits Porta. 'The more people who know about the gold, the bigger's the risk of losing it. But I don't think you'd have told me your little secret either if you an' hubby weren't in need of some good old German know-how! If God won't take you the Devil must. But we'd do best to think it over carefully before we decide who else to tell where the Jew fly-paper is, or, before we can turn round, there'll be more souls outside its hidey-hole than there are waitin' at the gates of Hell. Thirty million bucks! Good Lord preserve us! Thought about the effect it'll have on the market when you let that Commie load loose on it?'

'As I have told you, there is thirty millions and probably some little more,' she assures him, tracing dollar signs with her fingernail on the sheet. 'I have calculated on it is hot money.'

'Hot, you say?' he laughs, noisily. 'If you'd said it was glowin' you'd have been a lot closer to the truth. Thirty millions! I've never set eyes on that much loot even in my dreams.' Suddenly his Slivovitz goes down the wrong way, and he begins to cough and splutter violently.

'You keep saying thirty millions all the time,' he gasps, between spasms of coughing. 'But you don't say thirty million *what*? Don't say it's Eyetie money! *Don't*! Thirty millions of them wouldn't get a German bailiff out of his warm bed!'

'It is Yankee, capitalist dollars,' she breathes, looking at him with an expression of triumph. You would think she had printed them herself.

'Dollars,' he mumbles radiantly, working out rapidly in his head what that would be in marks. 'Holy Mother of

Kazan, that's a lot of reinforcements!' Enthusiastically he grabs his piccolo, jumps high in the air, rushes round the room, like a happy fawn and hops up on top of a table. From this new eminence he begins to sing, in a ringing voice:

There was a rich man, and he lived in Jerusalem,
Glory hallelujah, hirojerum,

He wore a silk hat, and his coat was very sprucium,
Glory hallelujah, hirojerum.

At his gate, there sat a human wreckium,
He wore a bowler hat and the rim was round his neckium,

The poor man asked for a piece of bread and cheesium,
The rich man cried: 'I'll call for a policium,'

The poor man died and his soul went to heavium,
He danced with the angels, till a quarter past elevium,

The rich man died, but he didn't fare so wellium,
He couldn't go to heaven, so he had to go to hellium,

'No,' the devil said, 'this here is no hotelium,
It's just a plain and ordinary hellium,'

The moral of the story is: Riches are no jokium,
We'll all go to heaven, 'cause we are all stony brokium.

'Who teach you English?' she asks in surprise.

'*I* did,' he grins, playing a gay run on his piccolo. 'It's a song a fence I knew used to sing when he'd taken a sucker. He met that many of 'em when I knew him I just couldn't help learning it by heart.'

'He was English?'

'No, a Yid from Berlin-Dahlem. I often used to go to the feasts in the synagogue with him with a hat on. Now he's gone off somewhere to wait till the new era goes back to bein' the old era, an' me and my hat can go to parties in the synagogue again.'

133

'Fancy another trip in the gondola?' he suggests, licking his lips. 'The thought of all that gold's got me really worked up!'

'It's not as easy as it looked at first sight,' he goes on, thoughtfully, as they lie, side by side, relaxing after their erotic exertions. 'I'm not happy there's so many mixed up in it. Thirty millions, even, ain't much if it's gotta be shared with half a division.'

'Who *says* we share with every man of them?' she purrs, falsely. 'They get a nice tip, big enough for a good night on the town! *One* night!'

'I couldn't agree more,' whinnies Porta, in a transport of delight. 'We ask 'em to wait for us somewhere, an' let 'em sit waitin' for us till their arseholes grow icicles. When do we go?'

'As soon as I have contact my husband,' she answers, 'and that will not be a long time. He will arrange *propusk* for you. They will be *real* ones, too. Not even a suspicious OGPU would sniff at them with his flat nose. You give me good, clear photographs for every one we take with us. Not in German uniform, of course!'

'I'll mobilize the flash-artists right off,' he promises, with a grin which makes his face look like an open cash-register. 'We're to be Russians, then?'

'You did not think you would be running around like Swastika-mad SS-men? You will be changed into weary Volga Germans. That will take care of the language difficulty.'

'Volga Germans,' he asks, blankly. 'And what kind of fellers are they?'

'German emigrants, who once settled along the banks of the Volga. They are Soviet Russians today, but they live like Germans and talk German to one another. They are given various special tasks in the Red Army in wartime, but otherwise the Army will not have them. Like the *Khirgiz* people. They too are used only in wartime.'

'But good soldiers I'm sure,' he said. 'The kind they need

to get shot at when there's war an' disagreements on.'

She takes two oversized bouillon cups with a handle on each side. With a suitably dignified air she prepares what the Russians call a small eye-opener. Two-thirds vodka, one-third coffee, four large spoonfuls of sugar, half a preserved pear, and to top off the whole a dab of blackcurrant jam.

Porta takes half of the concoction down in one gulp, and emits an emperor of a belch, which echoes round the four-poster bed.

'Not bad at *all*,' he praises it, and pours the rest down his throat with the gurgle of a sewer passing an air-bubble.

'My husband is very quick,' she assures him, sipping carefully at her own eye-opener. 'He thinks it is now the time for Jews who want to get somewhere to leave the Soviet paradise. It is said that every fourth prisoner they shoot in the Lubyanka is a Jew. Do you not think execution is barbaric?'

'Ye-e-es,' says Porta, drawing the word out. 'But on the other hand it's not nice to be gettin' in the way of true-believers, and hinderin' them in getting home to the wonders of paradise.'

'Cynic!' she snarls, pushing back her red-gold hair. 'I do not understand why ever I have anything to do with you.'

'Matter o' taste, as the cat said when it licked the dog's arse,' he laughs, noisily.

'Believe me,' she goes on, lighting a cigarette, 'if it was not for my husband's sake I would not have involved myself in this. As I have told you I come from an aristocratic family. One of my ancestors smashed the skulls of two hundred Turks in the wars against the Huns. He did it with only a club.'

'Must've been a very quarrelsome lot, your ancestors,' says Porta, making himself up another eye-opener. 'You ever thought your old feller might be moving over to the wrong FPO? Jews aren't just the most popular lot in Germany right now. They make soap out of 'em. Funnily

135

enough it's all right for washing in!'

'What have you against the Jews?' she jumps up angrily, and stares him rigidly in the face. 'You do not look much of an Aryan. If you run into Himmler perhaps he will make *you* into soap!'

'I've got nothing against nobody at all,' says Porta, with a long, hearty laugh. 'I'm a businessman. On Sunday I buy something from God and on Monday I sell it to the Devil – at a good profit!'

'You remind me a lot of my husband,' she laughs. 'He does not look like a Jew. People believe he is a dumb Polish yokel. Nobody dreams he can count to more than five. But what drives him is his unique greediness and longing for power. He has everything but the fuel: *money*! And money is now lying there ready under his nose!'

'Whyn't he picked it up before, then?' asks Porta, cleaning his nails with a fork.

'Picking up no problem,' she replies. 'Another thing to get it out of Russia! What is thirty millions worth if all you can do is turn it over and look at it. To get out of Russia we have to go through all of the country you have stolen from us.'

'And that's why you need Obergefreiter Porta,' he nods, emptying his bouillon-cup with a slobbering gulp. 'What about if things go wrong? Your commissar-hubby got that one sorted out, too?'

'We shall hang!' she cries, throwing her naked arms wide in a theatrical gesture. 'There is some risk in every game!'

'I doubt if we'd get off *that* easy,' sighs Porta, sadly. 'They'd have a nice bit of fun with us first in the Lubyanka, though I don't reckon it'd be us gold-robbers who'd be doin' the laughin'. And, if we were lucky enough to miss that, don't expect to find any nice-mannered boys amongst the hat-brim sellers in *Prinz Albrecht Strasse*. They'd put us in the acid bath first to soften us up, and then they'd peel the skin off of us in two-inch strips.'

'We must be optimistic. Then everything will be all right.'

136

she says with a brilliant smile. 'You know, perhaps, that optimists live longer than pessimists?'

'I'm a born optimist, myself,' Porta admits. 'That's why I'm still in the land o' the living. But it *might* be a good idea if we was to take a couple o' pieces of artillery and ten or eleven machine-pistols with us on this little gold robbery turn-up. And just one other important thing! Have you figured out how you're goin' to get the gold through Germany? They have a way of executing people who're found in possession of illegal gold. I don't suppose you were thinking of sendin' the glitterin' stuff by express freight, were you? One of them train chauffeurs was to get the idea there was valuables in the boxes an' it'd be: goodbye gold! If they pick us up in Germany we'd not have a chance. Be easier making sausagemeat of little girls and sellin' it to the Army for iron rations!'

'You say you are optimist!' she shouts, angrily. 'Why do you not go and let yourself get shot to small pieces for this foreign Führer of yours? You are always against me! You do not help, but leave everything to me!'

'I'm an optimist all right, believe you me,' answers Porta. 'But I'm careful, too! You don't see me dashing out on thin ice like some silly sods do!'

She is over in a corner of the room, attempting, with much effort, to drag a chest-of-drawers away from the wall. She looks angrily at Porta, still recumbent on the bed.

'You do not think of helping me?' she shouts, gritting her teeth.

'Sure,' says Porta, without moving.

'Shit!' she snarls, tugging at the heavy piece of furniture. When she finally has it a couple of yards out from the wall, to the accompaniment of a shower of Russian curses, she removes a panel, and takes a map from the recess revealed. Still swearing she throws herself on her stomach alongside Porta.

'It's easy to see you're tellin' the truth about your aristo-cratic ancestors,' he grins, slapping her hard on her naked behind.

'Tanks and trucks are the only safe transport possibilities, when we are to get through these forest stretches around Minsk,' she explains, pointing to the map.

'Oh, yes,' says Porta. 'I don't really understand why we don't stay in your part of Russia, lady? You know who's *in* those woods? The whole rotten Red Army, that's who! Guerillas all over! You do what you like, but not with Obergefreiter Joseph Porta in tow! Where's your armoured transport column goin' to wind up, anyway?'

'Liepaja,' she says pointing to a spot on the map.

'Libau, you mean,' Porta corrects her. 'On the Baltic. And from there we take the boat direct to America, luxury class, I suppose?'

'No! To Sweden! Karlskrona!'

'I'd rather go to Stockholm,' Porta wrangles. 'I've never had a girl from Stockholm. I suppose you an' hungry hubby know that those Swedish half-Eskimos keep a hell of a close watch on their harbours? They've found out 95 per cent of the Wehrmacht's looking out for a chance to get in there, with mpi's as passports. Your plan's no good, girl!'

'As you wish,' she smiles, sweetly. 'I look after my side of the front and you fix it with your German friends.'

Porta sucks his army teeth long and thoughtfully. 'All right, I'll look after things, but there's just one point. We go 50-50.'

'You are out of your mind,' she shrills, furiously. 'Why you should have half? You think I am crazy? That a German crematory rat like you can swindle me? I have crushed bigger rats than you will ever be! You do not know me, I think?'

'You're a poison viper, you are,' Porta snarls, sulphurously. He throws his empty bottle violently at the ceiling.

'Your German greed has turned you mad,' she spits at him. 'You talk like a Greek brothel-owner!'

'Give in, you stinking Commie bitch,' fumes Porta. 'You might just as well. Your polished Soviet manners won't get you far with me! Fifty-fifty! Want me to chisel it out for you in Nazi letters ten foot high?'

She storms to and fro, spitting and frothing. Chairs are knocked over, glass smashes, a shoe flies out through the window. She stops, but only to throw a large lamp at Porta, who is still lying in the four-poster, drinking *Slivovitz* from the bottle.

'I was not wrong about you, you puffed-up male whore!' she screams, shaking with rage. 'Heaven be thanked that I have seen through you, you wicked German tramp. I will have you shot, and your head chopped off, both at the same time! God help you when my husband gets hold of you!'

'Make me die laughing, you do,' shouts Porta, sending a mouthful of spittle after her. 'I can fuck up your little gold-diggin' game for you, easy as winkin'! It'll be prick up the arse for both of you.'

In the end they throw themselves at one another, and break up everything left in her boudoir to break. They crawl out from under the wrecked four-poster and finally agree on how the gold is to be shared.

The next twenty minutes pass quickly. They literally rape one another. They go at it so energetically that two Russian soldiers hiding down in the cellar choke on their vodka at the sounds getting down to them. One of them climbs a tree outside their window to see what is happening. The sight makes him fall out of it and break an ankle.

'Better get my German glad rags on, and step along over to His Grace Chief Mechanic Wolf,' Porta decides.

'Who he?' she asks doubtfully.

'A link in the chain we can't do without, unfortunately,' he replies. 'He's an illegal transport an' arms dealer company all on his own. I've also got to wake up the "War Minister" in Berlin!'

'War Minister!' she coughs, as her cognac goes down the wrong way. 'Are you crazy? We want no minister mixed up in this! God the Father preserve us! If such a one get the slightest hint of what we are doing we will be executed *immediately*!'

'Executions?' smiles Porta. 'Maybe some'll get executed, but it's not bloody well going to be us. Only dummies let themselves get knocked off that way, and you an' me ain't dummies!'

From down in the street come the sounds of loud singing, and shrill police whistles. A couple of pistol shots crack.

'Hell!' she cries, in fright, 'what happens?'

'That'll be Tiny, celebrating the day his mother come close to losing her life,' laughs Porta, looking out of the window.

A couple of hours later he wades, panting, through the powder snow, with a photograph of a gold ingot in his hand. Without taking any notice of the large, colourful signboard:

TRANSPORT SECTION WOLF
ENTRY STRICTLY FORBIDDEN

he vaults over the barrier and goes on down the narrow pathway.

'Can't you read?' yells an Unteroffizier with a face only Frankenstein's monster would have envied him.

'Can *you*?' asks Porta, continuing calmly on his way.

'No entry for unauthorized personnel,' howls the monster-faced Unteroffizier, tearing his machine-pistol down from his shoulder.

'*I'm* not unauthorized,' answers Porta, without bothering even to turn his head.

At the next road-block he meets a notorious Feldwebel who was posted away from Germersheim for cruelty to the prisoners. He works for Wolf now. Bodily injury is his field of endeavour.

'Halt!' he roars, standing squarely in Porta's path. He looks the size of a tank block.

Porta pushes him fastidiously to one side, with the air of a man opening the door of a railway station toilet.

'What d'you mean pushin' me, rat? Can't you see these? I'm a Feldwebel!'

'Can *you* see *these*? The highest rank in the *Reich*! Oberge-freiter, same as your Führer was. Tell Wolf I'm here, shit-head, an' quick about it!'

The Feldwebel runs to the telephone to sound the alarm.

but Porta is already in the next workshop shed before he can get through. He treads cautiously over a trip-wire which would have set a T-mine off under him.

Two grey-brown wolfhounds come towards him, growling savagely.

'Hello boys!' he smiles. 'Find somebody else to tear a piece off!'

The dogs bare yellow fangs, and continue to advance towards him, threateningly.

'Hi!' he says, saluting with two fingers at the brim of his yellow topper.

'Hi!' growl the dogs, wagging their tails in welcome.

Around a strategically well-chosen corner Wolf's two Chinese guards stand with *Kalashnikovs* at the ready.

'Hi!' Porta greets them, pushing the muzzles of the *Kalashnikovs* gently to one side.

'Hi!' reply the Chinese guards, slapping their weapons.

'You look like death on crutches,' says Porta, with a short laugh.

'We death all right,' they say, laughing an Asiatic laugh, and lifting their *Kalashnikovs*. 'You like try?'

'Some other time! I haven't a moment just now,' he replies, sidling past another booby-trap.

'I thought the neighbours'd turned you off,' says Wolf, sarcastically. 'I was looking forward to a good wake, but you've disappointed me as usual!'

There is a P-38 with a full clip lying on the desk in front of him. A *Schmeisser* hangs on the back of his chair. His desk drawer is booby-trapped. The charge is big enough to blow up a seven-storey apartment house, if anybody is foolish enough to open the drawer. On a camouflaged shelf over the door is a bottle of petrol packed in three stick-grenades, in case the unbelievable were to happen and somebody get past the first three traps. As an extra bit of security the yard-door is connected to a surprise packet for anybody who might go out that way after doing something wicked to Wolf. The uninvited guest would be turned into a lot of tiny pieces and thrown a long way up toward Heaven.

141

Porta makes himself at home with a bottle of whisky, which he knows is kept behind Army Service Regulations and an unread copy of *Mein Kampf*. 'Skole!' he laughs. and almost empties the bottle.

'Don't mind *me*,' says Wolf. sourly. 'You'll never learn manners. What do you want anyway? I don't recall havin' invited you?' He flaps a grain of dust from his hand-sewn Bronzini boots, which cost 1,400 marks. He has them sent from Rome by special despatch-rider. He regards highly-polished riding boots as the most important part of a highly-placed man's image. Porta says it is because he had to wear clogs from the Poor Children's Fund when he was a child.

'Can those things keep out water?' asks Porta, pointing to the glittering riding boots. Wolf wears spurs on them, in defiance of all regulations. They jingle every time he moves his feet. Wolf would never dream of mounting a horse though. He is. in fact, rather afraid of them.

'How'd I know.' asks Wolf. 'I never go out in the rain!'

'Let me just have a ride on your Jew machine.' says Porta. reaching out for the calculator. He takes some currency rate of exchange lists from his breast pocket. and puts on a thoughtful expression.

Wolf looks inquisitively over his shoulder. When he sees the size of the figures Porta is working with, he begins to shiver all over. His face changes colour several times, and his piggy, yellow-green eyes begin to light up greedily.

'*Mama mia*.' he whispers. He crosses himself religiously three times, bends down, and kisses Porta on both cheeks.

They close the steel shutters and lock them from the inside. The whole, complicated alarm system is set ready for action. Nobody is going to get away alive from an attempt to enter Wolf's lair.

'I may have been mistaken about you.' Wolf says. in a flattering tone, clinking his glass against Porta's. 'Your health. you wicked old villain!'

'Ditto, ditto.' smiles Porta, throwing the drink down with

mouth agape, like a man emptying a bucket into a sewer.

'To think I have always regarded you as a wicked criminal swindler, who would sell his own mother if it suited him,' says Wolf, shaking his head sadly.

'For*get* it!' says Porta refilling his glass. 'Anybody can make a mistake now and then!'

For some time Wolf sits leaning back in his generals-only swivel-chair, and enjoys the sight of the photograph of the gold ingot.

'God save all thirteen of us,' he whispers. 'With lumps o' this stuff socked away, the rest of our lives'd be without worries. We could let the rest of 'em stand in water up to their necks, and most of 'em'll wind up poor after the war. *We'll* be laughing, and enjoying the feel of fine clothing next to our skins!'

During the next few hours highest priority express messages fly backwards and forwards between Wolf's HQ and the War Ministry at Berlin.

Far into the night the plans for the most important and top-secret action of World War II are complete. They are given the codename RICHES.

Oberfeldwebel and departmental head Sally, of War Ministry 4th Office, is on his way to Russia two hours later in a JU-52 mailplane with highest start and landing priorities.

In a three-axled Mercedes, with a General Staff flag fluttering from the front fender, businessmen Porta and Wolf drive to the airport to receive His Excellency 'War Minister' Sally. Sally swaggers, like another Frederick the Great, down the steps from the aircraft standing some way out on the landing strip. He is wearing a tailor-made cavalry uniform, highly-polished boots and a big, insincere grin. Around his neck is the War Service Cross. Knight's Class, which has been arranged for him by his many shady connections.

The Luftwaffe men salute him stiffly. He nods kindly to them. A Field-Marshal could not have done it better. He tiptoes across the wet asphalt. He does not want his highly-polished boots to be smirched by the Russian mud.

'What a country to live in,' he says, shivering, as he creeps into the large Mercedes. 'Why couldn't you have chosen a warmer country to liberate?'

'Nobody asked us,' grins Wolf.

'How's the outside world looking these days?' asks Porta, tucking the almighty 'War Minister' up in a bearskin to prevent him from the aching cold. He is unused to the Russian climate.

'They're dropping bombs on us all the time. The Brits by night and the Yanks by day. It's hardly possible to lift a glass to your lips any more. Half of it gets spilled by the constant shaking everywhere. Wherever you look there's misery. The Home Front shuffles around in old clothes, and everybody's hungry. Don't think you lads out here are the only ones having a rough time. We are also suffering badly at home. But we do our duty uncomplainingly, and willingly go hungry to save old Germany!'

'Well, you don't look as if *you're* suffering much from the shortages,' says Porta, with a knowing chuckle.

'I didn't say I was, did I now?' the 'War Minister' replies. He offers American cigarettes round, and French cognac from a silver hip-flask.

'"The Lame Gendarme's" still where it was, for God's sake?' asks Porta, worriedly. 'If those bloody British and Yanks have dared to as much as scratch the paintwork they'll have me to reckon with! And *that* won't suit them one bit.'

'I'm sure they're aware of that,' smiles Sally. 'The only thing left on the square *is* the "Gendarme". I looked in there this very morning, and was asked to pass on everybody's regards. They asked if you weren't tired of fighting for Führer, Folk and Fatherland. I don't understand myself how you lot can stand living here.'

At the last second Porta manages to swing the heavy Mercedes round the still-smoking wreck of a lorry. Round

144

about lie soldiers, their faces to the ground.

'What's your opinion, as "War Minister", of this war we were forced into starting?' asks Porta, turning his head to look at Sally, sitting there shivering. 'No danger of us winnin' it, I hope?'

'Be easy,' says Sally, knowledgeably. 'The other lot's got its collective finger out, so we will lose the last battle just as we usually do, and will be able to use the usual excuses of ambush and treachery as the cause of our losing!'

'That's the German way,' says Wolf. 'It's in the tradition. We win our way straight into defeat!'

'Thank the Lord,' Porta breathes more easily, dragging the Mercedes around another wrecked lorry. 'Sometimes I get nightmares thinkin' we might win!'

Porta treads on the accelerator. He gives the car everything it can take. The Divisional Commander's standard on the front fender makes everything else on the road give way.

'See that fat chap there, with the narrow shoulder-straps an' the silver braid,' he remarks with a laugh. 'Don't often see a salute that smart out here!'

'They all get the shits, when they see the flag of General "Arse-an'-Pockets" on the front of a car,' says Wolf, condescendingly.

'We're more'n "Arse-an'-Pockets" is,' says Porta. 'He's only a general! We'll soon be *rich*. We can buy and sell generals, if we want to!'

Three MPs start screaming and waving their arms to clear the way for them.

'Going nicely, now, ain't it?' grins Porta, in satisfaction. He pushes down even harder on the accelerator.

'Keep to the right, you dogs!' roars Wolf in his well-oiled voice of command.

Two Unteroffiziers and a squad of soldiers jump for the ditch, and sink up to their necks in snow.

'*That's* the way,' nods Wolf happily.

'I'm givin' it all it can take,' says Porta. 'Livens up the day for the coolies!'

A bottle of Napoléon cognac goes the rounds.

'This just arrived from my French Connection,' remarks Sally, taking another big swig at the bottle. Half of it comes spurting out of his mouth again as Porta bangs his foot down on the brake pedal with all his might. The heavy staff-car goes into a spin on the slippery surface of the highway. With the touch of a master he directs his vehicle between the trees, jumps a tall hedge and stops it with its nose buried in a haystack. It was at the eleventh second of the eleventh minute of the eleventh hour.

Two RATAs with red stars on their wings come roaring out of the clouds. They rush along above the road, the muzzles of their machine-cannon flashing.

'Good Lord preserve us,' stammers Sally, his eyes rolling nervously. 'They do go to it in this country. The reports say the front is steady, and all's quiet!'

'Those devil's children come over like that every day,' explains Porta. 'You can set your watch by 'em. We call them the traffic police. They can get the traffic jams out of the way like nobody else can!'

'I lost two ten-tonners last week, right in the middle of church service on a Sunday,' says Wolf, looking sad. 'That's what you have to put up with when you're fightin' the godless. I only lost the crews, thank God! The waggons could be repaired!'

'Those devils won't be back again, will they?' asks Sally, looking nervously up at the grey clouds. 'Thank the Lord I'm only visiting here. I was born to wear a uniform, but not in wartime. Lord above, no!'

'Yes,' smiles Porta, 'it's impossible to imagine how the history of the human race might be changed, if you was to come out here and take an active part in the battle.' He laughs so much he doubles up over the steering wheel, and comes close to crashing into a wrecked gun. The bodies of its six horses lie dead in the road.

'Do they go on like this every day?' asks Sally, staring at the dead horses, lying there stiff-legged with mouths agape.

146

'As I said, you can tell the time by 'em,' answers Porta, indifferently. 'When they've done five missions they give 'em a medal. Pulls in the cunt, y'know. The flak gunners shot one down the other day, a puffed-up sod who'd only talk to officers. He had eight bars on his ribbon, so he must've knocked out a good few of truck-owner Adolf's rolling-stock!'

'What happened to him?' asked Sally.

'SS strung him up,' answers Porta, carelessly. 'He was too much of a hero for 'em to call him an *untermensch*. Alive he'd have been bad for propaganda. Fellow with a bit of a headache there,' he goes on, pointing, as they go by, to an old supply-soldier, sitting in a pool of blood with his steel helmet upside down on his head.

'By the way, did you ever hear any more of that chap they called "Polka Porky"?' asks Sally, maliciously. 'He took you to the cleaners all right. There wasn't much of your 80 per cent left after he'd been there, was there?'

'He's turned over a new leaf,' says Porta, spitting out of the window. 'Stopped stealing from people. One of my pals, feller who cleans the windows for the Gestapo at *Prinz Albrecht Strasse*, took him to the dentist to have his teeth looked at. There was some trouble so my pal borrowed the dentist's drill to fix it for him. Slipped a bit now an' then and made a hole or two in his tongue.'

'Don't suppose "Porky" liked that?' laughs Sally, wickedly.

'No, he didn't, to be sure,' answers Porta, with a hard laugh. 'There weren't any teeth left, and the holes in his tongue make him stammer. He has trouble asking for other people's 80 per cent now. People get tired of waitin' for him to finish what he's saying.'

'Yes, he boasted a lot about his having put one over on you,' says Sally, handing Porta the cognac bottle. 'Remember that fellow "Fat Pino", who used to be always boasting about how big he was? Well, a fellow steps out of a car on the *Hohenzollerndamn* right in the middle of the day. He throws

147

his arms round "Pino", gives him a big, smacking pansy kiss right on his mouth, and pushes a knife into his back at the same time. Straight to the heart, and all finished very neatly. He was off, knife and all, before people had finished staring at what had been happy "Fat Pino", only a moment before.'

'They call it the kiss of death in Sicily,' explains Wolf. 'I've used it a couple o' times here in Russia. Makes the opposition pull in its horns for quite a time, an' gives a bloke room to work in!'

Porta swings off the highway, and edges the heavy staff-car through narrow, snow-covered streets, sounding his horn continually. Pedestrians dodge to all sides. With a flamboyant swing he stops outside Wolf's residence with its forest of 'No Entry' signs.

The Chinese goons open the double doors to allow plenty of room for Wolf and his two companions to enter.

Two Russian POWs stand ready to polish Wolf's boots. They are graciously permitted to polish 'War Minister' Sally's boots as well.

Porta sits drinking cognac while these operations are carried out. 'Time enough to polish your boots when the war's over,' he thinks.

Chairs clatter as they enter the main office, and the clerks spring to attention.

Chief Mechanic Wolf touches the tip of his swagger-stick to his cap-peak. He has seen British officers do this in films. Things like that give a man class, he feels. His two book-keepers, specialists with erasers and forged signatures, put thoughtful expressions on their faces as 'Field-Marshal' Wolf goes by. He tramps heavily on each step of the iron staircase on his way up it, making his spurs jingle merrily.

'Hi!' he greets his two wolfhounds, who are lying with fangs bared, ready to attack. 'They had a swamp German for dinner last week,' he laughs. 'Wasn't a lot left of *him*! The idiot came in here, somehow, without warning, and said he'd pinched something or other from King Michael's army. Or whatever it is their boss's called down there in Rumania!'

'Now then! Let's get down to business,' says Sally, when they are seated at an extremely well-furnished dinner table. Wolf's bodyguards have been thrown out, and the door locked behind them. 'After what I've heard I doubt very much whether this deal can be carried through. It fairly stinks of *untermensch* treachery and Jew-boy traps!'

'Now don't come here puffin' yourself up, as if you *were* somebody,' shouts Porta angrily, pointing his fork at Sally. 'You do what I say. You don't need to do no more or no less to put this job through. *And* you get 5 per cent for doin' it. Personally I'd have thought half that was enough.'

'You *don't* think it's too much,' Sally smiles acidly. 'That's enough for today! You going to drive me to the airstrip, or do I have to take a taxi?'

'Have a good trip,' grins Porta, 'an' see you soon!' He helps himself, with apparent indifference, to a plateful of pickled pigs' trotters.

Wolf goes mad, and explodes with rage. He knocks the pigs' feet out of Porta's hands and rushes after Sally, who has his hand almost on the door knob.

'Hands off, you dope,' he screams. 'Want to blow us all to bits? You're not back in your bloody vicarage now. You're in a headquarters that's important to the war effort. An' I'll tell you something else, too, you brain-fucked little pygmy. We don't care a streak of piss what you do or don't have doubts about. You do what we tell you, or you'll soon be finished with creepin' around playing War Minister. We've knocked off bigger meatheads'n you, you imitation, operetta shagbag you! *Panjemajo?*'

'Very well, then,' grumbles Sally, sitting down again at the table, but keeping his silk cap on. Angrily he snatches a piece of black pudding, spoons sugar over it and then syrup. 'I usually play along with the people whose bread I have eaten,' he says, stuffing his mouth with the black pudding.

'What a shit you are,' says Porta, round a mouthful of

149

trotters. 'Don't you try to shove me around like that. When it comes to it you're not a real War Minister, you're just a bloody clerk in a lousy office. Any prat can be one o' them!'

'Oh, to the devil with it,' Sally gives in. 'Good health, boys! And let's get on with it! We'll all end up in shit creek anyway, sooner or later.' He takes a swig at his glass, and gives out a long, ringing belch. 'But why in the world,' he goes on, thoughtfully, 'don't you just pick up that gold yourselves. Nice and quiet. It'd be cheaper and easier for you, surely? By what they say in Berlin, Russia's fallen on its backside. There's nothing left to do but a routine clean-up, so, as far as I can see, the gold's just normal spoils of war!'

'An' you call yourself "War Minister"?' Porta shouts, contemptuously. 'Man, you sound more like a pregnant virgin in a Turkish knocker!! This kinda job can only go through with the help of sensible Russians, who, like us, don't give a shit for the Fatherland an' its need for *lebensraum*! We can stick together like shit to a blanket. Look, the plan's worked out an' ready. I'm fuckin' a bint just now as has been parked here by her feller. He's a commissar. She's got that fond of my joystick she's told me all about this Kremlin gold that her commissar husband had the job of hiding away till peace breaks out again. He's got the brilliant, genius-type of idea of goin' on his travels and taking the gold with him. We put together a combined German–Russian battle group. The commissar fixes things up back where he is, and we look after things here. Fits like a prick does up Lizzie. We drive off to Libau with the liberated gold, and from there we sail to Sweden. Goodbye to the Thousand Year Reich and the Soviet Paradise both!'

'The Swedes no longer have customs and passport checks then?' asks Sally, taking another mouthful of black pudding. Syrup dribbles from the corners of his mouth. 'You're out of your minds. Bullshit, the lot of it! I have to deal with paperwork acrobats every day. We run into a couple of inky-fingered coolies in the wrong place, and they've had it. That kind of thing's too easy!'

'Sven's looking after all that! He talks the lingo,' says Porta, confidently. 'All he does is tell the Swedes we're resistance. And it ain't even a *lie*! That's what we're doing, leaving Adolf and Joe's armies. Social Democrats, we bloody are!'

'Two thousand three hundred and twelve kilometres and four and a half metres,' says Sally thoughtfully, looking at the General Staff map spread out over the food on the table. 'That's only to where the gold is hidden! We also have to get back again. A Panther goes 100 kilometres on a full tank, and then there's the lorries. Got to have *them*! You can't carry the gold in your pockets. Where's the petrol coming from? They say the petrol pumps're all closed down in the neighbours' area.'

'You *worry* too much!' shouts Porta, waving a sausage around angrily in the air. 'This commissar whore o' mine guarantees all that. They've got a petrol reserve big enough for an armoured division, if you've got one to spare. All you've got to do is cover us with the sodding Prussians, so they don't go pissing around the world looking for us. *You* get us departure orders, battle orders, movement orders, and all the rest of the paperwork shit we need to get around in this bloody war. And the orders've got to be top priority. Get that straight, Mr "War Minister"! We don't want every barrack-square bastard with a brain the size of a walnut, an' coloured rag on his hat, tryin' to stop us!'

'Is *that* all you need?' replies Sally. 'That's easier than wiping your backside and shaking the drops off your cock afterwards. You'll get papers. Papers signed by Field-Marshal Keitel with all the usual loops and squiggles. No asexual iron-hat'll start shouting at you. He'll just salute, and pass you on!'

'Well then,' smiles Porta, 'why all the nonsense? All you do's what you used to do when mum sent you down to the shops with a list in your hot little hand!'

Wolf fills their glasses quickly, and shouts 'Skole!' before Sally realizes what Porta has said to him.

'We'll also want you to have a flat-bottom lying in Libau,' Porta goes on, emptying his glass in one gulp. 'The Navy job, with the propeller that goes round twice as fast as any of the other grey-painted bathtubs. I've got a feeling we're going to be in a hurry, just about then.'

'Small stuff for me,' declares Sally self-confidently, adding a new note to his long list. 'It's only a question of finding the right papers and stamping a red GEKADOS* across the lot. With the right documentation those Navy pricks'll sail you where you want to go, and never ask what's in the boxes. But who's going to help us in Sweden? My stamps and signatures have no force there!'

'The Swedes?' grins Porta, easily. 'I'll buy 'em. They're only Social Democrats. They stopped using their brains long ago.'

'Social Democrats!' mumbles Wolf. 'We got to share with *them*? Don't they believe everybody should have the same pay?'

'You're stupider than you were the day you were born,' bubbles Porta. 'When it's money you're talking about, the secret's to keep the share-out to as few as possible! The commissar's bint an' me have got everything worked out. In the end we do the lot of 'em in the eye and off we go with all the loot.'

'You were perhaps thinking of pissing us in the eye, too?' asks Sally in an obviously threatening tone.

'What the devil do you take me for?' asks Porta, with a deceiving laugh. 'You two are with *me*. The others *ain't*!'

'Sounds very nice, I'm sure,' says Wolf, sceptically. 'But the fellers we leave behind on the quay, waiting, are going to be very annoyed when they realize what's happened. And they'll start looking around under all kinds of bushes and stones, to have a little talk with the chaps who've done it to 'em!'

'Are you really that stupid?' asks Porta. He dips a frog's

* *Geheime Kommandosache*: German for Secret Command Matter

152

leg carefully into jam. 'I'll cut it out in cardboard for you, then, so both you *and* your Mongols can understand it. When we get to Libau with our load marked SECRET all over, we start straight off shouting and giving orders. Tiny an' me puts on long leather coats and trilby hats with the brims pulled down over our eyes, so's any squareheaded German can see we're tough tecs from *Prinz Albrecht Strasse*. No smiles from us. Who's goin' to dare question us?'

'That reminds me, by the way, of one Herr Barsch, who used to live in *Phasanenstrasse*. He was an estate agent, with a diploma, and he knew how to take people, if anybody did. Everything went fine for him until he was unlucky enough to hit on one of these surefire certainties, which more often than not get a chap inside the box with the key turned three times and the door bolted from the outside. Some time previous Herr Barsch had met a Jew Stockbroker who he considered to be a sucker. The Jew had bought a villa in Dahlem from him that was that full of creepy-crawlies an' all sorts of rottenness, it was a wonder it hadn't walked off on its own out into the Spree. Herr Barsch had been going round for some time with the feeling that he was lettin' the Jew get away with something by not taking him again. He had a word with a couple of his pals about it, at last, and they agreed with him it'd be money for jam for people like them. They arranged a meeting with the Jew, at an office they'd rented for the day, and after a bit o' natterin' to and fro and fro and to they agreed on a new deal. The Jew puts 500,000 marks on the table, and so did Herr Barsch an' his two mates. Their ducats were, however, in the form of forward-dated cheques on a newly-opened bank account. They'd never even *seen* that much money all at one time. After that they went out and took a gander at some hot industrial buildin' areas. It was raining so the Jew-boy stayed in his car, smokin' a cigar. He didn't want to get his Paris-tailored coat wet.

'After a good dinner at Kempinski they said goodnight to one another. Herr Barsch and his two scoundrelly pals took a long time getting home that evening. They kept breaking down into screams of laughter all the way home, at the thought of all the ducats they had picked up. The old Jew went off innocently to Bad Gastein to have himself a roll in the healthy mud they've got there. Four weeks later Herr Barsch & Co were invited to a little chat at "Alex". They were taken into department 9B which looks after fraud, swindle and rubber cheques. The interview with the three friends ended with them inside Moabitt where they sat counting their toes till they were brought into court. They were shackled at their wrists and ankles, so's it was quite clear they really *were* criminals.

'The judge was a woman they called "the Devil's Sister", because of her wicked nature and the heavy sentences she handed out. She stared at the three tycoons, when they were escorted into court in their rattling chains.

'"Why are these prisoners not chained by the neck, so that they could have been dragged in here like the dogs they are?" she snarled, wickedly. She bent over the indictment on the bench in front of her, and rattled through it at such a pace that nobody could understand a word she said. She raised her head and stretched her neck like a hungry vulture, staring the three estate agents down.

'"According to paragraph 900, section 3, part 4B, the punishment for the crime which you have committed, i.e. grand fraud and illegal sale of the property of third person, is imprisonment for a period of from two to ten years. In aggravated circumstances the sentence may be increased to hard labour for up to fourteen years." She banged three times with her gavel, covered up her permanent-waved hair, and announced the sentence: "In the name of the Führer and the German people I sentence you to fourteen years hard labour! I only regret that I cannot sentence you to life imprisonment." she added with a smile which resembled that of a shark turning on its back to strike.

'The three former geniuses of finance rattled their chains out of the court, taking their dead cert with them. Nobody outside *Bautzen** has seen them, since they jingled off through the courthouse gates in the Black Maria!'

'Yes,' sighs Wolf, 'money can be a source of wisdom. But what were you trying to tell us?'

'Well, you see,' smiles Porta, pleasantly, 'I wanted you to understand that you must never undervalue anybody! Even though there's only a few around with more'n sand in their heads, most've 'em have still got enough up there to take you for a sucker, if you don't keep on your toes all the time.'

'Yes, anybody can buy a Jew's gun an' a piece o' paper, but usin' it right's a different kettle of fish,' mumbles Wolf, writing down a figure on the tablecloth.

'What's the Old Man going to say to this trip?' asks Sally, practically, pursing his lips. 'Won't we have trouble with him?'

'Yes, he'll be our big problem,' admits Wolf, showing all his gold fillings in a ghastly, hyena grin. 'He'll call it bank robbery, and won't like us havin' planned to leave most of the mob in the lurch.'

'Oh, come *on*,' protests Porta, shovelling the remains of the blackcurrant jam into his mouth. 'You're making it into something ugly and criminal. To my way of thinking it's completely legal. Commie theory says everything belongs to the people, and aren't we the people? So all we're doin' is going off to pick up our own gold!'

'It limps,' hisses Sally, contrarily. 'The gold belongs to the Soviet people, and that's not us!'

'In a way you're right,' Porta says, triumphantly, 'but my bint an' her commissar husband *are* Russian Commie people, and they are going to share their gold with us! And very Social Democratic of them too, I say.'

'Know what,' Wolf suddenly begins to laugh noisily and wriggles happily in his generals-only swivel-chair. 'I'd love it if we could just leave Tiny behind on the quay at Libau. I

---

* *Bautzen:* A notorious German prison

still owe him for that time he wanted to blow me to bits with this radio.'

'You must be out of your mind,' cries Porta. 'Don't make any mistakes about Tiny. Maybe he does call the letter H a rugby goal and Y a catapult, but he's still the cunningest sod that ever slunk down the Reeperbahn. If we were stupid enough to leave him at Libau, and do him out of fulfilling his dearest wish: black silk underclothes and alligator-skin shoes with pin-holes in 'em, he'd be mad enough to drink the bloody Baltic dry, an' then we'd never get to sail to Sweden.

'I remember once when he was batman to the Commander of 9th Army at Hamburg, General of Cavalry von Knochenhauer. One of the wicked sods from Sankt Pauli put the word in about Tiny having done something Herr General von Knochenhauer didn't like one little bit. In went Tiny for interrogation, and they knocked him about something dreadful, but didn't get anything out of him. Still, when he got out on the Reeperbahn again, he was limpin', reduced to the ranks and a lot thinner than when he went inside.

'"That Kurt's a wrong un," he explained to the Jew furrier's son David, when they were sitting down in "The Headless Nag" drinking beer. "A louse's what 'e is, a filthy rat, *donkey* shit! Let's me'n you go an' talk to 'im a bit an' persuade 'im to stop shoppin' people!"

'"He's a dirty, rotten, bastarding lump of afterbirth," shouted David, angry on Tiny's behalf. He'd never met Kurt really. "He's nothin' but a chopped-off pair of Kaffir bollocks!" he wound up, wrathfully.

'When they'd finished gettin' one another all worked up, they got "Pickpocket Petra" to ring over to "The Cow With Three Udders", where Kurt was sittin' drinking raspberry juice'n rum.

'"Who'm I talkin' to?" asked Kurt.

'"Me o' course," said Petra, which was true enough.

'"Who's me, then?" squealed Kurt, suspiciously. "Got a

name, haven't you love?"

'"Fräulein Müller, Petra Müller."

'"Go *on*! Now ain't that nice of you to ring, Petra? How's it goin' then? 'Ad it off lately, 'ave you?"

'"Hello Kurt! Listen to me now, I got a hot one for you! Can you be at *Zirkusweg* in a half-hour's time? It's your lucky day, dear! You'll be jumpin' for joy, you will!"

'"Go on with you. You don't say so? I'm on my way already!"

'A quarter of an hour before the agreed time there was "Kurt the Nark" standing on the corner of *Zirkusweg* an' *Bernhard Nocht Strasse*, steppin' around like a black Yankee as had something hot to dispose of.

'"Pickpocket Petra" popped up out of a watchman's shelter, and whispered something into Kurt's ear. While she was talkin' she slipped one hand into his fly-opening and tickled him up, at the same time helping herself to the wallet in his arse-pocket with the other. Second nature to her it was. It was the way she made her livin', anyway.

'Out from *Kastanie-Allée*,, where the street lamps was out, come Tiny, the Jew's David an' "Ready Money Paul", in a beer-waggon they'd borrowed for the occasion.

'"We're pickin' up a 'ot load. Wanna come along?" rumbled Tiny's bass voice from the dark of the driver's cabin.

'Soon as "Kurt the Nark's" up in the waggon, which was one o' them with a canvas back, Tiny an' "Ready Money" are up there with him. "Ready Money's" twistin' his balls up to nearly round his neck. an' Tiny's got him by the throat. an' is bendin' him over backwards so his backbone's making crackin' noises. He was soon making the kind o' sounds people do when they're gettin' close to being strangled to death.

'The Yid furrier's boy David was tryin' to aim a Baretta at him. He wanted to plug him between the eyes, but every time he was ready to pull the trigger Kurt's head was somewhere else. So when the first shot went off it only creased the top of his ear, and went out through the truck's canvas and through a third-floor window. There it nearly frightened the life out a farmhand from Soltau who was gettin' ready to have a go with "Gallopin' Gerda". The next shot ended in the same place an' Gerda's visitor was that frightened he broke an arm tryin' to run down stairs an' put his trousers on at the same time.

'By this time the "Nark'd" found out he was starring in a real live liquidation scene, which you otherwise only experience in a horror film!

'"Jesus Christ!" he screamed, and God must have given him the strength of ten at least, 'cos he managed to butt "Ready Money" in the face, an' bring his American-made boot up in Tiny's tingle-tangle with full force, at one an' the same time. Then he burst through the canvas o' the waggon head-first like a delayed-action shell, knocked Petra arse-over-tip, and found himself standing on the pavement, shaking like a leaf from the nervous tension of it all. Petra was screaming for dear life, and Kurt was spinnin' round on his own axis tryin' to find out whether he was still alive or if he'd been killed.

'"*Get* 'im!" howled "Ready Money Paul", and crawled across Tiny, who was sitting, nursing his maltreated privates.

'"Holy Synagogue," moaned the Jew furrier's David, "that shit's makin' that much noise, you'd think somebody was trying to kill 'im!"

'"Choke 'im off, then," roared Tiny. "'E's already stayed breathin' too long!"

'Kurt had found out by now that he wasn't dead after all, but would be soon if he stayed where he was. So off he goes, fast as his legs can carry him, down towards *Davidsstrasse* so he can get into *Herbertsstrasse* where he'd be safe. He was king down there. God help those three if they were mad enough to go in there after him.

'"The yellow swine's runnin' for it!" roared Paul. "*Get* 'im!"

'The beer-truck roared down through *Hopfenstrasse* right on Kurt's arse. He was running like a hare with the sparks flyin' up from his American boots. He was just about to slip into safety behind the iron fence at *Herbertsstrasse* when the truck caught up with him, and crushed him flat against it. He looked like a great splash of beer-mash some crazy sod had chucked up against the fence. The beer-truck backed off to get away before the coppers arrived. You could usually count on them getting hung up by their truncheons and pistols in the swing-doors leading from *Davidsstrasse* Station.

'They left their bumper behind, mixed up with the remains of Kurt, and disappeared down the *Landesbrücke*, fast as a Rabbi with the SS breathin' down his neck. Next day everybody in Sankt Pauli was talkin' about how "Kurt the Nark" had been taken out by a hit-and-run driver. All the coppers from *Davids Wacht* were out looking for a beer-truck, but it had been lyin' on the bottom of the Elbe, the stink of beer washed out of it a long time since.

'"Mulatto Louis", so-called because he wasn't a real, pure German, was a kind of a viceroy on the Reeperbahn at that time, and decided who it was did what! But he kicked the bucket about a year after, from natural causes. They found him hangin' by the neck in the bus terminus. He'd got worried when he heard about Kurt's sudden departure, and got some people to find out what had really happened. It soon got around who was the hit-and-run driver, an' all the bosses on the Reeperbahn were goin' round whisperin' to one another:

'"Him there, Tiny, *you* know. Him an' his mate David, the feller with the astrakhan collar. They're a coupla hot numbers, they are. *They* know how to fix things!"

'The easy removal of "Kurt the Nark" from the asphalt of Sankt Pauli made Tiny an' David, the Jew's boy, very famous. They were well on the way to becoming wealthy specialists in the removal of unwanted citizens of Hamburg. But this lucrative business they were buildin' up came to a stop, unfortunately, when Tiny got posted to the bicycle dragoons at Breslau, an' the Jew's kid David took a single to England in the bilge of a collier, 'cos he didn't get on all that well with Adolf.'

'How you do go *on*!' says Sally, irritably. 'Why waste our time with all that shit? Who the hell cares what Tiny's done on the Reeperbahn?'

'You don't understand what I'm saying, do you?' asks Porta, throwing his arms wide. 'It's because I want to get it into your thick skulls that it'd be very *un*healthy to leave Tiny gapin' after us on the docks at Libau, *and* it might also shorten our lives considerably!'

The sun is rising over the melancholy Russian landscape when they take leave of Sally at the airstrip.

'Hope he don't fuck it all up,' says Wolf, pessimistically, as the JU-52 disappears into the clouds carrying the 'War Minister' with it.

'He's no stupider than he was on his birthday,' Porta comforts him. 'He knows where the pickings are, and he'll stay on his toes!'

The Old Man turns the plan down immediately. He does not want to spend the rest of his life in Germersheim, or somewhere in Siberia. But Porta will not give up. He chatters on and on about ownership by the people, and in a couple of days time he has the Old Man convinced that the gold is really ours, and that there is nothing criminal in our going to fetch it. The plan begins to take shape.

Sally's two specialists in alterations and signatures arrive with the mail-plane from Berlin. They are each carrying two large briefcases, decorated with the German eagle. In the following days, Chief Mechanic Wolf's sanctum sanctorum is in a state of white-hot alert. TOP SECRET documents are all over the place.

After the Old Man has examined the TOP SECRET orders for a while, he gives in, with a bark of laughter.

'Never in my life have I seen anything like this! It *can't* go wrong. There's even an Order of the Day from the Führer!'

Porta is sitting beside Vera, telling her about their progress since Sally's visit. Proudly he shows her the Führer's Order of the Day, signed with his own hand. It's all there. The special eagle and everything.

'Let's get moving,' he says. 'The orders for a special partisan-type action are already on the desk of the divisional commander, General "Arse-an'-pockets".'

'What if some weak-minded, walnut-brained person was to check this with the Führer's HQ?' asks Vera, with healthy suspicion.

'Don't be silly, girl,' laughs Porta. 'No German dope in uniform'd dare ring Adolf'n ask if his orders were really what he meant! Think your hubby'd ring up Joe'n ask *him* if he knew what he was up to, liquidatin' a load o' fellers who'd poked their noses in too far?'

'No, you may be right,' Vera gives in, thoughtfully.

'Up my arse, how I do look forward to bein' a civvy again,' says Porta, dreamily. 'A life without danger, where anybody can run around free, with any invitin' loot he likes in his pockets.'

'Do not start laughing too soon, my friend,' she mumbles. 'You have no idea how complicated the life of a civilian can be. There, they have no regulations written down to follow!'

'And there's nobody who's got to give anybody the first salute, is there?' says Porta. 'Any shit can just walk past any other shit, just staring blankly at fuck-all. But I do believe it'll be different for us who're travelling first class. They'll lift their lids to us, an' kiss our arses if we want 'em to. It's better to have money in your pockets'n a bundle of stick-grenades!'

'Yes, God knows you are right,' breathes Vera.

Porta sits waiting, with a bottle of cognac and a pot of coffee while Vera goes to find a telephone to try to get in

161

touch with her commissar husband. She is mad enough to spit when she comes back.

'I've had enough of it,' she screams, throwing herself into an armchair. 'If those shits and my clever husband do not pull themselves together we have had it. We are for the shit-heap!'

'Yes, I thought we'd have trouble working with a bloody policeman,' says Porta, worriedly, pouring more cognac into his coffee. 'I *know* 'em! They can do anything, long as somebody's tellin' 'em what to do. If there *isn't* anybody, they flap round in circles like a lot of old maids who've had a bucket o' cow-piss thrown all over 'em. If we don't find out something that can get your twit of a husband moving, PDQ, we'll soon find ourselves on the receiving end of a lot more shocks!'

'That all you've got to say, you limp German prick?' she scolds him, forgetting she is a highly-placed, aristocratic lady. 'What've you got a head for? *Do* something! Give your orders! You *are* a German, aren't you? Just sit there swilling coffee and cognac!' She goes on furiously for some time, spitting out the foulest oaths in the language. Words she certainly did not learn in her aristocratic home.

'Yes, it is a bit shitty ain't it?' Porta admits. 'I must say it's nice and pleasant having a bundle of cash in your pants, but it does bring a lot of excitin' situations with it. Tell me, girl, does your feller drink?'

'No, never,' she says. 'But why do you ask?'

Porta sucks on a tooth, and pulls at the lobe of his ear. 'Does hubby work hard?'

'Indeed he does. I guarantee you that. He has worked like a horse all his life for the lousy state. It is only seldom he drinks, and then he gets really drunk.'

'That does ease my mind,' nods Porta. 'People who drink too much, y'know, see things through rosy spectacles an' everythin' goes easy. I must admit I was scared of the lot of it being just drunken dreams. Let me talk a bit of my Russian German to your hubby. Where's your radio? We'll soon get things on the right track an' be wealthy people with houses an' fishin' rights in Sweden. D'you like salmon, girl?'

> *It is easy to keep clean when you do not engage in trade or mix with other people.*
>
> *Henri de Montherlant*

'Let me go,' babbled the old Jew, trying to tear himself away from the brutal grip of the three young men.

'Where've you hidden the stuff?' shouted the big stormtrooper, hitting the old man in the face.

The woman screamed and tried to help her husband. She was thrown back into the dark corridor. She screamed again when the SA man's boot sank into her. She screamed for the last time when a rifle butt smashed into her face. Then they looted the shop.

When the police arrived they found the old man lying weeping across his wife's body. They turned him in to the collection point at Old Moabitt, and hanged him for wife murder eight days later. That was the day Dr Goebbels decreed:

Ordnung muss sein!

It was 3 April, 1936.

164

THE BURIAL OF GREGOR'S GENERAL

The men who have been on leave are beginning to return. They come plodding down the long straight highway. Some have managed to thumb a lift, but most of them have had to walk the fifty kilometres from Svatogorskaja. The leave train didn't go any further. It is easy to tell which of them are town boys and which come from the country. The farm lads are giving way at the knees from the weight of all the good food their families have loaded them down with when they left. The townies have only their equipment to carry. One thing they all have in common. They are unbelievably sorry for themselves, and under their influence the whole regiment is very soon in the grip of the blackest kind of depression.

We snarl at one another, punch-ups are started for the slightest of reasons. Tiny had already beaten eight men up so viciously that he has been tied to a tree as if he were some kind of watch-dog. We have no guardhouse to keep him in. The Unteroffizier-cook, a fellow we call 'Fried Egg' because he looks like one, gets himself scolded almost to death when two men back from leave throw him into the soup cauldron. All he'd done wrong was to say: 'Welcome back to the joys of the Eastern Front.'

Porta is slouching grumpily down the broad main road, when he runs into Sonia Pushkova, her round fat face shiny with sweat as usual. She believes herself to be very attractive, although she would be none the worse for a close shave. She crashes into Porta with all the grace of a fully-loaded truck, and throws both her fat arms around his neck.

'Like to come into my chicken coop an' have a look at

the new hen?' she asks him, licking the inside of his ear with her fat, wet tongue.

But Porta is far too low in spirits to be interested.

'Shit on your new hen,' he mumbles, and gives her broad rump a hearty smack. 'I'll come an' fuck you some other day, and your hen can sit on her perch and cackle in time to the beat!'

All alone, Gregor comes limping into what was once a fine hotel, before the war, but is now a half shot-up heap of ruins. A primitive sort of bar has been opened in it, but the kind of bar which is only for people with money – and a lot of it.

'What a shithouse of a place,' Gregor says, sitting down alongside Porta on a rickety bar-stool. 'Beer and champagne,' he orders, sourly.

'What the devil are you doin' here?' asks Porta, and stares questioningly at his stick. 'And what's happened to your leg?'

'Sprained my ankle at the funeral,' explains Gregor, swallowing half the contents of his tankard in one go. He stares at the girl behind the bar.

'You are pretty man!' she says in Russian.

'I know that,' he replies. 'I don't believe in the German God any more,' he turns and says to Porta. 'When you've had it good for a bit, and then come back to this godforsaken country, *then* you really understand for the first time what kind of a bucket of shit the German High Command's offerin' its tired heroes! Hell's *bells*!'

The Old Man comes in, followed by Tiny and Barcelona.

'Now I've seen the lot,' roars Tiny, exploding into a shout of laughter at the sight of Gregor. ''Is 'Ighness the Chauffeur-General 'as come back to the poverty-struck!'

'You been decorated?' asks Porta, pointing to the colourful KVK* on Gregor's chest.

---

* *Kriegsverdienstkreuz* (War Cross for Merit)

'My general awarded it to me on his deathbed,' answers Gregor, assuming a sufficiently sorrowing expression.

'Well, well. So *he's* gone to Valhalla too?' says Porta, sadly. 'The Fatherland certainly does require sacrifices from us. I know the family of a colonel that's sacrificed three sons an' two daughters on the altar of the Fatherland, and God help me if they don't still wave paper flags on all the national holidays!'

'Yes, it's rough enough,' sighs Gregor. 'My general'd stayed alive, my fate'd have been different.'

'No doubt about that,' admits Porta. 'The winners would probably have strung you up alongside your general!'

'Could be,' agrees Gregor. 'But what's worst? Rolling round in Russian muck with a pound o' lead in your guts an' dyin' slowly, or dropping down a couple o' yards through a hole with a rope tied round your neck? Oh well! I had some good times with the General Staff. Me an' my general, an' our monocle, had some fine manoeuvres together. In the beginning it was like the day after a Harvest Festival!

'"All we need here to make the similarity perfect," said my general, polishing away at our monocle, "is the smell of cowdung. That would be *it*! We've got to get this crowd in line," he trumpeted through his eagle-beak of a nose. "Unteroffizier Martin, you will move into staff quarters," he barked, semaphorin' with our monocle. "In twelve minutes we drive to church and remind God that it is His duty to give German arms the victory!"

'I took over the quarters of a Leutnant who'd been reduced. They stunk of perfume worse than a whore's scent factory. This Leutnant'd been a brown-holer, so they'd made him a slave in Germersheim. On the way I met my old mate the Adjutant, the rotten swine. When he saw me he stopped dead as if somebody'd hit him between the eyes with a club.

'"You," he groaned. "God in Heaven, *you*! And I hoped and prayed you'd been shot to bits and spread all over the Russian steppe." He glared at me like an admiral out on the high seas just before he gives the order to open fire with a full broadside. Then he stuck his face up close to mine and opened his mouth so I could see his tonsils. "You know what, Unteroffizier Martin," he squealed, like a tom-cat that's got its balls trodden on. "You are the nastiest, and most repelling individual I have ever met. You're a barracks *rat*! That's exactly what you are! A meaningless shout on a wet barrack-square! But you're not going to fool me! I've seen through you! Your conduct can be compared to that of a money-grubbing Jew, but I imagine I've told you that before."

'"Yes sir, Herr Rittmeister sir!" I smiled, crashing my hobnailed heels together twice. "I realized a long time ago, sir, that the Herr Rittmeister did not regard me with the same warm affection as he would a son!"

'You should've seen that lousy bicycle dragoon,' Gregor goes on. 'He made a face for all the world like a travellin' salesman dealin' in moth-eaten rabbit skins. On the way to the mess my general got annoyed because some blokes didn't salute us, even though the divisional flag was waving merrily on the front mudguard. The Staff Padre got a rocket straight off, 'cos his dog-collar wasn't as clean as my general wanted. This made the dope of a sky-pilot nervous, of course, and he got mixed up in his bible text and told us Jesus was at the Battle o' Carthage, and handed out Hannibal the Iron Cross.

'"You need a rest, my good parson," barked my general right in the middle of the prayer, and banged him with eight days confined to quarters, before he'd got to the "Amen". But it wasn't till we got to the war game in the afternoon my general really went up the wall. He'd got a message from Führer HQ, you see, that told him that it wasn't us who'd be gettin' *53 Panzer Corps*, but some shit of a South German who'd got his party book in order. My general an' our monocle took that very near. We'd been looking forward, you see, to smashin' up an armoured corps and shedding a bit of good German blood on the battlefield.

'It was a deep secret, but we were really jealous of a

Russian colleague they called "the Butcher of Khiev", because of his remarkable efficiency at finishing off the troops he was put in command of. My general wanted to be talked of as "the Butcher of the Ukraine". Things like that look great in the history books!

'"There are dark times on the way," predicted my general. "No war game today!"

'Well, the message from Führer HQ went into the waste-paper-basket, we polished our monocle, and took a stiff drink. We were in such a bad mood we even forgot to mark the bottle so we could check if anybody had taken a swig on the sly.

'When I helped him on with his uniform, at exactly 23.00, he looked funny. It was as if his eagle nose had begun to droop a bit. He didn't check his bedtime with the three watches he carried around with him. He'd been hit pretty hard by them havin' given our armoured corps to some fat-gutted party dope from the Bavarian beer-halls.

'"Soon the ravens will come to fetch us," he said, through his nose, and sent me a steely glance through our monocle.

'"Yes, Herr General, sir!" I replied, banging my steel-shod heels together. "It really looks dark! The civilians have stolen our uniform and us gentlemen for God and the Kaiser've got to stand in the corner with our monocle in our hand! Yes sir, Herr General, sir, these are wicked times. We can expect nothing good from the civilians. They are the spawn of the devil. They will spit in our beer!"

'We were silent for a while, thinking things over.

'"Play a little for me, Unteroffizier Martin," he ordered, lounging down in the large general's chair he had had made from the skin of his late horse, Baldrian, which was so German it even topped the mares in Wagnerian rhythms.

'I sat down at the mechanical organ and sang:

> Even I, a strong man,
> Have felt the fiery
> Heat of love . . .

'My general didn't like that one much. It was too tame.
So instead I sang:

> The horses race
> Like a storm along –
> A shot through the head –
> The Rittmeister's dead!
> We smash the enemy –
> Chase him home . . .

'Then my general wouldn't hear any more. He sat there
and seemed to shrink in on himself on his dead horse.

'"Unteroffizier Martin, you have a spot on your mess-
jacket," he said, a little irritably, pointing to a spot no
bigger than a wart on a fly's arse.

'"Do you think I am going to die?" he asked, placing our
monocle in his eye.

'"I'm sure of it, Herr General, sir," I answered. "Those
the heavenly warrior loves he calls home to his table."

'"Yes, we all have to go some time," he sighed, with a
hopeless glint in the eye wearing the monocle.

'After this sad discovery, he had to take another cognac, a
double one. Between the second and the third glass my
general found out that the whole of life was only a preparation for death.

'"Unteroffizier Martin, since you are only an Unteroffizier, and in no way a learned man, I conclude that you
have never thought about how sad everything is. Alone we
come into the world, and still more alone we march out of it
again."

'We were silent for some time, each of us alone with his
thoughts. I was standing there thinking how great it would
be if the old clown'd pull the cheeks of his arse together and
slide into the world of dreams, where everything was all
splashed over with German and Russian blood. I had a bint
waiting for me, you see, at the Bismarck statue that's all

170

covered over with pigeon-shit. *Blitzmädel** she was an' fucked with the whole regiment. When she got into top gear she could make a corpse come.

'My general took another nip from the bottle of Corsican optimism. "You are firmly believed then that I am going to die, Unteroffizier Martin?" he starts up again with the verbal diarrhoea, between a couple of well-satisfied grunts.

'I was permitted to take a little one, as a reward for my honest answers, a very unusual thing where my general was concerned. Of course I had to drink it standing at ease, which is the way things are done in general officer circles.

'Then him and our monocle started marching backwards and forwards in the room. Our spurs jingled real Prussian-like. When we had our night uniform on we always wore boots and spurs till we climbed into beddy-byes.

'The way he looked walking up an' down there he reminded you of a whole regiment of hussars going at the throat of Germany's enemies, and knockin' 'em on the head with sabres. It was typical of my general, and our monocle, that they always marched about when they had to get the blue blood to run out of their heads an' down into their arses so's they could think.

'After some time of this, when I was getting dizzy from turning round all the time to keep facing my general, he finally stopped and stared at me for a long while. He looked like an executioner takin' an eye measurement of the neck of a bloke, who's due to turn up his toes.

'"I am going to give you an order, Unteroffizier Martin, and the devil will come and take you if you don't carry it out punctually and properly!" After a lengthy pause, while he rubbed his eagle-nose thoughtfully: "If I have to go off to serve in the great army, which will probably be before you dismiss for all time, you must see to it that the band of 5

---

* Army Signals girl

171

Hussars blows *Rote Husaren** at my funeral."

'"Very good, Herr General, sir," I replied, cracking my heels smartly. "All shall be arranged as the general orders. The buglers of the Hussars shall blow until their trumpets are red-hot!"

'"I'll trust you with that then, Unteroffizier Martin! But you also see to it that Stabsmusikmeister Breitenmüller of 5 Hussars places two *Leibhusaren* in full parade uniform with sabres in the mourning position at the head of my coffin. Two more hussars from 5 Regiment's corps of buglers are to play *Der Tod reitet auf einem kohlenschwartzen rappen†*. To be played *andante* of course. But should we be so unfortunate as not to be able to get 5 Hussars bugle corps, because they are out fighting for old Germany, then you are to see to it that a well-trained choir of soldiers is commanded out, not less than 25 men, and you, Unteroffizier Martin, will sing the solo. Is that understood?"

'"Yes sir, Herr General, sir! Beg to report sir, I'm already singing!"

'Then my general gets up into his pit at last. He was that taken up with kickin' the bucket that he'd got all the way down into bed before he found he'd still got his boots and spurs on. He got a bit rotten about that. But we got his boots off, and after I'd read him a bit about Old Fritz he went off into a deep sleep.

'Next morning we gave inspection a miss. Instead we went off an' inspected the flowers in the castle park. The Cavalry bed with the yellow tulips pleased him, as they usually did. They stood there straight as a string, bowing their necks just like the sodding horses of the 7 Uhlans in Düsseldorf, our regiment. They were the ones who rode straight to hell in a crazy cavalry attack at Cambrai in 1915, with my general in the lead. We were Oberstleutnant then. We always got ourselves very worked up when we talked

---

* *Rote Husaren:* Red Hussar
† *Der Tod reitet auf einem kohlenschwartzen rappen:* Death rides on a coal-black horse

about that ridin' trip. Sneaky as the English always are, they'd spotted machine-guns all over the place, so it wasn't easy to launch a nice-lookin' cavalry charge. If it'd been *them* that'd sent out their dragoons to charge *us* we'd have met 'em in the stirrups, face to face, with drawn sabres and lances at the ready. When we got to the white lilies my general got wrinkles all over his forehead, and started cursing like a whole gang of seamen in an Arab knocking-shop!

'"Typical infantry," he trumpeted, "look like a flock of nuns who've just been raped by French sailors. See that stupid lily there? Two centimetres out of line. Remove it, Unteroffizier Martin! On to the muckheap with it! If we're not careful, everything will go to pieces."

'At the red roses – the artillery bed – our humour went up a couple of degrees and our ice-blue eyes lit up, joyfully. The roses stand there, battery by battery. They look really soldierly.

'"That's the way!" said my general, and took the monocle out of his eye three times, as a sign that he was well-pleased.

'We walked backwards and forwards a bit, enjoyin' the sight. But it clouded over when we got to the supply troops, the blue cornflowers. Good Lord, what a mess! But that's the way it always is with echelon troops. Yokels, the lot of 'em. They don't even know the difference between right and left. You give 'em a bit of hay round one ankle an' straw round the other and then you shout "Hayfoot! Strawfoot!" Their horse detachments can't find a girl who'll have anything to do with them, and have to have a go at the horses when they get the chance.

'My general sentenced the whole cornflower bed to be executed, so at dawn I ran our hand lawnmower through the lot of 'em.

'The panzer troops, the pink roses, made a better showing. What a straight-backed lot! I felt proud to be a Panzer Unteroffizier. We stayed a long time looking at them and in the end we'd convinced ourselves things weren't as black as they looked.

'"Takes balls to be a panzer soldier," my general said, rattlin' his false teeth.

'We nodded in passing to the engineer troops, black tulips. They're the coolies of the army anyway. But when we got to the catering lot, the cabbage bed, we got a shock. The Moses dragoons were standing there droopin' like so many gonorrhoea-infected pricks.

'My general sentenced them all to death on the spot. "To the gas-chambers with them," he snarled, without a thought in his head of how important a catering corps is.

'Everything went wrong when we got down to the orchards, and inspected the scarecrows. They were wearing Russian uniforms. My general got a funny look on his face when we found the first one with unpolished boots. The two next had their coats buttoned crooked, and the last was wearin' his cap back to front.

'My general nearly swallowed the gardeners, who come on the run. We chased 'em up through the orchards with that many threats, and so fast, their tongues were hanging out of their arseholes an' their piles were up around their ears.

'An old, white-haired feller cracked open like a maiden-head on a summer night, an' threw up all over the general's boots. My general pulled out his pistol and aimed it at this *untermensch*, and, of course, he fainted from fright. They sent him to the front the day after, to spend the rest of the war with a corpse-collection unit.

'We were in a black humour, as we marched back to the castle. The Angel of Victory received only a perfunctory salute in passing. The sentries slammed the doors open, but one of them made a mess of it and his door swung back and hit my general right in the face. You should've *heard* him. He didn't shout, like some stupid Unteroffizier, but what he did say, through his nose, sat right in the bullseye. He literally shot those two guards down with his words.

174

'"Never beat around the bush with people of that sort," he twanged down his nose.

'Yes, my general did just what he liked with every man in our division. He signed death warrants without even reading 'em. We didn't waste much time on that sort of thing, anyway.

'In the corridor we ran into the Catholic padre, who was so fat he had the shakes permanent. Every part of him shook like a jelly. My general stopped in the corridor without acknowledging the fat padre's salute.

'"Well, it's you is it, reverend padre? It's not often you put in an appearance, but you are, perhaps, busy preparing the way for the many soldiers who fall for the Fatherland?"

'"Very good, Herr General!" mumbled the sky-pilot weakly, looking as if he was about to drop dead on the spot.

'My general had pulled his long neck down into his collar at the sight of the Staff Padre, but now he suddenly shot it right out again, and screwed his monocle more firmly into his eye.

'"Yes, you must be very busy, reverend father," he spat out. The nostrils of his eagle-nose vibrated as if he were smelling a corpse. "Your boots are not polished, but there are perhaps other clothing regulations for the gentlemen of the Corps of Padres, with which I am not familiar? Three days confined to quarters, reverend padre, and you will report every other hour to my Adjutant with well-polished boots and equipment. It is possible that you have been allowed to slouch around in a state of unregimental filthiness in the division you came from, but *not* here in my division!"

'So we left the Jesus dragoon standin' there to think over things. After we had slashed at our riding boots with our riding whip a few times we ordered war games for the whole garrison. That's what we always used to do when the officers were goin' to get some stick. They were all there when we arrived. My general understood this sort of thing. He was always master of the situation. Nobody ever took *him* for a sleigh-ride. My job was to look after the cardboard clock, so I had a good view of what was goin' on, and I stood so's I could have a good grin now and then without 'em seeing it. Our division had the best terrain model of anybody in the whole Army. My general'd looked after that. There was dozens of streams and rivers, and guns and tanks; and bridges all over the place that we could blow up just before the enemy got to 'em.

'My general stood there for a long time, glarin' nastily at all the nervous faces round the war table. Then he gave 'em a long speech about what was going to happen if Germany, as usual, got its arse kicked up round its ears by our rotten enemies.

'"This time they will drink their ale from our skulls," he predicted. "Our sexual organs will decorate the walls of their officers' messes." But, he swore by our monocle, before it gets that far – and may God forbid it, he added, in the tone of an archbishop – we must see to it that our enemies get to know us. "We shall bombard them with fire from our long-range artillery," he explained, waving his pointer backwards and forwards over the simulator table. "Then our armour will roll forward in a destructive flying V formation. Our heavy Tigers will take away their appetite for war. Those who are left we will smash under the tracks of our self-propelled guns, and those who have gone into hiding we will blast with our flamethrowers." He hammered his pointer down on a village, destroyin' it with one blow.

'All the officers turned their eyes sadly towards the shattered village. The terrain was a German landscape, you see, with German cows and our fat German peasants on it!

'"Germany will never capitulate, gentlemen, mark my words," hissed my general, lettin' our monocle fall out of his eye. Suddenly he realized what a terrible lot of nonsense he was talking. When he had taken a break, in which he punished a couple of Leutnants by postin' 'em away to the infantry for gigglin' at a dirty story, he nodded to the Chief-of-Staff. "The Wild Boar", a dried-up stick of a

Major-General with a stiff leg and a patch over one eye, took over, and the war stimulation was on the go.

'The first who got the hammer was a Rittmeister who was going too fast. He mistook his own lines for the enemy's and let a couple of Stukas smash up his own armour that was waiting in ambush for the neighbours' T-34s. That Rittmeister was letting his tears fall in a front-line regiment the very same night. My general didn't even give him the regulation three days leave. Nobody could feel himself safe with us. Just when they were enjoying things with the staff and countin' on an uncomplicated life, off they went, all of a sudden, to a front-line unit, the anteroom to the Valhalla mess.

'A bit later a Major and three Leutnants got themselves removed from division's protectin' arms, for goin' the wrong way with the enemy's tanks.

'My general got more and more annoyed, and his eyes were shooting out wicked ice-blue flashes!

'I could see what way things were going. Before these simulated games were over the division'd have a noticeable shortage of officers. It was lucky though, I thought, that they weren't *real* officers but only reserves – war surplus shit so to speak. But our German God had kept the best to wind up with. Every bit of our concentrated anger fell on the Adjutant, the rotten swine. He got himself that infiltrated in Ivan's infantry that he lost a whole battery of SPs. My general shot his scraggy neck half a yard up out of his collar, like a submarine commander who was tryin' to sink a battleship. The adjutant feller got a fit of the Andalusian shakes, and started his AA batteries shooting down our own air support. They came down over the whole simulator area like a shower of confetti.

'I was grinnin' like mad up there alongside my cardboard clock. It was a lovely sight to see that lousy Adjutant in trouble. He looked like a constipated rat. My general told him a lot of things in a voice that nearly cut the boots away from under him, and he slunk off looking like a half-drowned suicide candidate.

'Then my general stopped the war game before the incompetent officers ruined our army completely. He made a long speech to those remaining, in which he told them what his feelings were with regard to civilians in uniform. He wound up by telling them that Attila had been much better off than the general of today. He wasn't encumbered with reserve officers, but had born warriors around him who knew how to swing a club and split the skulls of other tribesmen.

'Off we went then, and banged the door after us. I left the cardboard clock at five minutes past twelve. Just to give the clever fellers something to think about.

'Then we changed uniform, and put on our battle kit with our hand-artillery on our hip.

'"To work," ordered my general, and out he goes through flocks of cacklin' geese and poultry that thought they owned the road.

'"Hell's bells," I thought. Time to pray. I knew my general, and had a pretty good idea of what he might get up to when he was in one of his black moods.

'Just after the birds' tattoo we get up in our staff car, and drive down through the darkened villages with our divisional standard on the front mudguard and blue slits on the headlamps, so's nobody'd be in doubt of who was coming. My general muttered away darkly during the whole of the trip. "Honour be to God in the highest and peace on earth," I thought.

'My general had decided to inspect the coolies stationed round about in the civilian quarter. We dropped down on the divisional gaol like delayed action lightning on the Day of Wrath. The guards were sitting around playing cards with the prisoners and their weapons were hanging on the coat-racks out in the latrines. You should've heard my general, and seen those guards and prisoners jump around like cockroaches on a red-hot fryin' pan. In the end when they'd all been ordered into the cells, I was commanded to lock the doors an' bolt 'em. When I handed the keys over to my general, he threw 'em as far as he could over on the other side of a muckheap.

'Finally we dismantled their machine-pistols and spread the parts all over Westphalia, so they'd be *really* busy when they got the order to parade for inspection with mpis. Yes, my general knew how to turn civilians into reasonable imitations of soldiers.

'The next place we rolled up at, the officer in charge appeared on the doorstep in pyjamas and slippers. My general made a terrible noise.

'"The enemy is in the outskirts of the town," he roared, pushing his beaky nose almost into the sleepy major's face. "The enemy is on its way into the town!" he repeated.

'"That's not so good," mumbled the major, and offered my general cognac for an eye-opener.

'"My dear man, have you not just heard that the enemy is here with his armoured spearhead almost standing on your toes?" said my general, with shattering calm.

'"Well I suppose there's only one thing left for us to do." The major smiled, and pulled his pyjama trousers up around his waist. "And that's to get off out of here, before we get the shop all smashed up! But what the devil's the enemy want here?"

'Now we practically jumped out of our riding boots. We dropped our field-monocle, which got smashed, but thank God we always had an extra one in our breast-pocket.

'"You give the alarm!" roared my general, in a rage.

'"Very good, Herr General, sir!" answered the major, and he shuffled out an' put on his tin helmet. Then he put his head out of the door, and shouted "Alarm!" three times into the night-still village street.

'Nothing happened for a while, and then the telephone rang, very angrily. My general picked it up.

'An angry voice asked what kind of idiot it was who shouted "Alarm!" here in the middle of the night.

'"It's me," shouted my general, in a voice which made

the telephone mouthpiece shrink in on itself. "An alarm has been ordered, because paratroopers have surrounded us!"

'"You must have eaten an old boot an' it's disagreed with you," laughs the voice at the other end of the line. "Go in and get some sleep, you war-crazy idiot, and wait with all that shit till daylight. No paratrooper in his right mind'd dream of landing here with us! We're not doing anybody any harm!"

'My general threw the telephone from him in disgust, and sent the major a destroying general's glance.

'"You'll hear from me," he promised him, darkly.

'"Very good, Herr General, sir," piped the major, saluting with the wrong hand to his steel helmet. He had only now realized who his guest was.

'"What a spineless individual," snarled my general, as we crashed through a new village," he'll end up wishing that it *had* been enemy paratroopers who visited him rather than us!"

'We came down like two emissaries from outer space on some quarters where a rifle regiment had found protection from the night damp, and were lolling in broad peasant beds.

'A tall, thin beanpole of a Feldwebel, with his steel helmet turned round backwards on his head, coughed out a kind of report. When he had finished and was standing and wondering what else he could find to report, he realized that he had forgotten to call the room to attention. The coolies were lying around with their heads on the tables, snoring, an' not givin' a damn for standing guard.

'"Sound the alarm, man," screamed my general. "The enemy is on its way into town!"

'"What?" grunted the Feldwebel, fearfully, breathing cheap schnapps straight into my general's face. "What?" repeated this sketch of a soldier, scratching himself violently on the backside.

'"Sound the alarm, for hell's sake," screamed my general again, nearly frightening the life out of the company cat.

which was lying fast asleep alongside the stove. It sprang straight up in the air, and came down standing stiffly on all four legs.

'"*Servus*, Herr General, sir!" it meowed.

'The tin-hatted beanpole began thinking so hard, dents appeared in his helmet. He reached for his belt and pistol, which were hanging on a hook. Then he pissed off over to one of the sleepin' beauties an' began to shake him awake.

'"Herbert," he yelled. "Wake up, damn your eyes!"

'"Sod off!" answered Herbert, throwing a sleepy punch at him.

'"It's important, Herbert! Come on! Get up!" the beanpole implored him.

'"Go over'n wake up the OC, and tell him the enemy's here with tanks an' all sorts of ironware!"

'You should have seen my general! He looked as if his favourite football team'd lost an' he was goin' to have a Greater German stroke any minute. Then he went green, an' finally blue in the face. He simply couldn't get a word out for several minutes, something which only happened infrequently. But then he got his voice back, with a vengeance.

'"We're at war, man," he screamed. They must've been able to hear him down in the south of France. "Any minute now the enemy's tanks will roll in and tear the flesh from our bones. Sound the alarm, *Stufe 3**, man, damn your eyes!"

'"Very good, Herr General, sir," mumbled the Feldwebel, scratching his head, thoughtfully, under his steel helmet.

'"Get your fingers out, Herbert! Sound the alarm *Stufe 3*! Wake up the section commanders. Tell 'em the British are here with their tanks. They'd better get their gear together, too, so's we can get off out of it before we get took prisoner. Jump to it, Herbert. Ain't you found out there's a war on yet?"

---

* *Stufe 3:* German: Stage 3 alarm

'"Me gun," muttered Herbert, still half-asleep. He puts out a hand to fumble after his rifle, which is hanging on a hook by the window and looking just as sleepy as its owner and the rest of the guard.

'"And they dare to do this to me," wheezed my general, pushing the whole of his eagle-face up out of his collar. "They are all mad as hatters and think they're here to live off the fat of the land! Unteroffizier Martin, show them how to sound the alarm when the enemy is knocking on the door!"

'I picked up a "guitar", smacked a full magazine into place, and burnt off the whole load. Then I changed magazines and, just to be on the safe side, sent another load off up the long village street in the opposite direction.

Lights went on in some of the houses, and sleepy voices shouted protests.

'"Good Lord preserve us," groaned my general, taking our monocle out of his eye. "This gang don't even respect the black-out regulations!"

'After about ten minutes had gone by, a fat reservist came rattling up on an Army motorbike Anno 1903.

'"What the hell are you crazy loons playing at?" he yelled furiously, coming close to falling off his bike with rage. "Firing off weapons here in the middle of the night. There'll be a court-martial out of this, devil take me!"

'"Yes, you can count on that, my good man," snarled my general.

'The reserve officer let his bike fall to the ground when he saw the general's red tabs and oak leaves. He was struck dumb on the spot, and remained standing quite still in an attitude which good-natured people might even have called the position of attention. It took us some time to get out of him that he was the regimental Orderly Officer.

'"Enemy armour is on its way into your billet area," thundered my general, as if he were Marius himself on the Raudian fields.

'"What kind of armour?" asked the fat cycle dragoon, moping at us.

'"British tanks, Herr Oberleutnant, sir," grinned "Beanpole", hitching up his pistol belt which had slid down round his backside over the hips he hadn't got any of.

'"God have mercy on us," cried the fat man, in terror, and shifted his weight from one leg to the other.

'"I'm sure he will have," barked my general. "But you had better help yourself a little first, my good man."

'A leutnant came sailing along just then, dressed in riding breeches, slippers and a pyjama jacket with red stripes.

'"The CO requests to know what the devil's going on, and why all this shooting in the middle of the night?"

'My general stared in amazement at this strangely-clad officer.

'"Tell me now, my good man. Is this a messenger service or a Prussian infantry regiment?" and I can tell you he gave that Leutnant in slippers and pyjama jacket a goin' over it was a treat to listen to! Oh, but it *was* a lovely rocket.

'When he ran out of curses and threats he went spurjinglin' over to an anti-tank gun that was standing, getting bored to death, in between some bushes. Without glancing either right or left, and without a thought for the consequences, he released the firing mechanism and pulled the lanyard.

'"BOOM!" thundered the 75 mm.

'"There goes auntie's rock cakes off of the plate," I thought, as the shell went screamin' off into the night, waking up all the German birds in their cosy nests. Germany is used to gettin' into wars, but it's still not all that often they fire guns off back home. The shell went through three houses in a row, causing quite a bit of rearrangement of the furniture. It finished up inside a *Panzer Spähwagen** inside the ammunition locker. Lord what a row the ammunition made goin' off. That scout car got itself spread out over half of Westphalia! Some bits went into the Rhine, and some splashed into the Weser. But what else happened was that

* *Panzer Spähwagen:* German: Scout car

183

the life came back into that sleepy regiment. How they did mill about. Most of 'em ran for their lives, but a few war-mad sods wanted to fight back. What a sight the German sun did see when it finally came up. It came close to goin' back down again, I can tell you! An armoured company battled bravely for two hours, an' only gave in when the house they were defending was reduced to ruins. Then they discovered, to their horror, that the enemy was their own motorcycle battalion.

'My general's alarm exercise cost 88 wounded an' 9 dead. Two committed suicide an' three were reported missing. That three caused a lot of scratching of heads, until it was realized that they just couldn't have been taken prisoner by the British, because there wasn't any British. That was something my general was just playin' there was.

'"Those men have, devil take me, deserted," growled my general. He called the MP boss to him, a big, brutal Hauptmann with eyes that wicked the Devil himself'd have envied him 'em. "I demand, my good man," he began, looking daggers at the chief headhunter, "that deserters from the flag and shirkers be treated ruthlessly! No slightest consideration is to be shown to dirt like that. Out with it!"

'The dummies got caught of course. They landed up in Germersheim, where a firing squad of Pioneers shot the cowardly lives out of them.

'"Can't make an omelette without breaking eggs," said my general, satisfied, as we drove back home to breakfast.

'My general used to like that kind o' service. Make 'em shiver all over! Get a move on! That was his proper element. Nobody ever could do it as good as he could, my general.

'In the afternoon we took a look at the Engineers. They threw bridges over streams, an' then they took 'em down again. My general timed 'em on his three watches. A few eggs got broken here, too, to my general's great satisfaction. A dope of an Unteroffizier got his legs crushed. He was too heavy in the arsepart when a crane we'd pinched from the Frenchies broke up. Two other fellers got drowned, caught between the pontoons. Not regulars, thank God, only compulsory service blokes. But my general got browned-off about it anyway, and had the rest of 'em, and their NCOs, crawlin' on their guts with rifles at full stretch an' noses down on the ground. They got their teeth cleaned good enough to last 'em the rest of their lives. It was a pleasure to see how he made soldiers out of that lot of monkeys. People who'd soldiered with us never, ever forgot the experience.

'When we'd worked our way through the evenin' trough – we used to call it "dinner" 'cos my general liked using stylish foreign expressions, specially English. It came of his having been on detachment with the 11th Hussars, the lot that've got "Moses in Egypt" as their regimental song – we took off our evening uniform an' pulled our white gloves down again on the glove form we had for the purpose. Then we put on our garrison uniform and went to church so's Field-Marshal God'd get what he had comin' to him in that direction. But when we got back again there was a nasty surprise waitin' for us. The staff was rushing about all over the place. They were due East every man of 'em, and the reason wasn't to station them closer to where the sun rises.

'"They're mistaken, those dressed-up dummies at Führer HQ," shouted my general. "I'll teach 'em! I give the orders here! Nobody's going to move any of my division as long as *I'm* in command!"

'The Chief-of-Staff danced round as if he'd pissed himself and was now goin' on shittin' himself. Without saying a word he handed a nicely folded and creased letter over, signed by Adolf in person. My general's face looked like Mayday. His chin dropped right down over his Knight's Cross. The Chief-of-Staff shrugged his shoulders sadly, and stared out of the window.

'"Relieved of command," stammered my general, spelling his way through the letter again. He wouldn't believe it really said what he'd read in it.

'"Those whom the Gods will destroy they first strike with blindness," he thundered. "Now the Bohemian corporal's gone too far. The dice are thrown!"

'Keitel came on the phone a bit later. He got a few home truths to pass on to "the man from Brunau".

'We'd hardly got our night uniform on before the telephone started to ring fit to break all records.

'"Must be important," said my general, straightening his regimental nightcap so the gold-embroidered bird and the cockade sat in line with his eagle nose.

'It was *General der Infanterie* Burgdorff, head of personnel, who wanted a little chat with us. In the hierarchy he was known as "the Black Eminence".

'My general's face changed colour several times, and his beaky nose turned quite cobalt blue during that "little chat".

'I was in no doubt what was goin' on. The shithouse was flaming away madly, and my general was goin' to get all the fine little delicate hairs round his arse singed off. After General Burgdorff had put down the phone we sat there for a long time, quietly, thinking things over. I could almost hear the crackin' noises comin' out of my general's skull. Whatever, it seemed to have come over him that it wasn't always very clever to go round saying out aloud what you were thinking. There's a lot of Germans've died of doing that since 1933.

'Before we marched into the land of dreams, we changed back into our light duty uniform, and we wrote letters.

'When the sun popped up to see what had happened to good old Germany in the course of the night, we'd signed the last letter, and everything was laid out straight in the middle of the blotter, which is the Prussian cavalry's way of doin' things.

'"My service pistol," said my general in a severe voice.

'I chased off after the hand artillery, wiped it off quickly with a polishing-cloth, loaded it and took off the safety catch. Then I handed it to my general.

'"Goodbye then, Unteroffizier Martin," he snarled, and extended his hand to me for the first time. "Do your duty by

186

our beloved Fatherland! I will follow your progress!"

'"*Zu befehl*, Herr General," I replied, clicking my slippers twice. "May our honourable monocle remain unsullied!"

'Then he put the gun to his forehead, while I stood off out of the line of fire at the salute, and we shot ourselves. The *way* my general could carry it off! He was fan*tas*tic, he was. But he was also my general. Three bullets went through his field commander's cranium, and only *then* he dropped our monocle. Oh, but it was dignified. If I hadn't been a little bit stinko from tasting our cognac I think I would have cried.

'I arranged him nicely, an' put his cap on him, and, after a lot of trouble, got our monocle in place regimentally. After that I alarmed the staff.

'They came along, clicked their heels and saluted and arranged their faces in regulation folds of sadness. Even the Adjutant, the wicked sod, shook his head so sorrowfully all the *mensur* scars on his jowls wriggled like eels in jelly.

'The following days were taken up with the arrangements for my general and our monocle's funeral. We inspected the goodbye-boxes, and picked out a heavy block of a coffin in ancient German oak with a long row of iron crosses cut into it all round. I had to search half Germany for a scarlet velvet cushion to lay out my general's fruit salad on. He'd done all right in the two world wars, and hadn't been backward in coming forward in peacetime either.

'The company clerk spent five hours polishin' up our parade sabre before the Adjutant was satisfied with it. It was a hell of a fine sabre we'd got. A sword of honour from the *Leibhusaren*. I often thought about swoppin' it for a cheap Solingen steel job. Some crazy collector'd certain sure pay a pretty penny for it.

'The company's Chief Mechanic paint-sprayed my general's tin helmet, so's it could reflect back the flames from the torches.

'Two Staff Padres came from Berlin, with the Padre General in the lead. They were all glittering with phoney gold crucifixes and things to help to pilot my general up to

Valhalla. Everythin' possible was done to make it a really lovely funeral. The only thing that went wrong was the buglers. Those bloody hussars were hiding out some place or other on the Eastern Front, letting themselves get shot to bits by the neighbours, and, worst of the lot, the kettledrum nag'd gone off an' deserted to the enemy. *And* it'd taken the kettledrums with it. Well, a cavalry regimental band without kettledrums isn't worth a shit! I really hope the MPs get hold of that rotten horse some time, so they can hang it up alongside all the rest of the lousy deserters. It could, at least, have left the kettledrums behind it. They're German property. It ain't fittin', the neighbours banging away on 'em!

'Every arm was represented by a Leutnant, standing guard of honour. Six they were. They stood there, stiff as statues, round my general, who was lying there enjoying himself in the Knights' Banqueting Hall. He was in full dress uniform with all his orders. *Blaue Max**, and Iron Cross with "knife an' fork", and he was wearing fine patent leather boots with silver bar spurs. I can tell you he was the loveliest body you could ever imagine. Dressed like that, my general could fly straight up to Valhalla and start an alarm exercise going as'd make the floor of Heaven red-hot under the feet o' the angels.

'There was a hell of a row about his headgear. I wanted him to have his steel helmet on. That's why I'd had it spray-painted. But the Adjutant wanted the garrison cap with gold oak leaves an' everythin'.

'"Steel helmets are out of place with dress uniform!" he screamed, wriggling all his *mensur* scars at me.

'His chops were going like a runaway howitzer. He was that mad he could've cracked Brazil nuts with the cheeks of his arse and sucked the kernels up the wrong way. In between times he told me what he thought about me. I felt like giving him one in the kisser, but it wasn't worth it. He

* Pour le mérite (a high WWI order)

188

was a Rittmeister and could've had me in the black hole without my feet touching if I'd hung one on him.

'"May you be struck with every kind of pest we've got in this country," he hissed. "If I saw you caught in a beartrap I'd leave you there to bleed to death. I can tell you, Martin, there's a terrible fate waiting for you. As soon as the general's in the ground, off you go, straight to the Eastern Front, so fast the dust and dirt'll be spurting up in clouds from your boot-soles. And I'll find the worst, stinking unit in existence to send you to! A unit that operates behind the enemy lines in *their* uniforms, and does all the things that are forbidden by the conventions of war, might be *just* the thing. Look forward to it Martin, even your sick mind couldn't imagine what the Russians do to swine like you who hide behind their uniform!"

'"Oh I know all about what they do, Herr Rittmeister, sir. First off the neighbours' boys have a bash at your balls with a good, heavy hammer. Then they put an electric wire up your arse, so's your worms are dancin' a polka round your piles before you know it. I've had a dose of it before, sir, but I've got away with it every time so far. I would, however, like to thank the Herr Rittmeister, sir, for all his good wishes, and express the hope that we shall have a pleasant reunion in the heroes' common grave."

'He wriggled his *mensur* scars at me then like a bag of snakes. He looked for all the world like a prematurely born wild boar. Lord, what a row he did make, until the Chief-of-Staff came in and told him to shut up.

'"You'll be waking the general again if you keep on like that," he said, warningly.

'My general lay there takin' it easy, while the whole garrison came and said goodbye to him. They came from near and far, clicked their heels together, rattled their sabres and turned their sorrowing faces towards the ground. Some of 'em cried, so's we could really understand how much they'd loved my general. Lies and falsehood all of it. There wasn't one of 'em who wouldn't have been glad to see my

189

general bubbling in his own fat in hell.

'Then one morning along came the artillery, with a great rattling gun-carriage and six black horses. Commands were shouted, sabres pointed at the ground and standards sunk. Six officers strutted stiff-legged over to my general, who was lying there looking lovely and expensive in his vampire-box.

'"Funeral procession! Slo-o-ow March!" screamed the Chief-of-Staff. An' off we went towards the garrison church.

'I went to get up in the staff-car, but there was some yokel sitting back of the wheel. I'd been relieved!

'"I'll get you for this, first chance I get!" I promised him, stupidly. He was a Feldwebel, even though he was only infantry.

'"You can crawl," said the Adjutant, "believe me you'll get used to it!"

'"Shit," I thought. "We'll meet again out East perhaps!"

'In the garrison church, fat, six-foot-tall wax candles were burning, and the infantry band was playing sorrowful march music. Goethe or Chopin it was. I don't know, but it was very sad. If it'd been me that was my general and had to go off to Valhalla, I'd have had hot rhythm and a black feller from America to howl out a solo. A blues, that's a thing you can get your teeth into an' understand. It's something that can put some gunpowder up a body's arse on its last trip!

'There was a whole mob of people in uniforms and civilian clothes dancin' a war-dance round my general's wooden uniform. There was even Navy there. A couple of crooked-eyed Japs, too. If the war hadn't been forced on us there'd have been British and Russians as well. They were all mates of my general.

'The war flag was draped over the vampire-box. On top of it was the red velvet cushion. I'd got it from an old woman in Bielefeld. It was her cat's bed. All the fruit salad lay glitterin' on it. The sword of honour and the steel helmet shone like catshit in the moonlight of a spring night. My general's horse, Magda, had also been invited to the party.'

'In *Church*?' the Old Man breaks in, in amazement.

'No, damn it. She stood outside chattin' with the six artillery horses.

'Then it started up properly. An honour guard from the Panzer Grenadiers pointed their guns at the sky and loosed off a volley at Valhalla. The signal to open up the gates, I reckon, so's there'd be plenty of room for my general when he got there. When the flags went down, off went the organ at top decibel level. It roared and groaned so that even the biggest dummy present must've understood that a general's burial was a very solemn affair.

'Then the Staff Padre spoke up. He talked about God, explained how God had always been a Prussian and that that was the reason He'd always been on our side. He got a bit mixed up and got the British God tangled up with our chap. There were some who growled a lot about that. In a world war it can be a very serious matter to go fraternizing with the other blokes' God.'

'Yes,' puts in Porta, 'where the devil'd we all be if half us German dummies lay talkin' in the night with the English God? And the Scots were prayin' to the German bloke? What a mess it'd make of a world war where that sort of thing went on!'

'The Staff Padre was getting close to high treason with all his natterin' about the English God,' Gregor goes on. 'Until the Padre General got the dope smartly away from the German God's altar. I think he's off somewhere on the East Front already, and has forgotten all about the British God.

'This Army bishop really gave my general what he deserved. I've always known we were big, but I never thought we was as big as that Padre General made us out to be.

'"May the general live in the memory of the German people as the brave and duty-loving leader in the field that he was," brayed this top sky-pilot, bangin' his fist down on the edge of the pulpit. "The general was loved by his men; they followed him through thick and thin, and died with a smile at his feet."

'I could have told him a bit different. Them *I* saw kick the bucket weren't smiling. No, they were gnashin' their teeth!

'"The most beautiful death a man can have," crowed the high-flyin' sky-pilot, "is to fall in battle for the Fatherland. The general, who is now leaving our ranks to march up and join the great army in the sky, was from his earliest cadet days a shining light for German youth, a fearless and undemanding warrior!"

'For more'n half an' hour he ranted on about beautiful, lovely death. Then the next Staff Padre came on. He was kind of a parson Hauptfeldwebel.

'"Let us all pray," he roared, in a voice that'd have blown the wings off half the Heavenly Host. "On your knees for *prayer*! Helmets *off*!"

'So we knelt down with the neckpiece of our steel helmets placed regimentally alongside the third tunic button from the top. Exactly according to Army Regulations, military church service section. A Feldwebel and two Obergefreiters got put on orders by the Adjutant for laughin' when in prayer position.

'"Amen!" thundered the padre.

'"Coffin *lift*!" the Chief-of-Staff ordered, and six Leutnants spit on their hands, hoisted the goodbye-box up on their shoulders, an' staggered off out of church.

'It was snowing. There is no doubt that the German God wanted to remind my general of wicked Russia where his first Army Corps got a couple of good beatin'-ups. The gun-carriage rolled off with my general, but it couldn't drive him all the way to the hole. The garrison churchyard was on the top of some hills, you see. Up there was all the top ten, an' a few more too, of the German leaders. Some of 'em had marshals' batons with 'em in their wooden suits. But the six horses weren't enough to pull the gun-carriage up the steep hills. Magda was the only one who could manage it. She struggled up, but only with a whole lot of puffing and panting. Now an' again she'd blow a fart, and soon the whole funeral procession stank of horse-shit. A couple of times she slid down on her haunches and covered all the pretty uniforms with slush. Bushes and weeping willows bent under the wet snow, and the steep churchyard paths were slippery. The Leutnants carrying the vampire-box had the greatest difficulty in getting up.

'"Couldn't that fucking sabre-swinging bastard have arranged to get himself buried on a sunny day?" snarled an infantry Leutnant, angrily.

'"He always was a shit, a creeping Jesus," whispered the officer behind him, a Leutnant of the motorcycle corps. "He never let us alone when he was alive, and now, even when he's dead, he keeps us at it!"

'"The bad fellow down in Hell'll make it hot for him," promised an artillery Leutnant on the other side of the coffin.

'The pock-marked marble eagles stared blankly at the procession, and the angels with Prussian profiles looked around them proudly. Here in the garrison churchyard there could be no doubt of who was somebody and who was only a coolie. The last-named had only a miserable tin or wooden cross. Some had the honour of a steel helmet perched on top of the crazy cross. A company commander had a stone pillar with an Iron Cross engraved on it, while staff officers were awarded a granite stone with the bird on it, and a short note of the places in which they had played hero for the greedy Fatherland. Generals had tons of marble on their graves and cornerpieces decorated with lions or eagles with the wickedest faces a man could imagine. But the Field-Marshals broke all records. Granite was rolled over them in huge blocks, with batons chiselled out of marble and piled on top of a giant Iron Cross. What a trip we did have up that cemetery hill! Snow slashed across our faces, and melted snow trickled down our uniform collars, and played Ice Age games down our spines.

'On the first stop in the side of the hill I suddenly remembered that my general had ordered me to sing before they let him down into the hole. To get into the right frame of mind I took a couple of good swigs of some *Slivovitz* I'd brought along in a hip-flask.

'An Oberst from Führer HQ fell on his bum and slid back down the hill. When he finally got back on his feet again and had untangled his spurs, he got his sabre caught between his legs and went down again.

'I was walking a long way back in the procession. The Adjutant had ordered that. He said the higher officers would suffer from shortage of breath if they had to breathe the same air as me. On the seventh swig of *Slivovitz*, a belch a bit *too* loud came back. An Oberstleutnant turned round and looked at me in surprise. It was one of these Staff shits with red stripes down his pants. He said somethin' or other to a shaky old Major-general who was tip-toein' along as if his boots were full of shit. Now they both stared at me, with court-martials in their eyes. But by the time they'd got the paper in the machine an' started to dictate I'd have been a long time back in Russia, and who the hell can find *anybody* in Russia.

'The civvy top hats had all put up their umbrellas. God, how it did snow! My general and our monocle had certainly picked an ugly day for the last sleigh-ride. Under the snow-laden birches some leather-coated chaps in trilby hats were slinkin' about, lookin' as if they didn't belong. A blind loony could've seen they were keeping an eye on things. Even my general's Mazda could see that "the Devil and the Gestapo were listenin'". Nobody said a word so long as the melancholy birches and the leather-coats were still in sight. A smell of corpses hung around us long after we'd passed 'em.

'Part way up the steep path, where we could see the birches from above and only just catch a glimpse of the leather-coats, a high-born lady in black and wearin' a veil, fell on her arse. She went all the way down like a bobsleigh out after a new world record, and straight in under the birches where the leather-coats were waiting, just longin' to make an arrest. The black-clothed lady with the veil didn't

194

come back to the procession any more. When we staggered past the war memorial for 1870–71, I happened to give another belch. It was quite painful, really. I should never've ate *Eisbein mit Sauerkraut* before going on the Valhalla march.

'It was when we started up a very narrow path, more like a sort of staircase, made of logs and slippery as all hell, things really began to go wrong. A cavalry Leutnant amongst the bearers got into trouble with his spurs, and let out a screech. Then he went down, with the result than an engineer Leutnant doin' the dead march just behind him went on his arse too. The whole procession halted wondering what was going to happen next, and I can tell you a lot *did* happen, an' in a hell of a quick time. The bearer officers tried desperately to hang on to the wooden box, but it got away from 'em and off it went thunderin' down the path with the six Leutnants after it.

'"Stop him! Stop him!" they were all shoutin'. You'd have thought my general was a shoplifter spurtin' off with his loot out of a supermarket.

'A Lieutenant-general, a mummy from 1914, who was standin' there rubbin' his toothless gums together, got knocked over. He gave out a shrill howl, as if the whole of Verdun, and the Siegfried Line after it, had been dropped on top of him. His *pickelhauber* went up in the air, and was never seen again. It probably ended up danglin' by the point from St Peter's backside. The prehistoric sabre with its silk tassels flew off to one side as the general-box steam-rollered over the uniformed mummy. The whole procession, with veils and top-hats and dress swords under their arms, went running off at top speed in front of my late general, to avoid getting their bones broken by the coffin coming rushing down from the heights. Magda was in the lead, spooked to death by the runaway coffin. Right to the end my general showed everybody he was a tanks officer who fully realized the value of a surprise attack. It was only when he got over on the other side of the tree-lined alley that he dropped down through the gears. It was lucky the gate with the helmets on the pillars was open, or God knows what mightn't have happened.

'Down there the devil got into the six black artillery horses, who had been standin' thinking over what Magda had told 'em about my general. Off they went with the gun-carriage, and the two postillions who were sitting slumped half-asleep on the backs of the two lead-horses went flyin' off into the ditch. Where the hell the six blacks and the gun-carriage wound up I've no idea, but they made a nice thunderin' noise away in the distance.

'The Padre General and the Staff Padres sent up a quiet prayer, while the Adjutant wobbled his *mensur* scars, and the Chief-of-Staff talked to the bearer officers in a manner which left them in no doubt that they were on their way to a front-line battalion. It isn't *done* to throw a general around, on his way to the hero's table in Valhalla, like *that*!

'"They were holdin' that wooden jacket like a nun holdin' a seaman's," I said to an infantry Feldwebel, who was standing there alongside me chuckling with laughter.

'The Adjutant gave us a shellackin' and promised us we'd get to know him. A reserve bearer from tanks took the place of the artillery nance. He'd broke his foot, and was still lyin' up there in a privet hedge groaning.

'"Coffin, *lift*!" commanded the Chief-of-Staff. "Funeral *party*! Slo-o-ow *march*!" And off the procession started again with the regulation sad faces in place. The drummers from the Infantry Band rattled out that thing "*Argonner Wald um Mitternacht*"*. You could literally hear all the chalky military skeletons rattlin' to attention in their graves!

'Even in death my general showed his sense of style. He'd planned the whole burial himself, and it was certainly a funeral that'd be remembered. I've only heard of one that was better. That was an admiral's funeral where a bridge broke in two and the whole procession, box, sailors an' all,

---

* *Argonner Wald um Mitternacht:* The Argonne Forest at Midnight

fell into the Kiel Canal. Fifteen of 'em drowned an' the admiral sailed off out into Kiel Bay. There he run into a surfacin' submarine. The sub's crew was that frightened they fired on the admiral, thinking he was some new kind of secret weapon they'd collided with. The admiral went down with his coffin.

'"Call this a funeral?" groused the Divisional Chief Clerk, an overweight Staff Feldwebel. "It's more like a battle course with all the trimmings!"

'The procession had thought that my general would have selected a grave plot on the first hill, but they were wrong. After a short rest and an inspection of a view of snow-covered misery we struggled down the first hill, and up the next. Two of the mummy warriors had strokes on the way.

'The Pioneers from the *Landesschützen* stood to attention with shouldered spades and drawn faces. The hole they'd dug for my general was enormous. A special detachment had decorated the grave with oak branches and flowers in the national colours. The wreaths were enormous too; the biggest of them from *Grofaz*. The red scarf on it said: "The Führer thanks you!" It seemed a bit funny somehow, when you think it was the Führer that'd sent him suicidin' off to Valhalla by his own hand.

'The funeral procession ordered off according to regulations. Top hats to the left, and uniforms to the right.

'Up came the Padre General again. He waved his fingers at us, and made a kind of a salute. Then he ranged a firm, both military and religious eye, in on the dark clouds.

'"Our God in the highest," he began, folding his thievin' fingers on the hilt of the sabre, "receive this . . ." He didn't get any further. By then he'd begun to slide down into my general's hole.

'The Orderly Officer, a creeping Jesus, who we suspected of bein' a brownie, tried to stop the servant of God. Instead the perfumed officer went down into the hole with him. "Bang!" went the oak coffin. My general probably thought the artillery was usin' him to sight in on.

'The Pioneer soldiers began to laugh, but their laughter died away quick when the Adjutant booked the lot of 'em for front-line service.

'"So long mate!" I whispered to the bloke standin' nearest me. "You've lived most of your life! Enjoy what you've got left of it!"

'He whined a bit, and said it was all a load of shit. I wouldn't deny it.

'The Padre General'd got his balance again, and the Orderly Officer had been fished up. So the bishop started off on his sermon again. My general had been a very great soldier, he said. An example to us all. He had always been ready to pile up a heap of bodies on the altar of the Fatherland, and the bullet-riddled heroes were all waiting to receive their great leader at the gates of Valhalla. "I bet they've got their hands full of some hefty clubs, ready to welcome him with," I thought, kindly. But, of course, I didn't say it out loud.

'"This German warrior," bawled the Padre General, sanctimoniously, in a voice which frightened all the church-yard pigeons to flight, "was a truly believing person, who followed the words of the Gospel. He was an officer of the Kaiser as he was of the Führer! Oh, Jesus Christ!" he went jabbering on, saluting, "here we bring to You a soldier, a man of steel, who without thought of self carried out the heavy orders which were laid upon him by the Supreme Warlord. Oh God, receive him as the hero that he is!"

'All the generals nodded in satisfaction. The Chief-of-Staff rattled his sabre applaudingly, and the Adjutant showed all his teeth in a grin, and ordered his *mensur* scars by the right.

'The God of the Germans'll open his peepers all right when he meets my general, I thought. It won't be long before the whole of Paradise is made over into a tank manoeuvre area with all the trimmin's. God and His Son'll be hauling targets an' acting as markers; St Peter'll be on the cardboard clock and St Paul keeping check of the ammo, so's none of the angels get away with a couple of live 'uns. Well, anyway, now I know how I'll be spending my time in the Heavenly Halls!'

'How?' asks the Old Man, without understanding.

'It's obvious,' grins Gregor. 'I'll be my general's chauffeur again, of course, and get promoted to Feldwebel, soon as I kick it. I pinched the Divisional flag by the way, before I took off for the front. My general'll be really glad when I turn up with it as a dead 'un. I'm sure he'll forgive me, even, for once having washed an' ironed it.

'"On your knees in prayer," commanded the Padre General, and off we went praying, the lot of us. The Adjutant still managed to catch a couple of the bicycle fellers who weren't prayin'. They were amusing themselves talking about a game the Finns play called "the grenade game". A lot of Finns stand round in a ring and one of them pulls the pin of a grenade. Then they throw it from hand to hand. The bloke whose hand it explodes in has lost. It's a most exciting game, but you have to be a Finn to really get bit by it.

'With a lot of sweating and whispered cursing the Pioneers had managed to get the coffin up out of the hole again, so it could be let down properly with whirling drums and ranting bugles. Ta-ta-ta-ta! But there was no luck being handed out that day. The bugles were frozen stiff and all that came out of them was some hoarse noises, like owls make. They frightened the cemetery crows nearly to death.

'The Chief-of-Staff whispered something viciously, and the poor musicians got orders to swop their bugles with hand-grenades an' rifles. Off to the front for them, too!

'Well, they finally got hold of some warm bugles, that could be played on, and down went my general into the cold ground to the tune of "*Alte Kameraden*"*. Everything looked as if it was going all right, until some dope of an infantry Leutnant wanted to rub his hands together because the rope was chafing him.

* *Alte Kameraden:* Old Comrades

'BANG! came the hollow sound, and the box tipped up on its end down in the hole. The worst part was that the end came unjointed, and there was my general's pale face starin' up at us complainingly out of the bust-up coffin. The most amazing thing was our monocle, that it still remained in his eye. It must have been good glue I'd used.

'Some of the top-hat and black veil brigade crossed themselves, and the Padre General gave the Staff Padres a rollockin' as if it was their fault the coffin'd broken up.

'Down the Pioneers had to go into the hole again to get my general out, while the coffin was repaired. We laid him out on top of a granite memorial of some place or other where German blood had been poured out in rivers.

'Three carpenters from the Engineers under the command of a Field Works Supervisor came dashing up in a *Kübel*. They splashed out slush all over the *pickelhaubers*, the polished tin-hats and the silk cylinders. First the supervisor had to make a drawing. This was done all very shipshape and to scale, while the procession stood around dancin' up and down on their freezing toes. Most of 'em had lost their burial faces by now, and just looked thoroughly browned-off. Still it was a funeral nobody who took part'd ever forget.

'I laid a blanket over my general. He looked that cold lyin' there on the granite slab in dress uniform without a cape. I saluted him. Our monocle glittered and it was as if I felt a heavy blow on the top of my head. It must have been my dead general giving me an order.

'Finally the supervisor was finished making his plan, and the carpenters could get on with the repairs to the good-bye-box.

'While the infantry musicians rattled away on their drums they piloted my general back into his last quarters, and suddenly I realized what it was that was annoying him. I'd forgotten to *sing*! Oh, Hell! I thought and off I went to the head of the oak coffin where they'd placed the sword of honour and the cushion with the medals back in position again. And then I started off, and sang all five verses about

Death rushin' off on his black steed. It raised quite a bit of a commotion. Yes, even the leather-coated lot slunk a bit nearer. Everybody stared. The tin hats, the *pickelhaubers*, the black veils an' the silk toppers. I reckon they thought I'd gone off my head, but to be perfectly honest I don't think I sang it too badly, even though it had to go through a cloud of *Slivovitz*, and I may have swayed on my feet a bit now and then.

'The Adjutant and his *mensur* scars were standing there ready to jump on me, but I got through the five verses all right. When I'd got through 'em I managed to wait with the next swig of *Slivovitz* till I'd saluted and reported to the open coffin.

'"Orders executed, Herr General, *sir*!"

'Then I did a half turn in proper regimental fashion, and saluted the Adjutant and all his scars.

'"God's Peace!" I said.

'You should've seen his expression. His scars wriggled like a load of eels. Just for a minute I thought he was goin' to cut me down with his dress sword.

'Then I sneaked off, back of a privet hedge, and took a gulp of *Slivovitz*, to get me back to normal.

'My song caused a bit of a commotion in the big funeral procession.

'I could clearly hear they were talking about me. There was no doubt I'd gone into first place, with my solo song.

'"Shovels *up*!" the Chief-of-Staff commanded, but before the Pioneers could start shovelling a G-Staff Oberst went over and whispered in his ear.

'"Stop!" shouted the Chief-of-Staff. The Pioneers dropped their shovels as if they had become red-hot. The *salut d'honneur* had been forgotten, and up my general had got to come again out of his hole.

'After a bit everything was ready again, with the exception of the soldiers to fire off the salute. They'd gone off home in the meantime. An orderly doubled off to the grenadier barracks, and after a long, cold waiting period up comes a squad under the command of a Leutnant.

'There were a couple more minor accidents. A Gefreiter fell down into the grave, and his rifle went off and wounded a veiled lady. He got sent to the front too. Finally a volley went off with a bang, and down went my general into the hole. The Pioneers started shovellin' dirt, and it rattled down on to the lid of my general's coffin.

'I bet my general's thinking he's getting fired on by the enemy, I thought.

'"Almighty Father! Eternal German God!" sobbed the Staff Padres, "We Germans are yours for ever and ever. Amen!"

'And at last it was all over. The procession sloshed back through the wet snow. They left their funeral expressions behind them. All they were thinking of was hot coffee, fresh pastry and a drink to wash away all that sorrow.

'Some of 'em went on their arses on the way down the slippery path, but nobody noticed that but the ones it happened to. The funeral service was over. The leather-coated lot mixed in with the procession to pick up any loose talk that might help the enemy. They didn't want to get back to *Admiral Schröder Strasse* without somethin' to report.

'I saluted a German hedgehog that was sneaking over a couple of graves. "God's Peace," I said.

'Lord, how it did snow, and now it started to blow up too. I got a lift from the Field Works lot. Nobody on the staff'd have me along. I was a pariah!

'Down at the mouth, I went in to "The Red Duck", to wet my singin' organ again, and while I was having a highly treacherous talk to the landlord I suddenly realized my general had disappeared out of my life altogether. Everything was over between us. Never again would he give me a rollockin' for washing and ironing the flag, or whatever it was I'd been up to between our trips in the staff-car.

'The very next day I got my movement orders. The Adjutant came and handed them to me personally.

'"See you again, Unteroffizier Martin," he barked,

hypocritically, as I crawled up on the lorry to the other candidates for death who'd made a balls of it at my general's funeral.'

'Lord save us,' sighs the Old Man, 'there's not all that ceremony when one of us lot kicks the bucket for the highly beloved Fatherland!'

Letters arrive, and we forget the general's funeral. There are three letters for the Old Man. His wife, Liselotte, has been promoted to Chief Tram-Driver. It's a safer job during the air-raids, since there are more shelters close by. When you're an ordinary tram-driver you're not always close to a shelter when the bombs start falling. All this talk about alarms going off in good time is nothing but propaganda. Usually the sirens do not start to howl until the bombs begin to fall, and the way they bomb now there is not much chance of reaching a shelter alive. Earlier they just dropped their bombs anywhere. Nowadays they pick out an area and flatten it to the ground. Even the rats get wiped out.

Heide is astonished to find that there is also a letter for him.

'Heil Hitler,' he mumbles, reverently, when he realizes it is from the Gauleiter of the Rhineland himself. He holds it up for us to see the over-dimensioned shiny party eagle. With the reverence of a Pope leafing through the Bible, he opens the envelope.

'At last! At last!' he is jubilant. 'They've given me the Black Eagle! And about time, too!'

'Black Eagle?' asks Porta. 'Where the devil we goin' to keep an eagle?'

'Idiot!' snarls Heide. 'It's a Party Order, one of the highest, too.' He holds up the document triumphantly in front of Porta's nose. 'What d'you say to that? Like one, wouldn't you?'

'No, thank you very kindly,' says Porta. 'It could cost me a snapped neck when the neighbours turn up an' Adolf and his party's part of the past!'

'I'm warning you,' hisses Heide, like an angry cat which

has had its tail trodden on. 'With this order I'm letting nothing pass! Anybody who insults the party goes on report!'

'The salad come with it?' asks Tiny, leaning forward inquisitively.

'No, that'll be along through regiment,' answers Heide, proudly. 'The CO'll decorate me with it personally!'

'I've heard they're hard at work, stamping 'em out day and night,' grins Porta. '25 marks for 100 kgs, an' the Gauleiters can shove 'em out in bucketfuls.'

'Obergefreiter Creutzfeldt!' shouts the clerk, throwing a letter over to Tiny. 'Gawd struth!' cries Tiny, holding the letter as if it was a grenade with the pin out, and sniffing at it cautiously. 'Who in the name of 'Ell'd be crazy enough to write to *me*?'

'You'll find out easy enough if you open it,' laughs Porta.

With a thick, dirty finger and tears the envelope open clumsily, and unfolds the greasy bundle of writing-paper inside it. For some time he sits staring at the pencilled scrawl on the cheap paper.

''Ere, you read it for me, will you?' he asks, handing it to the Old Man. 'My eyes aren't all that good today. All the shit there is in the air in this Commie country ruins a man's eyesight.'

The Old Man packs his silver-lidded pipe phlegmatically, and lets his eyes run along the closely-written lines. He shakes his head. 'What a family you *have* got!'

'Who's it from?' asks Tiny, staring at the letter.

'Your sister,' answers the Old Man, beginning to read aloud:

Obergefreiter loader Wolfgang Ewald Creutzfeldt
FPO no 23645
The German Defence Forces
Russia.

Dear Brother,

You mustnt think I like you because I start my letter with Dear and Brother. You are a drunk-Wolfgang – everybody says so. I am writing this to let you know you have no reason to go round happily thinking your youngest sister Emilie Louise Bock-Creutzfeldt as used to be – has been killed dead by some of the stuff the English and the other *untermensch* lot are dropping on Hamburg just now.

Mom's still alive too. You can bet your boots on it but she dont know you any more and I wasnt to send you none of her love. I know how hard it is for you to read letters. So Im writing this one very slowly sos you wont get confused when you read it. Im looking forward to it coming back sos Ill know your dead.

Your a rotten dirty pig thats what you are. Everybody here says the fightings hot in Russia and theyve all had somebody in the family shot. Mom was dead certain youd got blowed up too by one of them shells they shoot all over the place out there. But as usual you do us in the eye. We have not forgot the time you pinched all the money out of the gas meter and the coppers came from Davids Station along with the gas collector and were going to arrest Mom.

We was very disappointed I can tell you when the NSFO as has moved in to the old cloth museum back of the Main Railway Station you know it that big grey place with the old Kaisers eagles on it where you and David pinched the curtains when we wanted to do the place up a bit – when he told us you had not come to any harm in the war. Mom collapsed with disappointment when she heard and she cried an awful lot too. Shed been working out what her pension would be after you. The NSFO comforted her and said he was sure youd soon get yourself shot and he gave her an extra butter ration and some bread coupons.

I am sorry to have to write this letter me being your sister and all to tell you your a no-good that nobody really ought to write to at all. If you ever come to Hamburg again and ride the U to Altona – as I hope you never do do – you wouldnt never know our place again. Were moved out to Langenhorn on the other side of the SS barracks. Theres always a lot going on there. If we look out the windows early in the morning we can see them shooting traitors and such-like to death. When there aint any traitors to shoot they practise at cardboard figures so we dont need an alarm clock any more which is a lucky thing because our old one has stopped going. They begin shooting at five every morning and thats our time for getting up.

I am still cleaning on the trains and getting a free ride while Im cleaning. I have been made a State Railway Cleaning Assistant second class and have blue braid on my shoulder. I am allowed to eat with the five that work in the post waggon now.

I was in Dusseldorff last week. I had it off with a Supply Corps bloke as give me 20 marks to do it with him. We went into the toilet in the first class. You wouldnt believe how posh they are. Herbert Bock my husband and your brother-in-law – though I have to tell you from him that he wont have it your being his brother-in-law – so remember that. Theres that many blots in your copybook that nice people wont belong in the same family as you. Well anyway my husband Herbert Bock has got a new job with a uniform and two stars on his collar and a navy blue hat with a cockade on it and a lot of people under him. Hes looking after a churchyard. There is not a lot to do even though he is the only one there. All the people he used to work with have been called up and have gone off to help win the war.

Do you remember Limpy Egon? It was him you and the fur Jews son David was always with when you were on the streets doing unlegal things. Hed got a new job at the Hansa Breweries and then he died. Drank himself to death they called it. He got dizzy looking down into one of them big beer vats and fell into it. But he couldnt never keep away from the drink. They do say the beer tastes better since Limpy fell down into it.

You havent ever in all your life seen as much rain as weve been having in Hamburg for the last nine weeks and three days and all the accidents that have happened. Here they are then. The Elbe went up over the red line and thats you and your mates fault. We have got no lifeboats. You took them all with you to Russia. It isnt right you taking everything off to Russia with you and us having to do without at home. Were Germans too you know and just as good as you soldiers. The Führer keeps on saying were a *Herrenvolk*. Up you Jack. I reckon Germanys the arsehole of the universe and theres a lot more as says the same. To be honest with you Wolfgang you ought to get up and show theres some good in you. Tell your mates to stop this stupid war. You can do it if you want to. The parson said you could. You know him, the bloke that goes knocking on doors with the word. I can't remember what hes called. Something foreign but who cares anyhow. Stadthausbrucke 8 picked him up so we wont be seeing or hearing his Bible words no more. But it was barmy of him to be a traitor. The Führer dont like that kind of thing.

The other day me and Emma found one of them secret papers the ones your not supposed to read but we read it anyway. A persons only human after all. It said in it that the German soldiers ought to just go over and make pals with the Russians and the whole world war would be over. Remember now to tell your mates about it. But dont let nobody from the party hear you saying it. Now the secret paper dont come any more. Them who was writing it have got picked up by Stadthausbrucke too.

207

They got their legs broke before they got shot. It must hurt a lot to get your legs broke. Do you remember when I broke my little finger? It did hurt and it must be a lot worse to break a whole leg. You have to watch your tongue here if you dont want your legs broke and your head cut off after. Im going to be careful to say Heil Hitler to everybody. Then they cant say I aint faithful.

Things are happening all the time here in Hamburg and so we dont have to worry about what to do to pass the time with. Last night we had five warnings and the Martens that live in Altona got a bomb right in the middle of their bed. Lucky for them it was cause the Gestapo turned up an hour later to pinch them. They were very annoyed that there wasnt nobody to pinch. Them English ought to have been a bit more careful.

Our sister Eva says too its better to get killed than picked up alive by the Gestapo and our sister knows what shes on about. Shes gone up in the world she has and has got a job wiping the dust off the desks at Stadthausbrücke 8 where she sees things your not supposed to. She saw a bloke being interviewed they call it the other day. First they broke all his fingers then they pulled the nails off his toes. Then they whipped him with steel wire and put electric current through him that he had to pay for himself. They put everything on the bill says Eva so it must cost a bit to get arrested. Then this bloke fell out of the window from the fourth floor. He must have come down head first cause it was all bashed out of shape and nearly crushed. He got to pay for the window he broke too.

Our sister Trudy – you know her that was born in the milk shop – shes had a nipper but she cant remember whose it is. She never said if it was a boy or a girl so I cant tell you if your an aunt or an uncle.

The Baumüllers over in Altona have had a wedding. We went to it and never sobered up til after Easter. It was their lodger Long Hans that got married but the Gestapo came for him and they say hes dead now. His name was on the red posters they stick up all over the place when somebody gets his head chopped off at Fuhlsbüttel. It was the funniest party I ever went to. Long Hans never got married but he had a lovely *Polterabend*. Hed have been happy about it still if he hadnt got his head chopped off in the meantime. We all went off on bikes to the Louise on the Reeperbahn. Us girls sat on the crossbars cause there wasnt enough bikes to go round. There was two that got run over by a tram. They got killed. Then there was one that fell down a cellar stairs on his bike. He got killed too. His bike was ruined but lucky for him it was one he had pinched. One of them got himself caught in the door of the elevator to the Elbe tunnel. He wasnt really with us just a gate-crasher he was. But he was lucky. He was going that fast he went straight into the Elbe elevator. His bike hadnt got no brakes on it. If hed stopped a No 1 tram that was coming rushing down the hill from Fischmarkt would have killed him stone dead.

We was over at The Louise about seven. I know Ive got the time right cause my gent had his wristwatch on and said it was seven and it was a good watch as had once belonged to a Jew.

Us ladies got champagne and cherry wine. I drunk a whole bottle and got that happy I forgot about Wolfgang and all my other sorrows. The gents drunk Bummelunder* and beer from the time they come in the door til the coppers turned up from David Station.

Jensen from Hansa Platz 7 got into a row with the bridegroom. They pulled their knives and the bridegroom cut Jensens nose off. How he did bleed but we were that happy we didnt care. Then Jensen cut the bridegrooms hair off and he bled even more.

Then we had a bit of a dance and had some more champagne and cherry wine. Then the knives come out

* Bummelunder: South Jutland schnapps

again. Emmy her with the glass eye got her ears cut off. It didnt suit her a bit. The bridegroom went right off his nut after hed drunk a whole bottle of Bummelunder with beer in it. He lost his mind altogether and started swinging a long knife round over his head. Hes some kind of a foreigner from Austria. You must excuse me but if I was to meet the Führer Id ask him if he couldnt keep all these foreigners out of the country. They do nothing but make trouble. But we probably wont ever meet. People who get up on top of the tree dont remember where they came from.

Then the bulls come running from the David. Theyd got helmets on with straps under their chins so we couldnt knock them off. What a row there was. There was no windows left in The Louise after cause a lot of the coppers and guests left that way and all the chairs was broken cause of people sitting down too hard on them. Then they started throwing the tables at the tecs but the Flying Squad turned up and put a stop to the party. The kitchen was all smashed up and there was never a pot or pan left without a dent in it. So then they arrested us and took us all over to David and there we sung that loud they could hear us down at Landungsbrücke and people come running down to see what was going on. There *was* a crowd.

Detective-inspector Nass called us all sorts of things and nearly went crazy. Outside the whole Reeperbahn was singing and inside the wedding party was singing but nobody was singing the same song. If you dont all shut up soon Im finished with you lot shouted Detective-inspector Nass. Then they took us in in groups and questioned us.

You got no nose said Mr Nass to Mr Jensen. The man who cut that off must be punished. Thats been seen to inspector said Mr Jensen. It was that Austrian bridegroom but its all fixed up. Ive got his prick in my pocket.

Well later on the whole wedding party met in the jail. It wasnt too bad. They still have single cells but nobodys in them on their own. The prisons are that full up there aint hardly room for the warders. We got *ersatz* coffee with powdered milk and some army bread. Two slices apiece with a spoonful of turnip jam. There was a lot there could tell about things you never heard of usual. Well we got out again but not all of us. I dont know where them as didnt get out went to but nobodys heard of them since. Everybody at home sends their good wishes and Mom says your to do something brave for the Führer and the Fatherland. If you get a big medal your pension will be bigger when you get shot. You could at the least do that much for Mom and dont forget your not part of my husbands family.

> Goodbye for now
> Your sister
> Emilia Louise Bock born Creutzfeldt
> State Railways Cleaning Assistant
> Hamburg/Altona

'That brother-in-law as is married to my sister Emilie an' won't be related to me can just wait till I get 'ome,' growls Tiny viciously. ''E'd do well to count 'is bones, so's 'e'll know which of 'em's missin' afterwards!'

We have only been asleep a short while when the company orderly comes rushing in to tell the Old Man he's to report to the OC immediately.

'Heavenly posting for you,' he grins, maliciously. 'This time you're going to get your backsides burnt proper. The order's from right up top, and it got TOP SECRET stamped all over it, back and sides.'

'What the devil's up now?' growls the Old Man sourly, pulling on his ankle-length winter cloak, and swinging his machine-pistol over his shoulder.

'Clear as mud,' grins Porta, scratching at his pigeon breast with both hands. That's where the lice have a tendency to hold their get-togethers. 'It's Sally at the War

Ministry who's pushing all the buttons needed to get us off on our private gold-prospecting mission. Put your warm woollens on, my boys! It's goin' to get very cold, cold as all Hell, before we get home again with our gold.'

'Here goes the curtain for the first act,' says the Old Man, when he comes back. 'The official order says we're to cause disturbance and create panic behind the enemy lines, and we're to bring a General Skulowsky back with us, whoever the guy is!'

'Create panic! We'll do that all right,' says Porta, laughing shortly. 'But who the devil's this General Stinkanovitch? We can ask our way, anyhow. Maybe my bint's feller knows him!'

'And remember. All this stuff's TOP SECRET,' the Old Man goes on. 'Our heads an' necks both are on the line if anything leaks out! We're not even to talk about it amongst ourselves. "War Minister" Sally must've used up all the ink in the ministry stampin' TOP SECRET on everything. Field-Marshal Keitel's name's on the bottom of the order, only he don't know it, and the plan's been made by Field-Marshal Walter Model, who doesn't know anything about it either.'

'*Cojones*! They'll shoot us three times over if they ever find out,' sighs Barcelona, nervously. 'But they do say the cheekier you are the better things go for you!'

'If this goes the way we want it, I'm goin' to buy a big medal for Sally,' roars Tiny, slapping himself happily on the thighs.

In the course of the night we were issued with Russian uniforms, and the tanks painted with red stars and cyrillic lettering.

'If Ivan Stinkanovitch gets his claws into us, we'll have had the most of our lives already,' says Barcelona, gloomily.

It is snowing heavily, and visibility is no more than a couple of yards, when we load the tanks on to runners. Horses are to draw them through the Russian lines to avoid the rattle of tracks and the noise of the motors.

Snarling MPs keep everybody away from the secret transport.

'Miserable way to go,' sighs Porta, watching a couple of MPs drag off a civilian who has been a little too inquisitive.

It is only when we have got a good way over on the far side of the river that we remove the German transfers and the Russian signs come into view. DEATH TO THE FASCISTS is written in large cyrillic letters on the Panther's turret.

'*Job Tvojemadj*,' grunts Tiny, sticking out his chest like a second Ivan the Terrible.

'Watch out now. NO Commie fists!' the Old Man warns them. 'Here they salute just like we do. They're very touchy about that in the Red Army. It's only civilians who clench their fists and shout Red Front!'

*Wir waren einfach, weil das Volk einfach ist.
Wir dachten primitiv, weil das Volk primitiv
denkt. Wir waren agressiv, weil das Volk radikal
ist.** *

Joseph Goebbels

He opened the breech, threaded in a new belt of cartridges, and smacked the cover back on.

'Bloody shit,' he said. 'Can you hear 'em.'

'Tanks,' answered his no 2. 'You got any bread? I'm hungry as hell. Haven't had a bite for the last two days. Bloody, rotten war!'

'Ate the last I had this morning,' replied the machine-gunner, 'and that was a bit I found on a body!'

'We're not even worth a crumb of bread,' growled the no 2. 'They chase us like we were rats. Tell us to hold out! What for? So's those shits can save their own lives!'

'Shit the lot of it' said the machine-gunner, staring at the rows of ruins. 'Now they don't even give us grub any more. We have to steal it where we can find it. It's a wonder we got a bit of ammo dished out this morning!'

'That's the way it always goes,' answered the no 2, pulling his coat collar up round his ears. 'Ammunition they can give us, but food's quite another thing!'

'What do you say we knock off for good? Now! Change FPOs! Ivan can't be as bad as they say. Anyway it can't be worse over there than it is here!'

They both got to their feet, threw their MG into a stream, and went crouching forward slowly across the stubbled field.

An MG snarled in short bursts.

The no 2 was hit first. Then the machine-gunner was thrown across the wreck of a vehicle. A flock of crows flew up from the ruins, cawing harshly.

---

* *We remain simple, while the people remains simple. Our thinking is primitive, when the people's thinking is primitive. We become aggressive, when the people become radical.*

MEETING WITH THE COMMISSARS

The wind howls miserably through the stretched-out ruins of what has been, not long ago, a whole new *kolchos**. Now it is an untidy heap of collapsed walls and grotesquely bent steel girders. The frozen, half-burned bodies of its animal stock lie scattered about. War in all its wild ferocity has swept over the *kolchos*, and razed it to the ground with one satanic breath.

Three soot-blackened T-34s stand in the flattened orchard. Icicles cover them. Their crews are hanging half out of the hatches, blackened and burnt.

The Old Man is first out of the section personnel carrier. He looks about him, carefully. It is dangerous to feel oneself to be safe. Death lurks everywhere.

'Drive the waggon well in under the trees,' he orders Porta, who has his foxy, freckled face up out of the hatchway, sniffing the air.

'Jesus, but it's *cold*!' he says, his teeth chattering. He blows warm breath up along the sides of his face. 'It's colder than a polar bear's arse!'

The snow squeaks under the Old Man's boots, as he goes teetering up the icy path. He pulls the fur collar of his coat up around his ears, and turns his back to the biting wind, which tears at the stiff material of his camouflage jacket. He has a couple of stick-grenades in the tops of his boots, but this is no cause for suspicion. Russian front-line troops like to get hold of German stick-grenades. They throw better, even though the absence of a safety attachment

* Russian collective farm

makes them more dangerous. Once the cord has been pulled there is no way back. You've got just seven seconds left before it goes off, whether you like it or not.

The Old Man stops at the edge of a steep cliff and tugs the broad yellow leather belt with the long *Nagan* holster into place, irritably.

'Oh, how bloody *cold* it is,' whines Porta, banging his blue hands together. 'I'm glad I'm not a Russian and have to live here all my life.'

'Get the map out,' orders the Old Man. 'This has to be the rendezvous. The white *kolchos* has got to be those ruins, though there's not much white about 'em any more!'

'Who the hell *did* do that?' asks Porta, wonderingly. 'The war hasn't got to these parts yet! The enemy's a long way off! We're the first Germans here, and we're not the real enemy. We're just here to pick up something which legally belongs to us!'

'Flying bombs, I guess,' says the Old Man. He puts the heavy artillery glasses to his eyes. Silently he stares up at the long winding mountain road, which disappears in mist and driving snow high up amongst the storm-bent trees.

'Want us to put the tea-waggon in under cover?' shouts Tiny. His voice echoes in the ruins and rings back a hundred fold from the mountains.

'Shut it!' shouts the Old Man, nervously. 'They'll be able to hear you in Moscow!'

'Yes, but listen 'ere,' shouts Tiny, even louder. 'If we let this fartin'-box stand 'ere puttin' down roots d'you think Ivan Stinkanovitch will believe we're some of his mates?'

'Leave it there,' snarls the Old Man, irritably. 'But hide everything else and camouflage it. *Thoroughly*!'

Heide swaggers around importantly in the uniform of a Russian lieutenant, but despite the uniform nobody can have the least doubt that he is a German. He is far too correct. No Russian in his senses would think of going around looking like him. He has even cut away the long hairs in the grey-brown fur of his cap so that the large red star with its gold edges can be seen to greater effect.

'Get a sight of Ivan?' asks Porta, rubbing the snow from his eyes.

'Shut it, for God's sake,' snarls the Old Man sourly, polishing the lenses of the artillery glasses before again putting them to his eyes.

'There's a three-axled truck up there with a 76 on the back of it. There's something wrong with this set-up. It smells like a trap!'

'They wouldn't bloody be bothered,' says Porta, indifferently. 'Who in the world'd want to trap shits like us?'

'You never know with Ivan,' mumbles the Old Man, thoughtfully, continuing to stare intently through the glasses. 'Those devils don't think the way we do. They're an unaccountable lot of sods!'

'Give me that!' says Porta, tearing the glasses out of his hand. 'What the hell's the matter with you, letting an old Ford truck scare the shit out of you?'

'I know that gun,' answers the Old Man pessimistically. 'It's got a muzzle velocity like all get-out, and its shells can penetrate any armour in the world.'

'Weep on my shoulder,' suggests Porta. 'An explosive shell from our new 75 mm an' that peashooter can stick its muzzle up Stalin's arsehole, velocity an' all, and shit the casings out in granny's apron.'

'When we gonna start creatin' confusion?' asks Tiny impatiently, throwing a lump of ice over the edge of the cliff.

'What do you think we *are* doing?' answers Porta. 'You're screaming loud enough to give 'em earache in the Kremlin! And stop talking German in the neighbours' backyard, will you! It's dangerous!'

'Go shit! Everybody talks what 'e's born to,' snarls Tiny. 'I can't talk foreign!'

'Got us out here on a wild-goose chase again have you?' says Heide, with a malicious triumph. 'What did I tell you?'

'*I* can tell *you* that this caper's bang on,' says Porta,

217

raising the glasses to his eyes again. 'It's a dead certainty this time! And the prize is that big it's worth taking a risk for.'

'Last time it wound up as usual, with us empty-handed and standing there staring like a herd of dumb cattle,' says Heide, cantankerously.

'Was that my fault?' protests Porta, sourly. 'We ran into a couple of bits of bad luck. My plan was genial!'

'The plan was all right,' Heide admits, 'but all we got out of it was disappointment. All that was needed was for us all to have got shot. But this time the risk is considerably greater.'

'No battle, no victory!' says Porta, swinging the binoculars demonstratively in the air.

'If it goes wrong this time, I'll never listen to a plan of yours again,' snarls Heide.

'Listen here. Every sensible feller's goin' round waiting for the real big un'!' explains Porta.

'There's always something that goes wrong with your plans,' hisses Heide, angrily.

'You make me tired,' says Porta, giving him a wicked look. 'If you want to spend the rest of your life in Russia in company with a machine-pistol, all you need to do is to withdraw from this party.'

'Try, for the devil's sake, to keep your mouths shut for once!' the Old Man scolds them, viciously. 'A man can't hear himself think with all that crazy chatterin' goin' on!'

'Let's get under cover, *amigos*,' says Barcelona, shivering in the icy wind. It comes howling down from the mountain-tops, whipping razor-sharp crystals of ice into our uncovered faces. The cold bites through even the thick felt boots, making our toes ache.

The bitter wind is getting up to storm velocity. A deadly dangerous Russian winter storm may be on its way.

'We'll have to make snow-masks,' decides the Old Man. 'Make 'em out of camouflage stuff. Ordinary cloth gets wet and is worse than nothing. Barcelona, you put out sentries!'

'Why's it always have to be us?' protests Barcelona, stamping his feet in the snow to get the circulation going.

'Because I say so,' replies the Old Man, brusquely.

'Shit an' shankers!' barks Barcelona angrily. 'If I hadn't been through a real Prussian unteroffizier school where they teach you to eat old socks and look as if you like 'em I wouldn't bloody well accept this, I wouldn't!'

'What a lot of piss!' grumbles Albert. He is piling large blocks of snow one on top of the other. 'Why don't we just get inside the waggons and let the motors warm us up instead of workin' ourselves into the ground buildin' igloos?'

'You must have hit that black head of yours when you fell out of the tree,' sneers Porta. 'It costs fuel to keep the motors running, and if Ivan lets us down, we won't have all that much of it left to get home on again.'

'Start up every fifteen minutes,' orders the Old Man. 'The Devil help the driver whose motor freezes! It's 44 degrees below!'

The starting motors are already dead. All they give us is a long, hoarse, complaining moan. Even with the big starting handles we cannot get a response from them. Everybody helps to collect brushwood so that we can start a fire under the vehicles. The frost has turned the oil to a thick, doughy mass. The Old Man does not need to chase us. The thought of going back is in itself enough to speed us up.

'You idle pigs,' he rages. 'How often haven't I told you rotten lot to start your motors up at least every thirty minutes? Do I have to do every bloody thing myself? What the hell are we going to do if we have to take off in a hurry?'

'Grab on to the exhausts, an' slide on our bleedin' elbows,' laughs Tiny, noisily. 'It's slippy enough 'ere for it any road!'

Albert goes down flat on his face, and two large blocks of ice slip away from him. Only a stunted bush prevents him from going over the edge of the cliff. Furiously he gets up and kicks out at an invisible enemy. His feet slide from under him, and he goes down again.

'Don't count on me much longer,' he whines, and crawls up into the T-34 to make another attempt to start. To his great satisfaction the heavy Otto motor roars into top revolutions immediately. 'When you know your way around motors . . .' he boasts, looking triumphantly over at Porta, who is having trouble with the Panther's Maybach.

'German *shit*,' he hisses. 'Pretty enough to look at, but shit-all good on the job.' He kicks the instrument panel in vicious rage. After a long period of trying the motor finally begins to roar.

'What about the sentries?' asks the Old Man, as we huddle up together in the igloo.

'All in order!' declares Barcelona, snuggling down between the Legionnaire and Albert.

'Funny thing, but I happened to think of a certain Major-general Rottweiler just now,' says Porta, shaking a Juno cigarette out of its green packet. 'Not to be mixed up with the very well-known Herr Rottweiler from Hannover, who bred the Rottweiler police dog. The general wasn't even related to the dog-Rottweiler seller. They didn't either of them even know the other existed, and the general couldn't stand the sight of a Rottweiler police dog, because one of the black beasts had bit him once. It all started with a bicycle, one of the well-known Opel bikes from Bielefeld that only the upper classes roll round on. This Opel bike was standing up against the wall of the general's house one day, doin' nothing at all, and taking no notice of a big sign which said:

PLACING OF CYCLES HERE
STRICTLY FORBIDDEN

'Well, when the general got back from a court-martial he'd been holding where he'd condemned a deserter to death, and saw this bike, he was so angry he had an attack of hiccoughs. He screwed his monocle fast in his eye to make quite certain there really was a civilian bike parked up against his general's wall, and when he realized his military eye hadn't been foolin' him, he give out a lot of funny noises and changed the colour of his face. Then he made a quick strategic decision, attacked the bike, and threw the civilian shit into the park on the other side of the road. Back it came straight away. It was a park inspector who'd bunged it back again. You could just see his uniform cap above the top of the wall.

'"What the devil?" roared the general and he gave that park inspector a rollockin' of dimensions.

'With a lot of cursing and swearing he got the bike up into the regulation position for bicycles, and gave it a hefty push that sent it rolling along riderless down the hill towards the Soester crossroads. There it crashed into one of the post office's red bicycles, which was carrying reserve postman Grünstein, so that both of them were on duty. Grünstein wasn't carrying ordinary post that day, but secret post, sealed and registered and goin' from one Gestapo office to another. Herr Grünstein fell on his backside with a crash, and a treacherous gust of wind took all the letters and blew 'em all over the place. But it was much worse what happened next. Out of the park came a black-an'-brown Rottweiler police dog with its jaws lollin' open, just as the general was on his way in through his garden gate, which had eagles decorating it.

'"Bow-wow!" went the dog, an' brought its well-furnished jaws together on the general's fat rump.

'The general gave out a shrill scream, which did not quite fit in with all the medals for bravery which decorated his broad chest. He lost his grip on the gate and sprang into cover in the garden faster than any recruit. The cast-iron gate banged to behind him with a crash which almost made the Prussian eagles' beaks fall off.

'He looked cautiously out into the road to see who it was

221

that had taken out half the seat of his trousers, but there was nobody in sight. As you probably know, these Rottweilers're dreadfully cunning devils, and this one was not a backward member of its race. It'd nipped smartly in by the back door to continue its attack from a more strategically advantageous point.

'This time the battle was rougher. Not only the rest of the arsepart of the general's trousers went, but also a nice chunk o' the general's rump. Everything stopped though, as suddenly as it had begun, when the dog's owner turned up and called it to him with a whistle.

'"*Good* dog!" he said, patting the black devil. The general got slowly up on to his riding boots. "This is going to be an expensive matter for you, sir," he fumed. He rubbed his wounded rump: "That wild beast there is going to be *shot*!"

'"You don't seem to know who I am," roared the dog-owner, straightening himself up, "but you soon will do! I hope you're not off to the front line right away, general?"

'The general began to shout an' scream then, and asked what business it was of a civilian's what the German Army's generals did.

'"Who knows? Perhaps you are also an enemy spy?" he said, threateningly. Whole regiments of execution squads started glitterin' in his eyes, and a smile curled his lips: "I can tell you, sir, that that kind of question is one which often gives away the enemy espionage system. Let us take an example. If I was careless enough to tell you that I was going to the front on Tuesday the enemy would know immediately that 191 Jaeger Division was going into the line. One or two more of such innocent questions, and the enemy General Staff would know exactly where that division would be employed." The general pointed accusingly at the dog's owner: "And because of your regular activities, Herr Mole, the enemy already knows all about the 191st. That the men are from Sibengebirge, from which district come useful soldiers, faithful and dutiful, born infantrymen, who could be called to the flag as fifteen or sixteen-year-olds if need be. They do not have a lot of brains, but for that very reason they make extremely good infantrymen. To be sure there are not many of them left alive after a war, but that proves that that part of the country produces good soldiers. When the enemy General Staff gains possession of information of that nature, they immediately strengthen their lines, not with *one* division but with *three* elite divisions. If it had been a Berlin division, or a beerbarrel crowd from Munich, then firing off their mortars a little would have been enough to send such asphalt cowboys back to their beer-halls.

'"I saw through you straightaway, Herr Spy," he continued. "I am the Chief of the Military Counterespionage Service here in VI Military District, and I have sent a great many of your kind in front of the military courts. One careless question, and you villains stand tied to the execution post. *You* are under *arrest*!"

'"Now you've gone too far, general! You're not going to get away with that," shouted the dog's owner. "I'm a party member in good standing, and with a low number! I was in Munich." He banged himself on the chest. "I have sat alongside the Führer *twice* in *Bürgerbrau*. What d'you say to *that*?" He gave the Nazi salute, with fingertips exactly aligned with his right eye. "In 1923 I marched in the third row behind His Excellency General Ludendorff! I am a holder of the Blood Order! I'm not that easy to muck about with! I'd also like to know since when Army generals have started stealing bicycles? Do you know what it costs to steal a bike?"

'"Are you stark, staring mad?" roared the general, rattling his sabre and spurs.

'"No, but you are," said the dog-owner, with a sardonic smile.

'By this time a crowd had collected outside the general's eagle-decorated garden gate. The inquisitive stretched their necks to see what was going on, and laughed with pleasure.

'This disturbed the combatants, of course, so the general invited the Rottweiler and its owner inside, to continue the discussion without outside advice and interference.

'The dog's owner wasn't a normal, stupid person, and could talk nicely about most anythin'. He dealt on the Stock Market, too, and knew a good deal about foreign currency. He thought it would be only polite to introduce himself.

'"Strange," he bowed, clicked his heels and lifted his right arm. "Potato wholesaler, and barley exporter; party member; holder of the Blood Order. Heil Hitler!"

'The general growled a bit, but didn't consider it was necessary to introduce himself. He thought that any bloody fool, including a potato wholesaler living in that Westphalian hole in the ground Paderborn, ought to know who he was. It was people's duty, he believed, to know him!

'"Be so good as to take a seat, Herr Strange," he barked, with false friendliness, offering a gold cigarette-case with the German eagle engraved on it.

'Party member and potato wholesaler Strange scrabbled a cigarette out of the case, but had to light it himself.

'Anybody can understand that,' smiles Porta. 'Where'd we all be if this dog-lovin' spud-basher was only a demobbed Leutnant of the reserve who'd been sent home because he had his party-book in order. Or, maybe, an Unteroffizier, or even a lousy rifle-carrier? That low, a German Army general couldn't ever sink. Better make it look like forgetfulness on his part.

'For a bit everything was quiet. Like the lull they talk about before the storm. They just sat there watching the smoke spirallin' up from the general's cigar and the party member's cigarette.

'"Have you thought, general," the potato feller started off at last, "that it's about time we got moving and *won* this war? We can't go on overlooking slackness. Potato exports've practically stopped." He looked challengingly from the

224

general to the Rottweiler. The dog had stretched itself out comfortably on a lionskin in front of the fire. It was all that was left of a poor rheumatic lion the general'd shot in Africa while he was hangin' around waiting for World War II to start up. "Things look black to me, general, *very* black. Out of the few loads of potatoes one can get hold of, from good connections, 50 per cent have to be handed over to the damned Army, who pay bottom prices. Prices set by a group of sour-gutted civil servants in the Ministry of Food. People who can't even write proper German, but use a kind of idiotic civil servant language of their own. They should leave everything to the SS Reichsführer and throw the remains of the rotten monarchy on to the muckheap! It makes a man despair of life, general! I have written to the Führer, but received no reply. We win and win, but none of our victories *get* us anywhere! Barley I never see any more and potatoes are fewer and fewer. Give us a great, blood-soaked victory, and get it over with so's a man can begin to do business again. Like we were forced to do by Jewish high finance before the war. Look at the great victory we're winning just at present! The whole of 4 Panzer Army's sitting down in the woods along the Oka, where they're letting themselves get shot up by the Bolshie guns, and regiments, battalions and companies are being smashed to bits and spread out all over the delta marshes. And d'you know what people say? They say that no matter which way you look the whole sky is on fire. In every direction. Villages and towns are being laid waste too, so as there's nothing left of them but piles of ashes. But that's not what I'm really bothered about. War's *like* that. Tough and manly. Not for namby-pamby people! I learnt all about that in my twelve months at the volunteer school!" As he said this the party member an' spud dealer jumped to his feet and bowed politely to the general.

'"Beg humbly to report, Herr General, sir, one-year volunteer Strange, Leonhard, 33, Prussian Infantry Regiment, 6th Brandenburgers, discharged from active service by reason of potatoes and barley!" He fell back into the leather chair, a gruesome, antique monster with a back so uncomfortable that it was something only a masochist could love.

'"I don't complain at guns being fired off, towns being burned and people being killed. That's what war's *about*!" "Spuds an' barley," he went on, waving a fresh cigarette around in the air, "but the worst thing is those accursed artillerymen, that go shooting one distillery after another into ruins. What have the distilleries done to *them* to make them turn their rotten cannons on the *distilleries*?" He lugged a thick note-book from his pocket, shaking with anger. "Listen to this, general. I'm beginning to feel this whole world war is aimed specially at ruining me!" He wets his fingers and turns the pages. "'Red Star' at Kiev – took 185 tons of potatoes – razed to the ground; 'Fatherland's Oasis', Minsk – 200 tons potatotes *and* 100 tons barley – shot to bits. These *untermensch* owe me for the last two deliveries! What about the insurance? *Force Majeure*! Not a sausage back for all those high premiums!

'"Will the mighty German Army cover my losses? Excuse me, general, it was just a passing thought. Here's the 'Golden Eagle', Kharkov – good solid business – runs night and day the year round – the manager was a lovely chap. His wife's name was Wilma – always off to some spa she was. Nerves, general. Easy for *them* to get shot – nerves I mean – when you live in the Soviet Union, where the state can decide what colour your bedroom wallpaper's got to be, and can dip its greedy fingers into your pockets whenever it gets the fancy. Almost as bad as it is here!" Herr Strange put his hands to his mouth in fear, as he realized what he had said. He jumped from the masochist chair in confusion, stuck out his right arm and roared: "Heil Hitler!"

'The general gave a forced smile, and looked out of the corners of his eyes at the Rottweiler on the lionskin. It seemed to be amused at its master's disloyal remark. All its teeth were showing.

'"The day before yesterday I found, to my dismay, that eight distilleries had been burned to the ground. Honestly, general, if it goes on like this much longer, we'll *all* go bankrupt, and *I'll* be totally ruined. Who in the devil's name'll buy potatoes and barley when there's no distilleries left?"

'"Aren't you looking a little too much on the dark side of things?" asked the general, and suggested their taking a glass of something. "Our position is quite good just now. The German divisions are rolling victoriously over the Russian steppe. I will admit that a distillery goes up now and then, but we must all make some sacrifices to achieve the final victory."

'"It's time it arrived; preferably before those Red dummies shoot the last distillery to pieces!" sighed the potato-dealer sorrowfully.

'With a commanding wave of his hand the general ordered his visitor over to the war-map which decorated the wall alongside the fireplace.

'"See here, Herr Strange. Here we have the Dniepr and a little further back the Volga, the lifeline of Russia. We have only to get a short way over on the other side of *that* and our punishment expedition to the east is over. And here we have Africa. As you can see, it is no great distance to Cairo!"

'"How many kilometres?" asked Strange, practically. He picked up a match-stick, which represented about a thousand kilometres on the map.

'"*That* is of no importance," shouted the general, furiously, knocking the match from his visitor's hand. "As I say, it is not far, and now at this very moment Field-Marshal Rommel is preparing to make a decisive strike through the weak British lines. The German war banner will soon wave over the minarets of Cairo. The rest is merely a question of local mopping-up operations. The

Egyptians and the Arabs have always sympathized with us Germans. It can be only a matter of hours before they turn openly against the British terror regime and place themselves under the protection of our just, German leadership. Throughout Africa you hear the call '*Heim ins Reich!*'*" He sweeps his pointer from Cairo to the mountain ranges of the Caucasus and describes a graceful loop around the whole of Georgia. "Here the German war-machine rolls forward, crushing all that stands in its path." The pointer hops over to Burma. "And here the Imperial Japanese Army is smashing the British and American forces. The day is fast approaching when the victorious German and Japanese forces will join hands across the northern border of India. A masterstroke of strategy. What do you say to that, Herr Strange? Can you now see the Final Victory?"

'The potato-dealer cleared his throat, passed his hand across his face and ran his eyes over the large war-map. At the same time he couldn't help remembering all the wrecked distilleries.

'"Yes it looks all very nice, general," he admitted. "We're going forward a lot!" He seemed to consider a little, judging the distance between Burma and the Caucasus. "But we've retreated in a lot of places, too," he remarked, weakly. He put out a stiff, cautious finger and touched the chart. He ran his finger backwards and forwards at the western end of Georgia. "The Georgian Army road is unfortunately no longer in our hands," he said, speaking as if he himself had personally pulled the road out from under the feet of the German Army. He was getting close to high treason. "And what about Moscow, general? Even with the best of German eyes I don't think anybody could see a lot of Moscow from where our boys are at!"

'"And *you* have been a volunteer?" roared the general, purple in the face and sending the Rottweiler on the

* *Heim ins Reich!:* Back to the Reich

228

lionskin a severe military look. "We have had one or two small setbacks recently in unimportant sectors of the front. But what you call retreat, my good man, is no more than regrouping and straightening of the front. A necessary tactical operation which demonstrates the cool-headedness of our Supreme Commander. At this very moment our tanks are crashing along the Russian roads. Machine-guns rattle and German artillery pieces roar. Our shells rain down on the heads of the *untermensch*, who are now beginning to realize who makes the decisions. A good army leader can do great things with the German soldier!" He crashes his pointer down on the map. "In these forests we have amassed an army with a striking power of which neither God nor the Devil has ever seen the like. Once it begins to roll nothing will stop it until it is east of Moscow. Look, man! We have stormed from victory to victory. We have rolled up Jugoslavia and Greece, and thrown them into the ashcan. The crowing Gallic cock has lost his feathers, and been sent head over heels to defeat in just 40 days! Holland, Belgium, Denmark and Norway smashed and thrown on the scrapheap. They can only do what we order them to do. And here are Finland, Rumania, Bulgaria and invincible Hungary, our brave European allies. We could, if we wished, hand over the whole conduct of the war in the east to them."

'"The general forgot Italy," the potato-dealer put in.

'"Yes! We must also take Italy into account," admitted the general, letting the pointer wave a few times up and down the Italian boot. In reality he couldn't stand the Italians, or their spaghetti.

'"Can we *really* trust these Bulgarians and Rumanians?" asked Strange, thinking of all the money owing to him in those two countries. "I've heard they desert to the enemy by the battalion and they won't speak German any more?"

'"That's *enough*," roared the general. "I won't have high treason talked in my house! Understand *that*, you – you *volunteer*!"

229

'Now things began to develop at a pace nobody could have foreseen,' smiles Porta, happily. 'All the accusations they could think of, from cycle-stealing to high treason, flew to and fro in the room, accompanied by barked comments from the Rottweiler.

'"They can stuff this world war for all I care," roared "Spuds", scarlet in the face. "I don't give a damn who wins. All I want is for a few distilleries to be left standing by the artillery shits and the mad bombers, so that I can get my potato and barley sales back up again when it's over!"

'"I've seen through *you*," screamed the general, planting his fists on his hips. "Do you understand me? You – you bottle-lover!" He grabbed the potato-dealer by the shoulders and shook him like a rat.

'Unfortunately he carried out this unbridled attack on a party member right in front of the Führer's melancholy likeness.

'The potato-feller tore himself out of the general's grip, and took the opportunity of giving the Führer's picture a stretched-arm salute.

'"I warn you, general," he howled, insultedly. "I am not just a uniformed booby dancing round with a tin sword at his side! I am a holder of the Blood Order! I am a party member, I have a permit to carry a gun, and I'm not afraid to use it!"

'"What do I care about that," shouted the general, who had by now forgotten all he had learnt at Potsdam Officers' School, and was back on the parade-ground again. "I shit on your Blood Order, believe me, you schnapps burner, you! And where your party's concerned there won't be much of that left when the war's over! Ha!" he barked, whiffling his pointer through the air. "Do you and your Führer think that *we*," pointing a finger at his own chest, "the Prussian Army, which sprang from the earth at the command of Frederick the Great, will give your seventh-rank party the time of day? A party that's only able to think in terms of swivelling swastikas! D'you think we Germans can be led astray by foreign idealogies?"

'The potato-dealer couldn't believe his ears. He was close to going over to the wall and knocking his head against it to clear his thoughts. A _foreign_ idea! Shit on the party! This uniformed fop must have had his brains boiled from too much sun on his _pickelhaube_! Swivelling swastikas? What interesting thoughts those generals had! But the red-tabbed dope had it all wrong. They weren't curtseying round a semi-crippled Kaiser any more. A Kaiser whose only positive result in life was to lose a world war. They'd got to learn what the new era was all about! He opened his mouth several times to say something. His brain was overflowing with ready answers. But the general didn't give him time to speak.

'"Look at that," roared the general in a well-trained voice of command. He pointed to a large, dark painting which represented German justice. A giant oak, decorated like a rich family's Christmas tree. From every branch dangled a malefactor with a good German rope round his neck. It was a well-balanced composition. Women, children, young and old, even a skinny dog, were hanging there. "Look you potato-dealer, _look_!" he roared. "Here ends every German scoundrel, mongrel, _schweinhund_ and plague-rat, who dares to besmirch the Fatherland with word or deed. Take note of it, schnapps-burner! We Prussians deal harshly with villains who think they can go their own way. A rope round their necks, and up with them. The thought, my man, is father to the deed! Consider that!" He emphasized his harsh words and dark warnings by pointing to a number of beautifully framed pencil drawings, showing smiling SS-men carrying out executions after the Army's victorious march through Poland and Russia. Carrying them out completely in accordance with Army Regulations. "I had begun to regard you as being a good person, but now I have seen through you. You are a beast of the field, an _untermensch_ swine! Get out of my house! You wicked scoundrel! _March_! And take your mongrel with

231

you! It too will get to know what facing a German court-martial means!"

'The potato-dealer almost fell out of the door, followed by his dog. The dog turned its head and stared, with grinning jaws, at the raging general. "You can just wait," it thought, "till we two party members've been down to have a word with our Gauleiter!"

'Herr Strange jumped on his bicycle and pedalled off. He almost fell off again, when he turned in his saddle to spit a few farewell curses and threats at the general. *He* was still standing in the doorway, slashing holes in the air with his riding-whip.

'"That uniformed queer's going to learn what it's all about," the potato-dealer confided to his dog as they spurted down *Soest Weg*.

'"Bow-wow!" barked the dog, in agreement.

'They didn't stop till they arrived at the Gauleiter's pompous residence. Outside it the blood-red swastika flag waved lazily in the summer breeze.

'"The flag," said the potato-dealer, raising his right arm. "Heil! Sieg!"

'The Gauleiter came all the way out on to the steps to greet him. They had been friends ever since they worked together as farmhands on the estate of a baron who had since been executed.

'"Asphalt disease, Leonhard?" asked the Gauleiter in his thick, beery voice. "You look as if you'd been eating tar!"

'"A general," panted Strange, "an Imperial Prussian sod!"

'"Hope you didn't bite him?" laughed the Gauleiter noisily. "That could give us problems, you know!"

'"I didn't, but Wotan did! He ate off half his arse when he said he'd shit on the Führer, and the party was only a foreign idea!"

'"The devil! I didn't know your dog could talk," cried the Gauleiter in surprise. He straddled his legs and stared threateningly at the dog. "Be careful what you say, you black villain!"

'"No! Hell, Bruno, it wasn't Wotan who said it, it was that fop of a general!"

'"Shit on the Führer, would he?" asked the Gauleiter, a threatening tone coming into his beery voice. "We'll *flatten* him! No trouble! By the way, you owe me 500 marks from last Thursday. Not forgotten it, I hope?"

'"You'll get 'em tomorrow. Word of honour! I'll get 'em from the woman who hasn't got her divorce yet from the Yid we sent to the concentration camp!"

'"Mind you don't get yourself mixed up in anything smelly," the Gauleiter warned him darkly, scratching the dog behind the ears. "The good times, when us party comrades could do what the hell we liked, are passing away! The bloody Army's got too much say in things, these days. All the police shits are scared of 'em. Watch out for the front line, Leonhard. As you know there's a need for gun-fodder, and, unfortunately, the Army decides who's to be the targets! Once get posted there and even the party couldn't get you back home again!"

'"Don't say things like that, Bruno. *You* can get *me* out of it if they suddenly drop on me? I've been in one war for Germany. That's enough for me."

'"Let 'em reach out after you first," the Gauleiter comforted him, opening his arms wide. "Your job's still deferred. The country can't do without schnapps. We need it to keep our spirits up under all these hard and testing experiences we're going through."

'They sat down happily at the Gauleiter's large desk, which once belonged to a Social Democratic Minister for Justice. He's been rehabilitated since and now works on the rock-pile at Buchenwalde.

'Well, they sat there drinking cognac and putting a long report together. They were both holders of the Blood Order and the party emblem in gold, and they knew exactly which way to march to get somewhere. They'd played cards together every Thursday for years. They even had the same mistress, the sausage and delicatessen shop-owner Kelp's wife, Gertrude, a tall, black-haired, slightly plump lady whose ears stuck out. She wore size 8 in shoes, and could walk any infantryman tired on Winter Help Day, when they all marched to Pader Halle in a torchlight procession to drink beer, after rattling their collection-boxes all day. Gertrude was Herr Kelp's third wife, by the way. The first one died a natural death by drowning. Jumped into the Pader River with a lump of iron tied round her neck. Her name was Ulrikka, a very Christian, believing lady. She jumped in the river from the bridge behind the cathedral. Probably thought the Lord'd forgive her if she gave up her life near a holy place.

'If God did forgive her I've never heard about it,' smiles Porta, waving his arm in the air. 'Still there's not much gets out about what happens up there! Or down in the other place, for that matter!

'The sausage and delicatessen man's second wife's name was Wilhelmina. Feminine of the Kaiser's name. Her father sold cheese off the barrow. Mrs Wilhelmina was Aryan all over. Flaxen hair pulled back tight over her skull and braided. Looked like a frayed rope that had been left out in the rain. Down deep in her horsy-lookin' face a couple of wicked, German hen's eyes glittered. She always wore flat-heeled soles, and white stockings with black and red bobbles, that went halfway up her leg. This Aryan lady was not a sexually exciting creature. Quite the opposite! A man who got inside her would have got his prick broken up and ground into sausage-meat! They used to say she had a couple of rotating swastikas mounted up in it goin' both ways.' Porta suggests the motion with both hands. 'This Himmler-style woman took the mail train to Dortmund one day to buy curtain remnants at Liebstoss's shop in *Hindenburg Strasse*. An ancient liver sausage had exploded in the hands of the Kelbs' Polish servant girl, and has

234

spurted out all over the curtains. It cost the servant girl a spell in Ravensbrück, by the way. But Frau Wilhelmina had better have stayed home that day. She started her trip by visiting the baker, Otto, in *General Ludendorffstrasse*, who had a combined coffee-house and bakery. There she got four large cream cakes down her. She exchanged news with a couple of other party wives, who also had flaxen hair and buns at the back of their necks.

'When she was crossin' *Adolf Hitler Platz* a couple of hours later they began to toot a red alert. Bombs started to fall immediately. It howled, whistled and crashed all round her German bat-ears, and dust and dirt came down on her flaxen hair. Her Aryan braids came loose. She looked like a witch that'd been through a thunderstorm, on her way down from Norway to have a look at what was happening in old Germany under the national awakening!

'BANG! A bomb went off in front of her. It seemed as if the world had gone up in flames. BANG! Another went off behind her, and it seemed as if Satan was stoking up the fires of Hell! She became, of course, completely, Teutonically confused. First she ran one way, then she ran the other way.

'"Get under cover, you soppy idiot," screamed a bare-headed policeman. His helmet had been blown off his head.

'"*Wachtmeister! Wachtmeister!*" she screamed. "Tell me where to go!" She just managed to get her flaxen poll out of the way when a number four tram came flying through the air. The helmetless policeman didn't, though. The tram took him with it into Schultze's furniture store. Luckily for Schultze he had closed down two days before to wait for better times. Now he got rid of his stock, anyway, and only had to clean up after the tram and the policeman.

'Frau Wilhelmina ran round in circles, screaming. Then she saw a safe place: the National Socialist Constituency Office. But before she got there a 1,000 pounder bulls-eyed in on her. It tickled her all down her back and then went off. Frau Wilhelmina went with it!

'I've heard they shovelled her remains up, with the others, and they're all together in a mass grave in Döbliner Cemetery. RIP they put on the stone over 'em.'

'RIP? What's that?' asks Tiny, blankly.

'Rest in pieces,' answers Porta. 'But they didn't give her much rest under that flashy stone. A day or two after, one of those air gangsters dropped his whole load of 1,000 and 500 pounders in the wrong place. They landed bang on the cemetery, and he followed 'em up with a few thousand incendiaries for dessert. So now nobody knows what's become of Frau Wilhelmina's earthly remains. But this didn't faze the good Kelp. He married for a third time. This one was Müller's daughter, the well-known pig-dealer from Münster. She was a good-lookin' piece who knew what to use it for. She'd been working for Kelp for some time in the sausage section, making over old sausages into new ones.'

'Hey, now,' the Old Man breaks in, with a crooked smile. 'Aren't you forgetting your potato-dealer? He was on a visit to the Gauleiter?'

'Of course, damn it,' shouts Porta. 'You know how one story leads you into another. Where'd I got to?'

'They were laying plans, across the desk of the former Minister for Justice,' smiles the Legionnaire, lighting a *Caporal*.

'Oh yes! Well the telephone began ringing over at the Gestapo on *Ringstrasse*,' Porta continues. 'The Gestapo boss was one of their Thursday card-school mates.

'A *general*,' he roared happily, drawing his Walther 7.65 mm from his shoulder-holster. He was pleased as a bailiff who finds something worth money at a client's place.

'There wasn't almost anything the general wasn't accused of but *he* hadn't been wasting his time either. He'd had a ninety-minute talk with the Corps Auditor, Kurze. Everything went on report. The dog, the bicycle, the potato wholesaler, the wrecked distilleries and the long-awaited Final Victory.

'"We'll take *him*, all right," Kurze promised, self-confidently. "A crummy spud-dealer can't say what he likes to the German Army. He must be out of his mind! I suggest we start with the minor crimes, which give only fifteen years imprisonment: insulting the army, damaging military property, threatening the armed forces, jeering at the military uniform. Then we can go over to the ones punishable by death: defeatism, disseminating enemy propaganda, sabotage of the will to resistance, espionage."

'"What about the dog?" asked the general, vengefully.

'"We'll get to *him* all right," promised Kurze, letting out a bellow of court-martial laughter. "Sabotage of military equipment, and attack on a highly-ranked officer. Both hanging offences! Even the best of defenders couldn't save him from the rope. I'll use paragraph 241, section 5 of the military penal codex. That paragraph got me the War Service Cross First Class with clasp. Soon as the executioner hears that one, he starts off readying the scaffold for use."

'Things began to move the very next day, and I mean *move*! It could all have been settled by a good beating-up, and a German kick in the arse for the dog. Anyway! Department IV/2a picked up the general for a short interview, while GEFEPO* Department VIIb picked up Herr Strange. He was put in irons with collar and lead-chain immediately, according to Army Regulations.

'After some chatting about the weather, and dogs, the "interview" with Strange became more – what they call rigorous. The potato feller was given a few MP taps on the nose. He was lucky it wasn't the 30 Year War he was bein' interrogated in. In those days they used to nip people with red-hot pincers, and make 'em drink melted lead mixed with hot tar. This often used to help them to remember what it was they'd done.

'All afternoon funny sounds kept getting through from the interrogation office. People thought they'd got hold of

* GEFEPO: The Secret Field Security Police

a pig on the black, an' were slaughtering it. The noises didn't stop until the three GEFEPO blokes went down to "The Lame Duck" to freshen up for the second part of the interrogation.

'The potato feller didn't look too good by then. Unteroffizier Schulze, who'd been thrown out of Torgau for cruelty, and seconded to GEFEPO, had broken two of his ribs and had managed to turn his nose permanently upwards. Troublesome it was in rainy weather.

'The third day Herr Strange confessed to everything, and this made the GEFEPO quite human and friendly toward him. His wife brought him food parcels and they all sat round the table together and tanked up on Westphalian country ham and drank schnapps with eggs beaten up in 'em. Between meals they smoked the cigars and drank the cognac.

'The potato wholesaler signed a confession gladly. He was, in fact, by now so pleasant and easy to get along with that he was allowed to rubber-stamp it himself, and put it in a large Army envelope, which was then sealed with the bird and all the trimmings. And off it all went to the Judge Advocate General at Münster.

'The good times with GEFEPO were soon over, however. One grey, rainy day, "Spuds" got put into an asthmatic DKW, and sent off to 46 Infantry Regiment's barracks, where the Paderborn glasshouse was. They had rationing there. Two thin pieces of bread and a little blob of margarine. Even a hungry sparrow wouldn't have been attracted by the menu. On national celebration days they got a square of pâté de foie horse!

'His wife brought him plenty of extra food. Stabswachtmeister Rose of 15 Cavalry Regiment checked it in very carefully. Then the guards ate it all, down to the last crumb; after, of course, the potato-man had signed for receipt of it.

'They shot Strange in Sennelager early one August morning. They did it on target range 4, which wasn't used for

238

practice any more.

'The general ended up up shit-creek without a paddle. I don't know the details. There were a lot of rumours. Hung himself by his boot-laces, one of 'em said. It can't be true. He never wore lace-up boots in his life. Always swaggered round in long riding boots. A friend of mine in interrogation told me three apes from Fort Zittau came with an order for him to be handed over to them.'

Porta throws out his arm despairingly. 'Fort Zittau *eats* people. You go in, and you never come out. Even the Devil and his great-grandmother wouldn't dream of puttin' their heads inside Zittau's gates.

'This dog business was bad for a lot of other people too. There was the matter of the Gauleiter's toilet-rolls. They turned into a political matter. The paper was red, you see, and . . .'

Porta's story is cut off. Gregor Martin puts his frost-stubbled head in through the igloo opening.

'We've got visitors,' he says, rubbing the frost from his face. 'Hurry up and get outside!'

It is an icy night. The sky seems to drop icicles. The temperature is down below 45°. The storm howls along the steep cliff-walls. We feel as if our very souls are freezing to ice.

We stare anxiously towards the north-east, from where we can hear the noise of motors. Shadowy motor-sledges move rapidly down the winding mountain road.

Two sharp reports sound, sending us headlong to cover behind the snowdrifts. We get back on our feet again when we realize that it is only frost splitting the trees growing on the side of the mountain.

The motorized column is now clearly in sight, up by the gulch. An armoured motor-sledge is leading it, followed by an armoured car and a half-track transport waggon.

Suddenly a flare wobbles up into the air. It explodes with a hollow sound, sending three green stars out to one side. Shortly afterwards another one goes up, this time red.

'The Devil fuck my great-grandmother,' howls Porta, dancing round like a madman. 'It's bloody *him*! Where the hell's that signal pistol?'

'In the waggon,' answers Tiny, already legging his way over to it in a shower of snow. He is back in a flash with the pistol and hands it to Porta. 'It's loaded,' he grins.

'I should hope so,' replies Porta. 'You didn't think I was going to throw the bloody thing up in the air did you? We've got to get our answer back quick. Else that hellhound out there'll be on his way back where he came from again.' He breaks the pistol open and examines the cartridge. 'We don't want to send up a wrong 'un,' he says. 'It ain't every day people are out pinchin' Stalin's gold out from under him. That boy'll be nervous. They'll cut him into tiny pieces if this job goes wrong.'

'Yes, and us with him,' comes drily from the Old Man. 'I must've been crazy to get mixed up in this caper!'

'Don't shit your trousers yet,' says Porta, pointing the flare-pistol up into the air at an angle. The flare goes up and explodes hollowly in a burst of red stars. He reloads with a green flare and sends it up to burst alongside the red one.

Exactly sixty seconds later a green, and then a yellow, flare goes up.

'Fits like a prick in Lizzie,' grins Porta, satisfiedly. He smacks the lid of the stopwatch shut.

'*C'est le bordel*,' mumbles the Legionnaire nervously. 'That firework show must have been seen the devil of a way off!'

'Yes, before we know where we are alarm units from all over'll be on their feet looking for us,' forecasts Heide, darkly.

'I was beginning to get a bit nervous of whether that commissar bint hadn't taken my arse,' says Porta, tucking the signal pistol into his belt. 'She'd have been bitterly sorry for it if she had. Wolf's got a little rocket surprise for her if anythin' funny should happen to Joseph Porta on this trip.'

'Open out,' orders the Old Man, 'ready your arms! You never can trust Ivan!'

'We shoot first and ask questions after?' asks Tiny, readying his *Kalashnikov* noisily.

'None of that Chicago by night stuff here,' explodes Porta, furiously.

With a breakneck swerve a heavy armoured sledge comes roaring down the winding road, skids sideways across the clearing, and stops so close to Barcelona's T-34 that it would be impossible for him to bring the gun to bear on it.

'Bloody hell!' mumbles Gregor admiringly. 'That's some trick they've got there!'

There are a couple of minutes of excited waiting. The only sound is the whirling of the sledge's propeller. The wind from it tosses snow into the air. The hatchway of the vehicle opens slowly and a grey-white commissar cap with its large red star comes into view. For a moment two hard grey eyes stare over towards our two tanks. Then the newcomer turns his gaze up to the clouds, which hasten, darkly threatening, towards the east. He jumps lithely down into the snow, spews out a number of Russian oaths, and rubs his knee, which he has knocked on the hatchframe. A *Kalashnikov* is handed out to him. In silence he hangs it across his chest in the Russian manner. He puts his left hand down into his deep fur pocket. It is so deep that his arm goes down into it right up over the elbow. When he withdraws it he is holding a bottle in his hand. He puts it to his lips, takes a long pull, wipes his mouth with his furry mitten, and gives out a long, satisfied snort, like a cold horse which has come home to its warm stable. His cold grey eyes examine Porta, who is leaning nonchalantly up against a soot-blackened tree, playing with a bundle of hand-grenades tied around a petrol bottle.

'Joseph Porta?' he asks with a wry smile, tipping his machine-pistol slightly forward.

'The Golden Commissar, I presume?' smiles Porta, lifting his yellow topper respectfully.

'Right you are,' smiles the Commissar, offering Porta the vodka bottle.

'*Stolichnaja*,' nods Porta, sniffing appreciatively at the neck of the bottle. He puts it to his lips and enjoys the silky taste of the Russian luxury vodka. He feels it go right out into his fingers and toes. They pass the bottle back and forth between them until it is empty.

'You arrived late,' says Porta, 'but you *did* arrive!' He accepts a perfumed Russian officer's cigarette, offered him from a gold cigarette-case.

'It's been a tough trip,' answers the Commissar. 'We had to go the long way round, more than once. How was your trip, *tovaritsch*?'

'Apart from the hellish low temperatures you run to in your country, and the snow that piles up on what you call your roads, I've no complaints,' replies Porta.

After a while we are all standing in a circle round the two 'Mafia bosses'. More vodka comes out. This time a cheaper brand.

Tiny snatches a bottle from the hand of a little Siberian sergeant, who is preparing to take a swig from it.

'*Herrenvolk* first,' he protests, downing almost half the bottle. He licks his lips appreciatively before handing it back to the sergeant.

'Pull in your tongue,' says the Siberian. 'Sticking out like that, it makes you look as if they'd just strung you up!'

A new bottle of *Stolichnaja* had been brought out, but only for Porta and the Commissar. The rest of us have to make do with the cheaper *Raj*.

Before very long even the Old Man is looking on the brighter side, and beginning to kick up his heels in a few dance steps. It is 6 January, the Russian Christmas, to which everyone looks forward the whole year.

The sledge-driver fishes out a balalaika and Porta his piccolo. To their accompaniment the Commissar sings in a deep bass:

> 'Snow covers hill and plain.
> From longing's bitter deep
> Our souls cry out in pain.'

We forget our mission here, and no longer feel the icy cold; no longer see the moon with its frosty, barren light; no longer hear the trees cracking, with reports like rifle shots.

A bony corporal, in the olive-green uniform of the frontier troops, starts up an ancient Slavic song to the melancholy strumming of the balalaika:

> 'Bless Thee, O Lord!
> Look down with grace upon us . . .'

It is more than the Commissar can stand. He cries out. A wet drunken snort, like the barking of a dog with a heavy cold. His face reddens, and tears run down his cheeks. His wet, carroty hair hangs down over his watery eyes.

'*Ssss Rozh deniem Khristvym,*' he gulps, deeply moved. He grasps Porta in his arms, and he too begins to weep, in his drunkenness. 'I get so terribly sad at Christmas-time,' he sniffles, with such a sorrowful expression on his tear-wet face, that the rest of us are close to crying with him.

'A feller can't *stand* it,' sniffs Tiny, wiping his eyes with a filthy mitten.

'Look down with grace upon us, Eternal Master,' intones the corporal of frontier troops, taking a swig at the vodka bottle. 'Look down with grace upon us,' he repeats, handing the bottle to Tiny.

'We're goin' to need it, too,' sighs Porta, blowing his nose noisily. 'This is no ordinary criminal caper we're going on.'

'Bet it's the first time in history anybody's ever used tanks and guns to bust open a bank,' Gregor laughs loudly.

Tiny goes down on his haunches and tries to dance *prisjodka* with the frontier corporal, with the result that he comes close to breaking his back. On the advice of the corporal we tie him to two motor-sledges and pull in opposite directions. His vertebrae go back into place with a sound like a splintering plank.

'Bet that bloody well hurt,' says Gregor, wincing.

With a piercing howl the Commissar jumps high in the air, cracks his heels together a yard above the ground and begins to whirl round in breakneck circles:

> 'I am always drunk
> and fear no man or beast!'

he sings in a ringing voice.

The frontier corporal is hopping round with a full glass gripped between his teeth and his hands clasped behind his neck. The Commissar falls over with the vodka bottle still clutched in his hand. He looks at it in amazement.

'So *there* you are!' he hiccoughs. 'Thought I'd seen you around.' He staggers back on to his feet with great difficulty. Through a vodka haze his eye falls on Tiny, and he hands him the *Stolichnaya*.

'Take care of that till I get back. Drink any of it and you'll wind up in Kolyma! *Panjemajo?*'

'Trust me,' grins Tiny, looking thirstily at the bottle.

'A man's more stupid than the Pope, if he trusts anyone,' slavers the Commissar, staggering dangerously. 'You know Tomsk,' he asks a snowdrift, trying to embrace it. 'You can hear yourself walk there. When you're on your way back from the brothel "The Merry Bed" your footsteps *echo*! They've laid the roads with wood in Tomsk! Only thing they've got plenty of in Tomsk. If you've been in Tomsk, *tovaritsch*,' he tells the snowdrift, 'the rest of the world you won't bother with. You won't be able to manage it, see! Tomsk is the arsewhole of the universe!'

Finally Porta manages to get him back on his feet. They kiss one another on both cheeks in the old Russian fashion. Arm in arm, and singing at the top of their voices, they stagger towards the remains of the soot-blackened *kolchos*'s main building. They fall several times on the way.

They are almost there when the Commissar remembers the *Stolichnaja*. He turns back, swearing viciously, and after colliding with several trees on the way he reaches Tiny. He puts out a demanding hand towards him.

'I'm sorry,' says Tiny falsely, handing him the empty bottle.

'The devil!' roars the Commissar, staggering threateningly. 'I'll be damned! And I thought it was only Russian corporals who stole from their officers! What am I to do with you?' He hiccoughs and emits a long, long belch. 'I'll send you to Kolyma!'

'Gimme a bottle of vodka then, first?' asks Tiny, belching in his turn.

'You know all the tricks, do you?' says the Commissar, blinking his watery eyes.

"Give him a bottle,' he turns to the frontier corporal. 'Now we're having a party it might as well be a good one. It's only Christmas once a year.' He looks prayerfully up at the clouds and mumbles: 'Look down in grace upon us, Lord!'

'That Tiny, he's a wicked chap,' Porta confides to the Commissar, as they stagger arm in arm towards the main building. 'He was hardly born before the Children's Aid took him. Nobody can *stand* him, down at the David. He goes round with Jews too!'

'Does he really?' asks the Commissar, stopping to salute a tree, which he seems to think is a rabbi. 'It's not all Jews who're suitable company for weak people,' he says, giving out a thunderous belch.

'You're right, there,' says Porta, putting the wrong end of his cigarette in his mouth.

'Look down in grace upon us, Lord,' pants the Commissar, throwing a snowball at an imaginary enemy. 'This cursed war will lead to nothing good! Before we know where we are properly, all our ideals will have been destroyed, and our banners trampled into the mud!'

'I just want to tell you one thing,' shouts Porta, letting himself down on to an up-ended bucket. 'They're whores an' pimps the lot of 'em, no matter how high up you go. They fuck one another's wives to get an advantage out of it and do it backwards and forwards too.' He stares at the Commissar, with streaming eyes. 'It's bloody immoral! You can't do that an' *stay* moral! You ever fucked anybody else's wives?'

'You are my friend,' screams the Commissar, in drunken happiness. He throws his arms round Porta, so hard that he falls backwards off his bucket. 'And you have fucked my wife,' he laughs, cunningly. 'How is she, by the way?'

'Last I saw of her she was playin' monkeys up a tree with some counter-jumper from supplies, but he had the clap and the MPs picked him up.'

'Red Front!' shouts the Commissar in a ringing voice, clenching his fist. 'When you're driving in a waggon you cannot get off,' he breathes, mysteriously.

'The trick's in the deal,' explains Porta, with drunken honesty. 'Everything's based on buying and selling, and what you've *got* to have is your head screwed on straight. The dearest thing you've got to sell is yourself!'

'Who the devil'd buy me?' asks the Commissar, doubtfully.

'A lot more people than you'd dream of would,' answers Porta.

'As ugly as *I* am?' smiles the Commissar, mirthlessly.

'If you can't get what you want you have to take what you can get, as the ostrich said when he tried to have a fuck at a duck.'

'Look down in grace upon us, Lord,' sighs the Commissar, throwing his arms wide despairingly.

'Nobody move!' roars Gregor in a high, screaming voice. 'This is a hold-up!'

'He's practising for when we get to the gold,' Porta tells the Commissar.

Drunk as we are we can see there is a storm coming up. One of the feared mountain storms which, in a moment, change everything to a raging hell of snow, with winds strong enough to send a twenty-ton truck flying over the edge and down the mountainside like a piece of loose paper.

We crawl into the igloos and roll up close together to protect ourselves against the terrible cold. Sausages and legs of mutton are passed from hand to hand, and after some brief, mumbling talk we fall into a heavy sleep. Only the machine-pistols lying around us indicate that there is a war on.

Tiny grunts in his sleep and smiles like the cat who has eaten the goldfish.

The Commissar sleeps with his cap turned round on his head. Now and then he makes strange noises and sobs in his sleep.

With a scream he suddenly sits up and clasps his head with both hands. It feel like one huge inflamed boil. He groans aloud, as he tries to turn his body and realizes that his backbone creaks like a door hanging on rusty hinges. He cannot discover where he hurts most. He is in pain from the tips of his toes to the roots of his hair. He finds out his head is the worst. It feels like a basin of gruel made with old, sour milk. 'Look down in grace upon us, Lord,' he sobs, and falls, groaning, back down amongst the rest of us.

'*Gauno**,' snarls tank-driver Ermolov, turning angrily away from the unhappy Commissar, who mumbles again, weakly: 'Look down in grace upon us, Lord!'

'*Guano*,' repeats the driver, viciously.

'Don't be too hard on me,' whines the Commissar, drunkenly maudlin. Then he throws a wicked look at Ermolov. 'Arsehole,' he growls, offended at a miserable Staff-sergeant permitting himself to say 'shit' to a Commissar of the Army, the highest ranking authority at Corps

---

* *Gauno:* Russian for shit

247

HQ. Where the devil's it all going to end if this filthy war goes on much longer? Never heard anything like it. A lousy NCO throwing a word like 'shit' at *him*. A Commissar of the Army! He falls back down and snores his way straight into an alcoholic nightmare.

'I'm goin' to Maxim's
Where all the girls are dreams . . .'

sings Porta happily in his sleep.

It is more than Albert can stand. He springs up excitedly and begins to shake Porta roughly.

'What the hell are you up to, you black shithouse?' rages Porta, punching at him. His beautiful dream has been broken into and he is angry.

'You were singing!' snarls Albert furiously, diving under the canvas again and burrowing down between Gregor and me.

'Singin'?' gapes Porta. 'I was bloody well sleepin'! The Bible's softened your brain, you black apeman!'

'Shut it!' roars the Old Man from his corner. 'Go to sleep! That's an *order*!'

Quiet falls again on the igloo, and we all dream of what it is going to be like to be rich. None of us have ever tried that before.

It is still dark when we get up, and all around us is a blinding hell of snow. Ice crystals drive at us like bullets, tearing our skin so that the blood comes.

Tiny starts a violent argument with Staff-corporal Oscar Rowitsch, called 'Frostlips', because he always looks as if he is freezing to death.

'You 'eap of Caucasian camelshit,' screams Tiny angrily, and begins to swing his arms, threateningly.

'Frostlips' ducks like lightning, and just manages to avoid Tiny's devastating punch.

'Stand still, so's I can get at you,' roars Tiny, rushing forward like a bulldozer.

248

'Frostlips' lands an iron-shod infantry boot on the tenderest part of Tiny's instep.

He lets out a roar which a lion would have envied him and grabs at his injured foot. A serious tactical error. He barely sees the heavy Russian infantry boot coming at him until it thuds into his face. With a scream of pain he falls on his back, blood spurting from nose and mouth. Now he is really angry. Like lightning he rolls himself into a ball, kicks his feet into the air and straightens out like a released spring. With the force of a steamhammer, his forehead crashes into 'Frostlips's' broad Mongolian face. Then he spins round and kicks out backwards like a crazy horse.

For a moment he seems to hang in the air. Both his size 14 boots hammer into 'Frostlips's' chest, knocking all the breath out of his lungs. The next kick sends him back several yards and he slides towards the edge of the cliff. We see him already on his way over into thin air, but his dangerous slide is stopped unexpectedly. Warrant Officer Stepanov comes round a corner of the ruins, with his arms full of fried sausage and mutton, and gets in the way.

Stepanov lets out a roar as his feet are swept from under him, and sausage and mutton fly up into the air.

He is on his feet first with his *Kalashnikov* gripped by the muzzle and on his way to split 'Frostlips's' skull with the butt. The Commissar's quick intervention saves the man's life.

'Stop those crazy games,' he growls. 'Wait to play 'em until you've all become Swedish Social Democrats!'

But Stepanov, whom they used to call 'Whorecatcher' when he was serving on the Moscow Vice Squad, is so angry they have to tie him to a tree until he simmers down.

It is well into the afternoon before we get away. There are problems with several of the vehicles, since their drivers have been in no condition to turn their engines over during the night. We have to tow the half-track behind the T-34.

We are totally exhausted when we stop, well into the night, for a couple of hours of rest. We have laboured through oceans of snow. A couple of times we have come close to losing the trucks. Ice broke under their wheels on the way across rivers not yet frozen through.

The Old Man has to threaten us with his machine-pistol to get us to build an igloo. But it gets built at last, and we huddle together, freezingly cold, inside it. Now we come suddenly awake again. Porta gets the cards out. He shuffles and deals with practised fingers.

'Tell me,' he asks 'Whorecatcher', 'what did you Moscow fellers do with rapists when you got hold of 'em?'

'Sent 'em to Kolyma,' the former Vice man says, making a clumsy attempt at palming the ace of spades under cover of the talk.

'Better have that one, too,' says Porta, sweetly, holding out his hand.

'That's funny,' answers 'Whorecatcher', looking innocent.

'Yes *very*, bleedin' funny,' rumbles Tiny, angrily. He draws his *Nagan* from its place in his boot-top. 'You just watch somethin' funny don't 'appen to you, mate. Like you suddenly growin' a couple extra 'oles in you somewhere or other!'

'I can't see there's any risk grabbin' a bit o' free cunt now an' again!' Tiny laughs noisily and scratches his crutch. 'If you get picked up for it all you got to say's the bag's a bleedin' liar!'

'You don't get away with it that easy, lad,' says 'Whorecatcher' sadly. 'The Vice Squad knows all those games. Keep off rape! Any caveman of a copper can prove it's you that's been inside it easy as winking. Cunts're like guns. The rifling tells you what's been through 'em, and even the most corrupt judge'll take that kind of thing seriously. I can only remember two cases where the sod got away with it. There was this Anna Petrovna who'd accused some limp prick of having raped her. Well, the report revealed that she'd let 946 high-born gents get across her. They used to contact her by telephone. Not too clever of her that, 'cos our telephone bugging service checks all telephones. We had a serious talk with her, and she told all. Rape, that was just a bit of fun she was having. The real reason was he wouldn't share his black money with her. They both wound up in Kolyma!'

'But you said he got away with it,' protests 'Frostlips', disappointedly.

'I said he got away with the rape charge,' answered 'Whorecatcher'. 'He went to the mines for having black money. Three years later he committed suicide with an ice block.'

'What was the other case?' asks Porta, interestedly, raking in the pool. It is the fourth time he has had twenty-one!

'It was a Chinese bint,' smiles 'Whorecatcher', lifting up the corners of his eyes with his fingers to show us what she'd looked like. 'She found out one day that her belly was growing at a surprisingly rapid rate. So she stepped off up to the social worker, who was one of them that was born in the bottom of a laid-up barge, an' believed every word the slit-eyed bint told her about rape and being misused and that. So if the yellow bitch could get a prick tacked on to her coming nipper then she was certain of getting a bag full of roubles from the social lot. We had a bit of a talk with her and read what she'd said to the bull she'd got on the board as being pappy. Luckily for him our sex experts were able to prove that what this Pekin duck was saying was not on. They sent her to Kolyma, together with what she was carrying around in her.'

'What about the feller?' asks Porta. 'He go to Kolyma, too?'

'No, not for that,' answers 'Whorecatcher', sorrowfully. 'He went up for a different job, couple of years later. He'd been celebrating the first of May, and got drunk. While drunk he'd talked a lot to a bloke who didn't agree with him. You know what I mean, I reckon? He was picked up before he'd even got rid of his hangover!'

'Jesus,' cries Tiny, impressed. 'You reckon the German

Vice bleeders are as good as your lot?'

'*I* dunno,' says 'Whorecatcher', playing a jack, on which Porta promptly drops an ace for another 21, 'but I can guarantee not much gets past 'em, and I know that when there ain't a war on they visit one another and pass on the news!'

'What a bleedin' world we do live in!' sighs Tiny, letting his cards down, thoughtlessly, so that 'Frostlips' gets a look at them.

'Twenty-one,' chuckles Porta. He has immediately picked up the signal from 'Frostlips', who is his partner.

Tiny is speechless. With a silly look on his face he stares at the ace and two queens lying in front of Porta. He has two jacks, and a king on the side. If it hadn't been for all that talk about the Moscow Vice Squad he could have bid 'Twenty-one' long ago. But he is still so shocked at what he has heard that he does not even get annoyed.

'Are you really telling me,' he asks, bending absorbedly forward across the table, 'that you Vice cops can find out if I've been having a bit of illegal crumpet off with some bint or other? Sounds like a bleedin' fairy tale, to me!'

'Well, it's still a fact,' says 'Whorecatcher', putting a king in place. 'And the sentence is thirty years. After twenty years you've got a chance of transfer to a labour camp. Oh, and don't forget, if you like a bit o' rape, that most of those chaps get sent to the *Pjopre* prison on the Tomsk river. I was there once on an escort job for two blokes who hadn't committed rape, but who'd had a couple of "frigates" cruising the *Nevski Prospekt* for 'em. They'd got twenty-five years for it. They were both of 'em in good humour all the way, making plans for the future and such, but you should've seen their faces when we come up over the hills and got a sight of the place they were headed for on the other side of the river. It was still a good way off, but it felt just like a wicked, cold fist being smashed into your face. We three that was escorting them, we took a good firm grip on their leading chains. We knew they only had one thought in their heads: to get away from us in any way they could. Those "ship-owners" had just realized what a long time twenty-five years really is.'

'Holy Mother of Kazan, but it *is* a long time,' Porta comes in thoughtfully. He strokes his chin, consideringly. 'A whole Porta lifetime. Lord save us. It's a *long* bloody time!'

'Shut *up* for Christ's sake,' mumbles Tiny. 'It'd knock over the wickedest black monkey as ever lived. Twenty-five years! Just for 'avin' a couple of biddies out workin' to put a bit more butter on your bleedin' bread. And I suppose there *could* be twenty-five years more 'angin' fire in the re'abilitation camp?'

'You can count on it,' says 'Whorecatcher'. 'I never heard of nobody who came straight home when he was finished with a stretch. Whether it was prison or punishment camp. There's always a "surprise" for dessert. They call it expulsion to Siberia anyway.'

'Jesus,' groans Tony, putting his hand to his head, so that 'Frostlips' can see all his cards again. 'Be better to *pay* for it, and get a receipt too. Fifty years, just for a shag! Bleedin' 'ell no! I'm going into a monastery!'

'Bet there's a lot of those cunt-crazy sods in gaol on the Tomsk who wish they'd been born without goolies,' remarks Porta, bidding twenty-one triumphantly for the twelfth time.

*You don't have to be in a war for more than five
minutes to find out how stupid it all is. There must
really be a better way of doing things!*

*Porta to Tiny on the outskirts of a burning Russian
town*

The great, cool church hummed with the voices of people in prayer.
They prayed aloud for the things they were allowed to pray for, but
in the silence of their thoughts they prayed for peace. For an end to
the hellishness of war; never to see soldiers or tanks any more; never
to experience bombs and incendiaries again. They prayed that the
man in the grey party uniform might be amongst the dead in the next
bombing raid. They begged in their prayers that they might soon be
granted the sight of British and American soldiers.

Suddenly the mumble of prayer stopped. Panic grew in the eyes of
the congregation.

The priest rose from his knees and stared fearfully towards the
closed door, heard the hard tramp of jackboots and the hoarse, brutal
song:

Wir werden weiter marschieren,*
wenn alles in Scherben fällt,
denn heute gehört uns Deutschland
und morgen die ganze Welt!

'SS,' mumbled the priest and let his folded hands fall down to
his sides.

Everything was in ruins already. Berlin was a pile of
rubble. Stuttgart burnt. Hamburg pockmarked like a lunar
landscape. Leipzig a hell of fire. Breslau fighting to the last
man and the last bullet. In Cologne the ruins of the cathedral
loomed above wrecked houses; but the Führer's guard marched
on, crunching the ruins under their heavy boots.

---

* *We will march on*
When all is in ruins,
Today Germany is ours
Tomorrow the whole world!

THE PARITIP

The Commissar's armoured sledge leads the column. But then, he is the only one who knows the way to the hiding-place of the gold.

The narrow, winding path grows steeper and steeper. The higher we go the more our spirits sink.

Time and again the tanks slide backwards, and risk going over the edge and down into the depths below us. Looking down, it reminds one of a cauldron of water at the boil. Driving snow spouts up from it in jets like those of a fountain. Only the drivers remain in the vehicles. The rest of us put on Siberian snow-shoes and run along the inner side of the path, close in to the rock wall where there is less risk of being blown over the edge by a sudden violent puff of wind. Close to the tree level, where the eternal winds have hardened the snow, we change to short skis.

The tanks and motor sledges can now increase speed and we have difficulty in keeping up.

At breakneck speed Porta's Panther goes into a hairpin bend, slides sideways and hits the mountainside with a crash. It spins completely round on the icy path, slides backwards and comes rushing down towards us, with ice and frozen snow showering up around it. We throw ourselves headlong to one side to save ourselves from being crushed by the 45-ton monster.

The rear T-34 is in the middle of the first hairpin when the Panther comes rushing down on it in a giant cloud of snow.

'Holy Christ!' screams Albert, grey-faced with terror.

'Turn the waggon, you bloody black fool,' shouts Barcelona, desperately, but Albert is completely paralysed. He glares, wild-eyed, at the death coming roaring down at him.

The Old Man is up on the T-34 in one long jump, but before he has got down through the turret the Panther has arrived. Steel clangs against steel, and both tanks rush on down the slippery path.

Somehow Albert gets the tracks to go the opposite way, so that the T-34 slides into the wall of the cliff and stops the wild race. How, is a mystery. The Panther rears up, mounting halfway up on the T-34. Through the clashing of steel we can hear Albert calling wildly on God. The Old Man brings his hand across the black man's face twice, hard. Albert stops shouting, and begins to grin foolishly.

'No man can stand up to this sort of thing,' he whines miserably. He is standing out in the snow, a little later, staring down into the abyss below.

'Shut your black trap!' shouts the Old Man furiously. 'Get back up in that tea-waggon of yours, so's we can start up again.'

'I bloody won't,' protests Albert, grey-faced. 'I don't want anything to do with that gold! I'm satisfied with bein' a poor, black Obergefreiter in the German Army, I am. What good's a load of gold to me, man, if I'm lyin' smashed up in my tea-waggon at the bottom of a rotten cliff?'

'I ordered you to shut it,' rages the Old Man. He turns his mpi on Albert. 'Up with you!'

Whining softly to himself Albert shrugs his way down through the hatch and bangs it to behind him.

There is wild discussion as to which of us are to go with the drivers in the vehicles. We all refuse, and then Porta arranges a driver strike. They won't drive without an observer in each waggon.

It is hard to tell whether it is the Old Man or the Commissar who shouts the loudest. But it all ends as it usually does, with the weakest going to the wall. Resignedly, swearing in an undertone, I climb up to Porta and edge my way down behind the instruments.

'You look like my pal Rodeck the day they picked him up on a 30-year rap!' he grins.

'I don't *know* your bloody friend Rodeck,' I answer him, sourly.

'He was a nice, pleasant chap,' Porta goes on happily. 'They called him a car-thief, and it *was* cars he stole. But he was really a painter, and he was that good at it he could repaint any size of car you liked to come with, in 1 hour and 11 minutes flat. There was usually some paint left over, too, so the owner of the car and his family could sniff themselves silly for a week after. He lived, free and happy, in the company of his paints and his sprayers, until one Wednesday mornin' between 3 and 5 o'clock. Then the door-bell rang so long and loud you'd have thought it was the Devil arrived to pick up a lost soul.'

'"Who the hell's that?" shouted Rodeck from his side of the door. He was naturally a bit narked at being woke up at that un-Christian time of the day.

'"Give you three guesses," creaked a voice out from the landin', and then the door gets smashed in on him, and two snap-brims are asking for a view of his wrists. "Click" go the cuffs and there he is with his pyjama jacket fitted with steel extensions.

'So off he went with all his paint-pots, and nobody outside the "Alex" tec-shop has seen him since.'

The road has begun to improve, and everybody gets back up into the vehicles. Before we cross the pass, the Commissar orders us to rope the waggons together with double towing-wires. The path will become so steep that there is danger of the vehicles toppling over backwards. Their theoretical angle of climb we have long ago exceeded. The new T-34 is in the lead with Albert driving. It is a tank which has everything the others ought to have but haven't. It can climb like a chamois on its incredibly wide tracks, and Albert knows how to drive it; but we have to fill him up with plenty of liquor to make him forget his constant fear of death. When he has got half a bottle of vodka inside him he is on top of the world. Only Porta is a better driver.

'Take it easy now, black-arse! No further'n the edges,'

Porta warns him from the Panther's turret. 'Don't get to thinkin' that Russian thunder-box can scramble down sheer rock faces!'

Albert gives him the international 'Up you' sign, with a slap of his hand on the inside of his bent elbow.

The tow-wires break twice, as if they were cotton, and the Panther slides back down towards the dizzying abyss.

'Don't we soon get a break?' says Barcelona, dog-tired. 'Hell, it's black as the inside of your hat!'

'A break? Here? At three in the afternoon?' shouts the Old Man angrily. 'You must be off your rocker!'

The Commissar orders us to tie outselves to one another with our climbing-ropes, in order that nobody get lost in the roaring hell of snow.

'I just can't go on any more,' moans Gregor. 'You can have my share of the gold! If this had been a legal job, they'd have had to strike a new medal for it. We deserve one!'

'An' if it goes wrong,' laughs Tiny, raucously, shaking chunks of ice from his shoulders, 'they'll tie 120 years on our back, with a little bit of a chance of gettin' out on parole when we've done 80 of 'em an' 'ave forgot entirely what cunt's all about!'

'Save your breath!' snarls the Old Man sourly. 'Stay here,' he orders, shortly, releasing himself from the safety-rope. 'I'm going forward a bit to have a look. Don't blow me away when I come back!'

With his binoculars bumping against his chest, he climbs on up, and is hidden, in a few seconds, by the driving snow.

'He's that bloody careful, he wipes his arse an hour before he goes to the shithouse,' snarls Porta irritably, taking a big bite of frozen brawn, and washing it down with a swallow of vodka.

'There isn't a chance of Ivan Baggytrousers laying an ambush for us. It's overcareful sods like that who slow down the war effort. If it was up to me it'd be off we go for Uncle Joe's gold as fast as the tracks'd let us! That'd soon make the neighbours take off, if they really *were* crazy enough to be sitting nursing their frost-bitten pricks and waitin' for *us*.'

'How cold *is* it?' asks Gregor, shivering.

'*Je ne sais pas, mon ami*,' answers the Legionnaire despondently, beating his body with his arms. 'But I have never been through anything like it!'

'48 below,' reports Heide, arrogantly.

'You're barmy,' protests Tiny, hopping on the spot and swinging his arms. 'You mean 148 below at least! My toes've turned to icicles inside these felt boots, and my blood thinks it's become part of the bleedin' Arctic Ocean!'

'Oh, no!' groans Barcelona, brushing icicles from his face. 'It's not worth it. Who the hell'd ever believe it could *get* this cold?'

'Pack yourselves out with paper,' orders the Commissar, throwing down some bundles of old newspapers which he and 'Frostlips' come up with. 'Rub yourselves down with snow all over first, then pack yourselves in a layer of newspaper!'

'You must be round the bleedin' bend,' screams Tiny. 'Take our clothes off at 148 below? We'll go off bleedin' bang like the soddin' trees!'

'Wait till it gets *really* cold,' laughs the Commissar. 'This is only the beginning!'

'If it's goin' to get colder'n this then my share of the gold's goin' cheap,' declares Tiny, through chattering teeth, while he packs a few copies of *Pravda* round his stomach.

'No, not like that.' 'Whorecatcher' warns him. 'First you've got to rub yourself down with snow. It's not near as bad as you think. Feet most of all. Rub 'em till you feel they're glowin'!'

'Oh Jesus!' sobs Gregor, rubbing snow all over his naked body. 'Some ski tour this is. And we're doing it as volunteers!'

'Yes, you don't 'ave to go to the soddin' psychopaths to be certified as a bleedin' super-idiot,' rages Tiny, struggling with his frozen fur jumpsuit.

'Who the hell would've thought it could get this cold any place on earth,' pants Porta, pushing an extra copy of *Izvestia* down round his chest. 'I'm cured of winter sports for the rest of my life!'

'I can't help wondering, man, whether that fuckin' gold's really worth all this trouble?' chatters Albert. 'You want to hear what I think, we'd turn back now, before the new Ice Age overtakes us!'

'*I'm* not givin' up *my* gold,' shouts Porta. 'If I have to roll on my bollocks through ice an' snow all the way to where it's hidden, an' do it on my own, I'll still do it! But if you want to go on living your little lives out in lousy, stinkin' poverty, then step off now before you've got too far into the Ice Age!'

The Old Man comes back, blue in the face with cold.

'Why the devil didn't you take me with you?' asks the Commissar, smearing frost salve on his face. 'Never do that again! You don't know how easy it is to get lost. You can't count on the compass. The mountains make the readings go wild!'

'Give me a drink,' says the Old Man, brusquely, reaching for Porta's water-bottle.

'D'you know this area?' he turns to the Commissar.

'No, I've never been here. But we save about 400 kilometres by going over the pass. Everybody says it's impossible from October to the end of May. I chose it for safety. Nobody would dream that anybody would try it in winter-time.'

'The devil,' curses the Old Man. 'Let's get out of here. We've got to get through that pass quick as possible. There's a storm on the way. Just on the far side of the pass, there's an old fort, or a monastery or something, where we can tank up and get a breather for the night.'

When we are halfway up the pass, one of the half-tracks skids off the path and we have to dig it out of the snowdrifts.

Porta wants to push it over the edge, and is on his way

with the Panther, but the Commissar protests violently. The truck cannot be done without, if we are to bring back the gold.

Then the older T-34 gets stuck. We weep with rage and despair and are ready to give up completely. Finally we get the new T-34 backed into a position from which it can pull its elder brother out of the snow. The tow-wires stretch and hum.

'Back!' shouts 'Frostlips' warningly, jumping behind a snowdrift.

'Somebody comin'?' asks Tiny, confusedly, staring from behind a large tree.

The wire snaps with a whining crack and the pieces fly close by Tiny's head. A fraction of an inch to one side or the other and he would have been beheaded. A madness of rage grips him. With a shovel in his hands he rushes towards the T-34, where Albert's black face is just visible above the turret coaming.

Like lightning Albert has the hatch slammed to and dogged fast from the inside. Tiny smashes the shovel down on the closed hatch cover in a mad rage.

'Come outside, you black cannibal, so's I can kill you!' he roars madly.

'Knock him out!' shouts the Old Man. But none of us dare go near him when he is like this. A mad grizzly is a lapdog compared to him.

'Come out, you black ape,' he screams, pulling the cord of a grenade and swinging it round his head.

'Hell! Get rid of it,' warns Porta from the Panther's hatch.

''Ere then!' shouts Tiny, throwing the grenade at Porta, who is down under cover inside the tank with the speed of a ferret.

The grenade strikes the top edge of the hatch coaming, but the antenna causes it to change direction and it goes off with a sharp crack.

'The devil take me if I'm going to stand for this any longer.' rages the Old Man. He grabs his *Kalashnikov* by the barrel and swings it round his head. The butt comes down with a hollow thud on the back of Tiny's neck. With a long, hoarse exhalation of breath he goes down in the snow. His arms and legs jerk a few times, then he lies still.

'Shoot him,' foams Albert from inside the T-34, 'shoot that mad bastard.'

'Where *did* you catch *him*?' asks the Commissar, shaking his head wonderingly. 'He ought to be kept in a strait-jacket for the rest of his life!'

'Tie him up,' orders the Old Man, grinding his teeth together. 'Tie him up like a Christmas tree! When he wakes up he'll be worse than a ton of HE. Tie him to the gun. Even he can't shift that!'

'What was up with him?' asks Porta, putting his head up again cautiously through the hatchway.

'He nearly got his napper chopped off when the wire went,' explains Gregor, with a laugh. 'Now he thinks Albert did it on purpose. They had a bit of an argument over some black puddin' earlier on.'

'It's what I always say,' laughs Porta. 'He's too touchy, that boy!'

It is well into the night before we are through the pass and go slipping and sliding down the far side. The huge fort rises before us, dark and threatening. It is built of great, shaped blocks of stone, piled upon one another without any kind of mortar. If mortar had been used it would have crumbled away long ago. Frost has bitten deeply into the corners of the blocks.

'That's what I call building blocks,' cries Heide, for once really impressed. 'How on earth did they manage to get them up on top of one another?'

'Slaves,' replies 'Whorecatcher', as if it were the most natural thing in the world. 'Never been a shortage of them, here in Russia. They're willin' and effective, and there's plenty of 'em. People can be made to do most anything, if you know how to apply a knout to 'em, or cut 'em a bit with a Cossack knife!'

'I've always been a great admirer of your humanitarian

principles,' says Porta, sarcastically.

The Old Man wants us to tank up before resting, but he has to give in to our wild protests.

'Frostlips' and Gregor get a huge fire going inside the great hall.

'Stinks o' dead men in here,' says Barcelona, sniffing the air.

'To hell with that,' hisses the Commissar. 'Dead men aren't dangerous!'

'You're that ugly a feller could spew up just lookin' at you,' shouts Tiny angrily. He hits out at Heide with his machine-pistol.

'Stop that everlastin' squabbling,' shouts the Old Man. 'Now I want quiet! One word more and you get guard duty!'

'That Nazi shit looks like 'e's on 'is way to a funeral,' roars Tiny, pointing at Heide with his mpi. ''Is own funeral, too!'

'Shut up and come over here. Let's have a game of idiot bank,' suggests Porta, shuffling the cards. 'How many's in?' he asks, looking around him.

'I'm too bloody tired,' moans Barcelona, dropping down heavily on the packed earth on the floor.

'There's two things a man's never too tired for,' says Porta, cutting the cards into talons. 'Gambling and shagging! I can tell you a story about what can happen to people who think they're too tired to fuck!'

'The very widely-known *Wachtmeister*, Alois Fresa from the "Alex" station, got temporarily posted, one Palm Sunday it was, to the plain-clothes branch. He put on his good pin-striper, and then got himself an Afro hair-do – that's a typical symptom of paranoia. When he found it not so easy to pick up a bit o' the other, he got hold of a couple of yellow leather shoulder-holsters an' stuck a couple of P-38s into 'em. He'd seen that was how the tough cops on the films did it. Of course, this made a hell of an impression on the shield-struck floozies. He let the word go round he was Gestapo, but that was a lot of balls. He was on the bicycle-theft flying squad, really. Then his lucky day rolled round. He met three villains' comin' out of the *Commerzbank* in *Hohenzollern Damm*, each with a bagful of shekels in his hand, and he blew 'em away with his hand-artillery. This blood-bath got itself talked about all over Berlin, and the women were soon standin' ten-deep round Alois. After a bit of this, though, he found it was more'n he could manage and wished they'd all get to hell out of it and leave him be. So there he was, late one night, sitting in "The Crooked Cop", head down, an' fucked all to pieces. Up came a little made-up doll from the Wedding district, totterin' along in heels like stilts, an' began touching him up for starters.

'"How'd you like to show me your *other* gun?" she whispered, passionate as all hell. "I've heard a lot about *you*! You know you look the way Clark Gable always wanted to look!" She touched him up a bit more then, and got one of her long, painted nails inside, and started working direct on John Thomas with the roll-collar. But Johnny T. wasn't havin' any. He was limp an' wrinkled as a 90-year-old eunuch.

'"Sod off!" snarled Alois, giving her a push. "If I was to really get hot for you, you'd have to look a lot different!"

'This Wedding bint started givin' him mouth then, which Wedding bints have a way of doin'!

'"An' *you're* the feller they're all talking so much about," she yelled. "You ain't even got hair on your balls. You don't get away with turnin' *me* down!" And before anybody knew what she was up to, there she stood with his two P-38s in her hands. She'd flipped 'em neatly out of his shoulder-holsters. Then she cocked 'em with her thumbs the way the cowboys used to do when they walked into Prairie Town bank to arrange a loan.

'"God! No!" he screamed, holding out his hands in front of him. As if that was goin' to help!

'The one-legged bartender choked on his drink. He was tryin' to shout "Heil Hitler!" an' swallow at the same time.

'"Understand me! Please! Darlin'! I'm too *tired*!" babbled

Fresa. But he'd gone off the bar-stool on to the floor before he even knew he was dead.

'The bartender tried to scream, but all he got out was a sound like a sea-lion with asthma.

'So there you see what can happen to a feller who's too tired to fuck! Anybody else want in?' asks Porta, looking around again.

'Twenty!' shouts Gregor, slapping twenty marks on the nearest talon.

But the game soon peters out. We are far too exhausted, and hardly care whether we win or lose. The two last players are Porta and 'Frostbite'. Then they, too, give up.

Tiny has hardly got his head down before he breaks into a roar of laughter. He is one of those lucky people who can laugh for hours at their own jokes. His unbridled laughter takes the rest of us with him. Soon laughter shakes the whole room.

The Commissar whinnies, tears running down his cheeks. Every time we look over at Tiny, sitting with his pale-grey bowler cocked at an angle on his head, we explode into laughter again. We simply cannot stop. The only serious face is that of Heide. Each of our roars of laughter seems to tighten his face into an even stiffer mask of severity.

Finally we fall into a sleep of exhaustion. Suddenly Tiny is there again. He stands over the Old Man with legs apart, jabbing at him with a machine-pistol.

'What the hell now?' curses the Old Man.

'You're under arrest!' says Tiny with an MP look on his face.

'Arrest? Are you mad?' hisses the Old Man, angry at being pulled back out of dreamland. 'What the hell're you talking about? Don't you know I'm your Section Leader?'

'That's why,' growls Tiny, darkly. 'In mine, Adolf's an' the German people's name you are under arrest. You have illegally laid hands on a subordinate!'

'Now I've heard that one too?' protests the Old Man, blankly.

'It won't 'elp you to deny it, Oberfeldwebel Beier,' says Tiny, with the strict air of an interrogator. 'Did you, or did you not, crack me on the bonce with an mpi butt? You see? Now I'm going to shoot you for it! I will not stand any more of it!'

'He's mad as a hatter,' whispers 'Frostlips'. He edges over towards Tiny, who has released the safety on his weapon and whose finger is already curling dangerously on the trigger.

The Old Man sits there paralysed, staring at him.

'Frostlips' jumps forward and bores three stiff fingers into Tiny's diaphragm. Air leaves the big man's lungs with explosive force. He bends over forward.

The Legionnaire lifts his arm and brings the edge of his hand down with all his strength on Tiny's neck. He falls unconscious.

'What the devil's wrong with him?' gasps the Old Man, wiping the sweat from his brow. 'It's not the first time I've knocked him cold with a butt-stroke. I'm getting fed up with the bloody idiot!'

'*Bien sûr*, he is dead drunk,' says the Legionnaire. 'That is the trouble! You can see it on him!'

The Commissar begins frantically to rummage in his pack. He pulls out two empty *Stolichnaja* bottles.

'I'll say he's drunk,' he says, throwing the bottles disgustedly from him. 'The swine's drunk two litres of vodka!'

'Let's kill him,' suggests 'Whorecatcher', as soon as he discovers there is not a drop left in the two bottles.

'A beating is what he needs,' says the Legionnaire. 'A good whipping with our belts would make him think twice!'

'No good,' answers Porta, shaking his head. 'He's a double-nature. One of 'em, when he's drunk, is completely unaccountable for his actions; then there's the sober feller, who can't remember a single thing the drunk did while under the influence. When he's not drunk he's right enough.'

'Then we'll have to see to it he don't get drunk, won't

we,' says 'Frostlips'. 'He's a danger to all around him!'

'That's nothing to what he's like if you *refuse* to give him anything,' laughs Porta, heartily.

I don't know how long I have been asleep when the others awaken me. Soundlessly I grasp my machine-pistol, and strain my ears in the darkness.

Porta sits up alongside me and is about to give a shout. I put my hand on him to indicate silence. Instinctively he covers the glowing embers of the fire with a tin bath. The room is in total darkness.

'What is it?' whispers the Old Man, nervously.

'I don't know,' I whisper back, my hands tightly around the mpi. 'Something woke me up!'

'Skis,' mumbles Tiny, who has ears like a weasel. He claims he can hear a fly rubbing its legs together five miles away. Against the wind, too!

'Are you sure?' asks the Commissar, in a voice which shakes a little. 'It's not the wind, fooling you?'

'Don't you believe it!' answers Tiny. 'Me an' my flappers don't make mistakes! When you been a slave in Torgau, you can 'ear the lice dancin' a tango on the belly of a Chinese whore in Shanghai!'

'Skis!' mumbles the Commissar, thoughtfully. 'Then they're after us! But how the hell can they have found us here?'

'Impossible!' whispers 'Frostlips'. 'Can't be us they're after. Must be somebody else. There's manhunts on in Russia all year round!'

'Well, they ain't come out here in this hellish snow for the fun of it, you can bet your boots,' says 'Whorecatcher'.

'Let's get outside!' orders the Old Man, nervously. 'We're like rats in a trap in here!'

Unfortunately, it has stopped snowing. A full moon has come out from behind the hurrying clouds, and the snow glitters in its pale beams.

We huddle together, freezingly cold, behind the frost-weathered stones, and stare out over the snowy distances.

We can see nothing, only hear the wind, howling.

'Jesus'n Mary!' cries Tiny suddenly. 'The 'ole Red bleedin' Army's on its way up 'ere after us!'

The Old Man turns his glasses in the direction Tiny is indicating, but can see nothing.

'You're still bloody drunk, and seein' things,' he snarls angrily.

'*Job tvojemadj,*' cries the Commissar. 'Siberians! A whole company of 'em, and they're coming this way!'

Soon after, the rest of us can see them too. They come racing down the mountains on skis in one long line.

The Legionnaire slides down behind the MG-34, inserts a belt, loads, and closes the cover with a tiny click.

I draw my pistol from its shoulder-holster, cock it and let the hammer down carefully on the round. It's the best way with a *Nagan.*

'What the hell d'you think you're goin' to get up to with that popgun?' asks 'Whorecatcher', with a gesture of resignation. 'Do you realize what those fellers'll do to us when they get hold of us? I hurt just thinking about it. We'll never see the light o' day again! And when they've finished with us we'll only be able to crawl!'

'Shut up,' I snarl, holstering the pistol again. 'They won't take *me* alive!'

'You're wrong! If they want us they'll take us, however much you bang away with that pistol of yours. The sun's gone down for us. We're *dead* men. Think I'll just stroll down there and get it over quick!'

'You stay here,' commands the Commissar, in a voice sharp as a knife. 'Damned if we're going to give up just because a couple of slit-eyed NKVD coppers come sliding down on boards!'

'I'm not givin' up either,' swears 'Frostlips', readying his *Ka'ashnikov.*

Gregor cracks a magazine in the LMG. He too is ready to fight things out.

The Legionnaire puts a *Nagan* in his boot-top, and draws his Moorish combat-knife.

'What the hell good'll it do, bangin' away now, man?' sighs Albert despairingly. Still he loads himself up with hand-grenades.

'You look like a lump of black pudding left behind in a shithouse,' grins Porta.

'That's what I feel like,' admits Albert sadly.

'Shall we give 'em a dose up the arse with stovepipe Lizzie here?' asks Tiny, battle-hungry. He handles the heavy mortar as if it were made of cardboard. 'We can blow them shits away like confetti, when they come on to that long flat bit.'

'You must have been reading our propaganda leaflets again,' Porta scolds him irritably. 'They'd hear it a million miles off in these shitty mountains. Then we'd have the whole rotten OGPU on our necks!'

'*Njet mortira**,' warns sledge-driver Ermolov, hugging his *Kalashnikov* closer to him. He has loaded with explosive bullets which smash anything they hit.

'Is it the OGPU?' asks Albert with wide-open eyes. Even the thought of the OGPU or the Gestapo makes him shiver like a blancmange.

'Yes! Who'd the hell you think it was?' asks Porta, with a short laugh. 'Think it was a load of Salvation Army blackbirds, out picking up loose souls?'

'*Ssatana*,' curses the Commissar. 'Of all the fucking patrols to run into! Siberian bloody OGPU. *Ssatana*!' he repeats, banging his fist down viciously on the *Kalashnikov*'s round magazine.

'What the hell difference does it make if they're Siberians or whatever?' asks the Old Man, blankly. He keeps his eyes on the long line of snow-camouflaged skiers on the far side of the mountain slope, as he speaks.

'Hell of a difference,' growls the Commissar. 'Siberians are the best manhunters in the world. They're on their feet night and day all year round, in peace or war. They range the country from the Polar Sea to the Black Sea, from the

* *Njet mortira:* No mortars

269

mountains of China to the forests of Finland and Poland, and they get a *bounty* for every single body they bring in.'

Staff-corporal Dalin comes rushing down the ice-clad path, completely out of breath, throws himself down alongside the Commissar and fishes a crumpled cigarette from his pocket. Hungrily he sucks smoke into his lungs, and lets it come slowly out through his nostrils.

'Igor's still up there,' he explains, pointing to the mountain top. 'There's a whole company of OGPU special service troops on the way up and they've got a short-barrelled mountain gun with 'em. Igor thinks they've picked up our trail.'

The cigarette burns down one side. He looks at it, sadly. '*Tovaritsch*!' he says, giving the Commissar a pleading look, and scratching his head under his fur cap. 'Let us go home, and leave the gold where it is! A man who has never been rich will never miss it!'

'Shut up, you mangy cur,' says the Commissar angrily. 'There *is* no way back. Take a swig of vodka, maybe it'll swill the cowardice out of you!'

'Get your pecker up, mate.' Tiny puts his arm, comfortingly, round Dalin. The man looks like a sick hen, whose eggs have been taken from her. 'Buck up, now! You're gonna be rich, an' can pick out your own wall-paper.'

'Have we got any chance at all of getting out of this?' asks Gregor desperately, looking up at the snow-capped mountains.

'I'm no prophet,' growls the Commissar impatiently. 'But first of all we've got to get up through that gulch before they start cackling on that bloody radio of theirs!'

'We can soon blow that lot away,' cries Porta, optimistic as always. 'We've got two tea-waggons, the PIV and the Panther *and* that armoured sledge. We're a whole bloody army. They've only got a pissy little mountain gun, and for sure not a single armour-piercing shell for it. They can't do more'n scratch our paintwork a bit!'

'The *radio* dammit, the *radio*!' shouts the Commissar

furiously. 'Before the noise of our first explosive shell has died away they'll have alarmed their base and we'll have a whole division on top of us – supported by Jabos! There'll be headhunters swarming all over these mountains like flies on a hot midden!'

'Who says we use guns?' asks Porta. 'We just go quietly up to 'em with open hatches so they think we're on their side. Then when we get close enough to start up on 'em with balalaikas an' guitars. Goodbye the slit-eyed shits!'

'*Njet!*' answers the Commissar, shaking his head negatively. 'Anybody can tell you don't know the headhunters. Immediately they sight us a radio report goes off, and somewhere or other somebody starts finding out who we can be. Nobody can *move* in Russia without the OGPU having been informed, and what d'you think'll happen when they can't obtain radio contact with the company we've liquidated? I promise you. Everything comes to the boil!'

'You don't think, then, that it's us they're looking for?' asks the Old Man, doubtfully. 'Who the hell else can it be?'

'It's *certainly* not us,' answers the Commissar, decisively. 'They're one of those blasted tracking patrols who're not looking for anything in particular. Patrols like that are permanently on the hunt for anybody wandering round without a *propusk**.' He pushes his fur cap thoughtfully back on his head.

His grey eyes suddenly begin to glitter cunningly. 'I think I've got it," he says after a long pause. 'A natural disaster! Their base could accept *that*!'

'You don't call it a disaster being rocked into eternity with lead guitar music?' asks Porta, with a short laugh, and patting his mpi.

'Certainly,' answers the Commissar, 'but we can't use that kind of disaster in this instance.'

'If you want to know what I think, man, then I'm for pissin' off out of here in one hell of a hurry,' whines Albert,

---

* *Propusk*: Permit

in a hoarse voice. He pulls his snow-mask further down over his face.

'What kind of weak sisters are you?' roars Porta angrily. 'Here I'm trying to make you rich, so you can wave goodbye to the stinking army for the rest of your lives, and lie on the beach playin' with the luxury whores. When you've started something then you finish it. *Panjemajo?* The earth's round, and if you ain't smart you can risk falling off it. And it *ain't* smart to give up now just because a party of Sweatyfoot Indians come slidin' along on planks. Let's get on with it. There's daylight up ahead!'

> 'Und wenn die ganze Erde bebt,*
> und die Welt sich aus den Angeln hebt,
> da kann doch einen Goldsucher nicht erschüttern!
> Keine Angst, keine Angst, Rose Mari . . .'

hums Tiny thoughtfully, drumming his fingers on his *Kalashnikov.*

'Could we get along that windin' trail there that goes up alongside the ruins?' asks Barcelona, pointing.

'Yes, you could if you were a mountain goat that'd lost its wits,' answers the Commissar. 'This time of the winter nobody gets through without going through the gulch, and after that there's the *Paritip†*, but we can leave that for now. I can tell you it's not for people with weak stomachs, and in a high wind even the strongest-nerved get the shits!'

'*Paritip?* What the hell's a *Paritip?*' asks Porta.

'Wait till you see it,' grins 'Frostlips'. 'It might make

---

* Freely translated:
  And should the whole earth tremble.
  And the world roll off its tracks.
  That cannot shake a prospector.
  Never fear! Never fear! Rose Marie . . .
† Russian: roughly 'the Floater' or 'Glider': a suspension platform over a gorge

even you wish you'd stayed home. That is if you ain't one of these religious types who thinks death's better'n life!'

'Und noch bei Petrus wollen wir*
den Würfelbecher schwingen . . .'

hums Tiny, and kisses a hand-grenade.

'Shut bloody up, you half-witted idiots,' rages the Old Man, banging the butt of his machine-pistol into the snow.

'Won't even let us sing any bleedin' more,' grumbles Tiny.

The Commissar goes down in the snow between the Old Man and 'Frostlips' and draws a sketch with the tip of a bayonet.

'An avalanche,' cries the Old Man, in surprise, studying the sketch with a sceptical mien. 'Think it can be done?'

'Our one chance,' answers the Commissar. 'There's tons of snow up above ready to come down if we just help it a bit.'

'Shut *up*, then!' cries Porta, licking his frost-chapped lips cautiously. 'The light begins to flicker out there. An avalanche! Fuck *me*! Those headhunters down there'll get rolled straight into Paradise. Both St Peter an' Jesus'll go arse-over-tip when they arrive up there with all that snow!'

'How much gel' we got?' asks the Old Man, getting to his feet.

'Three full boxes,' answers Barcelona. 'Enough to put the Kremlin up on the moon!'

'One box o' ten's enough,' says the Old Man.

'Catch!' shouts Tiny, throwing a package of explosives into the Old Man's lap.

'Are you completely mad?' shouts the Commissar, in terror, throwing himself down like lightning behind a

---

* Freely: And up with Peter we will make
  The dice-cup shake and rattle . . .

weathered stone block. 'In this temperature? Anybody knows it'll have degenerated by now and can go off at the slightest touch.'

'Take it easy,' smiles Porta. '*We* don't have to abide by the patent laws, so we've changed the formula round a bit. What we've done'd send the inventors crawling up their own arseholes for fright, but we found out, when we were soddin' about up there where it'd freeze the balls off a brass reindeer, that a bit of nitroglycerine in the dough and a freshener of nitre made it more stable in cold weather. If we'd used what the eggheads at Bamberg'd told us to we'd have been on the moon by now playin' hide and seek with the Mars-men!'

Tiny fishes a whole bundle of loose primers carelessly out of his pocket, and hands them to him. Any ammunition expert would have jumped out of his boots at the sight. Primers have to be treated with great care. The least shock can send them off.

'Shall we blow off all the soap, then?' asks Tiny, eagerly, beginning to make preparations.

'Hell no!' answers the Old Man crossly. 'Five or six ought to be more than enough!'

'*Mon Dieu*! Where are the pincers?' asks the Legionnaire, excitedly. 'We must hurry! They are coming towards us quickly!'

'Pincers?' asks Tiny. 'They've gone missin', but who needs 'em? You can bite 'em on to the cable. I've done it often. Quicker, too! Don't 'ave to bite too 'ard though, else your teeth fall out – *an*' your old napper goes with 'em, too!'

'*Merde*!' says the Legionnaire, shaking his head. 'Only a man who is tired of life bites on those things!'

Unworriedly Tiny pushes the wires into the primers and bites them fast.

'He's too stupid to realize the danger,' grins Porta. 'Not even the dumbest dog'd even *sniff* at a primer!'

'He's raving mad,' says 'Frostlips'. '*We* have to put on rubber shoes when we go into the depots where they keep

274

that shit. That sod *eats* 'em!'

'It's because he's a Sunday's child, born on Christmas Eve,' laughs Porta. 'Nothing can happen to *him*!'

Tiny is already chewing on the fifth primer. When he has finished he connects the explosive mass in a way that sends shivers down our spines. Then he puts the whole lot down into his deep pocket. The dangerous primers stick up on their wires and bob about like the bells on a jester's cap.

With Dalin in the lead we make our way towards the mountain-top. When we have got some way up we have to change from skis to snowshoes.

'You're goin' to have to learn to stand on those planks a hell of a lot better,' Dalin criticizes us, with the irritability of the expert, 'or you'll never manage this job!'

Up under the small conifer trees, we fumble our way in pitch darkness, and have to use our handlamps in short flashes. There are narrow, deep crevasses everywhere. To go down in one of these is certain death.

The storm howls, in long, miserable moans. Frost explodes in branch and trees with the sharp crack of rifle-shots.

Cursing and fuming we try to protect our faces against the short stiff branches of the trees. They whip across our faces, drawing blood when the skin breaks.

Dalin pushes us along, angrily, jeering at us for our clumsiness.

'Even an old, worn-out Cossack grandmother could catch up with you,' he rages, impatiently. 'Dopes like you lot'll never win this world war!'

'Wait'n see, you bowlegged Jewboy,' screams Tiny, throwing his mpi at Dalin, but not succeeding in hitting him. 'You don't know us Germans yet!'

After two hours of inhuman toil we reach the open slope above the tree-line. Tired out we drop down. The wind is not merely icy, it is a roaring hurricane. We can see the peak, like a great, threatening colossus, a little way in front of us.

'*Ssatan*,' Dalin curses. 'Up on your feet! In half an hour

275

the moon'll be out, and they'll be able to see us 100 miles off.'

'Jesus'n Mary,' groans Tiny. 'I can feel them OGPU *Kalashnikov* explosive berries borin' their way into my good German guts already!'

Suddenly I stumble, and begin to slide down the slope. I am rolling like a snowball at constantly increasing speed when a large rock gets in my way. For a moment I think I have broken, or sprained, an ankle, but the fear of being left alone soon gets me back on my feet, even though I can feel the pain right up through my back.

'I can't go on!' groans Gregor, dropping like a felled tree to the snow.

'Up you get!' snarls Porta, giving him a brutal kick. 'Think of your share of the gold and you'll *want* to go on!'

'Shit on the gold,' pants Gregor, worn out. 'If it's all the gold in the world you can keep it! Let me *sleep*! I want to die! *Now*!' He presses his face into the snow, and his whole body shakes with hysterical sobs.

Together we get him back up on his feet, and drag him between us like a sack. He shouts, and calls us every name he can think of. Finally Porta cannot stand it any longer. He gives him such a beating that all his frost-sores break open like ripe boils. It helps for a while.

Ermolov is lying in the shelter of a projecting shelf of rock staring through his night-glasses. Silently he points down the mountain. We can see the OGPU company, like small, moving, black spots below us.

'We've got to get further up,' says Dalin. 'But get some speed on now! There's not much time to lose! But don't look down,' he warns us. 'Look up!'

'Good Lord deliver us,' Porta breaks out, in amazement, when we are all the way up, and see the enormous masses of snow which are resting on only a relatively small rock-shelf.

'When once that starts to roll,' says Barcelona, 'that band of murderers down there'll do well to move arse in one hell of a hurry!'

'Four charges ought to be plenty to set that snowball rolling down on their nuts,' says 'Frostlips', scratching his head thoughtfully under his fur cap.

'Let's use five. Better safe than sorry!' suggests Porta, looking up at the huge lip of snow. 'But now the devil are we goin' to position the loads without settin' the avalanche going too soon? If it starts before the neck-shooters have got into the wide bit there, they'll get back with their balls intact and we're in the shit up to our necks!'

'We'll have to get over on the other side,' says Barcelona. He leans over the steep cliff-face and draws back, shivering. 'That's impossible! Take an eagle to do it!'

'Leave it to me,' says Tiny, pushing energetically forward. 'I ain't no eagle, but I'm clever'n one. You lot ain't got no idea of 'ow to blow anythin' up! *I'll* show you how to do it!'

'Don't do it,' warns 'Frostlips'. 'You'll break your neck!'

'Don't give me that piss!' sneers Tiny, contemptuously. 'Take a look at the way a bloke from 'Amburg does it! I'll be up on that mantelshelf and 'ave the fireworks in place quicker'n a bull up a butcher!'

'He's right,' says the Old Man, convinced. 'The shelf's bound to increase the force of the blow an' make even more snow come down on 'em. The noise of the charges'll get damped down by the snow, and the slits down there won't get frightened and do the devil out of a nice fresh delivery!'

'Why not?' asks Porta, shrugging his shoulders, indifferently. 'Try it! Tiny's always gettin' away with things other fellers'd break their necks trying!'

'D'you think it's *dangerous*?' asks Tiny doubtfully, peering cautiously down into the dizzying abyss.

'Not a bit of it,' lies Porta impudently, pointing up to the snow-cap hanging threateningly out over the lip of the shelf. 'If all that weight of ice an' snow can't fall, how'll you be able to? Just be careful not to spit on both hands at the same time!'

'Let's do it then,' says Tiny, decisively, wrapping the

rope around him. 'Gimme that ice-axe. Keep a tight hold on the string now so's you can pull me up again if I go on me arse!'

Gregor sits down, presses his heels well into the cliff and passes the rope out slowly, as Tiny moves across the icy slope.

'He'll never make it,' whispers Barcelona nervously.

'More rope,' shouts Tiny impatiently. 'I got to go round a corner, for Christ's sake! It's black as up Albert's arse down 'ere!'

'He'll kill himself,' says Gregor, darkly, paying out more rope.

Frostlips sits down beside him and helps him hold on to it. It is literally Tiny's lifeline.

'Jesus Christ!' howls Tiny, in a voice which sounds as if it is coming to us through cotton-wool.

'Anything up?' asks Porta, looking up, but unable to catch sight of him.

'Fell on me arse,' comes faintly from the cliff-face. 'It's blowin' like 'ell over 'ere. My prick's turned into a bleedin' icicle.'

'This is madness,' mumbles Barcelona. 'He'll never *make* it!'

'Wait and see,' says Porta. 'I know Tiny. If he gets really angry there's nothing can stop him!'

We can hear the sound of the ice-axe, which he is using to cut steps in the rock and ice. Gregor and 'Frostlips' pay out more and more rope.

'How the hell's he *doing* it?' asks 'Frostlips', shaking his head. 'He needs all his strength to even hang on to the cliff-wall, and he must already be frozen through and through!'

'Yes, and don't forget he's got his pockets full of explosives,' says Barcelona. 'And like the dope he is it's primed! Don't need much of a knock for him to blow himself and half the mountain to bits.'

'Did he ever take an ammunition course anyway?' asks 'Frostlips'. 'Nobody who's ever had anything to do with explosives treats 'em the way he does!'

'He *was* on a course at Bamberg,' laughs Porta, carelessly. 'But they threw him off it before he managed to blow the whole place up. He did kill off a few ammo experts though, without getting as much as a scratch himself. Even though he went up there on the Milky Way a time or two, he still came down licking the cream off his chops!'

If we lean out over the edge of the cliff we can just see Tiny's dark shadow moving slowly upwards, veiled in billowing clouds of snow.

'He looks like one of those stuntmen climbing up a skyscraper,' mutters the Commissar nervously.

'Bit short of windows to nip through, though, if he gets tired,' says Porta, drily.

'If he slips now,' mumbles 'Frostlips', 'he's got 5,000 feet under him. The rope'd cut him clean in two!'

'Damn an' set fire to it,' curses Tiny from out in the snow. 'This bleedin' ledge ain't no wider than a fly is between the eyes.'

'Hang on with your toes,' suggests Porta. 'Bend 'em like the birds do!'

'What do you think I *am* doin'?' comes Tiny's voice from out on the mountain-side.

'Get on with it,' shouts 'Frostlips' nervously. 'Those headhunters'll be in the valley in a minute, and at our throats before we know where we are!'

A nasty crash and a rain of powdery snow cuts him short. The rock-shelf has given way. With a howl of terror Tiny goes out into thin air but in some miraculous manner manages to hang on with his ice-axe.

Cursing and swearing he begins to work his way upwards again. We lean out and see him hanging and swaying where the ledge was before.

He hacks viciously at the snow and finally makes a hole large enough for the charges. Spitting with rage he rolls the cables a couple of times more round the explosive and forces stones and pieces of ice into the hole to wedge the charge in place. It wouldn't be smart if we were to take it with us when we moved the wires.

A strong gust of wind takes off his fur cap and nearly sends him down into the gulf with it. He slides down hazardously, but finds a foothold on the second ledge, which is somewhat broader.

Even though he is bear-like in size, he looks small against the tons of snow which hang, suspended, above his head. He checks the charges once more and gives the primers an extra crimp with his teeth. Balancing on the edge he takes a swig from his water-bottle. Then he starts back across the vertical, wind-blown, rock wall. A huge eagle flaps close by him. Furiously, he throws a punch at it, loses his grip and slides some way down the mountain face.

Gregor, alone on the safety rope, had become unobservant from cold and exhaustion and does not feel Tiny's tug on the rope. It is hanging so loosely that it has become dangerous. The big man has no more than just rounded the sharp corner when the eagle attacks again. He strikes out at it and loses his footing. His hands claw at the ice, blood spurts from long gashes and nails rip away. His axe curves out over the edge of the cliff, and goes sailing on down in a cloud of snow.

The eagle gives a hoarse, triumphant scream, and dives to the attack again.

Porta lets out a terrified shout, which warns Gregor just in time. He manages to press himself in between two vertical rocks, before he is taken over the edge by the terrific pull on the rope.

'What the devil are you up to?' asks the Commissar, wriggling his way over to us. 'Good Lord Almighty. He must have been killed!'

Far below we can see Tiny swinging back and forth on the rope with the raging eagle flapping around his head.

'He's lost his axe!' says Porta.

The Commissar lowers his own ice-axe down to him, quickly, and he manages to grasp it after several attempts.

Slowly we tighten the rope. If we go too quickly we can risk it snapping.

As we pull him up higher and higher we can hear him cursing and swearing.

'Got a full head of steam up,' says Porta. 'Gregor'd better get going till he's gone off the boil!'

'I'm off,' says Gregor firmly, beginning to buckle on his skis.

None of us has noticed that Tiny is already up over the edge, foaming with rage. The Commissar gives a warning shout as he comes rushing towards us through the snow, looking for the guilty party.

'You drop Tiny's bleedin' rope?' he roars accusingly, pointing his ice-axe at me.

'No, *no*!' I yell, to avoid certain death. 'It was Gregor! He dozed off!'

'Dozed off, did 'e?' roars Tiny. He bulldozes through the snow, towards where Gregor is sitting buckling on his skis.

The Old Man throws an mpi at him. It hits him right in the face, but he carries on, without even a second's pause.

Gregor just manages to turn around. Tiny grabs him by both skis and swings him round above his head like a hammer-thrower. When he has got speed up he lets go of him. With a crunch his body strikes a rock, his skis splintering. Then Tiny is on him again, hammering at him with his fists. They seem to be rotating as fast as propellers. Gregor knows he is fighting for his life. With the courage of desperation he succeeds in kicking upwards and hitting Tiny on the knee. Now the big man goes really crazy. With a scream he jumps up into the air, turns, and comes down on Gregor with such force that the man's body is literally pressed down into the frozen snow.

'Back!' hisses the Commissar, white with rage, and pressing the muzzle of his *Kalashnikov* into Tiny's throat. 'Back I say, or I'll shoot your head off!'

But Tiny is deaf to everything. Foaming at the mouth with rage he goes on beating the unconscious Gregor.

'Let me,' says Porta, bringing his machine-pistol down on Tiny's neck. With a tired grunt he falls down and lies motionless across Gregor.

'Chuck him over the edge!' suggests 'Frostlips' furiously, giving Tiny a brutal kick. 'The mad bastard's *dangerous*!'

'Take it easy,' says Porta. 'Who wouldn't be annoyed at some idiot lettin' him take a 300-yard sprint down the side of a mountain, and gettin' his whole bag o' bones knocked sideways?'

Shortly afterwards Tiny regains consciousness, shaking his head like a duck which has just been down to have a look at the bottom of its pond.

'I couldn't help it,' Gregor excuses himself weakly, wiping blood from his battered features.

'We'll discuss that later,' Tiny promises him with a wicked look, and lumbers off towards the edge of the cliff.

'Where the devil are you going?' asks the Old Man, running after him with his machine-pistol at the ready.

'Ain't we gonna roll that snowball?' asks Tiny. 'Ain't that what we crawled up on this Commie bleedin' mountain to *do*?'

Cursing and swearing furiously he begins to climb the icy granite wall again. He is so angry that he has forgotten to attach his climbing-rope.

'If he slips now,' says 'Frostlips', 'he's had it! Mad as they come, he is!'

'Don't for God's sake tell him it's dangerous,' warns Porta, 'then he'll be sure to fall!'

It seems an eternity before he finally finds the cable. It is still attached to the explosive charge. As carefully as if it were made of glass he pulls it over to him, and winds it around his elbow.

'God have mercy on us all!' groans the Commissar. 'Never in my life have I seen anything so insane!'

Twice, on his way back, he slips on the slope. Only a frozen snowdrift which is accidentally in his path stops him from going over the edge and down into the abyss.

'What about if it's a dud?' asks Barcelona, nervously, when Tiny is back and has gleefully connected the wires to the batteries.

'We'll be paddlin' up shit-creek,' answers Porta. 'Nothing left but to go straight at 'em with hand-grenades, balalaikas and guitar music!'

'The radio,' says the Commissar. 'That blasted radio. They always station it at a distance from them under cover! The signaller will be screaming for help as soon as we make a move, and up'll come the Jabos!'

'I'm against this battery shit,' rumbles Tiny. 'An old-fashioned fuse, what splutters off to where you can *see* it goin'. That was better'n more fun too! Used to remind me of Christmas Eve, when old Mr Creuzfeldt used to get drunk an' make us sing:

> And when they came to 'Erod's 'ouse,
> 'E was there in the window, an' lookin' out . . . .'

'Come *on*!' orders the Old Man, lowering his field-glasses. '*Use* the batteries! It's a matter of minutes! Send it off when I give the order!'

'What you talkin' to me like *that* for?' Tiny flares up, angrily. 'Think I live in a bucket with a 'ole in it, and've got me brains where me balls is, do you? I can tell you the psychopaths give me intelligence gradin' 0.7, which is very 'igh!'

'Depends which end of the table you start at,' grins Porta. 'But steady on with those leads and that battery. *Would* be funny if we got the lot of it down the back of our necks ourselves. Those bloody assassins down there'd kill themselves laughing, and we'd go down in world history as the biggest dopes ever to have taken part in *any* war!'

'*Job tvojemadj*,' mumbles 'Frostlips'. 'Here come those devils!'

The moon comes out like an explosion. We can clearly see a line of soldiers moving upwards on skis. They stop several times, and stare up at the peaks as if they knew we were there.

'Must be time we sprinkled a bit of snow down on 'em,' says Porta. ''Fore it's goodbye gold an' the life of Reilly!'

'Wait!' warns the Commissar. He examines the terrain through his binoculars. 'We've got to take them *all*! If one gets away, up goes the alarm!'

'There's guests on the way up the cliffs,' says Tiny, listening tensely. 'I can 'ear their climbin'-irons!'

'Balls,' says 'Frostlips'. '*I* can't hear a thing!'

'No, but I *can*,' says Tiny, wiggling his nose like a rabbit in a cabbage-patch.

The officer leading the column stops and turns his field-glasses up towards the brow of the cliff behind which we are hiding.

'Keep *still*!' whispers the Commissar, his voice shaking. 'The slightest movement, those bastards'll *see* it!'

'I'm ready to move this mountain,' says Tiny, grinning broadly.

'Hell!' whispers the Old Man. 'No shit now, or we're finished!'

The OGPU soldiers below us have fanned out. They have their skis on their backs and push themselves up by their staves. We can now hear, too, that there are more of them on their way up the face of the cliff.

'What we bleedin' waitin' for?' asks Tiny, impatiently. 'Ivan'll *be* here in a minute, shakin' 'is bleedin' balalaikas under our noses!'

Nervously, I screw the cover off a stick-grenade, and put my finger through the ring. I am ready to throw it as soon as the first Russian face appears above the edge of the cliff.

Most of the soldiers in the long single column have now disappeared along the side of the mountain, where we can no longer see them. Their voices become more and more audible, however, through the wild howling of the storm. Suddenly the tail of the column – five soldiers – stops. They point field-glasses towards the top of the great mass of granite. Some instinct must be warning them of an unknown danger. They are not recruits. They are manhunters of the most experienced kind.

'Shall I *do* it?' asks Tiny, moving the wires even closer to the battery. So close that we cannot understand why the charge has not gone off.

'Not yet!' whispers the Commissar. 'We've got to have those five come closer!'

Porta is down behind the LMG, the butt pressed into his shoulder, and his finger on the trigger.

I open the covers of the cartridge boxes, and hold the long belts ready for use.

'*Now!*' hisses the Commissar, bringing his fist down in the snow.

Tiny gives out a scream of pleasure, and makes the contact.

For a moment it is as if the world stands still. Then the icy quiet of the night is split open by a series of thunderous explosions. They roll across the mountains and die away in far-distant echoes.

'Ought to give the headhunters something else to think about,' grins Porta with satisfaction, bringing the night-glasses up to his eyes. The OGPU soldiers have been gripped by panic, and are scattering to all sides.

It seems as if the huge overcap of snow has remained untouched by the explosions. Several minutes go by in which nothing happens.

The OGPU soldiers have also seen this. They stop, and begin feverishly to buckle on their skis. A little officer waves excitedly with his *Kalashnikov* and shouts hoarse orders.

'Roll then, you bleedin' snow, you!' mumbles Tiny, shaking his fist up at the snow-cap. 'I'm going up to see what's wrong,' he says, getting up on one knee.

'Crazy sod!' snarls the Old Man. 'You're staying *here*!'

There is a sound like that of distant thunder, swiftly coming closer. The first of the colossal snow-masses whirls up in a huge white cloud. For a moment it seems to hang suspended in the air; then movement commences. Hundreds of tons of frozen snow hit the opposite slope and are thrown up again as if from a new explosion. Then the first gout of snow thunders against the rocks further down the mountain.

Faster than thought countless tons of snow are on their

way down the mountain, sweeping away everything in their path.

The nearest of the OGPU soldiers are whirled by the snowy masses into nothingness. A couple of soldiers on skis are racing in front of the tumbling snow, and seem as if they may have a chance of getting away from it.

'*Vive la mort*,' snarls the Legionnaire. He picks up a sniper's rifle and adjusts the telescopic sights.

'Not at that range,' says the Old Man.

'*Bien sûr*,' replies the Legionnaire. He presses his cheek against the butt and fires rapidly three times.

The leading skier falls forward, and continues on down the slope with his head down like a figurehead between his skis. The soldier bringing up the rear turns to see where the shot came from. Then he makes a fatal mistake. He makes a half-turn but is caught by panic. Turns again, and is overtaken by the avalanche, which thunders over, and buries him.

Trees whirl in the air before the advancing masses of snow. A whole forest is torn off the face of the mountain.

'What a bleedin' snowball *that* was!' shouts Tiny happily, when we are down at the vehicles again. The others have been waiting for us down there, getting more and more nervous.

'Those headhunters certainly lost their skis,' says Porta. 'What a roller-coaster that was!'

'I'll take it,' offers Tiny, crawling into the radio-room, from which we can hear a howling call-tone.

Tiny fiddles with the receiver, and bangs it a couple of times impatiently on the side of the tank before it works.

''Ello!' he says into the microphone. 'Who am I? I'm me, that's who I am!'

'Idiot! What's your position?' fumes a sharp, annoyed voice.

'Down round the arse'ole o' the universe,' answers Tiny, with a little laugh. 'We just threw a snowball at the neighbours' kids!'

'Where are you speaking from?' asks the voice, impatiently.

'From 'ere!' answers Tiny. 'Where else?'

286

'Are you out of your mind? I want to know where you are?' snarls the voice.

'You're a dumb 'un! We're in bleedin' Russia, of course!'

'Now you watch yourself, soldier!' The strange voice shakes with rage. 'You don't seem to know who you're talking to?'

'Think I'm a fortune-teller or somethin', do you?' answers Tiny, bursting into a roar of laughter.

'Are you laughing at me?' The voice becomes dangerously calm. 'I want to know who I'm talking to?'

'You're talkin' to me, you dope!' shouts Tiny, beginning slowly to come to the boil. 'Ain't you realized that yet? You're about as useful as a prick that's been touched up by a circular saw!'

'You are speaking to the communications officer.' snarls the voice, angrily. 'Now I want a straight answer from you: rank, name and unit!'

''It your 'ead on somethin' 'ave you?' explodes Tiny. 'We're only allowed to talk secret! The neighbours ain't got to be able to know what we're goin' about, see! You ain't gonna get a thing out of me! You could be one of these bleedin' spies they talk such a lot about. *Panjemajo?*'

'God help us to have patience! D'you know the code word?'

'No, why should I?' Tiny laughs noisily. 'It ain't me that's the sparks. I'm just standin' in for Julius that's gone for a walk!'

'Listen now, soldier.' hisses the communications officer, his voice shaking with rage. 'You're mopping up. Now I want to know *what* you've mopped up!'

'You coulda said that straight off, 'stead of askin' where we are.' answers Tiny. 'We just threw a bleedin' great snowball at Ivan, as is now on the way to Paradise fast as 'is skis can take 'im!'

'Give me your section commander and get off the radio, you madman! I'll give you bloody snowballs!'

'Old Un'!' screams Tiny in a ringing bass baritone. 'There's some sod of a psycho on the radio as wants to know what we've mopped up! Watch out for 'im though, 'e might be one of them bleedin' spies as is sneakin' around all over the place listening in! Says 'e's an officer but I think 'e's probably lyin'!'

'What the devil have you done now?' asks the Old Man, looking worried, and edging down in front of the radio.

A long conversation follows, which, for the Old Man's part, consists of: 'Yes, sir! Yes, major! Yes, sir!'

'You know what I fancy, now?' asks Porta, when we are again on the move. 'Hard-boiled eggs and shrimps in lobster sauce, then a large helping of pork with *sauerkraut* and preserved pears.'

'Shut up,' hisses the Old Man, crossly. 'Shut up about food! And I'll shoot you, Tiny, if you ever go near that radio again!'

A grey dawn has broken through when we reach the *Paritip*, which we hope, with a good deal of luck, can take us across the ravine. It is an odd-looking construction.

'Bottoms up, St Peter!' says Porta, looking down into the depths. 'Can that thing carry a tank?'

'So they say,' answers 'Frostlips' with a shrug of his shoulders. 'And we've got to hope they're right, because we ain't got a bit of choice in the matter! We've got to go over! We've blocked the pass ourselves with that avalanche!'

'Doesn't look all that solid,' says the Old Man, eyeing the contraption sceptically. It is a heavy platform, which hangs, swaying, suspended from thick cables.

'Come along! Let's get on with it! Who's going first?' shouts the Commissar, impatiently.

'You can go first, Albert,' says Porta, with a graceful wave of his hand.

'Not me, man!' says Albert, after he has been out on the rocking platform. It has to be propelled over the chasm by the turning of a hand-winch.

'You'd rather go last, perhaps, when the cables are a bit more worn?' asks Porta, sarcastically. 'You grab that offer of mine in a hurry, my son, and take off first!'

Albert gives in, and edges his way down through the T-34's turret hatch.

Cautiously, as if he were driving on glass, he edges the

heavy tank out on to the *Paritip*. The platform rolls like a ship in heavy weather at the overload. Slowly it begins to glide over towards the far side, its cables singing with the strain.

'Slowly,' the Commissar warns. 'Only slowly!'

Silently, and with butterflies in our stomachs, we follow the swaying platform. Despite the weight it is carrying, the violent blasts of wind still move it from side to side.

'Looks bloody dangerous, that,' mumbles Gregor. 'And think, we've volunteered for it!'

'Kind of thing a man only does once in his life,' grins Porta, carelessly. 'We'll have a story to tell when we're all Swedish Socialists!'

The heavy Panther goes over last. The logs of the platform creak warningly and the cables sing as they take the strain of its weight.

Porta runs his hand through his red hair, spits into the ravine, and he and Tiny take the winch.

'I daren't watch,' mumbles the Commissar, turning his back. 'It can't be long before those cables go!'

As he speaks the words there is a sharp crack, and one of the cables breaks. The platform begins to heel over to one side. The Panther slides slowly backwards.

'*Par Allah*!' cries the Legionnaire, nervously. 'It's going off. It's all over with them!'

'Hell!' howls Porta, in terror. He throws himself at the winch. 'The whole shithouse is goin'!'

The platform heels more and more. One gust of wind and they are finished.

'Grab the cables!' shouts the Commissar. 'Move! Bring up the T-34!'

Albert backs the tea-waggon into place. Working against time we get a wire to the platform and haul it on to firm ground before the other cable breaks.

'God the Father preserve us!' says Porta. He is up on the edge staring at the *Paritip*. The platform now hangs at an angle of 45° down towards the bottom of the ravine. 'That was *close*! A feller needs a good bit of luck to get through a world war still breathin'!'

Brutality creates respect.

Adolf Hitler

They ran across the playground, jumped the fence and went on down Wundt Strasse, panting heavily. They heard the shouts from behind them:

'Halt! Stehen bleiben!'

But none of them stopped. The hard staccato bark of a machine-pistol sounded.

The first man to go down, with his face in the chuckling, spring-flushed waters of the stream, was the Section Leader, an old Feldwebel. He had already lived through one world war and had been firmly determined to live through this one as well.

The next to fall was the youngest. He was just sixteen. He crawled some distance on his knees, his face down close to the cinders. A long trail of blood marked his path. He was still alive when the military police reached him. They put a bullet through the back of his neck.

The rest of the section reached the race track and disappeared into Scheibenholtz Park. They hardly noticed the Leutnant, dangling by the neck from a tree with his hands tied behind his back.

A little further on an Oberst and a Gefreiter were hanging.

All three had a sign around their necks:

ICH BIN EIN FEIGLING, DER DEN FÜHRER VERRATEN HAT!*

Two hours later the military police picked them up crossing Johannes Parkweg.

All nineteen were hanged on the nearest trees as a terrible warning to other deserters.

This happened on 3 March 1945 at the Leipzig race track. The bodies of the deserters were not cut down until six weeks later.

* I AM A COWARD
   WHO HAS BETRAYED THE FÜHRER

290

THE MAD OGPU CAPTAIN

The Commissar raises his hand in the signal to halt.

In the middle of a round market-place, half-covered with powdery snow, a number of motorcycles stand parked. They all have side-cars on which machine-guns are mounted.

'Queer they don't take the guns inside with 'em?' Porta wonders.

'Not a *bit* queer,' sneers Heide. He is, as usual, annoyingly well-informed. 'As long as they're outside they're ready for firing. That's due to their effective frost lubricant. Take them inside and the temperature variation would make them freeze up and they'd be useless.'

'Watch out that swivellin' swastika in your *'errenvolk* prick don't freeze to ice,' Tiny roars with laughter at his own witticism.

'Not a sign of a sentry,' mumbles the Old Man, putting his head cautiously up over the edge of the turret hatch. 'These chaps must feel pretty bloody safe round here!'

'Over behind that house there's an old lorry,' says Porta, pointing.

'Then there'll be a lot of Ivans, count on that,' warns Tiny, craning his neck inquisitively.

The Commissar jumps heavily down from the motor-sledge. With his long cloak billowing in the wind he tramps towards us through the deep snow.

'Stay on your toes,' he says, bending his head back to look up at the Old Man in the Panther's turret. 'I don't understand this! There's not supposed to be any military personnel here! I'm afraid they may have got wind of us. Drive up through that street over there! I'll make this place safe with the T-34s and the sledge. Don't fire unless absolutely necessary. The dark'll help us. These yokels can't tell the

291

difference between a tank and a tricycle. If anybody asks, tell them you're transporting muck. They can understand *that*!'

Porta starts up, with a roar which makes the nearest houses shake. He speeds the 700 HP Maybach up to maximum revolutions to show what it can do. Typical driver showing-off. It is something he will never grow out of.

'What'll I put in the peashooter?' asks Tiny, patting a shell.

'HE, dammit! What did you think?' snarls the Old Man, irritated.

'I thought markers'd be all right,' grins Tiny, happily. 'We've still got some with red paint! Ivan'd be pleased as punch to get twenty gallons of red paint plastered all round 'is chops! Red's the colour o' the season in this country, they say!'

'Good God Almighty!' the Old Man breaks out. 'Have we still got those cursed markers? I've told you to chuck 'em out! They'll be the death of us if you make a mistake some time!'

'I never make mistakes,' boasts Tiny, in a superior tone. 'An' I don't want to lose those shells! Sooner or later we can 'ave some fun with 'em!'

Porta swings the Panther into a narrow street, which only leaves it fractions of an inch on each side.

'Get out and steer him,' the Old Man orders Tiny.

'It's always me,' protests Tiny, sourly. 'Why can't it be Sven? 'E's a volunteer an' wants to be an officer! Let 'im give the orders, then!'

'Shut up,' snarls the Old Man, 'and do as I say!'

With a lighted cigarette Tiny steers Porta down the narrow alleyway. When we have got some distance along it the Old Man orders a halt.

'Where the devil're we going to end up?' he mumbles, resignedly.

'In a boozer,' grins Porta, indifferently, and points to a large sign KUKHMISS – TAERSSKAJA* *Bajomaj*. 'They

* Restaurant

got rooms to let, too! Let's go in and sign the book. I can't remember what it's like any more to sleep in a proper bed.'

Tiny is already on his way up the broad steps leading to the restaurant.

'Where the hell're you off to, you crazy sod?' explodes the Old Man, pulling himself up on to the edge of the hatch.

'Goin' to order coffee an' 'ot Danish,' shouts Tiny, with his hand on the door-knocker.

'Idiot!' roars the Old Man. 'D'you want to get us shot?'

'No, I want a cup o' coffee,' chuckles Tiny, with a grin like a split pumpkin.

'You steer Porta, and nothing else,' snarls the Old Man, not far from boiling-point.

'Slowly, very slowly,' warns Tiny. 'Just a bit to the left an' you'll knock the 'ole bleedin' 'ouse down. The landlord wouldn't like *that* a bit!'

'Hell!' groans the Old Man, wiping the sweat from his brow. 'That was *close*!'

Suddenly Tiny dashes back to the tank and goes in through the side-hatch with the celerity of a rabbit disappearing down its hole.

'What's up?' asks the Old Man, in amazement.

'The *entire* Red Army's standing there just round the corner, scratchin' its arse,' pants Tiny, out of breath. 'If I 'adn't been careful stickin' me bonce round the corner of the 'ouse, they'd 'ave shot me up far as the other side of the bleedin' moon!'

The Old Man looks through the night-viewer, but can see nothing. The street lies dark and deserted.

'You've been drinking again, as usual, I suppose,' he says, sending Tiny a nasty look.

'Oh, you think that, do you?' shouts Tiny, in an insulted tone. 'Well then. You take a trip up there yourself an' stick your own nut round the corner!'

'What now?' asks Porta, taking a quick nip at the vodka bottle. 'Shall we rock along and take a look at these Commie soldiers? Or shall we give 'em an acid drop so's they'll know we're coming?'

'Slow forward!' orders the Old Man, shortly.

293

The heavy tank bobs a deep curtsey when Porta treads cautiously on the accelerator. Its near-side track takes the pediment of a house with it.

'That whatsit over there on the corner. Ain't that one of the flowers of the neighbours' army?' asks Porta, stopping the tank with a jerk.

'Slow forward!' orders the Old Man, in a low voice. 'He'd never be standing there, gaping, if he had any suspicions of us. He'd have screamed an alarm long since and woke up the half of Russia.'

'What about givin' 'im a pot o' paint?' asks Tiny, with a little laugh.

'The gun safe?' asks the Old Man, nervously.

'Too true she is,' answers Tiny. 'Think I'm barmy enough to be steppin' along in front of a tin-can with a readied gun pointing at my backside?'

A guard with a *Kalashnikov* is standing at the street crossing and staring with interest at the tank rattling towards him. If he gets suspicious, we're caught in a trap. We can't use the gun in this narrow street. They can put us out with hand-weapons without the least bit of trouble.

'What the hell's that clown thinkin' about?' whispers Porta, staring out through the driver's slit at the dark form standing planted like a statue a couple of hundred yards in front of us, with both hands buried deep in its pockets. 'Must be one of those Cossack abortions they've picked up on a midden and given a gun in exchange for his muck-rake!'

'And it's all gone that quick the army's forgot to give 'im the course on tank silhouettes,' grins Tiny, 'so 'e thinks we're a mechanized shit-barrow!'

Just before we reach the guard, Porta's eye falls on a narrow side street. With a great noise of falling bricks he turns the Panther into it, only to brake suddenly.

'They after us?' asks Tiny, taking a comforting swig at the vodka bottle.

'No, but we're in a blind, bloody alley,' snarls Porta. 'Why the hell can't they put up signs? We'll bloody well complain about this!'

'Couple of Commie squaddies from the neighbours on the way towards us,' warns Tiny, peering cautiously out of the side hatch.

Porta takes a quick look in the mirror. 'The devil! And they look like a couple of real public enemies!'

'Damnation,' curses the Old Man, nervously. 'Back! To hell with the consequences! Let's get out of here, before we get our arses singed!'

Nervously I take down an mpi from its bracket, and cock it. There is a whine of metal biting into concrete.

'Watch those tracks,' warns the Old Man. 'Bust one, and we've had it!'

''Ere comes another public bleedin' enemy,' says Tiny, stretching his neck.

Porta throws the tank round to the right so sharply that the shells come out of their open racks and clang about on the steel deck.

The Old Man lights his silver-lidded pipe with shaking fingers.

'Drop your speed, damn it!' he shouts, desperately.

'Fuck all to be frightened of,' howls Porta, switching on the forward spotlight. Too late, he sees two four-wheel-drive Tempos parked so close to one another that nothing wider than a bicycle could get past them. 'Everything's under control,' he screams, presses home the accelerator and rips the Tempos in two.

The Old Man drops his pipe, and covers his face with his hands.

'I trust you,' he says. He has no other choice. He gives up, leans back in the tank-commander's seat, and watches the night come rushing towards him.

The motor is thundering at maximum speed. Round about in the houses, lights come on without consideration for the black-out.

'Oh hell!' cries Porta. 'Now we're stuck! Elevate the gun! I'm going straight on!'

'You're not bloody well going straight through that wall, are you?' asks the Old Man, in fear. '*That* ought to make 'em realize we're not on their side!'

A balcony comes down, raining bricks and mortar on the tank. A motorcycle is flattened under its tracks.

Three Russians come towards us waving their arms.

'Shall I give 'em a pot o' paint?' asks Tiny. 'That ought to make 'em think a bit!'

'*Stoi, stoi idjiotsetvo*,' they shout and make threatening gestures at the tank, which goes roaring on down the narrow street smashing everything in its path.

The three Russians stop, and stare in terror at the onrushing tank. The next moment they are thrown up into the air, fall again to the cobblestones and two are crushed under its tracks. The third is back on his feet, and rushes off madly down the steep street.

'Get *him*!' shouts the Old Man. 'He mustn't get back and give the alarm, or all hell'll be loose!'

'I'll *eat* 'im!' shouts Tiny, and is already out of the side hatch with his garrotting-wire in his hand. He falls, of course, on the icy road. '*Ruki verch!**' he screams after the fleeing Russian, who is out of his mind with terror. He stops and spits angrily towards Tiny, and bends down and picks up a lump of ice which he throws at the tank. Then he sprints off again with Tiny thundering at his heels. They go down in a heap in a snowdrift.

Tiny jabs with his combat knife, but slips on the ice and misses his stroke.

The Russian gives out a scream of terror and disappears at top speed round a corner before Tiny can get back on his feet.

Careless of what he hits, Porta backs out of the narrow street at such a speed that you'd think the whole town was coming down round our ears.

A woman screams, hysterically, somewhere out in the night.

'Where the hell's that woman?' asks Porta, craning his neck. 'Screamin' women make me nervous!'

* *Ruki verch!:* Hands up!

296

'She's moved in with us. Up on the turret!' answers Tiny, laconically.

'Moved in?' asks the Old Man, blankly.

'Yes, and she's brought 'er bed an' blankets with 'er, too,' grins Tiny. He puts his head out of the side hatch.

The girl lets out a couple of strange long gulps at the sight of Tiny's sooty face. Then she gives another rattling scream.

''Eavens above. She's fell off,' he says, rubbing the palms of his hands together.

'Jesus *no*! Didn't hurt herself I hope?' cries Porta.

'Don't think so,' answers Tiny, who is hanging half out of the hatch opening. 'She's running that fast you'd think she'd got a wildcat in 'er pants!'

'Did she take the bed with her?' asks Porta, interestedly.

'No, it's still 'angin' there,' chuckles Tiny.

'Great! We can take it in turns to sleep in it!' Porta turns the tank in the direction of some old wooden houses with balconies and loggias projecting out over the street.

'Be careful, you're too close,' warns the Old Man. There is a sound of splintering wood and the tinkling of broken glass.

'The devil!' curses Porta, treading on the brake.

'What's wrong?' asks the Old Man nervously, bending down from the turret. 'Brakes gone?'

'*They're* all right!' snarls Porta, tramping away at the pedal. 'It's this rotten can. It keeps skidding, and smashing into these shitty houses!'

'Looks like the bleedin' 'ouses are tryin' to overtake us!' shouts Tiny, throwing half a loggia off the side hatch.

'That's what they *are* tryin' to bloody do,' answers Porta. He continues his attempts to brake lightly, but the tank only goes faster down the icy road. 'Somebody must be pushin' us. Shoot the bastard!' he shouts.

'Are we in difficulties, then?' asks Tiny.

'Difficulties?' answers the Old Man. 'We've been in bloody difficulties ever since this fuckin' world war got started!'

'What about goin' outside an' 'avin' a look at things?'

suggests Tiny. What he really wants to do is to get his feet on solid ground again. The atmosphere inside the tank seems to have become very hot all of a sudden.

Porta steers us in between two apartment blocks built of reinforced concrete. We are stuck there, quite helplessly.

'By all the devils in hell!' curses the Old Man, tensed like a spring. 'What the hell did you want to come in here for?'

'I'm tired of bustin' up houses,' answers Porta, resignedly, 'and, as you know, all roads lead to Rome!'

'We gotta go to Rome now?' asks Tiny, in amazement. 'Them Commies moved our gold to Rome, then, 'ave they?'

'Idiot!' snarls Heide. 'You *are* as stupid as you look!'

Tiny is about to go for him, when a yell is heard above from a first-floor window. A big Russian in shirt-sleeves with a steel helmet on his head leans out and waves his arms furiously.

What happens next is really a reflex movement.

Tiny's machine-pistol spits blue flame at the gesticulating figure. It rolls out through the window, slides down the front shield of the tank and lies still in the snow.

'*Dis*-mount!' orders the Old Man, jumping down from the turret. 'Let's get back to the market-place and see what's happening there! It sounds as if all hell's broke loose!'

At full speed I run headlong into Albert coming the opposite way past the baker's shop on the corner. He lets out a hoarse yell, and stumbles over a dead dog.

'If I get out of this alive I'll go to church every single Sunday!' he whines miserably. 'I'd rather be a sausage-man in Africa!'

'Who's firin'?' asks Porta, dropping down behind the LMG.

'Neighbours,' shouts Barcelona, taking cover behind a road-sweeping machine.

The market-place is a scene of wild confusion. Muzzle-flashes blaze from all directions.

'Take cover, for Christ's sake,' shouts 'Frostlips', as Gregor dashes recklessly across the square with tracer whistling around him.

'What's going on?' he asks in terror. He goes over the fence in a long arc and lands alongside 'Frostlips' in a cloud of snow. They are only a foot away from one another, but shout at the top of their lungs, covering one another with spittle.

'They shooting?' Gregor asks excitedly, readying his machine-pistol.

'Yes, you dope,' spits 'Frostlips'. 'That's what they're doin' nothin' *but*!'

'Why don't you shoot back at 'em?' roars Gregor, sending a waterfall of spittle into 'Frostlips's' face.

'That's what we *are* doin'!' answers 'Frostlips'. He sprays a rain of bullets out in front of him without taking any kind of aim.

'Think we can make it?' shouts Gregor in a voice which echoes between the houses.

'How the fuck should I know?' squeals 'Frostlips', sending an idiotic burst through a plateglass window. It breaks up into a million pieces and sets a burglar alarm going.

'Burglars!' shouts Gregor. 'They've got a nerve with both the German an' the Red Army in town!'

'Shut your stupid bloody mouth!' rages the Commissar, wiping spittle from his face.

The snarl of a *Kalashnikov* cuts him short. The windows on the far side of the market-place disintegrate, and all six tyres on the lorry parked under cover of the long house, go off with deafening explosions.

In the confusion I throw two hand-grenades. One of them goes into the cabin of the lorry which immediately catches fire.

'What the 'ell's goin' *on*?' shouts Tiny, staring round him in confusion. 'What kind of bleedin' idiots are shootin'? An' who the bleedin' 'ell they shootin' *at*? We're *friends*!'

A long, raging burst from a pair of machine-guns answers him.

'This is bloody well *enough*!' shouts Porta resentfully, losing his yellow topper.

'Those bastards have mounted guns up there on the third

floor,' screams Albert, pointing wildly. 'I don't think they know we're friendly!'

'I'm not taking any more of this shit,' shouts Porta, lifting his machine-pistol.

The shutters splinter. Snow, ice and shards of glass fly in all directions, as he empties the *Kalashnikov's* entire magazine into the window in one long burst.

A very fat and very angry lady in a bright yellow nightdress, and with a red nightcap on her head, appears at the shattered window.

'Sons of bitches!' she screams, furiously. 'You're going to have to pay for every bit of what you've smashed! Cowardly mongrels! Go out and shoot Germans, and leave us Russians in peace!' She lifts a large pottery floor-vase above her head, goes back a little way and runs forward to get more distance on her throw. Unfortunately for her she gets too much distance. She forgets to let go of the vase and goes with it out of the window. With a shrill scream she lands in a snowdrift. The vase flies out of her hands and hits 'Frostlips' on the head. He gulps, and goes out like a light.

'Wow!' cries Tiny.

'Right on the coconut!' laughs Porta, happily.

'Wow!' repeats Tiny. 'Was that lady *mad*?'

'I should think so, too,' replies Barcelona. 'Who wouldn't be, with a gang of gun-crazy bums going round shooting people's windows up in the middle of the night?'

'Was it 'er as shot off the gun?' asks Tiny.

'No, we must've been wrong,' says Porta, shaking his head. He cranes to get a better view of the fat lady, who is crawling round swearing in the middle of the snowdrift. 'God, what a lovely creature! Just my style! Between her legs the Thirty Years War wouldn't seem a minute too long! Hej! Olga!' he yells, 'come on over here and let's have a jump together!'

'Let's try shootin' the other way and see what happens,' suggests Gregor, his fighting blood up.

A long MG burst kicks up the snow along the whole length of the market-place. A bullet burns a furrow in

Porta's left boot.

'Ow-ow-ow! Blood!' howls Albert. A ricochet has slashed his check.

'Frostlips' has regained consciousness, after his meeting with the floor-vase. He jumps back and takes cover behind Porta. He holds out the heavy *Nagan* in front of him, clenched in both hands. Unwittingly he is aiming it directly at Porta.

'Jesus, Son of Mary!' cries Porta, turning round and looking straight into the black muzzle of the *Nagan*. He can see the rifling clearly, and can sense the round-headed 11 mm bullet waiting down there to be fired.

'You're *dead*!' howls 'Frostlips', quite out of his mind with fear.

Porta ducks just as the gun goes off. The bullet passes only a fraction of an inch from his cheek. His eyes turn up, showing the whites, and he falls backwards into the snow. He claims he is dead.

'Hell, man! That bullet went straight through me! I never heard a bang like that before in all my life!'

We have to show him his face in a mirror, so that he can see there is no entrance hole, before he realizes he is still alive and that 'Frostlips' has missed. It takes him a while to get over the shock.

'Reminds me a lot of a fight I was in once in Wedding in Berlin,' he says, ducking under a burst of machine-pistol fire. 'Me old dad comes home blind-o an' thinks the long haired's been having a bit on the side! While he was punishing her for that, he finds out the pork roast has got itself burnt. So he makes up his mind to smash up the whole street, *before* he goes back to knocking the old woman about. Well, then the coppers turn up and *they* start in beating *him* up and everybody else with him. They never thought to ask where the blame lay!'

'Let's get over there,' shouts Tiny. He grabs a *Schmeisser* and starts off at top speed across the market-place, careless of the bullets that are flying round his ears.

The crazy Maxim gunner on the far side of the houses

knocks snow into the air again with a new long burst. He is traversing the square.

Porta rushes down the street, stops at a cellar window and sends a whole magazine through it. Suddenly the machine-gun stops firing, and everything becomes strangely still.

Tiny goes up the long cement stairway in two big jumps. He crashes the door in with his boot.

'Shut the door, you fool,' roars a voice. 'There's a crowd of madmen out there shooting at us!'

Tiny grips the long magazine of the *Schmeisser* firmly, and presses the stock in under his elbow.

A captain with green OGPU shoulder-boards gives a shout, and goes down behind a desk with both hands clamped down on top of his head.

A big figure stands in the middle of the room, waving a '45 around. A single shot sounds, but from another direction. Tiny believes for a moment that he is dead, so shocked is he. He swings the snub-nosed German machine-pistol in a half-circle.

The big Russian with the '45 gives a shout, as he looks down the black barrel of the *Schmeisser*. He drops his pistol and raises his hands in the air.

Along the filthy wall stand a group of half-dressed supplies soldiers, staring in astonishment at Tiny and the *Schmeisser*.

A corporal goes forward a couple of steps, and blinks his eyes. Realizing that what he sees is really there, he stops and pulls his head down between his shoulders like a tortoise.

The *Schmeisser* chatters like a runaway circular saw. Blue flames spit; long gashes appear across the walls. Chalk-dust comes down like heavy snow.

A little soldier, who is very drunk, zig-zags across the room at top speed, dives across a table and crashes headfirst into the floor. He stays down there, with both hands protectively covering the back of his neck. Cautiously, he turns his head to see if what he thought he saw was really what he did see. It was.

A group of Russians sit there staring, quite paralysed by

the number of things which have happened in such a short space of time. Then they fall over backwards, the legs of their chairs shot out from under them.

A funeral party, armed with black umbrellas, comes running up the stairs to see what is going on. They need a little amusement after the melancholy atmosphere of the churchyard, and push forward behind Tiny to peer over his shoulder. Those in the lead catch sight of the *Schmeisser* with its bulldog snout and long magazine. Then they see the ugliest face they have ever set eyes on, and quickly realize that something is happening which should *not* be happening. They fall over one another's feet to get away; slip on one another's hats and galoshes, which have fallen off, and involve themselves inextricably in wet black umbrellas, some of which have turned inside out.

A large, damp, unbelievably ugly dog lollops over and sniffs at Tiny. It looks up at him and licks his hand. It seems as if it is smiling at him. It closes its eyes when the firing starts. Splinters of glass fly through the air and are pulverized into powder. Woodwork splinters. Stray bullets gouge into walls. The dog opens its eyes again, and is so happy its tail seems ready to fall off.

Roars and hysterical screams are heard, in time with the flaying, raging stutter of the German mpi. Bullets ricochet and fan out, whining across the room. A waterpipe bursts, and water spouts in all directions.

A large oval object rolls to rest in front of Tiny's feet.

The wet dog sniffs at it cautiously, and backs away.

'Holy Mother of Kazan,' howls Tiny, in terror. 'A rifle-grenade, a bleedin' rifle-grenade!' With a well-aimed kick he sends the dangerous thing into the furthest corner of the room. There is an earsplitting explosion. Then a 6-foot tall, red-hot stove comes flying through the air.

Tiny and the dog duck in unison as the stove passes over them, and stare after it fearfully as it goes crashing on, taking the double doors with it, and making the civilian funeral party run even faster. They think the red-hot stove is the devil himself out collecting souls to take back down to hell!

A hand-grenade comes flying through the air, hits the door-post and screws back again like a billiard ball which has been given wrong side. It explodes on top of a buffet. Blood flows everywhere. It resembles a butcher's block.

A sergeant, wearing only one boot, and with his helmet on the back of his head, comes rushing along with wildly staring eyes and throws his arms round Porta, who is on his way through the swing doors.

'*Tovaritsch, Tovaritsch*, do something or other!' he screams, beside himself with fear.

'We *are* doin' something!' answers Porta, tearing himself from the man's embrace.

'You're all wrong,' roars the sergeant at the top of his voice, although he is only an inch or two away from Porta. 'We are Russians! We are *friends*!'

'That's just what we *thought*,' screams Tiny, equally loudly. 'We're *Germans*, man!'

'I know it,' roars the sergeant. 'You belong to the Volga Brigade!'

'What're you shooting at us for then?' asks Porta, in a ringing voice. 'We thought you were counter-revolutionaries that we were supposed to shoot the heads off of?'

'No, no! You're wrong!' shouts the sergeant. 'We are all in a service and supplies company! We never do nothing to *nobody*!'

'Come on out then,' shouts Tiny, waving invitingly with the *Schmeisser*. 'It's all over. All a mistake!'

'Mistake?' sighs the Old Man, his eyes widening as he looks at the wreckage around him. 'Preserve us! What a mess you've made out of this place!'

'It was their own fault,' Porta defends himself. 'It was them that started with grenades!'

A Russian with his fur cap right down over his eyes and his cloak fluttering out from his shoulders, comes rushing down the steep street as if the devil were at his heels.

'Paratroops, paratroops,' he screams in panic fear. He misses his footing and slides a long way on his stomach. When he finally gets up enough courage to look up from the snowdrift in which he has ended he stares, paralysed, into

304

Albert's coal-black face. He makes some strange noises, and then his heart stops beating. He has, quite simply, died of fright.

'Well I'm damned,' cries Porta in amazement. 'Before we know where we are Albert'll be our secret weapon. We hold him out in front of us and they all die a natural death. Their hearts stop beating at the sight of him!'

'*Job tvojemadj*!' curses a sergeant, picking bits of glass from his face. 'And one *Schmeisser* can do all that! If I hadn't got down behind that cupboard quick that fucking machine-shitter'd have cut me in two. Shot every bit of rotten life I've got out of me, it would have!'

'I was close to shitting myself, when that sod started up with the *Schmeisser*,' admits a corporal, his face chalk-white. 'If I hadn't fell down the stairs it would've been all up with me.'

A white-haired warrant officer is sitting in a heap of broken glass and wall tiles. He is holding his leg, which has been slashed open from the instep to above the knee.

'My leg! My leg!' he gasps in despair, 'and those cursed liars told me it was a piece of cake in supplies! I'd never hear a shot fired in anger, they said. In the last five minutes I've heard more shots fired than ever there was in the whole of the First World War!' ·

Suddenly a new burst of fire rakes across the market-place, and a guttural voice rings through the night:

'Pull in your heads, you pigs! Here comes Michael Yakanashi! And he's not coming alone!'

A long shimmering salvo from a *Kalashnikov* terminates the threatening message.

'It's that crazy captain again,' explains the pale corporal, crawling under a bench. 'I wish the devil'd crawl down his throat with a sack o' dynamite on his back! He won't give up till he's killed the lot of us. He can thank his good connections he hasn't been strung up long since. It was "shiverin' pig" that caused it all!'

'"Shiverin' pig"?' asks 'Frostlips', blankly.

'Jellied pork,' nods the corporal, solemnly, throwing his arms wide. 'The crazy bastard *hates* "shiverin' pig"! They say he killed his wife for givin' it him every day.'

A very young soldier with a heavy blood-soaked bandage round his neck, and with eyes which bug out like a frog's, drops down, out of breath, between Porta and Tiny.

'I've got such a headache,' he moans. 'All that *noise*!' He lifts his *Kalashnikov* and empties its 100-shot magazine at the spot where he thinks the mad captain has taken cover.

'Come on! We'll take care of him,' shouts the Old Man, furiously. 'I want to get some *peace*, dammit!'

Singly, in short crouching rushes, we move towards the building. In between the chatter of the mpis and MGs we hear shouts coming from the third floor.

'Down with the counter-revolutionaries! Death to the Trotskyite traitors!'

'That mad bleeder's got shit where 'is brains ought to be!' growls Tiny angrily. He runs across the market-place at top speed, tracer whistling around him.

'You meet these flag-waggin' idiots everywhere these days,' says Porta, hitching his equipment to a more comfortable position. 'They've got the national rag hangin' out of both their ears and their arseholes, just so's nobody'll make the mistake of thinking they don't love the lousy Fatherland!'

In a shouting, confused mob we land in a deep gutter which gives us some cover.

'This the first time you been on a job like this?' asks 'Frostlips', with a grin. 'Ever been with the cops?'

'Only arrested by 'em,' answers Porta. 'I've never been out shooting with them!'

'Then you've missed a lot,' grins 'Frostlips', sending a couple of shots from his *Tokarev* up at the third floor. 'Blokes like him up there I know all about! See here, the end of the show's nearly always the same! They bang away till they get tired of playing. Then they put the cannon in their mouth and send it off with their big toe!'

'That one with the big toe ain't easy,' says Porta, knowingly. 'Usually goes wrong and they live on with half their nut blown off.'

'Right!' grins 'Frostlips', 'and then they're on a forced diet for the rest of their lives! No pork! No blinis!'

'Down with Trotsky,' comes a roar from the top of the stairs. The captain has opened the battle for control of the house.

He keeps us pinned down on the landing for over an hour.

'He must have enough ammo for a whole corps,' mumbles Porta, shaking his head. He presses himself close to the wall as a salvo from above smashes in the door of an apartment.

'Why the hell did we have to stop here, anyway?' the Old Man turns to the Commissar. 'If only we'd gone on! This caper is pure madness!'

Now the situation has got completely out of hand. 131 gun-crazy German and Russian soldiers literally shoot to pieces the building which the mad captain has chosen for the scene of his last battle.

'He's switched on the lights,' screams the young corporal with the bug-eyes. 'Let's get the hell out of here! That mad bastard's put the lights on!'

'He's got us now,' shouts 'Frostlips', in terror. He tries to creep down the stairs backwards, but a couple of shots from above pin him down where he is.

'He can stay there and put holes in the lot of us, easy as pie,' roars Porta, getting even closer to the wall.

'Put the bleedin' light out,' shouts Tiny, 'before that dummy shoots our 'eads off!'

21 automatic weapons are aimed at the staircase light. On the films one shot would have been enough. But it is not like that in real life, and we feel the fear of death creeping up to the very roots of our hair.

Several hundred shots are fired. The ceiling and walls hang in shreds. We cough at the chalky powder filling the air and the acrid smell of cordite.

'You're all mad!' says the Old Man, getting to his feet and stepping across Porta and the Commissar, who are lying with their machine-pistols in firing position.

'The lights,' babbles the young corporal. 'That crazy bastard can *see* us!'

'God help him when I get hold of him,' promises a fat sergeant, picking at a jammed cartridge.

'We'll 'ave to cool that barmy bleeder to get 'im out of

'ere,' hisses Tiny, his finger curling itself reflexively on the trigger of his mpi.

The Old Man edges along close to the battered wall, keeping a careful eye on the staircase opening. When he reaches the fuse-box he calmly reaches up and screws the fuses out of their sockets.

'Wow!' says Porta, in surprise. 'Why didn't we think about that long ago? That's the army for you! Why do it the easy way when there's a hard way?'

There is a bang and a flame shoots out of the primitive fuse-box.

The young corporal gives out a high screech, and almost falls down the stairs. He thinks they are throwing grenades.

A hysterical burst sprays the staircase. Bullets chisel away at the handrail.

21 mpi muzzles are directed at the madman. Muzzle-flashes light up the stairs. The noise is terrific.

A heavy object whirls down from the top landing, taking the handrail with it. With a sickening thump it lands at the bottom of the stairwell. Blood splashes up on to us.

'Looks like a plate of "shiverin' pig" himself now,' says Tiny. He stand up and swings his mpi up on his shoulder.

'Get him out of here!' orders the Commissar, making a grimace.

There are crowds in the street. All the umbrella people are back, and have brought their children with them. The fathers hold them up over their heads to let them see the body, which is being carried out by four supply soldiers. Some give a cheer.

We go back with the Russians to the wrecked canteen. Porta has found a cauldron filled with *Bortsch-koop**. He adds a few things to it, which make it even tastier, and soon the whole canteen smells beautifully of meat soup.

Porta and a sergeant go out after supplies. There is a wild argument over a case of mutton sausages which the sergeant refuses to hand over without a requisition. The Commissar signs one gladly, and gives it all kinds of official stamps.

* *Bortsch-koop:* Russian soup

Now the sergeant is free of responsibility, and Porta can have anything he wants. But when he comes back carrying two large baskets of eggs the Old Man protests. He can see what could happen with eggs inside a tank.

'You're out of your bloody head!' shouts Porta, angrily. 'Wait till I do you Greek *Musaka*. Then you'll be glad I brought the eggs along!'

'Do you not use eggplants – *aubergine sautée*?' asks the Legionnaire, astonished. 'I have never heard one uses eggs!'

'There's sure to be a lot you haven't heard, while you were soddin' about in the desert shooting the arse off the Arabs,' Porta jeers. He hands the basket of eggs to Tiny. 'When I say, I make *Musaka* with eggs then I *mean* I make *Musaka* with eggs! Now all we need is a bit of minced beef, some onions and tomatoes. Butter we've got!'

The Old Man gives in, but demands that Porta clean up the waggon if the eggs do get smashed.

Tiny is having a row with a supply sergeant. First the sergeant kicks him on the ankle and then he hits him over the knee with a club. Tiny makes the V-sign. '*Pig!*' he yells and pushes his fingers hard into the sergeant's eyes. The man runs off screaming, and goes straight into a wall he cannot see.

'Bleedin' mad lot, these Russians!' says Tiny, sitting down to take the cards from Porta. ''Oo's got all the money, then?' he asks, kissing the cards. 'It ain't me, that's for sure!'

> *You have to hate to be a good soldier in wartime. If you cannot hate whole-heartedly, you cannot kill. Hate is the strongest energy source in a human being.*
>
> *Sven Hassel*

'It's all up!' said the Feldwebel brusquely, pointing at the road-block in front of them.

'Turn right!' ordered the major. His left uniform sleeve waved emptily in the breeze.

'It's all over, sir,' grinned the driver. 'They'll mow us down if we try to get away!'

The major fumbled his pistol from its holster, and prepared to jump from the Kübel. He stopped with a jerk. Machine-gun fire kicked up the dry earth in front of and behind the car. The driver and the Feldwebel jumped out immediately, and raised their hands above their heads.

Five Russians came out from the trees.

'Tovaritsch,' shouted the Feldwebel, and waved a piece of something white. He fell forward on his face in the dust of the country road.

The driver ran off to one side, but stopped suddenly and went down. Muzzle-flashes spurted from the five Kalashnikovs.

The major was knocked out of the Kübel. His face broken in, his chest split open in an explosion of shredded cloth and flesh.

The three wounded soldiers in the back of the car slumped down in a fountain of blood.

'Job Tvojemadj,' laughed the youngest of the Russians, as they poured petrol over the bodies.

When the petrol-can was empty, the sergeant threw a hand-grenade into the car. It became a flaming bonfire. They stood for a while watching the burning Kübel, then turned and sauntered back into the woods.

'Germania kaputt,' grinned the corporal, and lighted a papyrus.

THE VLADIMIR PRISON

The captain, who is big, and has a face which resembles what a Neanderthal Man must have looked like, pushes us over towards the guard-room wall.

'*Propusk*,' he growls, extending a demanding policeman's hand towards us. As he does so his tongue suddenly protrudes from his mouth, and the beginning of a scream dies away in a horrible rattle.

'Come death, come . . .' hums the Legionnaire, whipping his garrotting wire from around the dead man's throat.

The Old Man hurries us on.

Silently we go up over the narrow wall, to come in from behind the other guards before they can sound the alarm.

Igor is over at the cable-box, as quick as a cat. Fat sparks shower down as his cutter bites into them. In only a few seconds of action the Vladimir prison is cut off entirely from the outside world.

With machine-pistols at the ready we dash towards the guard quarters. Tiny is in the lead. He swings a *Nagan* above his head in true policeman style.

'Come on out with your hands in the air!' he roars, in a Chief of Police voice.

'Idiot!' snarls Porta. 'It's not in the plan, the gold-robbers sayin' that! That's what the OGPU says to the robbers!'

Tiny ignores him. He has become paranoiac since we put him into a Russian warrant officer's uniform.

'Come out of there!' he shouts, even louder than before. 'Or we'll shoot your heads off!'

'Have you gone *mad*?' rages Barcelona, kicking open the door of the guard-room. 'That's queer!' he cries.

'What's queer?' asks the Old Man.

'There ain't a soul in here,' says Barcelona, in amazement.

'D'you mean we're in the wrong guard-house?' cries Porta, shakily.

311

'Out of the way,' says Igor, pushing forward. 'I threw a gas-grenade in here. Those boys are sleeping like never before.'

'Here they are, all snoring,' says Porta, jumping over the counter. 'Makes you sleepy, just to look at 'em!'

He yawns audibly, and drops down into a deep armchair.

'Out, out!' screams Igor, excitedly. 'Are you mad? The gas is still working!' He almost drags us out of the guard-room.

Porta brings up the rear, staggering and blowing like a whale.

'Where are the gas-cylinders?' asks the Commissar. He comes down the broad prison gangway like a second Trotsky with a *Nagan* held in his hand.

'Here!' grins Tiny quietly, pushing a serving-trolley in front of him loaded with gas-cylinders.

'Don't drop those!' the Commissar warns him. 'That gas works faster than an iron bar across the head.'

'Yes, we saw that just now,' answers Porta. 'I still feel like Snow White in the glass box!'

'I don't bloody like this,' mumbles Barcelona. 'Have you thought what they'll do to us, if they get hold of us?'

'All the things the censors cut out of the horror films,' answers Porta, with a short laugh.

A woman soldier waving a *Tokarev* rushes out of the kitchen.

Igor jumps on her and places his *Nagan* between her eyes. There is a hollow crack and the wall behind her head is covered with blood, brains and bone splinters.

Two jailers come out from the south wing of the prison, and stare blankly at Igor standing there with the *Nagan* in his hand.

'Enemy of the people,' he snarls, kicking irritably at the body.

The jailers give a Russian shrug of their shoulders, and go on without a word. It is best not to know, or see, too much in Vladimir prison. It is not unusual for people to be liquidated without explanation.

Our two lorries rumble into the prison yard, followed by one of the T-34s.

'Get your gasmasks on,' orders the Commissar nervously. '*Keep* them on no matter what happens! This whole prison's full of gas already!'

'Will they die?' asks the Old Man, worriedly.

'Not all,' laughs Igor indifferently. 'Only those who would have died in any case!'

'Come on,' says the Commissar, catching Porta by the shoulder. Porta's head bangs into a door-post.

'What the hell?' he cries, yawning like a sleepy horse. 'What's goin' on? Hell, where am I?' He leans against the door, and tries to remember where he is.

'Move it!' says the Commissar, pushing him. 'You've got a vault to open! You told us you'd been a locksmith's apprentice, and could open any lock in existence!'

'Right enough!' mumbles Porta, and wobbles sleepily down the stairs.

'Frostlips' is behind him with two large bundles of keys. He swears one of them must be the key to the vault.

'Are you sure the right key's *there*?' asks 'Whorecatcher' in a worried voice. 'You've been wrong before!'

'I'll guarantee one of 'em fits,' says 'Frostlips' in an insulted tone. He clashes the bundles of keys together.

'One's enough,' says Porta, leaning tiredly against the heavy door of the vault. He looks through the big keyhole, but can see nothing. He begins trying keys in it. None of them fit.

'Frostlips' gets a funny look on his face, and stammers something about how maybe he has got hold of the wrong bunch of keys.

'I should've known!' says 'Whorecatcher', angrily, 'the last time you were wrong you had a toothache, and this time you're suffering from nervous stress!'

'The whole bleedin' prison's asleep,' reports Tiny. He comes clattering down the stairway with a pleased look on his face and swinging a gasmask in his hand.

'I never in my life seen anybody go on their backs quick as the key-rattlers and the slaves in this cage! That bleedin' gas ought to be able to close down this world war quick as knife! I'd just love to see Adolf's an' Uncle Joe's coolies sleepin' like babes in one another's arms!'

'Unfortunately it only works in a closed room,' says the Commissar. 'Otherwise, I can assure you the whole German Army would have been put to sleep long ago!'

The Old Man comes down into the cellars. He is angry.

'Don't you think we're going to get our arses singed on this one?' he asks, standing with feet apart, in the middle of the room.

'We'll manage,' says Porta, running his fingers over the armoured door. 'All I've got to do is find out how this thing works, and then we're rich!'

'How long will it take?' asks the Commissar, impatiently. 'We haven't got a lot of time! There's enough gas to put 'em to sleep just once more and then we've had it!'

'Why not liquidate them all now?' Suggests Igor, his *Nagan* already in his hand.

'Don't you ever get tired of killing people?' asks the Commissar, irritably. 'You must soon be sick of yourself. *I* get sick just looking at you!'

Igor shrugs his shoulders indifferently, and slams his *Nagan* back into its holster with a jeering look on his face.

After half an hour's work on the difficult lock, Porta sits down despondently.

'I can do it,' he says. 'But that's not the question!'

'Then be so good as to inform us, please, of what the question *is*!' says the Commissar, with heavy irony. 'I'm just dying to know!' Under stress conditions the Commissar's right eye winks involuntarily. It opens and closes as if the eyelid were on a string. It has brought him into contact with a number of ladies in the course of his life, but it has also brought him a number of scoldings from ladies who did not approve of being contacted in that manner. His right eye is winking furiously now, but there are no pretty girls in sight.

'It's a question,' explains Porta, with a dubious contortion of his features, 'of time!'

'Time?' whispers the Commissar, working his eyelid so hard it is wonderful the eye does not fall out of its socket.

'Yes, time!' Porta smiles with an effort. He sits down

314

cross-legged in front of the unapproachable vault door.

'It's going to take more time, then!' nods the Commissar, falling resignedly into a chair. 'How *much* more time?'

Porta counts on his fingers, and it seems for a moment as if he is about to begin on his toes as well.

'This is a very intelligent vault we've to do with here! The bloke who gave birth to this was no pal of safe-crackers. It's *different*! Different in every way!' He knocks, thoughtfully, on the door towering above him. 'The steel's different! The lock's an unknown make, and the bloody door itself's different! It's a real shit vault this one. Must've been a Jew that invented it!'

'Thank you!' smiles the Commissar, with a snarl in his voice.

'I've not been let in on everything, I see.' says the Old Man, pushing his fur cap back on his head. 'That's for sure! I've been done!'

'Porta.' says Gregor, bending over him. 'tell us straight. now. How serious *is* it?'

Porta grunts, as if a bullet had sunk into his midriff.

'Shitty!' he answers.

'How much shit?' asks Gregor.

'A great big bloody pile of shit!' answers Porta, lighting a cigarette. 'More shit than I'd ever have thought there could be!'

'How long will it take you to open it?' asks the Commissar, puffing nervously at his cigarette.

Porta counts on his fingers again.

'All night an' part of next day.' he says sadly, holding out his hands like a fisherman showing the size of the one that got away.

'That's *great*!' the Commissar explodes, jumping up from his chair. 'We'll have plenty of time for sightseeing, then?'

Porta gives him a long stare.

'Let me just tell you I'm no happier about this than you are. But don't forget it's a Soviet bloody vault we're dealing with, made in the USSR. No German vault would have been so mean!'

315

'Listen here!' says Barcelona, pushing forward. 'The fact of the matter is, put short and sweet, that you reckon you can get this rotten box open some time before next Christmas, so we can get away with the gold?'

'I've told you. There's not a lock in the world I can't get past, but it takes the time it has to take! When I was helping Egon, the best locksmith in Berlin, there wasn't a lock didn't give up when we arrived. We even used to open locks for the coppers, and we were highly respected, I can tell you. Look at those wheels there! They ain't even round like normal wheels. They look like somethin' out of a wrecked aeroplane!'

The Commissar tramps backwards and forwards impatiently, making figures of eight on the floor.

'I do believe I'm dreaming,' he says, knocking himself on the forehead. 'Yes, I'm dreaming! I'm in hospital being anaesthetized, before they cut off both of my legs!' He kicks the vault door viciously, and grimaces with pain. 'And I hope it's true, too, because this situation is much worse!'

'We goin' to live?' asks the Old Man, puffing fatalistically on his silver-lidded pipe. 'That's all that interests me. Don't tell me it's a lot to ask!'

'This job ain't for us,' shouts Tiny, resolutely. 'If you lot'll listen to me, we'll get out of 'ere quick as we can, an' find a proper bank. We go in there with mpis, scrape the beans together an' sod off out of it! Any dope can fix a thing like that! I knew a kid o' twelve as done it! He'd got to sixteen before they shot 'im!'

'An' where'd you get rid of all those roubles you'd knocked off?' asks Porta, with a sneer.

'Roubles? What roubles?' asks Tiny blankly.

'The roubles you and your chopper had picked up in the bank,' answers Porta, ironically. 'You don't bloody well think Russian banks are stocked up with dollars, do you? Roubles you can wipe your arse on, and they don't even do much of a job of that!'

'An hour from now the gas won't be working any more,' remarks the Commissar, with a hopeless look on his face.

'Give me all the tools down here,' Porta demands. 'That

rotten, shitty lock's going to get to know Obergefreiter, by the grace of God, Joseph Porta!' He pulls the vodka bottle from his pocket, and reduces its contents by a third. Then he screws the cap back on and returns the bottle to his pocket.

'You're dead sure you can open that damned door?' asks the Commissar, with the air of a Grand Inquisitor.

'I said I could,' answers Porta, annoyed.

'And you can do it before the turn of the century?' the Commissar goes on. 'I only want to know, so that I can arrange my affairs accordingly!'

'Don't get me worked up. Come and give me a hand instead! I need light! Plenty of light. Then everything'll go a lot quicker!'

'Yes, I'm sure,' says the Commissar, turning the hand-operated spotlight on to the lock.

Porta takes a few deep, long breaths to quieten his nerves. He squats down on his haunches, like an Inca warrior readying himself for breakfast.

'Normally a lock like this ought to fly open when a feller blows on it!' he says, thoughtfully.

'Blow on it,' suggests Gregor.

'The rotten thing's shaken my confidence!' says Porta fiercely.

Igor rattles down the stairs with his *Nagan* ready for action in his hand.

'Found a piece of cunt sergeant rattling off to the OGPU on the blower,' he says, holstering his *Nagan*. 'I blew her away and smashed the phone. We hadn't cut it off when we moved in.'

The Commissar presses his lips tightly together, and keeps back some remarks which he was otherwise prepared to spit out.

'What'd she tell the OGPU?' asks Barcelona practically.

'Nothing much! I was right behind her when she made the connection. I blew her brains up the wall.'

'Did anybody ever tell you what a stinking pig you are?' asks the Old Man, staring contemptuously at him.

'Only you,' grins Igor, executing a highly complicated Russian shrug.

Porta leans down toward the door of the vault. His pointed nose touches the lock.

'I can't give you more light when you're standing *there*,' protests the Commissar. He turns the spot on to Porta's right eye, which is peering into the lock.

'God dammit,' shouts Porta, spitting angrily on the lock, 'it's *mean* to make anything so bloody complicated! If all locks were like that, think of all the unemployed there'd be!'

'Unemployed?' asks 'Whorecatcher' in amazement, kneeling down alongside him to relieve the Commissar with the spotlight.

'Yes, of course! Bank robbers would have to give up altogether, and the police shut down their robbery sections! I need a drill with a diamond tip, that can get through that blasted metal!'

'Here,' says 'Frostlips', handing him a diamond drill.

'I'll fix that bloody thing now,' says Porta grimly, and presses the drill against the lock. It whines like a runaway outboard motor. Then it slips. It has hardly scratched the metal.

'You'll do it all right. Take it easy,' Igor comforts Porta, patting him on the shoulder.

Porta moves away like a dog which has been patted by a cat. He pushes a thin tool into the lock, but soon gives up again.

'Dammit,' he mumbles despondently. 'I'm *good* at locks, but this bastard's a real headache.'

'If we get taken,' grins Gregor, carelessly, 'we can write a book about it. How about this for a title: *Gold-robbers in Siberia*!'

'Oh, you *are* funny!' snarls Porta wickedly. 'You're close to making me *die* laughin'!'

'What about acid?' suggests the Commissar. 'We've got a bottle here, and a syringe!'

'Why not?' answers Porta. He empties the entire contents of the acid bottle into the lock.

It bubbles and hisses for about ten minutes. One or two drops splash on to the Commissar's uniform, burning holes in it immediately. Nothing happens to the lock.

'Rat piss!' says Porta, sending the empty acid bottle rattling across the floor with a kick.

'What about a saw?' suggests 'Frostlips'.

'If you're in need of exercise,' hisses Porta, 'then saw as much as you like. But, if it's opening the vault we're talkin' about, then sawin' at it won't do any good!'

'I can't get away from it,' says Tiny, giving the door of the vault a kick. 'It's too much trouble breakin' into a bleedin' vault! Why don't we go for a sausage factory. It's a lot easier!'

'A *sausage* factory?' asks Porta, turning his head.

'Yes,' grins Tiny. 'I know a couple of fellers who make a livin' at it!'

'Were they hungry?' wonders Gregor.

'Not on your life,' answers Tiny, grinning even more. 'They go in the day the slaves pick up their coppers. They go quietlike into the pay office, pick up the shekels an' off they go again. Easy as shittin'!'

'What about if the wages are paid by cheque? That's common practice nowadays,' smiles Porta, sourly.

'Nip down to the bank an' cash 'em, then,' shrugs Tiny.

'Try that,' suggests Porta. 'You'd be sorry for the rest of your life!'

He picks up a tool, and does something complicated to the vault lock.

'No,' he says, shaking his head. 'I'll have to drill again. This is what the trade calls a tricky box!'

'Tricky?' asks the Old Man, wonderingly. 'What do you mean by that?'

'The tricky part is that there's traps in it, and they're what you've got to give a miss to,' answers Porta, knocking on the door of the vault. 'If I make a balls of it, at least ten big, wicked steel rods are goin' to shoot out an' lock that door so's nobody in the world can ever open it. There might be one feller who could get in to the gold, and that'd be the bloke who made it in the first place.'

'Why didn't we bring 'im with us, then?' asks Tiny irritably, throwing his arms out wide in despair.

'Even if he was here, it wouldn't help a shit,' says Porta. 'When those steel bars come out you need a special machine to break the wall down. A shit of a thing like that weighs Christ knows how many tons, an' you don't walk about with it under your arm.'

'Sounds promising,' moans the Commissar. 'Time's up! The key-boys need more gas! Get your arses in gear!'

'Shall we give 'em the lot?' asks 'Frostlips', from the cellar door. 'Will it send 'em off for ever?'

'It's a humane way to die,' the Commissar feels. 'Everybody likes a good sleep!'

'Damnation!' hisses Porta, pressing his lips together. He picks up a tool. His grip is so tight that it hurts his hand. 'Hell!' he curses again. 'I know all the most advanced ways of fixing a lock, and Egon and me's tried 'em all! Give me that electronic listening thing!' He puts the earphones on with the air of a famous surgeon who is about to cut the stomach out of a patient. He turns the combination lock carefully, listening for the pawls to drop. After a moment, which feels like a week, he tears the earphones from his head.

'Somebody's comin',' says Gregor, gazing up the stairs.

'I belched,' says Porta.

'No, somebody *is* coming,' mumbles the Commissar. He picks up his *Kalashnikov* from the floor.

'Shut up, or I can't think! If somebody's comin' then shoot 'em! I want quiet!' says Porta.

'So do we,' says the Commissar, clicking off the *Kalashnikov*'s safety.

'Maybe it ain't clever to shoot 'em straight off,' says Tiny. 'I've heard it's best to greet God's local representatives with a smile!'

'An' who's God, then?' asks 'Frostlips'.

'Depends where a feller is when 'e's smilin',' grins Tiny. 'Uncle Joe 'ere p'raps?'

'I will go up and speak with our guests,' says Igor, with a Siberian grin. 'You look after things while I am gone!'

'I've made my decision! I'm going to hit that vault in every way possible,' rages Porta. 'An' I'm going to do it all at the

320

same time. I'm not going to let a shit like that fuck me!'

'Right!' says the Commissar. 'What d'you want me to do?'

Porta gives him a funny look.

'Watch your napper now,' he warns, "cos something's going to happen! Make some coffee! It clear's a feller's head!'

'To be quite honest I've begun to lose my liking for our planned life of luxury,' says Barcelona doubtfully. 'Maybe it ain't all that much fun owning a little island over there by Haiti, where you run everything yourself and can be king, emperor, grand duke, general or anything else you want to be!'

'Oxygen bottles and a burner!' demands Porta, brusquely.

The flame hisses, and sparks fly round our ears. Soon after, Porta gives up the torch. It was about as much use as a dull cheese-knife.

Albert backs the T-34 in, and attaches the towing-wires to the three odd-looking cogs on the door of the vault. We hope he can loosen it from its hinges, but all that happens is that a wire snaps and causes a lot of damage.

When we try again, this time with triple tow-cables and the tank moving backwards in small jerks, all three cogs come away from the door.

We sit down, despondently, and drink coffee.

'I could have made this coffee a lot better,' grumbles Porta, sniffing at the dregs in his cup. 'All I'd have had to do was to make it from dried-out cow-dung!' He gets up, takes a bundle of dynamite charges and begins to affix them to the big door of the vault.

'Think that's all right?' asks the Commissar, his right eye ticking away madly.

'If it ain't,' answers Porta, 'and we don't get under cover in one hell of a hurry, then we'll suddenly be dead, and won't have to worry about this bloody door any more!'

The noise of the dynamite exploding is deafening, but when the smoke clears all that has happened to the door is that a large black spot has appeared in the middle of it.

'Well, we'll just have to get even tougher,' hisses Porta,

shivering with rage. 'Soup*, an' a few more charges! That's *got* to be able to leave that door lyin' in peace with its backside up!'

The first explosion was like a paper bag popping in comparison to this one.

The cellar looks like a split melon. We scramble over collapsed walls to get to the gold. But when the dust finally clears away we stand choking and spitting in front of the vault door, which is standing where it has stood all the time.

'I won't take this from anybody, or anything!' rages Porta. 'My honour's at stake now! I'll show 'em who's an Obergefreiter by the grace of God!'

'Get on with it, in the name of Hell!' says the Commissar, spitting out brick-dust. 'We've got to get out of here as fast as possible!' He stares at Porta with his ticking eye and blows out more brick-dust.

'Are we going to *live*?' asks the Old Man expressionlessly, withdrawing slowly up the stairs.

'I think so, yes,' answers Porta. 'It won't be all *that* much of a bang.' He presses plastic explosive on every available inch of the door. Tiny helps him, crimping the primers with his teeth.

'I think you'd all better get up out of the cellar.' Porta advises us, when he is ready. 'One or two things might start rattlin' around in here!'

'I could do with throwing a few things around, myself,' says the Commissar, running quickly up the stairs.

We wait tensely outside the cellar, while Porta completes the wiring of the door. Then he backs slowly up from the cellar with a cable in each hand.

'All clear?' he asks. ''Cos in a minute it's goin' to go bang-bang!'

'Blow that fucking shit into bits and pieces!' shouts the Commissar, going down on one knee.

'Yes!' mumbles Porta. He brings the ends of the two cables together.

* Soup: Nitroglycerine

322

The explosion is so loud that none of us can find words to describe it afterwards. But we feel the blast. It comes roaring out of the cellar opening, and throws us across the parade ground and through the door of a guard-room on the far side of it. The room is full of sleeping soldiers – and smashed furniture after we arrive.

We pull ourselves together after a while. When we are back in the cellar and stand staring at the unharmed steel door the Commissar begins to sob.

'The gun,' says Porta sharply, and is already on the way over to the Panther with Tiny at his heels.

'We certainly got all that rubbish cleared out of the cellar, anyway,' says the Old Man. He kicks at the one remaining piece of brickwork the blast has not taken with it.

With rattling tracks the Panther comes rolling across the barrack square. It waddles into the cellar entrance, brickwork collapsing on all sides.

Porta puts his head out of the driver's hatch.

'Better take cover before I start bangin' away! That door'd better tighten its ring, now!'

The long gun sinks down, with a humming sound, and traverses towards the armoured door.

We hold our ears and await the sound of the shot, tensely.

There is a heavy thud, and everything is suddenly blood-red.

We look at one another, and cannot believe our own eyes. We have become live, surrealistic paintings. Tiny has loaded with the wrong ammunition, as the Old Man has feared he would for some time. He has used a marker, and there is red paint everywhere.

'Unmilitary, miserable drunkard!' shouts the Old Man, trying to wipe the paint from his face.

'I'll strangle that cheeky Social Democratic son of a bitch!' rages the Commissar, hitting away madly at a dented bucket.

'Take it easy, fellers,' says Tiny, with his head out of the side hatch. 'Anybody can make a mistake! I'll soon get a couple of tins of paint remover, so you can begin to look 'alfway 'uman again.'

'We'll need new uniforms,' says 'Frostlips', who is dripping with red paint. 'We'll be arrested, soon as they set eyes on us. Red as we are nobody *is*! Not even in *this* country!'

'Back everybody!' screams Porta, warningly, from the turret. 'We'll give it one up the arse now!'

'Not *another* bloody marker!' shouts the Old Man, nervously.

The pressure wave from the S-shell is terrific. It feels as if a giant warm hand clenches itself round our bodies. The deafening noise seems to split the air apart. When the dust disperses the powerful shell appears to have done little damage. There is a small hole in the door.

'Got him!' shouts a jubilant Porta from the turret hatch, grinning all over his face. Bluish-grey smoke seeps from the hole.

'You bloody *did* it!' shouts Gregor happily.

'What's that smoke coming out of there?' asks the Old Man, in a frightened voice.

Suddenly an ominous silence sinks over the cellar. We all stare at the smoke issuing from the hole.

'Can gold burn?' asks Albert, blinking his eyes behind the mask of red paint which covers his black face.

The Commissar crosses the room in three long strides, and peers through the hole.

'Hell! That rotten German shell has started a fire inside! Quick! Get some water!'

We fall over one another on our way up the stairs for water.

'Fire!' shouts Tiny. He comes dashing back with a hose and a ladder he has found hanging outside on the wall.

When 'Whorecatcher' turns on the water, the pressure on the hose sends Tiny tumbling over backwards, and the stream of water swills the rest of us out to the sides of the room.

With much shouting and screaming of threats we finally get control of the hose and direct the jet through the hole.

'Give it two more shells,' orders the Commissar, pressing his lips together.

Twice in succession the tank-gun fires. It seems as if the entire prison is falling down on our heads. We are totally deaf for several minutes, and pains wrack us through and through.

'I'll bet we're the first people in the history of the world to have used a tank for a tin-opener!' says Porta, with a short laugh, as he jumps down from the Panther's turret.

'Let's go in and take a look at the goods,' suggests the Commissar, rubbing his hands together.

The big vault door gapes open like a peeled banana.

Porta stops to take a closer look.

'Yes, that's it,' he mumbles, 'it's quite different! Never seen anything bloody like it!'

'Jesus'n Mary!' whispers Tiny, impressed. He stares in fascination at all the gold ingots which have been thrown down from the shelves in the vault. 'I'm goin' to buy the entire bleedin' world, an' kick all the arses I feel like kickin' an' never salute nobody, never again!'

'Get moving!' the Commissar chases them. 'The gas'll soon have stopped working, and there'll be a crowd of sleepy-headed, panic-stricken idiots asking unpleasant questions! Get the Panther out, and back the waggons in so we can load up and get out of here!'

The Old Man is sitting on the big tool-chest, watching the loading with a peculiar look on his face.

'Aren't you going to help?' asks Porta, wonderingly.

'No!' snaps the Old Man, making a face as if there were a bad smell under his nose.

Everybody stops work and looks at the Old Man, who is sitting carelessly on the tool-chest, puffing at his silver-lidded pipe.

'What's the matter with you?' asks the Commissar. 'You've got to admit we did it! It could easily have been a fiasco!'

'I'm not with you any more,' says the Old man, looking angrily at the Commissar, 'and I'm bitterly sorry I ever was! It's a load of shit, that's what this is! Here we are, murdering right and left for some miserable gold! You can do what you like, but I'm *out*!'

'You gonna shop us when we get back?' asks 'Frostlips', his eyes narrowing.

'I don't understand your filthy way of thinking!' snarls the Old Man contemptuously.

'Don't you want *any* of the gold?' asks Tiny, practically. 'Thought 'ow much of it there'll be apiece when we get it sold?'

'No!' replies the Old Man decisively. 'In any case I don't believe any of you are going to get much fun out of that shit!'

'Shit?' Barcelona gives a forced laugh. 'You're off your head! We're rich men! A week from now we can demob ourselves, and if you want the biggest carpenter shop in the world you can buy it for yourself. That is if you want to go on planin' planks for fun!'

Porta sweeps up the gold-dust from the battered ingots and puts it in his pocket.

'What're you doin' that for?' asks Gregor blankly.

'Berlin intuition,' smiles Porta, foxily. 'Who knows, somebody might manage to take our arses at quarter to midnight, and then it'd be nice to have a bit in reserve in your pockets!'

'Stop!' comes a warning shout from Barcelona. 'The waggon can't take any more!'

''Ow bleedin' annoyin',' says Tiny, vexedly. 'There's a load of bars left yet! We can't leave them for Ivan Stinkanovitch! It makes me bleedin' ill to think of it!'

'Share 'em out between the tanks,' shouts the Commissar nervously. 'Time's run out! The gas has stopped working! They'll all be here soon, and they won't like what we've been up to one bit!'

From the parade ground two shots sound in quick succession.

Igor comes down the stairs, grinning.

'Couple of 'em woke up too soon,' he says, pushing his *Nagan* back in its holster.

'Get ready to blow up the communications centre,' the Commissar orders Igor. 'They must, above all, have no possibility of communicating with anybody outside for the next twelve hours! Set the primers for thirty minutes, and surround the lot with phosphorus cans! They'll burn like hell, and give them more than enough to think about!'

'Nothing more's going to be blown up here,' says the Old Man harshly, 'and there'll be no more killing either!'

'I'm in command here!' roars the Commissar, in a rage, 'and what I say is to be blown up *will* be blown up! Get going, Igor! What naïve fools you Germans are when it comes to it!' he jeers, his lips curled in contempt.

'Shut it! You stinking Soviet Jew shit! Shut it!' Heide swings round with his mpi at the ready.

Like lightning the Commissar has the weapon out of his hands, and slings Heide over against the wall.

'Don't call me a Jew shit, you stinking little Nazi creep!'

White with rage, Heide tears the *Nagan* from its leather holster, and aims it at the Commissar.

'Be a good boy now, little Moses, or Daddy smack,' grins Tiny, kicking the gun from Heide's hand.

Heide jumps forward as if on steel springs, and his right fist crashes into Tiny's face. There is such speed and power in the punch that Tiny goes over on his back and gasps for air.

'You 'it me, Moses!' he howls. 'I'm goin' to *kill* you!'

Battle is on. Heide rushes forward with a mad scream. Tiny is too slow in getting away from the rain of blows which come at him. A murderous punch lands on his temple, and he staggers and shakes his head like a pole-axed bull. The edge of Heide's hand catches him across the larynx and sends him to the ground. It would have killed another man.

'This time I'm going to *kill* you,' hisses Heide furiously, aiming a kick at the big man's kidneys.

Now Tiny is really angry and in that condition he is more dangerous than a whole case of dynamite. He gets back on his feet, wipes the blood from his face, and spits out a couple of broken teeth. With a noise like the splitting of skulls he crashes his forehead into Heide's face.

'Uh!' he grunts, and spits blood, as Heide's fist buries itself in his middle, pumping the air from his lungs. 'Uh!' he grunts again. He turns half round and smashes a karate kick at Heide's stomach.

Heide tries desperately to jump to one side, but Tiny's size 14 boot gets home on his hip with the force of a diving Stuka. He bends forward, and Tiny brings up his giant fist, with a happy grin, into his pain-distorted face. The left fist follows the right, and lands with a sound like a ton of dough falling from a skyscraper.

'*Mama mia*! What a punch!' cries Porta, who is sitting on a pile of gold ingots enjoying the fight.

We are all taken up by the battle. We shout and encourage them, and give good advice.

His face pouring with blood, Heide tries an attack, which, by all the tenets of boxing, is suicidal. One hard blow after another crashes into Tiny's twisted face. It resembles a bowl of minced meat, blood oozing from it. Tiny takes it all with the indifference of a rock, not even guarding against the merciless punches. You can no longer see from where the blood is coming. It is pouring from the whole of his face.

'Kick him in the balls,' shouts Porta kindly, banging his fist into his other hand to show how.

'Butt him! That rotten swastika rat,' roars Igor, furiously boxing holes in the air.

'Tear his head off!' screams the Commissar. 'Kill the stinking Nazi pig!'

There is no doubt where the Russian/German audience has its sympathy.

Tiny steps backwards towards the cellar door. Kostia, the little slant-eyed Siberian with the big Cossack fur hat, opens the door. The whole prison seems to shake as Tiny falls backwards down the stairs and through the trapdoor which leads to the heating system. All we can see of him are his size 14 boots caught on the edge of the trapdoor. The rest of him is dangling over the hissing hot-water pipes which have been smashed by the explosions.

Heide gives out a victorious yell, and throws himself murderously at Tiny, who is desperately attempting to release himself from the trapdoor. Kostia and Porta help him by pulling off his boots. He somersaults up onto his feet.

For a moment the two bloodthirsty berserkers stand watching one another. Heide, the boxer, is continually on the move, and using his left. It is no secret that he has a left hand everyone is afraid of. He has learnt to use it in the same way as the Britishers. Every punch is hard and deadly accurate. He is a feared regimental boxer, and has won countless matches. Anyone but Tiny would long since have been dead. Heide is grimly determined to kill him. Years of hatred are culminating in the battle between these two.

Tiny gives a scream like a bull elk at mating time, and flails away, but without any of his punches landing. He has no thought of defending himself. A hail of hard blows makes him stagger for a moment. He spits out a couple more broken teeth. His mouth looks like a crushed tomato.

Heide gets home two karate kicks on Tiny's body. The spectators howl in disgusted protest. When Tiny manages to do the same, they cheer and clap excitedly, and all seem to feel that everything is as it should be.

Shortly after, Tiny goes down on one knee. Heide immediately kicks him in the face, with a cracking sound like eggs breaking.

Tiny is now literally mad with rage. Roaring furiously he gets back up on his feet and lands a right on the side of Heide's head which sends him spinning round like a top. He gets a few more punches home, but this time on Heide's ribs. With blood running down over his face and both eyes closed he goes in like a mad bull to crush the Nazi's face.

But Heide ducks like lightning and feints a left towards Tiny's bloody face. Lithely he springs to one side and avoids a murderous kick at his crotch which would have crushed not only his testicles but his entire pelvis if it had landed.

Heide grins satanically, and begins to hammer away at Tiny's smashed face with his ramrod of a left.

'We've got to stop this,' says the Old Man, worriedly. 'Hell, that Hamburg crook's no more than a gutter fighter. He hasn't the faintest idea of how to box. The Nazi pig'll murder him. It's like a cat playing with a mouse!'

'The big dope don't even know how to defend himself,' says Gregor, shaking his head in commiseration.

'Stop 'em!' repeats the Old Man. 'It's cold-blooded murder!'

'Have to shoot Heide to do that,' says Porta, accepting one of the Legionnaire's *Caporals*.

Heide's fists are going like drumsticks, and every time they land on Tiny's face it sounds like a butcher slapping a parcel of minced meat.

Tiny keeps hitting out, but without his punches landing. Heide is dancing round merely flicking his left into his face, certain he has won.

Tiny gives out a ringing scream, and rushes forward like a mad bull in the arena.

The attack makes Heide step to one side professionally, and accept a couple of light blows. He bobs and feints, cool as a cucumber, takes a step forward and lands a straight left which stops Tiny as if he had run into a wall. His animal roar turns to a strangled gulp, as the air is knocked out of his lungs. He stops, in confusion, and wipes the blood from his eyes, trying to find Heide, who is dancing lightly around him on his toes. Every time Tiny throws his club of a fist at him he is out of reach. Cut to bloody doll-rags, Tiny shakes his head in an attempt to clear it. His left ear hangs down on his neck, half torn away.

'Yellow Nazi swine!' he growls furiously, and kicks out backwards like a horse.

Heide sees his chance. Two murderous blows and a kick and Tiny is staggering across the concrete floor like a dying man, with blood streaming from his nose and mouth.

Heide struts over towards the wall, brushing his hands together contemptuously, as if he had been handling something filthy.

'Butcher's offal!' he snarls, and goes to a water-tap to swill the blood from his face.

Tiny, who is lying on the floor struggling desperately to regain his breath, lifts his bloody head, and peers around. He looks like a grizzly bear awakened too early from hibernation, and he is just as vicious as one.

The babble of conversation amongst the spectators dies away. The sudden silence warns Heide, who has begun to comb his hair. He whirls and barely manages to duck under Tiny's giant fist as it comes hurtling at him in a hook which would have taken off his head if it had landed.

Heide goes to work with a whole series of professional body blows.

Tiny's lungs whistle for air, but Heide is in close, hammering at his middle. It feels as if his stomach is being smashed in, and his lungs dilate emptily in his chest.

Murder and hatred glitter in Heide's eyes. None of us doubt that he is not going to stop now until Tiny is dead.

'Adolf's little Moses,' gasps Tiny, with a horrible grin, swinging his arms in circles. He hits Heide on the chin with a punch which lifts him from the floor and throws him against a row of shelves. Machine-pistols clatter down over him. Tiny thunders forward and runs straight into the barrel of an mpi in Heide's outstretched arms. He is moving so fast it is a wonder the barrel of the weapon does not go straight through his body. He gives out a shrill scream and goes down on his knees with both hands pressed to his stomach.

With a crazy grin Heide swings the machine-pistol at him, but Tiny manages to duck away from it and the butt only grazes his head. He rolls across the floor and gets back up on his feet. On his way he too has got hold of a machine-pistol, and now the two men go at one another with the butts. Heide is the faster at this, too. Tiny remains the slow-thinking gutter fighter with no idea whatever of finesse. What takes Heide a fraction of a second to work out, takes Tiny an hour. Every time Tiny thinks he has Heide set up and swings at him, the mpi butt hits something else. Igor goes down without a sound, blood streaming over his red-painted face.

Heide has got round behind Tiny, who is standing staring blankly at the unconscious Igor whom he thinks of as a friend.

'Sorry!' he mumbles, sniffing sorrowfully. Behind him

Heide takes careful aim, and brings the butt of the mpi down on the back of his neck. He goes down on his face like a felled tree, his arms spread out like a man crucified.

The Old Man bends over him, worriedly, feeling for his pulse.

'Get a doctor!' he orders, harshly.

'Doctor?' the Commissar screams with laughter. 'Where the hell d'you think you are? You're in Vladimir isolation prison, man! They only use doctors here to certify death, and if there was one he'd be crazy from gas for the next 48 hours! Now it's *off*! And it can't be too soon!' He turns to Igor and coughs an order in some strange Russian dialect.

When we are a few miles from the prison, a blinding flash of light illumines the sky, and we hear the long, thundering roll of an explosion.

'Those villains blew up the prison anyway!' snarls the Old Man furiously.

'What the devil! At war aren't we?' remarks Porta, cheerily. 'And it's not only legal, it's also our *duty* to knock off the lads from the other FPO. It's only the communications centre Igor's blown up! If the commandant went with it, nobody's going to cry for him, either!'

The Old Man growls and looks angry.

A little later the differential goes on one of the trucks. We blame one another for it, and World War III nearly breaks out on the spot.

In the end Porta downs tools and refuses to do any more to repair the damage.

'I'm a bloody tank-driver,' he shouts furiously. 'Accordin' to regulations I'm not allowed to repair anything! The mechanical engineers are supposed to look after all that! Dial three zeroes and get ADAD*.'

'I'm a tank-driver, too,' bawls Kostia, his narrow black eyes glinting. 'I do no repairs either!'

'Let's go in and shoot some dice,' suggests Porta, crawling down into the Panther.

* ADAD: Equivalent to the British AA

332

'Why not?' grins Kostia, following him.

'No you bloody don't. I won't stand for it,' shouts the Old Man. 'I said I'd have nothing to do with your gold robbery, but I'm still the goddammed Section Leader of 2 bloody Section! Out of there, Porta, and get on that differential! That's an order!'

The only answer the Old Man gets is the smack of the hatch, closing down and being dogged on the inside.

'Frostlips' and Gregor crawl under the broken-down truck with a lot of cursing and swearing, but give up after a while, shaking their heads.

'Can't do a thing with it,' says 'Frostlips', 'it's a total write-off! The Yanks knew what they were doing when they made us a present of those rotten Studebakers! Capitalist shit!' he rages, kicking at the big tyres.

'What the hell's that?' asks the Commissar, and listens tensely.

'Crow,' cries out 'Whorecatcher' nervously, staring up at the dark sky.

As if in reply an old scout biplane appears from the clouds and circles low over us. Then it disappears again into the cloud curtain.

'If it's us they're looking for, they know where we are now,' remarks the Old Man, uneasily.

'It's not us,' says the Commissar thoughtfully. 'I had some German equipment and weapons scattered about in the prison, and the Kübel with the smashed radiator I left outside. So they're not looking for Russians. They're looking for a German Brandenburg Commando*!'

The broken-down truck is taken on tow behind one of the T-34s.

'We'll get another truck all right,' promises the Commissar, confidently. 'But until we do we'll just have to tow that Yankee shit.'

Six days after our departure from the Vladimir prison we halt in a deserted, forgotten village to make necessary repairs

---

* German special unit for raiding behind enemy lines.

to two of the vehicles. Their radiators are boiling so much that it is a wonder they have not split open long ago.

When the repairs are completed we sit down to play cards with the village mayor and the local OGPU chief, a man who got into political hot water twenty years earlier. We play in silence for a while, until 'Frostlips' accuses the mayor of cheating. When 'Frostlips' keeps on with his charges the mayor gets angry and threatens to cut off his ears if he does not stop talking such nonsense.

'May God grant you the pains and tortures of a slow death, you immoral dog,' snarls 'Frostlips' at the mayor.

The mayor goes pale, but still continues to cheat. Suddenly the light goes out, and while the mayor is gone to see what has happened, 'Frostlips' sweeps the money up from the table and hurries out into the kitchen.

When the fuse has been changed and the sleepy light again shines down over the table, the mayor discovers that his winnings have disappeared. He gives out a loud yell and looks under the table in the vain hope that the money has fallen on the floor. Of course, it has not.

'And you're the one who's supposed to see to it there's law and order here,' he screams accusingly at the OGPU chief, as he realizes slowly that he has been robbed. 'May the Evil One grant you thousands of cramps, pestilences and cankers, and so order it that these bounties not only fall upon you, but also upon your children and your children's children even unto the twelfth generation, if you do not find my money!'

'When we're finished with this lousy war,' scowls Barcelona, 'I don't want ever to see snow again! Damnation, how I *hate* snow! No matter where you look everywhere's white! The only chance you've got of seein' a bit of colour is to go out and look at your arse in a mirror!'

'What did you do before you became a soldier?' Kostia asks Porta.

'Oh, a lot of things,' answers Porta. 'Beat up the mothers' darlings from out in Dahlem, and fucked their girls; mugged a yokel now and then that'd come to Berlin to find out what it was like to ride on a tram. Had a job for a bit delivering for the greengrocer on *Bornholmer Strasse*, and then went up in the world and went round with coke on a delivery bike. Used to measure up the coke in a wooden keg. That was 5 litres and cost 95 pfennigs. Every household'd buy one of them, and it was just enough to keep the place warm through the evenin'.'

'Bloody hell!' cries Kostia, in amazement, 'I always heard you Germans were high finance people and that rich, you put notes in between your sausage and your bread!'

'Don't believe all you hear,' Porta advises him, condescendingly. 'In Old Moabitt we were that poor we used to steal the bottoms out of the beer-glasses when we went past a boozer!'

'We were poor, too,' says Igor. 'I washed houses, and made just about enough so's things could go round. One little vodka of a Sunday at the most, and even though it's forbidden to be poor in the Soviet Union we were still poor anyway. But then I got a bit more rich too, and I would've been really rich if you rotten Germans had stayed where you belong. My young brother an' me hit on a really great idea. We started holding up the deliverers from the meat market, and selling the proceeds on the black.'

'Did you rustle cows then?' asks Tiny, with interest. 'That ain't no good! I know all about that 'cos me an' the fur Jew's kid David pinched one of them things once. All we got out of it was all three of us landed up with old Nass in the David Station. Since then they don't bring cows inside. They took the bleedin' thing up to Nass's office on the first floor, and then couldn't get it down again. They 'ad to 'oist it down, and when it wouldn't go out of the window they 'ad to knock a 'ole in the wall for the walking milk-shop. They made it too little, and before they'd finished the cow got that scared of 'avin' been picked up by the coppers that it shit all over Nass an' all 'is detectives!'

'No, we did not take live cattle,' explains Igor, with a cunning grin. 'We waited for the ones who came to fetch meat on bicycles. When they went in to warm themselves with a quick early morning vodka, they'd leave their bikes outside. Then we would take the lot, bikes, meat and all.

They tried to come after us sometimes, but they never caught us!'

'Did your kid brother join the OGPU too?' asks Porta, interestedly.

'No, he was eaten by lions!'

'Eaten by lions?' asks Porta, in astonishment. 'How, then? I've never met anybody who's been eaten by lions!'

'Well, it was like this,' sighs Igor, sadly. 'We never used to pay to get into the Zoo, we went in over the wall. Sometimes, of course, we made a mistake and landed in with the sea-lions or the polar bears. We always got away with it though. The polar bears were that surprised when we came chasing over the wall that they never thought of eating us until we were out of there again. After a bit we knew all the animals pretty well. And they knew us, too. It was only the keepers who didn't like us.

'Well there was one day when we hadn't had anything proper to eat for several days, and were standing there watching the big cats getting outside their dinners.

'My kid brother was standing down in front of the lions' cage watching the keepers putting great big lumps of meat in to them. When the keeper was out for a minute, my brother nipped into the cage and grabbed a big chunk of meat from right under the nose of a motheaten old lion. It gave out a terrible roar when the meat disappeared, and struck out at him. He got such a blow that he went flying up in the other end of the cage and landed on another lion that was having its lunch siesta. All hell broke loose. Round and round they went in the cage! The whole crowd of 'em after my brother. What a din! When the keepers finally turned up there wasn't much left of him. Those mangy lions had eaten him all up!'

Kostia tells us that he has always been a headhunter, and has caught many prisoners who had escaped from Kolyma.

'The *Jakaeirs* always told us when anybody had gone over the wall. They got ten roubles for the information. Bounty was a hundred roubles for every body we handed in. We were merciful. We never tortured a prisoner. We would shoot him sleeping, so that he would not experience the fear of death. Winter was the best time. We could collect the bodies and store them until we had a sledge-load. In summer we had to get them handed in before they rotted and could not be identified. We got no pay for bodies unless they were identified at Central Camp, and there was another risk in handing in rotten bodies that nobody wanted. I know several who have been hanged for an unsolved murder. In that way the police got them off their lists and had less trouble with their percentage of open-ended cases.'

'Hell's bells!' cries Gregor, spitting, as if to get rid of a nasty taste. 'What kind of company's this we've got into?'

'But it was parasites on the body of the community we captured,' Kostia defends himself.

'You've got to be a Siberian, to think like that,' explains the Commissar, and sends Kostia a wicked look. 'These slit-eyed monsters come into the world through Satan's arsehole!'

Kostia laughs long and loud, and does not appear the slightest bit insulted.

'It's snowing like all get-out,' says Barcelona, looking out of the window. 'We're not going to get any further. Those snowdrifts are thirty feet tall!'

'I'll get a snowplough,' promises the Commissar, shrugging into his long fur coat. He slings his *Kalashnikov* across his chest, and waves to Kostia who follows him with a Siberian grin.

'Snowplough!' jeers Heide, who is sitting by the stove, looking insulted.

'He doesn't mean an ordinary snowplough,' says 'Whore-catcher'. 'He means a snow*eater*!'

'Never heard of such a thing,' says Porta, shuffling the cards deftly. 'What is it?'

'It's a machine which swallows tons of snow a minute,' explains 'Whorecatcher'. 'If you let a couple of 'em loose at the North Pole there soon wouldn't *be* a North Pole any more!'

'And he's going to find one of them in this hole in the ground?' Porta screams with laughter. 'What a bloody optimist!'

'He's a three-star commissar!' says 'Whorecatcher', and does not feel that any further explanation is needed.

After some time the Commissar and Kostia return.

'Get ready,' snaps the Commissar. 'The snowplough's here, and we have to follow close up behind it. T-34 first, Panther behind!'

'Tell me,' says Porta, blowing smoke in his face, 'you always want me in the rear! Don't you *trust* me?'

The Commissar gives out a long, long laugh.

'You're a funny bloody chap,' he says, between bursts of laughter. 'Anybody who trusts you ought to be kept in a padded cell! You don't mean to tell me that the thought of doing us all in the eye hasn't even crossed your mind!'

'Oh, well! There's a lot of things a fellow can meditate on.' Porta forces a smile.

The snowplough is an enormous machine which really does 'eat' snow, as 'Whorecatcher' has told us. We have never seen anything like it. The tallest of drifts disappears in minutes when it starts work on it. But shortly after we have passed by, new mountains of snow lie behind us, making the road completely impassable.

'Makes us safe from possible pursuers,' grins the Commissar, with satisfaction. 'This was the only snowplough in town. If anyone wants another they'll have to get it from Irgorsk, and that's where we're going!'

'Smart, smart!' Porta admits. 'A man doesn't even have to pretend to be thinking about it to be able to see we're home and dry!'

A militia man shouts at us halfway inside Irgorsk. The Commissar waves him off in a manner which only people who are in a position of power can permit themselves.

'He was scared of our red-painted faces,' grins Porta, exaltedly.

A row of searchlights send their rays up into the pitchblack night. They cross one another and play nervously over the dark clouds.

'What the devil!' cries Porta, in amazement. 'An air raid? Who the hell'd bomb this place? Must be some mistake!'

The thundering roll of an explosion makes the air shake.

'That a mistake too?' asks Gregor. 'Sounds real enough to me!'

An enormous column of fire goes up, sending a sea of white-hot sparks out over the whole town. Battalions of flames dance whirling along the rooftops. Melted lead drips into the streets, and whistles and bubbles in the snow. The heavy rafters of the large buildings begin to sink down, cracking and splintering. Gargoyles, cut in granite, fall from on high, smashing everything they land on. A granite head with a long tongue hanging from its mouth rolls along the street and ends up with a ringing sound against the Panther's tracks. An old-fashioned fire-waggon with solid rubber tyres breaks up under the rain of bricks. Firemen sitting along the sides of it do not even realize what is happening.

We stare, in fascination, at a concrete wall. The building is expanding like a balloon, slowly being blown up. The huge flat roof falls down through the inside of the house, which is one seething bonfire. Sparks fly hundreds of yards up into the air; steel girders bend as if they were made of soft rubber.

Two screaming girls come running down the street, with their hair and clothes in flames. A fireman aims his hose at them. They are thrown back down the street, and stick to the boiling, bubbling asphalt.

'Get *on!* Hell, let's get out of here,' shouts the Old Man, hysterically. 'That's all we needed! To get killed by our own air force!'

A container full of incendiaries splashes up alongside us. Phosphorus splashes on to the sides of the tanks and begins to burn. Paint ignites and bubbles on the sides of the vehicles.

'Don't touch it!' the Old Man warns over the radio. 'It can only put itself out!'

We swing up a broad boulevard, and see a row of corpses lying at a cellar entrance. They have been burnt to the size of tiny dolls, and are curled up in the strange positions which burnt bodies always assume.

A General of Infantry, his cape blowing out behind him,

roars commands, and rages threats at us when we ignore his orders.

'*Job tvojemadj*!' grins Igor, grimly. 'Let him burn! Poor soldiers can't expect anything of rich generals!'

The general runs after us, shouting and gesticulating. He stops and jumps to one side to avoid being crushed by Kostia's T-34, which rushes at him at top speed. He falls into a large puddle. When he gets to his feet again his boots are burning. There was phosphorus at the bottom of the puddle and it ignites as soon as air gets to it. Desperately, he rubs his boots on the cement. It is apparently the first time he has encountered phosphorus. Otherwise he would have removed his boots immediately. Now he is spreading the phosphorus, and making it burn even more furiously. He stumbles backwards into the pool. Gripped by panic he crawls out of it, and finds himself in a worse position than ever. Tiny blue flames dance all over his back. His cloak crisps rapidly. In only a few minutes he lies on the street, a heap of flaming rags!

'That phosphorus can get anybody,' mumbles Porta, staring at the bubbling heap which was once a general. 'I've heard they've gone over to using it down in hell. It's more effective than old-fashioned coal!'

A Stuka is hit, and explodes in a ball of fire. Shrapnel and red-hot metal parts shower down, and rattle on the steel sides of the tanks.

AA-guns bang. Wherever one looks something is exploding. It is as if an umbrella of blue-red-yellow fire had been opened above the town.

Some elderly firemen with an old-fashioned fire-engine work like mad things at the handles of their pump. Not much water comes out of it, but they still keep working.

A little further on, a fat man in a green uniform stands staring, paralysed with astonishment, at his arm. It is burning and bubbling. He was foolish enough to handle an incendiary.

Fleeing people run around him. They keep well away. Nobody helps him. A heavy air attack makes everyone insensitive. They all have enough to do to look after themselves and their nearest relatives.

The fat man falls on his knees, and burns up, apathetically, in a sea of blue flame.

The infernal howling of the dive-bombing Stukas tears at one's nerves. People are gripped by panic and rush round like terror-stricken hens.

'Not a bad idea, those sirens on the Stukas,' says Porta, holding his hands over his ears. 'That howling could make a lamb take part in a steeplechase!'

Soon the whole town has become a roaring inferno. Now the big Heinkel machines roar over and drop their high explosive bombs into the sea of flames.

A heavy lorry is thrown high into the air. Soldiers fall from it like confetti, and a few moments later they too are burning, down on the bubbling asphalt.

Automatic weapons begin to go off on their own. Bullets ricochet in all directions, like rice scattered over a bridal couple.

On the great ring boulevard in the expensive quarter of the town two ambulances stand across the road, in a blaze of dancing flames. Stretchers hang out of them and unrecognizable bodies burn in a mixed-up, soot-blackened heap.

Porta has a moment of panic when a tall concrete building collapses. The outer walls crash out across the boulevard and block the street. At the same time the street behind us breaks out in a hellish sea of phosphorus flames, at the new influx of oxygen.

Confused commands stream from the radio.

'Turn that bloody thing off,' snarls the Old Man desperately. He pulls out the plug to the chest-receiver, and the communicator goes dead. 'Come on Porta! *Quite* slowly, back! Cool down and do exactly as I say! If we start going into a spin, we'll never make it!'

Finally, Porta gets the heavy tank moving, and backs. He goes straight through a baker's shop. Glass shelves, bread, and paper bags fly everywhere. In a cloud of flour the tank goes through a partition wall and finally breaks through the

341

outer wall in a shower of bricks.

'The tracks are burnin',' shouts Tiny, in alarm. 'Bleedin' 'ell they are! An' stinkin' like 'ell too!'

'It's phosphorus!' says the Old Man despairingly. 'We've got to get it scraped off before the whole blasted waggon goes up, and us with it!'

He chases us. We leap out through the hatches, and begin to scrape away feverishly at the burning tracks and rollers.

'Watch out,' shouts the Old Man, warningly. 'Get that stuff on you and you're finished!'

He does not need to warn us. We know only too well what war-phosphorus is like. That frightful substance which attaches itself to everything and blazes more fiercely the more air it gets. The more you scrape, the more it burns!

The heat around us is terrible. Our hair singes and curls up, our skin burns. Incendiaries throw out their white magnesium glare wherever they strike.

An OGPU officer in a half-burnt uniform, but with a new, shiny *Kalashnikov* bumping across his chest, comes rushing from a side street, stops, and spits a hail of curses at us.

The Commissar comes running up like a vicious Dobermann, swells himself up in front of the OGPU officer, and lets off a stream of invective at him which makes him completely lose his breath.

The OGPU lieutenant is about to slink off, but changes his mind when a whole group of OGPU soldiers turn the corner with *Kalashnikovs* at the ready. One of them grabs Gregor and pushes his mpi barrel into his neck.

The first salvo goes over our heads and has an unexpected effect on the gun-crazy OGPU lieutenant. He is thrown a good way up into the air with his arms spread out like wings. The battle-happy officer is hit in the chest and it is as if the tracer bullets go straight through him. He manages to give out a rattling scream, before he is thrown backwards on to a burning lump of phosphorus. It flames up immediately.

Four machine-pistols spit fire at us.

Heide is in cover behind the Panther, shooting from between its burning tracks.

The OGPU men go down with crushed kneecaps. Heide has to shoot low from his position. He gets to his feet, and walks coldly towards the groaning OGPU soldiers. With a crooked smile, and a merciless coldness in his blue eyes, he clicks his mpi to single shots and puts a bullet into each of the pleading faces.

'Why the hell did you do that?' protests the Old Man, furiously. 'I've had enough of you!'

'The situation required it,' barks Heide arrogantly, changing magazines.

'Julius is nothing but a twisted caricature of his own beliefs,' sneers Porta. 'He stinks of dead bodies like all his swastika mates!'

'The day is not far off when I'm going to take care of you quite specially,' promises Heide, sending Porta a wicked look.

A jet of flame several hundred yards high shoots up into the air, and a long, rolling explosion sounds over the burning town.

Boris, the T-34's turret gunner, is thrown along the street and spitted on the machine-cannon mounted on the tank. He spins like a paper windmill, the long barrel of the gun projecting from his middle.

It was the city gasworks which had blown up. Everything has become an indescribable inferno. Brickwork splinters like glass. Iron rods expand and contort. Roofs are lifted from houses, as the blast flame sweeps across the town like a glowing fire-storm.

A JU-88 comes roaring in above the roofs with flames streaming from its wings. It sways and rolls from side to side, and crashes into a house. It explodes in a blinding red ball of fire.

A Willy's jeep comes towards us at a mad speed. The driver is hanging lifeless over the low metal door. With a crunching sound it hits the T-34 and is mashed to scrap under its tracks.

A long, sliding, scratching sound, like a sack of coke rolling down a ramp, sends us diving to cover. The strange sound ends in a thundering explosion, which makes our ears hurt, and almost blows the sense out of our heads. A large bomb has fallen a couple of hundred yards from us. It blows away everything standing, and leaves only shaved earth around the spot where it has fallen.

'Christ on the cross,' groans Porta, putting his hands to his head. 'Devil take the rotten Luftwaffe!'

One of the T-34s is burning. Black, oily smoke goes up towards the sky. Shortly afterwards the ammunition in the tank explodes and splits it to pieces.

'Take cover!' shouts the Commissar, as a coloured marker sinks down, throwing out a cascade of green fire all around it. High explosive bombs rain down. Dancing flames shoot up from the streets, like an army of flamethrowers.

'It's the gas pipes,' says Heide, importantly.

'You stupid bastard,' hisses Tiny, with a sneer. 'The gasworks has gone up long since!'

'Idiot!' snarls Heide, 'there's gas other places!'

The sky sparkles red, suddenly. A new bomber wave is closing in. The threatening thunder of the motors grows by the second. Markers fall, making a large square of light. We are right in the middle of it.

The first two thousand-pounders go off around us. It is like a volcano in eruption, and throws steel and fire many yards up into the air. The road surface cracks and piles up in heaps, and the huge artillery barracks behind us is pulverized. It seems as if the broad boulevard is thrown up towards the sky. Trees in the middle of it fly through the air like arrows from a bow, and the night becomes as light as the clearest day.

The Legionnaire and I come to ourselves out on the barrack square amongst broken guns, artillery tractors and corpses.

The motor-sledge has been turned upside down, its turret forced down into the softened asphalt. The motor hangs out, half off its mounting.

The Commissar curses, viciously, when he realizes the motor-sledge has been turned into scrap.

A fifty-pound incendiary bomb falls a couple of yards from the Panther, which is immediately wrapped in a roaring curtain of flames.

We go at the incendiary sticks with the fire-fighting equipment we have. Without the Panther we are never going to get back alive. Desperately we throw earth and sand over the red and white magnesium blobs, which burn all over the tank. The heat is unbearable. Time and again we are forced back by it.

The red paint we have been covered with begins to bubble up, but this has the advantage of thinning it. It begins to run away from our faces. Soon we only look as if we were suffering from measles.

We drive the vehicles under cover on the far side of the barracks, where there is a park adjoining the woods.

'I'll try to get hold of a lorry in place of the one that broke down,' says the Commissar. 'Kostia! You come with me! Grab a couple of grenades! You never know what kind of regulations-crazy fools we might run into!'

Half an hour later he is back with a brand-new Studebaker.

'What d'you say to that?' he asks, throwing out his arms proudly.

'The Soviet's going to suffer a great loss, when you leave it!' Porta grins in acknowledgement.

A thousand-pound bomb drops in the middle of a flock of sheep. Torn-off limbs are thrown along the street, and a heavy rain of blood spatters down on us, again turning us red. The stench makes us retch.

When we swing off the road to take what we think is a short cut, there is a deafening explosion, and white clouds of steam come hissing up out of the earth.

'Must be steampipes,' says 'Whorecatcher'. 'They'll be goin' off before we know where we are! Let's get to hell out of here fast!'

'Get back!' shouts the Commissar, waving with both arms from the T-34's turret. 'Hell, get back! If it's what I think it is, all hell's loose!'

The road begins to sink down, as if it were being sucked away by invisible forces. Houses on both sides of the road crumble and disappear into the hole, which closes after them

345

with a horrible, sucking sound.

'Good Lord above,' cries the Old Man, in horror. 'That's got to be more than burst pipes!'

'Too true,' shouts the Commissar furiously, 'but let's get out of here quick as all hell. I'll explain later!'

On the far side of the boulevard the road bulges up into a huge mound. It is as if the world were turning inside out. Houses fall down in whole rows, as if the earth were sucking them down into itself.

'This is bleedin' nasty,' mumbles Tiny. 'Seems like the devil's on 'is way up to 'ave a look at what's goin' on!'

In the middle of the park we are stopped by an OGPU patrol, which has driven two armoured sledges across the road.

'Get ready,' growls the Commissar viciously. 'Nothing's going to stop us now! Not the whole bloody Kremlin!'

Two nasty-looking OGPU men, dressed entirely in black leather, and with *Kalashnikovs* at the ready, stand in the middle of the road waving us down like policemen.

The Commissar jumps down from the T-34, puffs himself up and marches towards them. He shouts loudly and waves his fist in the air. A *polittruk** comes out from behind the road-block. He too seems to have puffed himself up. His broad, Slavic face promises us no good.

'Necker!' says Porta, world-wise. 'It'd be clever of us to shoot his balls off!'

'*Propusk*!' shouts the *polittruk*, holding out his hand in true policeman style.

'Up my arse!' screams the Commissar. 'I am on special duty with some Volga Germans! God help you when I report to Moscow! You're sabotaging a mission of national importance!'

'I've got my orders,' roars the *polittruk*. 'Even if the great Stalin came past, he'd have to show a *propusk*! *Panjemajo?*'

'A drink?' asks Porta, with a false smile. He offers his water-

---

* *Polittruk:* A Russian police commissioner

346

bottle from the driver's hatch with a gesture of invitation.

'Vodka?' asks the wicked-looking *politruk*. He grabs eagerly at the water-bottle, and takes a long drink from it. He hands it on to his two leather-clad minions, who swallow it down like thirsty horses. 'Nice an' warming!' he says, and his tone has become a little milder.

Suddenly, something strange seems to be happening to his face. He goes white as a corpse, then scarlet. The red goes slowly over to a blue tint. He grasps his stomach and gives out some very strange sounds.

One of the black-leather fellows puts both hands to his mouth, and throws up like a man in the grip of seasickness.

'Hell!' gulps the *politruk*. He feels as if the whole of his insides were being eaten away. He stares, confusedly, with eyes which seem about to fall from their sockets. The three men's bowels give way. Their legs bend under them, and they collapse to the ground with long rattling groans.

Porta puts the water-bottle back under the driver's seat, and makes a mental note to fill it up again with his special brand of grog.

The Commissar stares quite blankly at the three prostrate forms.

'What the hell . . . .' He has got no further when a sound reminiscent of distant thunder stops him. The earth under us begins to quiver.

'What the devil's that?' shouts Porta, looking around confusedly.

'Landslip!' shouts the Comissar, in terror, and comes towards us on the run.

From behind the two motor-sledges barring our way come two new OGPU men. They shout in confusion as trees begin to sway and move as if they were stems of grass.

'What the hell's happening?' shouts Gregor, with terror in his voice, as another row of trees comes crashing down.

'Landslip!' howls the Commissar, 'fucking hell it's quick *clay*! Run! Run for your lives!'

The whole forest dissolves before our eyes. A jumble of

347

rocks are thrown here and there. The earth begins to toss, like waves in a stormy sea. The noise is shattering.

In front of us the road begins to move like a plank caught in a whirlpool. Both of the OGPU motor-sledges slide down a deep incline which has appeared, and splash into a bubbling lake of mud and splintered trees. Through the deafening turmoil comes a new sound. A long, sucking noise, like that of a blocked pipe which can suddenly take air again. But a million times louder.

'*Run!*' shouts the Commissar, sprinting down the road with the rest of us at his heels, including the leather-clad OGPU soldiers.

The road begins to give way under our feet, and we jump up some inclines onto a narrower path which lies rather higher than the broad main road.

Apparently firm ground gives back hollow noises under our running boots. It is as if we were running in dough. Slowly the earth slips down and is churned into a muddy swamp.

Tiny gives a scream of terror when a large fir tree falls on him.

Gregor and I work desperately to release him from it, but it is only when Porta comes to our help that we manage to move the big tree.

A giant boulder comes careening down the slope and takes Boris with it. He gives one shrill scream, and is forced down into the ooze under its weight.

In desperation we run on down the narrow path, but it is like trying to cross a rushing whirlpool, which is continually attempting to suck us down into its depths. When we are only a short distance from the road fountains of mud and water spout up hundreds of yards into the air.

'Where's all that *water* coming from?' asks Porta. He is clinging desperately to an uprooted tree, which is whirling round in the bubbling mud.

'It's being pressed up out of the quick clay,' pants the Commissar. 'There's millions of gallons of it.'

'How the hell's it happening?' asks the Old Man, helplessly. 'I've never *heard* of quick clay!'

'It exists in Russia,' explains the Commissar, a little later, as we struggle through the slimy, boiling mud, slipping and sliding helplessly all over the place. 'A remainder of the Ice Age. 50 per cent of it is water, which has been trapped in pockets of clay and rubble. It can hold on to it for ever if only nothing starts it off. If something does, then what has seemed to be hard ground turns to mud which sucks down everything, as you have seen here. We've had whole towns disappear here in Russia when quick clay has started to move!'

'What silly bleeder started it off 'ere then?' asks Tiny, sneezing, and pulling himself up with difficulty from a sucking mudhole.

'Those damned German bombs did!' hisses the Commissar, savagely. 'I had an idea of what was happening down in the town, when the streets started to disappear!'

Finally we manage to work our way up to the solid road. Completely worn out we drop to the ground. We are no longer red. We have been turned into mud-coloured statues.

'*Job tvojemadj*!' shouts Kostia, pointing over at the OGPU guard barracks. It has begun to move down the road like a house on rollers. It begins to break up. Walls fall in, tiled roofs shatter, and in the winking of an eye it has been sucked down into the earth.

The whole of the slope on the far side of the road begins to slip downwards with ever increasing speed. Great trees are thrown into the air, and huge boulders crash together, splintering one another.

The water pressed out of the clay spouts up towards the sky. Millions of tons of clay are moving like a storm-whipped sea.

'It can't be *true*!' howls Porta desperately, hopping up and down. 'The Devil's come to steal our gold!'

Open-mouthed we stare at the heavily laden Studebaker truck, as it disappears quite slowly into the bubbling mud. Round about us geysers go roaring up. It is a fantastic sight, but we are too shocked to take in the splendour of the natural phenomenon which is going on around us.

A stream of mud and water roars down the road, and in a

matter of seconds both of the trucks loaded with gold have disappeared. A little later one of the T-34s slips down sideways from what is left of the road. With a deafening rattle it swings round and is sucked down into the mud. Its gun points upwards to the last like the bowsprit of a torpedoed warship.

'There goes the rest of the gold!' groans the Commissar, despairingly. He tears his fur cap from his head and tramples on it wildly, as if it were that which was to blame.

We struggle madly to get back through the seething mud to the Panther and the remaining T-34. They are jammed between two huge boulders.

Depressedly we walk round them to see how they have fared. The damage is a catastrophe. The tracks of the T-34 have been torn off, and lie spread in individual links down the remains of the road. The Panther's rollers have been torn from their beds. Several shock-absorbers have been smashed.

I climb up in the turret to look at the gun. *That* seems to be undamaged.

'*Can* these two shit-buckets be repaired?' asks the Commissar, with a look of defeat on his face. 'Without them we haven't got a hope!'

'How d'you think the foot-sloggers manage?' asks Porta, nastily. 'They've got nothing to carry their arses round in!'

'They *don't* manage,' answers the Commissar pessimistically. 'They walk till their ears are dragging on the ground!'

'Well there's not much left to talk about then, is there?' replies Porta, taking off his muddy fur coat. 'I'll forget I'm only a driver for once! Let's get the gas-cylinders out so's we can start welding! Need teaches modest maidens to fuck! Really we need a whole workshops company to get these two tin cans on the road again!'

For two days we work literally incessantly, but at last both waggons are roadworthy. Porta wipes his hands on a piece of waste and looks sadly round at the crumpled, muddy earth in which all the gold is buried.

'Well, now we know what quick clay is!' he says and throws the waste from him, resignedly.

Tiny is inconsolable. He walks around all the time jabbing a long spike into the ground in the hope of striking the gold. He simply refuses to believe that it has gone forever.

'Think we could organize an excavator?' asks Porta, looking at the Commissar. 'It must be possible to turn that forest upside down an' find our gold again?'

'Not a chance,' says 'Whorecatcher'. 'I once saw a whole town disappear in Siberia. They dug for three months with an army of excavators and didn't find as much as a brick of it. The Devil had swallowed the lot.'

'I *won't* believe it!' shouts Porta, angrily. He pulls down a pickaxe from the T-34. He starts to swing it energetically at the hardened mud. 'Think of all those dummies who dug up the whole of Alaska and half Canada in the hope of finding a handful of gold-dust! And those clowns didn't even know if there *was* anything, there where they were diggin'! We have at least got the advantage of knowin' there's a hell of a big lump of the stuff down there! Come on boys! Grab a spade or a shovel! Don't you *want* to go to Sweden and fish for salmon! It's more fun than bein' a German soldier in wartime!'

'You got somethin' there,' cries Tiny, grabbing a spade. 'When the Mafia 'ears about our gold they'll all be down 'ere! An' them white'eaded old bastards'll be diggin' too, even though it may 'ave been a long time since they used their 'ands!'

'They'd have their *spaghetti carbonara* goin' down the wrong way!' jokes Gregor, beginning to dig.

'Shut up a minute,' sighs the Commissar, resting his chin on his hands. 'I've got to think!'

'Don't do it for too long,' advises Tiny. 'It can be dangerous to think too long! When I was with the military psychopaths they said I *mustn't* think. Since then I 'aven't done it, an' it suits me down to the bleedin' ground!'

'The only way we could possibly get the gold back is with half a score of dredging machines,' says the Commissar, in a voice which sounds as if it is coming from the depths of a tin can.

'We can't get *them* down here,' protests Porta. 'They're

351

things that sail on *water*!'

'That's right,' answers the Commissar. He is so depressed he looks like a whole town in mourning. 'So forget the gold. We've lost it forever!'

'I got a plan!' shouts 'Frostlips', lighting up like a candle.

'Both God and the Devil protect us!' cries 'Whorecatcher', making a gesture of despair.

'We could drill for the gold the way they drill for oil,' 'Frostlips' goes on. 'I know a feller who can get hold of a drill for us!'

'Idiot!' snarls the Commissar. 'Why not a corkscrew?'

For a while we sit gazing miserably out over the dried-up sea of mud, which has swallowed up the gold which was going to turn us into good Swedish Social Democrats.

'You thought what's going to happen to us if they get hold of us, even if we're not carrying any gold?' Gregor throws out the idea. 'I don't reckon it'll be nice!'

'They'll hit us with all sorts of nasty charges and things. More'n we could count,' says Porta, heavily. 'For a start: High Treason or whatever it is they call it when you don't love the Fatherland enough! That gives you fifteen times life imprisonment, and that's a good bit of forever! The fact of our having lost the gold we pinched don't make a bit of difference!'

'They wouldn't even believe that rotten mud swallowed up the gold,' says 'Frostlips', with a mien sad enough for a man sentenced to death. 'They'd just keep on torturin' us till there wasn't nothing left *to* torture!'

'One thing we must be in agreement on,' says the Commissar, his face dark as summer thunder. 'We keep our mouths shut and forget all about the gold! If they get just a sniff of it having been us who took it we'll be chased by the lot of 'em. And they'll be tough about it. Not only the OGPU but the Gestapo, and the CIA and MI5, and the yellow thought police, and even the solitary member of the Soviet Secret Service! They'd all be on our tracks!'

'What about the Boy Scouts?' asks Tiny. 'I know a feller that's a Rover Scout!'

Two days later we stop at a crossroads where there is a whole cluster of signs pointing to all sorts of places.

Porta sits on the front apron of the Panther, chewing at a sausage and washing down each mouthful with vodka.

'What now?' he asks, glancing at the Commissar, who is hanging out of the T-34's turret hatch, looking miserable. 'You still want to go back with us? Now we're still as poor as we were when we started. Our fishin' trips in Sweden we're going to have to put off for a bit, I fear!'

'It's probably best we stay in our respective countries,' answers the Commissar, jumping down from the tank. 'I've heard a bit about what you Germans do to Commissars. And particularly *Jewish* Commissars!'

'Oh, I don't think we're as bad as all that!' says Tiny, trying to force a smile onto his dejected face.

'It's not you I'm thinking of,' says the Commissar, holding out a hand for Porta's vodka bottle. 'You're just Fritzs like our lot are Ivans. It's your Gestapo, SS and all the other rottenness I meant!'

'They're no worse than your filthy OGPU,' shouts Heide furiously.

'All Secret Police are an invention of the Devil,' says the Commissar, harshly.

'I still think you ought to come with us,' says Gregor. 'We'd get you in the Hiwis* easy, until we say goodbye to the army some day and *really* go fishin' in Sweden!'

'No!' says the Commissar decisively, shaking his head. 'Life's a game of chance! A man doesn't give up when he loses once! If I go with you now, I'm a loser! I've only gained a little time. I reckoned on it perhaps going wrong for us this time, and I've got my back covered. Another thing is I haven't got the nerve to stay around you lot much longer!'

'Moscow,' mumbles Porta, thoughtfully. 'So you'll be going via Tambow?'

'Yes, and after that Stalinogorsk,' 'Frostlips' grins without humour.

* Hilfswillige: German Work Troops

'Devil of a way you've got to go, there,' nods Porta, peering to the north-east. 'And there's bad weather coming up!'

'You can be on the other side of Kursk in four days,' explains the Commissar, 'but don't go through Voronez! Can't spit there for OGPU!'

'This is goodbye then,' says the Old Man quietly. 'It's a bit sad. We've got to know you!'

'We like you too,' smiles 'Frostlips', putting an arm round Porta's shoulder. 'How stupid war is!'

'You'll be shittin' your pants when you cross Dzherzhinski Square,' says Gregor, shivering in his cape.

'Not us. We'll get by all right,' laughs the Commissar, self-confidently. 'I'm more doubtful about you fellows! You must have something to tell 'em when you get back!'

'Our orders were to pick up some general, and invite him home with us,' says Porta, 'but where we going to find one of them?'

'Frostlips' spreads out a map on the Panther's front apron and makes a ring with a crayon.

'Here's 38 Motorized Brigade. It's been strengthened with a cavalry regiment, which is *here*! You've counted seventy-somethin' tanks of types KW-2 and T-34/85, and the usual filler of obsolete BTs!'

'Now you *are* certain that brigade *is* there?' asks the Old Man, doubtfully. 'They'll soon find out if it's a wrong 'un. and that'd be worse than coming back empty-handed!'

'Be easy,' answers the Commissar. '"Frostlips" knows what he's talking about!'

'We'd better give you something in return,' says Porta, bending over the map. 'Here, along the Merla by Solotev's 23 Panzer, and they're piss-poor! They've lost the most of their tanks. A medal-hungry general can win a couple for himself right there!'

'That's treason,' rages Heide. 'It'll cost you your head if I report you to the NSFO!'

'But you're not going to,' smiles Porta, coldly. 'Don't forget you were here! We're in the same boat, my son!'

'What about swoppin' tanks?' asks 'Frostlips', with a sneaky grin. 'We come home with your Panther, and you take in our T-34/85. They'd like *that*! The latest new creations of the tank modistes!'

'Maybe it's *not* such a bad idea,' says the Old Man, thoughtfully. 'We'd get through the Russian L of C a lot easier, and if nothing else we could lie in wait for an attack and slip through easy as winking!'

'Let us say goodbye properly,' laughs the Commissar, opening the first bottle of vodka.

Porta wipes his porcelain cup on an old sack. It doesn't make the cup any cleaner, but at least he *has* wiped it.

'Bring out our little surprise!' The Commissar turns to 'Frostlips'. He chuckles and trots over to the tank, and comes back with a case of red caviare. None of us have ever set eyes on red caviare before.

'You are all my friends,' hiccoughs the Commissar, knocking the neck off a fresh bottle of *Moskovskaja*. 'Every one of you is my very good friend, and I shall always be happy to see you again!' He takes a long pull at the bottle, shovels down a couple of spoonsful of caviare and belches loudly: 'Life is a good thing, don't you think?' he says, dreamily. 'There are always new surprises. You'll see! Some day there will be some other gold we can take off after!'

'Without me,' says the Old Man. He is half seas over by now and is explaining to 'Whorecatcher' how to make a chest-of-drawers.

'The most important thing,' the Commissar goes on, in a drunken voice, 'is to have good friends spread about all over the world! Then you can always help one another!' He lifts a finger and points it at Porta. 'Where we Russians stop thinking, that's where you Germans step in! Let us drink to friendship and the small, forbidden thoughts! It is quite wrong of us to fight one another,' he sniffles.

'A health to the Soviet people,' shouts Kostia. He rolls his black, Asiatic eyes confusedly when he realizes that there is something wrong with his toast. Although there are 250 million people in Russia, even the dumbest OGPU man knows that nobody cares to be called a Soviet citizen. He pushes a handful of caviare into his mouth and pours vodka on top of it. Then he toasts himself.

'A toast to Berlin!' suggests the Commissar, pleasantly.

'To Moscow!' hiccoughs Porta. He carries the chipped porcelain cup to his lips, and almost falls over.

'Not forgetting Hamburg!' roars 'Whorecatcher'.

'Thank you,' sobs Tiny, moved. 'You are all 'ereby invited to 'Amburg! We'll meet at the fur Jew's kid David's place at *'Ein 'Oyerstrasse* no 10, and there'll be a red alert out to all the 'ighclass 'ores from "Chéri".' He gets to his feet, swaying. 'To Tashkent!' he sobs, lifting his tin cup. It is a mystery how he knows there is a town called Tashkent, but, as always, he is full of surprises. Some people have died from them.

Heide is exercising Kostia. He is teaching him the German salute and the Prussian goosestep. Unfortunately every time Kostia gets his foot up on a level with his belt buckle he falls over backwards. In the end he gives up and sits looking sadly up at the racing snow-clouds.

'Thank God I am not a German!' he groans. 'They are far too energetic!'

It is icy cold when we wake up in the old roadmender's hut.

Porta puts both hands to his throbbing head. It is possible he may have felt worse at some time in his life, but just now he cannot remember when.

'*Job tvojemadj!*' groans Kostia, looking as if he has just been shot. 'What *have* they done to Kostia?'

Albert laughs loudly. He is one of those happy people who never have hangovers. Hangovers are always amusing – for those who do not suffer from them.

'You black cannibal,' screams Tiny cantankerously, making a face at him. 'If I wasn't sick I'd give you *such* a bashin'. You rotten apeman, you!'

The Commissar wakes up with a piercing scream. He thinks that the worst thing that can happen to a Russian has happened to him. He has been locked up in the cellars of the Lubyanka. He begins shouting at us in Odessa Yiddish, then goes over to German and claims he is chief of the SS.

'They must've put something really Russian in that *Moskovskaja*,' moans Gregor, his eyes brimming tears. 'It was strong enough to knock over a tree and turn it into sawdust!'

'It was bleedin' strong, I can tell you,' mumbles Tiny, wiping the sweat from his brow. 'I got a little bleedin' drop of it on my finger, an' now the nail's gone!' He has forgotten he has caught his fingers two days earlier in the turret hatch.

'I have suddenly realized, Josefvitschi,' says the Commissar to Porta, with a broad smile, 'that you are a crazy fellow. The most crazy fellow I have ever met! How the devil did you ever become a soldier?'

'Yes, I've wondered about that myself,' Porta laughs, heartily. 'But, as you must know, the most important jobs in the world are being a soldier or a whore!'

'There's only two kinds of bints,' shouts Tiny, with a cunning look on his face. 'The 'ores an' the dumb 'uns!'

'Let everybody think you're an ordinary, dumb twit,' explains Porta, 'an' you can stay standing upright on the crust of the earth enjoying watching the rest of 'em fall off!'

It is late next day when we finally take leave of one another. We cannot stop embracing, and agreeing meeting-places after the war.

High on a hilltop Porta stops the T-34, and we wave a final goodbye to our Russian friends who are disappearing in the distance on the road to Moscow.

> 'Sag' mir beim Abschied leise Servus,
> ist ein schöner letzter Gruss,
> wenn man Abschied nehmen muss . . .*'

Porta hums. Resolutely he starts the Otto motor up again.

As we get closer to the front line, traffic increases. We get tied up in traffic jams several times. There are Russian MPs everywhere. We are glad we are riding in a T-34, which does

* Old Viennese song

357

not draw the slightest attention.

We come to a halt. Papers are to be checked. Our hands grip mpis and grenades nervously. Porta shows our *propusk* and chatters in a mixture of Russian and German.

'Volga Germans,' mumbles the fat MP, and looks as if he would like to eat us.

'Right *tovaritsch*!' smiles Porta, offering him a swig from the water-bottle.'

The long column of artillery and tanks begins to move forward again.

The MP jumps down from the T-34 and waves us on.

For several hours we drive on in the middle of the column. Then Porta manages to turn off into a narrow forest path. Well into the woods he stops. We jump down and run about in the snow to thaw out our icy feet.

'I'm fed up!' says Tiny. 'I want to go home!'

'Good heavens, a general!' whispers Gregor, fearfully.

Three fur-clad forms appear from the closely ranked trees. It is a Lieutenant-general and two staff officers. They are carrying heavy briefcases, chained to their wrists.

'Who the devil are you?' snaps the general, in a deep, guttural voice. His sharp blue eyes peer at us from below white bushy brows.

'Volga Germans, *gospodin general*,' answers Porta in his best Russian.

'What the devil are you doing here?' the general goes on, suspiciously. He takes a red and white packet of cigarettes from his pocket. He lights one and blows smoke thoughtfully through his nose. 'Aren't you, rather, deserters? It seems to me very strange that you have stopped here to take a rest. You're a long way from the tank positions!'

'We lost our way,' answers Porta, throwing his arms wide.

'*Propusk*!' the general demands, putting out his hand.

A lot of things happen in a very short space of time. The general is down in the snow, stretched there by a blow from the edge of Tiny's shovel of a hand.

A short burst comes from the slim colonel's machine-pistol. A bullet burns across the side of Tiny's head. Blood pours down over his face.

The Legionnaire smashes the colonel's face in with a butt stroke.

The third officer, a lieutenant-colonel turns and begins to run off through the knee-deep snow.

'*Stoi!*' shouts Barcelona, readying his mpi. '*Stoi!*' he repeats, sending a short burst of bullets whipping around the officer.

The lieutenant-colonel stops and raises both hands above his head.

'*Germanski?*' cries the general, in amazement, getting slowly to his feet. He rubs his neck and swears softly.

'Well, we did get our general!' grins Porta, happily. 'See what they've got in those briefcases!'

'Well, look at *this*!' cries Barcelona, in surprise. 'They're draggin' a whole army corps battle order with 'em out here in the forest! They won't only kiss our cheeks, they'll kiss our arses too when we get back with this lot!'

The general tries to do a deal with us. He offers us the world if we'll let him turn the tables and take us in.

'Think we're *that* stupid?' jeers Tiny, with a roar of laughter.

'Don't forget dancing's better than hanging!' says the general, with an obviously threatening tone in his voice.

A German SP section breaks through the sapling trees.

Like lightning the Legionnaire is out there, waving a snow camouflage shirt.

With a deafening crash of tracks the leading SP comes to a halt. A hard-looking major with a machine-pistol in his hands leans out of the turret and snaps, harshly:

'*Halt! Hände hoch!*'

Two artillerymen jump from the gun with mpis at the ready. They order the Legionnaire over to the major, who breaks into a roar of laughter at the very idea of our being Germans. He changes his mind, however, when he sees the contents of the Russian briefcases.

'Well I'm damned,' he mutters. He salutes the captured general, who looks like a man who has lost everything he owned at poker.

'We'll meet again,' he says to Porta, and sends him a look which ought to have sent his army teeth down his throat.

We are on our way back to regiment, and there we get a reception equal to that of the prodigal son.

Oberst Hinka is delighted. When the interrogation officer is finished with the two Russians, wild activity commences in 4 Panzer Army.

Porta is resting in Helena's brothel, getting up strength to go over and tell Chief Mechanic Wolf the sad news of where the gold has ended up.

Some of the girls are dancing closely together to the music of a balalaika. Porta is the only male guest. A Tartar girl is sitting at the bar showing off her beautifully-formed legs. Her narrow eyes regard him with interest. Soon she sways over to him and sits on the edge of the table. Her narrow black skirt rides up to well above the edge of her stockings.

'You have measles?' she asks, letting a long, slim finger slide over the red paint spots which are left as a reminder of Tiny's marker shell.

'Only German measles!' answers Porta sadly.

'German measles?' she trills. 'That is catching?'

'Only for Germans,' answers Porta, looking national.

'You are prettiest tankman I ever see,' she whispers, giving him a look which could have melted a glacier. She slips down from the table and presses her body intimately against him. 'Would you like to come and see my room?' she asks, taking his hand, and pressing it between her warm thighs.

Porta smells her. Cheap perfume and old beer mixed. A lustful gleam comes into his small eyes.

She takes a small sip from his glass.

'You like to fuck now?' she asks, sighing deeply. She takes another tiny sip from his glass. 'I am good fuck! When you go with me it will be first time in your life you really fuck!'

The door bangs open, and Chief Mechanic Wolf marches in, his spurs jingling and his Brosini riding boots flashing.

'So here you are, then. Thin and crazy. Don't give a sod about telling any of us others how things've gone off! I've been lookin' for you everywhere!' He turns round and sees the Tartar girl. She is back on the table edge again with her skirt so high you can see she is wearing no underclothing.

'Buy yourself a piece o' cunt, then! Slant-eyes there's all right! Then we can get over to my place! I think we must have a lot of things to talk over!'

'You've been to the barber's,' grins Porta, running his hand over the girl's crutch. 'And you've had a shave too.' he smiles to her.

'Like it?' asks Wolf, in a self-satisfied voice. He passes his hand over his coal-black hair, which is shiny with brilliantine. 'My barber's famous, you know! Had a shop at "Kempinski". Even rich old bald bastards with no more'n five hairs left used to go to him to get permed. "War Minister" Sally sent him out here when the army finally found out they could use him in a war. As you can see he's sculptured my hair in the latest Hollywood style!'

'Well, well!' said Porta, blowing smoke between the girl's thighs. 'I prefer the professor style myself, with a couple of balls of cottonwool stickin' out over a feller's ears. Makes you look clever!'

There is silence for a while. Porta blows smoke between the girl's legs again, leans back in his chair and balances it on two legs. He pulls back his upper lip in a jeering hyena grin. It makes him look like a snarling dog. He has been practising it for a long time!

'You gonna fuck, or you goin' over to my place?' asks Wolf, impatiently.

Porta puts his hands on the girl's knees. Wolf's hand-sewn Brosini riding boots squeak.

'Don't waste my time with all that shit,' he rasps, bitterly. 'Come on! We're off! You can fuck her some other time! If you live long enough that is!' he adds, dropping his voice to a subterranean rumble. 'I can tell you Sally's on his way here from Berlin, and he's got a couple of these sudden-death fellers with him!' He stops speaking for a moment, and awaits a reaction to his sad news.

'Really?' answers Porta, looking as if he had heard nothing of any importance.

'You fuck now?' asks the Tartar girl, rubbing Porta's crotch. 'Better fuck than get shot! Come! We go this way!'

'No we don't!' roars Wolf. 'This is the way we're goin'!'

A little way down the street Wolf stops again and stands in front of Porta with his British swagger-stick lifted as if he were going to hit him with it.

'Listen 'ere, you shit, I don't seem to've expressed myself clearly enough! I said Sally was on the way! And he's determined that either he gets the gold he's got a right to, or else you go off suddenly on a one-way ticket! I'm tellin' you this as a friend.'

'Both you and that imitation "War Minister" can go and get fucked!' grins Porta, confidently.

Wolf does not answer, but contents himself with staring at Porta with a look which would have frightened away a poisonous snake.

They continue on down the street in silence, Wolf jingling his spurs and Porta banging down his hobnailed heels.

Without acknowledging either the growling wolfhounds or the icy-cold Chinese they stroll into Wolf's lair.

'Where did you put our gold?' asks Wolf, before they have settled in their chairs.

'Yes, what *did* I do with our gold?' answers Porta thoughtfully, taking a bite of sausage.

'That's what *I'm* bloody askin' *you*,' shouts Wolf, furiously. 'I saw you arseholes come in, but even with a monocle I couldn't see anythin' but a fucked-up old museum exhibit of a T-34, and I can't imagine there was space for both you lot *and* our soddin' gold in that tin can!'

'You're right enough there,' Porta forces a smile. 'There was only us and not as much as a grain of gold!'

Wolf walks slowly round the table.

'You didn't have to tell me *that*,' he hisses, and smashes his British swagger-stick down so hard on the table that it breaks in two. Raging, he throws the pieces from him. 'I've been over an' had a look inside that Russian shit-bucket, and now

I want to know where you've hid our gold? You might just as well tell me now before Sally gets here! He ain't got time to do a lot of talking with you! He's gonna just say gold, an' if you say there ain't any then you're dead! Where *is* the gold?' he repeats in a roar, spittle flecking his lips.

'Let me get a word in,' smiles Porta, in friendly fashion. 'That's what I'm tryin' to tell you!' He takes another bite of sausage and swills it down with *Slivovitz*. 'The gold! Yes! A very sad affair that was. It's gone. Been eaten up!'

'Eaten?' gapes Wolf. 'Who the bloody hell eats *gold*?'

'The earth,' smiles Porta, mildly. 'The earth ate our gold! Took it in, lorries and all! Drivers and mates went down with it!' He makes some slobbering sounds like a stopped-up sink and throws his arms so that Wolf can understand how the gold had gone down under the earth.

'I *see*,' says Wolf, pressing his lips together into a thin line.

'It sank down! You don't *say* so! D'you think I'm a complete bloody idiot? You're a lyin' bastard, an' that yarn of yours stinks of con! Jesus, I never heard anythin' like it! The earth ate the gold *all* up! You ain't the feller who wrote the *1001 Nights*, by any chance? Can't you make up a better bleedin' tale?'

Porta spreads out his hands resignedly.

'I didn't know the earth swallowed up gold, either,' he admits, sadly. 'But it *does*, though! I saw it with my own eyes, and it didn't only take the gold, it took three tanks, four trucks and two motor-sledges in the same mouthful. For dessert it took thirty-two men and a whole bloody OGPU guard barracks. If you don't believe me ask the others!'

'A right lot to ask,' yells Wolf, beside himself with rage. 'They're bigger bloody liars than you are! I might as well ask my dogs, an' be satisfied with bow-wow for an answer. But let me tell you somethin', you dirty bastardin' son of an alley cat an' a backyard bitch! If you don't tell me where you've hid that gold I'm gonna tear your lyin' tongue out an' kick your balls straight up into your rotten brains!' He gets more and more furious, crumples his favourite silk cap into a ball and tears at it with his teeth. Words come flying from his mouth like bullets. When Porta takes another bite of sausage he snatches it from his hand and throws it against the wall. 'Do you think you're in a boozer?' he screams. After a while he becomes so hoarse and out of breath that he is forced to stop.

'Finished?' asks Porta quietly, picking up the sausage from the floor. 'Then let me explain! And if you want to lash anybody with that filthy tongue of yours then take it out on the Luftwaffe! They're the shower that's responsible for it all! They bombed the wrong place! It's a wonder I came out of it alive, but, of course, you don't care a shit about that!'

'Too fuckin' true I don't!' snarls Wolf, grinding his teeth.

'Thought as much!' says Porta apathetically, slapping a large piece of sausage on a slice of bread.

'Like some rat poison to put on that?' asks Wolf, nastily.

'No thanks. Jam, though, if you've got it?' smiles Porta ingratiatingly, dipping his sausage in a bowl of redcurrant jelly. 'You ever hear of something called quick clay?'

'Never,' says Wolf. He stares blankly at Porta, whose jaws are working double time to keep the sandwich he has made from choking him.

'Quick clay,' explains Porta, gesturing with the hand which is holding his sandwich, and splashing redcurrant jelly on to Wolf's tailor-made uniform, 'is made up from silicon, sand an' a lot of other shit in clay tubes that can hold together on the outside but are full of water, a hell of a lot of water, inside. So long as it's left alone fuck all happens, but with certain kinds of disturbances, like, for example, bombs dropped by German knotheads, then all hell can break loose! The whole lot of it turns into a bloody great pool of mud when the walls of the tubes break up! The more it gets shook up the worse it gets! The whole surface of the earth starts movin' an' everythin' on it gets sucked down into hell. Trees, people, waggons, tanks and *gold*! I can tell you it was a very unpleasant experience, that lot was!'

'I wish it'd been a hundred times worse,' rumbles Wolf, viciously making himself a sugar sandwich. 'Couldn't you have hung on to our gold, *somehow*? You don't let anything valuable as that slip through your fingers! I hope, for your own sake, you can get Sally to believe your horror story! Otherwise something very nasty might happen to you!'

Sally arrives the next day. He has so little time to spare that he has himself flown from the airstrip in a Fiesler Storch which can land on the wide boulevard.

'They tell me you're up to something!' he shouts as soon as he catches sight of Porta, although still a long way off. 'But that *must* be a lie! You're not that stupid!'

'Drop dead!' answers Porta, with a disarming smile, aiming his forefinger at him.

'Let me hear it! What happened? Where's the gold?' demands Sally. 'I don't give a shit for your Grimm's Fairy Tales stuff, and I want you to know I've brought three interrogation experts with me from Berlin! When they've had you and your pals under treatment you'll confess it was you lot that nailed Jesus and the robber to the cross and stuck a spear in Him and gave Him vinegar instead of vodka like the pigs you are! What a shower!'

Arguing loudly they push their way into Wolf's sanctum sanctorum. They are so excited they come close to fighting when they stick in the door, trying to go through it all three at the same time.

Sally strides up and down the floor, foaming with rage. With a flourish he pulls the oversized pistol he carries round to the front of his belt and unbuttons the flap of the holster. He changes his expression from one of anger to deep, fatherly perturbation and then back again. He shows his teeth in a horsy grin and bends confidentially down over Porta.

'I think you're lying! And d'you know what else I think?'

'I'm no thought-reader!' says Porta.

'Shut up! I'll do the talking!' Sally roars. 'I think you and that filthy Jew Commissar have put that gold somewhere, and are just going to wait till the warring powers have knocked the stuffing out of one another. Then you'll take off and pick up *our* gold, and shit all over your good buddies here! See, that's what I think, you greedy son of a bitch!'

'Really?' smiles Porta sarcastically. 'Look at that, now!'

'Defend yourself, blast you! And shut up about that cursed

quick clay,' shouts Sally furiously. 'Not even a drivelling idiot'd believe that! And let me tell you the risk you and your Jew Commissar are running with this crazy scheme! The morons over there know you've pinched the gold from under their noses, and now they're looking for it. It's enough to make 'em forget the world war! And before you know where you are the whole world'll be after it! You'll never be able to get rid of it! Even the sneaky bankers in Switzerland or Liechtenstein won't touch it!'

'The Mafia might!' says Porta, laconically.

Sally sits down again, scowling, and digs out a large black cigar from his breast pocket, while he considers how to shoot Porta where it will hurt most.

'Let me talk,' says Porta placatingly. 'And I'll explain it to you so it can get through even that thick guard commander skull of yours! I know the gold's red-hot, so I'd never dream of goin' it alone. Believe me or not, the bloody earth's swallowed it up! And all those shits from the OGPU and the Gestapo ain't ever going to find it!'

It takes a very long time before Wolf and Sally are convinced that Porta is telling the truth.

Wolf looks as if he is waiting for the firing squad, and Sally looks as if he has already been hanged. Porta is eating jam with a spoon. It calms his ragged nerves.

'We'll need a whole lot of excavators,' Wolf breaks the heavy silence.

'I can get those!' promises Sally. 'We'll turn that rotten Russia inside bloody out!'

'You'll have to go through the front line again,' decides Wolf. 'And this time don't come back without the gold!'

'You might as well chuck it!' says Porta, disillusioned. 'The earth's swallowed it down and has digested it long ago!'

'How about that Commissar woman?' asks Wolf, after a long silence. 'We can't have her running about free! She knows a lot too much, and it can't be long before the Gestapo's here doin' a bit of gold-prospecting!'

'Funny you should say that,' smiles Porta in friendly fashion. 'That's just what the Commissar said when I asked him what to do about her. Kill her, he said. Don't let her get back! She'd talk to people she shouldn't be talking to!'

'I'll send 'er a gift parcel!' Wolf smiles strangely, like Father Christmas in the snow.

'One you die of when you open it?' asks Sally.

'That's it,' answers Wolf, and goes out to give some orders to the Chinese.

'I do believe I've developed a weak heart fom all this disappointment,' says Sally, as he climbs into the Fiesler Storch on his way back to Berlin.

'Now we're on speaking terms again,' says Porta, 'I've got another plan that can get us to Sweden so's we can go fishing for salmon!'

'Another plan,' shouts Sally, looking scared. 'I get closer to a heart attack every time I hear of one of your plans. But go on, what is it this time?'

'Sable,' whispers Porta secretively, looking around him cautiously.

'Sable?' asks Sally, looking blank. 'Those things they make fur coats of for the whores? You're surely not thinking of going into the furrier line. That's Jew business. You'd do well to keep out of it!'

'It's a lot bigger than that!' smiles Porta mysteriously. 'My friend the Commissar let me in on it. There's more than one kind of sable it seems, and one of the kinds is black and very rare. It's worth ten times as much as all the other bloody sable. It's called Barguzhinski sable, and is only found in Russia and there only in very secret places! They export only a few of 'em every third year so Uncle Joe can keep the price up for the little devils. There's a death penalty for breakin' the monopoly! But I've got a plan! We nip back through the front line and pick up an armful of females and a couple of lusty males. Then goodbye the Soviet at a hell of a lick! We hide the little beasts in some safe place, and then all we've got to do is get 'em to fuck. Then we're rich! Stalin has a stroke an' his moustache falls off!'

'And then he comes and shoots our heads off,' Wolf continues, pessimistically.

'Maybe that idea's not so crazy after all,' Sally is thinking aloud. 'I'll have a look at it when I get back to the War Ministry. We'll see what we can find out about Barguzhinski sable!' he mumbles with increasing interest as he slams the door of the Storch.

'Come on,' says Wolf. 'Let's you and me go over and get stinking drunk. We're rollin' again some time tonight! So it probably won't be long before you go on your arse for Führer, Folk and Fatherland. I'll come over an' spit on your grave!'

'I'll come back an' pee in your tea, then!' promises Porta.

THE END